Lorraine Inni...

The Girl in the Diamond Studded Heels

Lorraine Innis, the kind of girl who became an accidental heroine
is back, and this time she's changing the world! And her friends and
adversaries are all back, too, along with many new ones.
You'll learn the answers to these questions...

will Peter Liverot dodge the bullet and live to swindle another day?

will Nikolai Kropotkin achieve world peace and avoid baked goods?

will Purvis Twankey achieve his dream of being a singing cowboy?

will Patsy Einfalt get on television or at least get her foot out of one?

will Quinton Merton regress further into his second childhood?

will Davis Flemming spin out of control?

will Eugenia Bupp succeed in her plans for political assassination?

will Valerie Fierro awake in time to join in all the fun?

And...

Who is the mysterious visitor in love with the unconscious Valerie?

Why is an ex-CIA agent drugging Lorraine's lemonade?

And the big mystery at the center of it all:
What is Lorraine's real identity and is she really stuck being
a person she isn't?

If you enjoyed *The Kind of Girl*, the fun is just starting!
Buckle up for the next ride on G.C. Allen's Lorraine Innis
roller coaster and it's faster with even more
twists and turns!

Visit *www.iLorraine.com*

ALSO BY G.C. Allen

The Kind of a Girl

Coming Soon...

The Girl in the Aubergine Sandals
The Girl in the Lime Green Wellies
The Girl in the Saffron Espadrilles
The Girl in the Blood Red Stilettos
The Girl in the Sky Blue Plimsolls

The Girl
in the
Diamond
Studded Heels

G.C. Allen

*The Second Book in the
Lorraine Innis Series*

Daley•into•Print LLC
Mundus Est Vestra Locusta

ISBN-13: 978-0692181294 (Daley Into Print LLC)

ISBN-10: 0692181296

For the Squire of Streatham:
life-long friend,
advisor,
and severest critic
who guided me
to the pinnacle of success

"And who knows whether you have not attained royalty for such a time as this?"

Esther 4:14

Welcome to

The Girl in the Diamond Studded Heels

the Second Volume of the Lorraine Innis Heptalogy

The story so far...

Lorraine Innis, a seemingly average thirty-something woman, is, in reality, a man. Lorraine has assumed this disguise to bring Delaware banker, Peter Liverot, the president of Fourth Fiduciary Trust, to justice for the death of Martina, the fiancée of Lorraine's alter ego. Reluctantly assisting Lorraine in the plan is Valerie Fierro, an employee of Liverot's. Lorraine hopes to become the temporary replacement for Patsy Einfalt, Liverot's secretary, and thus gain access to Liverot's crooked business affairs. Lorraine explains to Valerie that to be convincing in her disguise, she has immersed herself psychologically in her role, going so far as to create a full life story and persona for Lorraine. This backstory includes the details that she is married and has just learned she is pregnant.

Aaron Laffler, an anal-retentive businessman, is married to Marcia, a beautiful, but dim-witted blonde. After years of marriage, Marcia informs Aaron that she is leaving him because their life has become insufferably dull. Laffler also learns that Liverot's bank is calling his loan, and will be assuming control over his business. Laffler then discovers that in addition to stealing his business, Liverot is stealing his wife. He snaps and decides to do something uncharacteristically bold to win back Marcia.

.

Eugenia Bupp, a frail, aged, right-wing anarchist, has hired hitman Rupert Karpis to assassinate United States President Quinton Merton and Russian President Nikolai Kropotkin at the end of their current summit meeting. Unbeknownst to Bupp, however, is that the summit, taking place at Camp David, is in jeopardy because of the erratic behavior of President Merton. Merton has suffered a nervous breakdown and is under unconventional therapy in which he role-plays as a toddler to cope with the stress of his office. Kropotkin has his own secret flaw. He is suffering from candida, a condition that turns his stomach into a distillery whenever he consumes wheat. Rather than admit the disease, Kropotkin would rather be seen as an occasional public drunk. Kropotkin accidentally witnesses Merton's childish therapy and is about to bolt the summit when Davis Flemming, Merton's spin doctor/chief of staff, convinces Yuri Bellikov, Kropotkin's aide and nephew-in-law, to take Kropotkin on a side trip to Delaware to cool off. To embarrass him, Flemming arranges to have Kropotkin address a meeting of French Dairy Farmer, or at least that's what Yuri believes. Upon arriving in Delaware, Kropotkin learns he is speaking to of a group of breastfeeding women.

Also arriving in Delaware are Rupert Karpis, who has agreed to try and assassinate Kropotkin while he has the opportunity. Deranged Aaron Laffler also arrives in Delaware, deciding that shooting Kropotkin is just the kind of daring feat that will impress his estranged wife. Meanwhile, on the way to meet Patsy Einfalt for dinner, Valerie and Lorraine are in a car accident. Valerie is unconscious, while Lorraine, seeming unhurt, is traumatized into forgetting her true identity and fully believing she is indeed the woman she appears to be. At the hospital, Lorraine meets Purvis Twankey, an aspiring cowboy singer from England, and the man who caused the accident. Purvis explains that in addition to his musical aspirations, he is a would-be inventor of gadgets. Lorraine is given tickets to that evening's meeting on breastfeeding taking place at the Hotel du Pont in Wilmington. Patsy Einfalt arrives at the hospital to check on Valerie's condition and meets Lorraine and Purvis for the first time. Purvis displays one of his inventions, a combination cellphone and warning device for deaf pedestrians that emits an electric shock in response to loud noises such as car horns. Patsy and Purvis escort Lorraine to the meeting on breastfeeding.

Aaron Laffler arrives at the Hotel du Pont and meets Eugenia Bupp. When Bupp discovers that Laffler is carrying a gun, she at first mistakes him for her hitman, Rupert Karpis. After she realizes he isn't Karpis, she emboldens the wavering Laffler to shoot Kropotkin, on the assumption that two hitmen are better than one.

Kropotkin addresses the meeting on breastfeeding, but unfortunately has accidentally consumed wheat, and acts drunk. Lorraine arrives at the hotel too late to attend the meeting, and for security purposes is made to wait outside along with the crowd of protestors and other on-lookers. In an attempt to call her non-existent husband, Lorraine uses Purvis Twankey's modified cellphone. When she receives no answer, she sticks the phone in her pocket.

Kropotkin emerges from the hotel to address the crowd. Aaron Laffler, out in the crowd, fires several rounds from his pistol, but they go wildly into the air. The sound of the gunfire causes the modified phone in Lorraine's pocket to emit a severe shock. Lorraine leaps forward, pushing Kropotkin and his young daughter to the ground just as Rupert Karpis, perched on a nearby building, fires. Karpis' shot hits Yuri in the shoulder. The Secret Service interrogate Lorraine, but soon discover she hasn't attacked the Russian but saved his life. Kropotkin meets Lorraine to thank her and winds up in a philosophical discussion in which he admits his candida. Lorraine convinces him to go public with the admission. He agrees to do so the next day. After she leaves, Kropotkin is inspired to draft a plan for world peace and dedicates it to Lorraine.

The Secret Service interrogate Laffler who admits to his role but doesn't confess his motivation. Liverot's crooked backers learn of the connection between Liverot and Laffler: that he not only stole his business, of which they naturally approve but stole his wife, which would draw attention to their operation. They send men to dispose of Liverot. Elsewhere, Bupp meets Karpis to pay him off, but upon realizing he wants to retire from the profession, kills him.

After an exhausting day, Lorraine arrives back at Valerie's home. Upon disrobing, she discovers her true sex and is at first distraught and confused. Lorraine then remembers her true identity and her secret plan to get Liverot. Instead of flying under the radar, she realizes that because of her accidental heroics she is now famous. She breaks out in laughter and then faints.

And now you're ready for...

The Girl in the Diamond Studded Heels

- 1 -
The Cheshire Waiter Requests

With skillful deliberation, the small spider lowered itself from the light fixture towards the bathroom floor below. As it produced its fine thread of silk, there was no way of knowing what, if anything, the spider thought of the body lying on the ceramic tiles beneath it. There was no way to tell if the spider had been observing the half-clothed figure for the last nine hours as it remained motionless; or even if the spider had seen the body just prior to its collapse. Back then the body had been as animated as it was now still: first in the throes of anxiety, then sudden uproarious laughter, then a brief silence before it fainted.

The spider swayed over the body's face as the figure exhaled. It paused for a moment before landing on the tip of the nose. The spider continued, resting on the subject's forehead under a lock of brown hair. The bug seemed to have no concern on what if anything was going on millimeters below its eight spindly legs. Fair enough, for within the mind beneath that forehead, the subject of spiders was also of little consequence. Much weightier matters were under consideration in the similitude of a dream.

Lorraine Innis was dreaming again. Unlike before, Lorraine's dreams were not of plots and scenarios, revenge and justice. Now Lorraine's mind was trying to process the dizzying events of the last twenty-four hours. The most basic facts of the day, and her life as well, were swirling around her in a blizzard of information. The weighty and the trivial spun around her, like so many illuminated factoids against a background that wasn't quite dark enough to be black, nor light enough to be gray. Significance and trivia, vied for preeminence, though distinguishing between them was difficult. Providing a backdrop for it all was the return of the persistent throb at the back of her head that had annoyed her most of the previous day.

As the information flew by Lorraine tried to sort it. One moment she might be considering the essential meaning of her being, the next, she was recalling the cats-eye glasses worn by her third-grade teacher. Gradually the maelstrom abated, and her dream world started taking on more recognizable forms.

She was back in Wilmington, back at the Hotel du Pont. Now, however, instead of being in front of the hotel, diving in front of bullets and saving Russian presidents from assassins, or standing in the ladies room arguing with Valerie Fierro, Lorraine was in the middle of the ballroom. She flinched at the glamorous woman across the room before realizing it was her reflection in one of the room's large mirrors. With detached appreciation, as if she were observing a stranger, Lorraine admired her gown. She twirled around to admire her appearance further, stopping midway through her second turn when the double doors cracked open. Valerie Fierro slipped in sideways to keep out the crowd in the foyer. Valerie leaned against the doors and exhaled.

"Valerie," cried Lorraine, "I'm so happy to see that you're up and around. The last time I saw you, you were in the hospital with tubes all over you, or was it…" She stopped to think, though her mind was still a swirl of confusion. "Yes, you were in the hospital, I think…"

"What the hell are you wearing," snapped Valerie.

"Isn't this formal?" asked Lorraine.

"That's not what I meant."

"Oh, we're wearing the same gown," said Lorraine.

"That's not what I meant," muttered Valerie, "but we are…shit!"

"It *is* the gown," said Lorraine. "I'm sorry, but I didn't know what you were wearing. Last time I saw you; you were in a hospital gown…weren't you? No, you wouldn't know that. You were unconscious."

"Will you forget about that?!"

"Forget? Yes, I've been forgetting so much. I need to remember to forget, or was it forget to remember? I can't recall."

"Forget it, just go and change!"

Just outside the doors, the anxious crowd began to chant her name, and Lorraine took a step towards the doors.

"Never mind them," said Valerie, "just get out of here. Get out of those clothes!"

"It's not fair that I should have to change," said Lorraine, "What about you?"

"I have a right to wear this!"

"My figure's not that bad."

"It's not your f**kin' figure," said Valerie, raising her hands as if to strangle Lorraine.

"Lorraine! LORRAINE!" shouted the crowd.

"So what you're saying is that I should have worn a dress, not a gown…"

"Damn it, how many times do I have to tell you?"

"Apparently one more time," said Lorraine. "I can't explain it. My head's gone all fuzzy again. Like after the accident."

"LORRAINE! LORRAINE!"

"Will you forget about the accident?!"

"Remember to forget," said Lorraine automatically. "That's odd; there goes that phrase again. It's one of the things that keeps going through my head. It's like a paper shredder is ripping through my brain leaving everything in fragments like..."

"Shut up! Will you just shut up! You've got to get out of here!" Now Valerie was shouting to be heard over the noise outside.

"What? Why?"

"LORRAINE! LORRAINE! LORRAINE!"

"Because, you dimwit, you're not..."

By this time Valerie continued to yell, but her words were carried away on the waves of chanting.

"WHAT?" shouted Lorraine.

Valerie bellowed into Lorraine's ear, but to no avail. Lorraine could make out a few words, half of them profanities and the others, "woman," "man," and "you dope," added very little information. Obviously, Lorraine thought, Valerie was agitated about something. She had the vague sense that she knew what was upsetting Valerie, while at the same time being tantalizingly oblivious to it, like an itch she couldn't quite scratch.

The double doors flew open, and her guests poured into the room. In the onslaught, Valerie retreated to the edge of the hall where Lorraine could see her shouting at a waiter.

"Mrs. Innis," said the first woman to greet her, "I mean, Lorraine."

"Denise Clott, I mean, Denise Zane," said Lorraine, "I didn't expect to see you here. It's been so long since I saw you, hasn't it?"

"It was just yesterday. We met in my law office?"

"Yesterday? Yes," nodded Lorraine, "I suppose it was yesterday. It just seems so long ago. How is your sister, Clodagh, not the other two."

"You're not supposed to know my sisters," said Denise.

"Oh, yes, you're right," said Lorraine, "how forgetful of me. No, I'm not supposed to know any of you. Am I?"

"No. You came to my office and gave me that money in trust," said the lawyer, "and said you were going on a dangerous mission."

"A mission? Yes, that sounds a little familiar. What did I say I was doing?"

"You didn't say. You just said you might die. Did you forget?"

"No," said Lorraine, "I remembered to forget. There's been a lot of that going on lately."

"You told me that I might never see you again," said Denise. "Now here it is, just one day later, and you've done so well, too; saving the life of President Kropotkin! That must have been the dangerous mission."

"Really?" Denise's theory sounded plausible, but not quite correct.

17

"I'm so proud of you; you're a credit to the women of Delaware...no you're a credit to all women...no you're a credit to humanity."

"Humanity, but really I..."

"Excuse me," said Denise, "but I must get a glass of wine...waiter."

Denise Zane tapped a passing waiter on the shoulder. He turned, and Lorraine gave a start. The waiter, pudgy and somewhat disheveled, looked disturbingly familiar. In fact, he looked like he could have been Lorraine's brother.

"I'll have a chardonnay, waiter," said Denise. "Lorraine? Lorraine?"

Lorraine just stared at the waiter.

"Lorraine? Are you all right?" said Denise. "You look as if you've seen a ghost."

The waiter turned away.

"He, I mean...that waiter...he looks like..."

"Yes, he reminds me of someone, too," said Denise, indifferently. "Oh, I know, he looks like a boy from my hometown, the boy I used to babysit. Isn't it sad? I thought he had more potential than to wind up a waiter. Still, look at him; he couldn't expect much more looking like that."

"Who is he?" Lorraine asked, but Denise Zane turned away.

"How do, Miss Lorraine," said a voice in a Northern English accent.

Lorraine turned to see the toothy grin of Purvis Twankey. He looked a sight in his western-style tuxedo complete with the rhinestone encrusted boots that added a good three inches to his height.

"Purvis," said Lorraine taking in his appearance, "you look...so very... interesting...I've never seen rawhide patches on formal wear."

"Nice of you t'notice, Miss Lorraine," grinned Purvis, before adding in a loud whisper, "They're nowt real leather. They're imitation. Ee, but you look proper champion yerself! Yer joost about the most beautiful wooman in place, 'cept for maybe that'n over there. Ee, but she's a peach."

"That's me, Purvis. You're pointing at a mirror."

"Ee, what a puddin' I am! Well, an' all, that's a relief. I thought that bloke standing next to her had me suit on." Purvis looked at Lorraine, then at her reflection, and finally at Lorraine once more. "By gum, you're even prettier in person."

"Do you think anyone else in the room looks like me?"

Purvis scanned the room. "No, Miss Lorraine, you're the prettiest lady in place!"

"What about any of the men?"

Purvis Twankey blushed. "There's nowt many pretty men here, Miss Lorraine. Are there?"

"I mean...never mind. What about the waiters? Do you notice anything unusual about them?"

Purvis brightened as he looked at the nearest waiter. Aye, that one there's got his shirttail hanging out!"

Lorraine shook her head, as the man in the Naugahyde tuxedo went to give fashion advice to the waiter with the untucked shirt.

"Hello, Lorraine," said Patsy Einfalt. In her discount knock-off evening gown.

"Oh, hello Patsy."

She stared at Lorraine's dress and sighed.

"What?" said Lorraine.

"I wish I could wear clothes like you."

"I doubt this gown would be very practical for working in the office or playing with your daughter."

"No," said Patsy, "I suppose you're right. I guess I'm doomed to be practical, just like you're just made for…"

"What?"

"You know, the regal look…like, well, like you should be on television."

"You were on television," said Lorraine. "I saw you being interviewed on the news."

"Oh, that," said Patsy, "but that's not really being famous. They only wanted to talk to me about you."

"Still, fame is fleeting."

"Unless you don't have it, then it's nonexistent. I didn't tell the TV people, but I wish I were just like you."

"No, you don't," said Lorraine. "At the moment I'm not exactly sure why, but you don't."

"Yes, I do. You're so famous, and I'm so unimportant."

"What about him?" said Lorraine, nodding towards the passing waiter.

"No, I doubt that he's famous," said Patsy, "unless he was on that reality TV show: *The World's Greatest Living Waiter.*"

"I didn't mean that. Does he look familiar?"

"Of course he does."

Patsy said this as if it were apparent, but before Lorraine could ask who the waiter reminded her of; she was interrupted by a herald's trumpet.

"Lorruska!" A voice cried out.

Lorraine turned to see the crowd part, and Nikolai Kropotkin, the president of Russia, striding across the floor, his arms extended.

"President Kropotkin," she said with a curtsey.

"What is this? Such formality from my Lorruska to her Uncle Nikki," he bellowed as he enveloped her in his strong arms. "Lorruska, let me look at you." he cried, though his hug prevented him from doing so.

"Nikki," grunted Lorraine.

The Russian let her up for air while keeping one arm upon her shoulder so that he might admire her at arm's length, like a priceless porcelain statuette.

"This woman, this remarkable woman," Kropotkin cried, "this is the woman who saved my life."

"It was a pleasure," said Lorraine quietly, "but an accident just the same."

"And still, she is so modest," said Kropotkin. "Diving in front of the bullets of two gunmen...so brave, like another Joan of Arc, or Catherine the Great." He tilted his head to appreciate her features from a new angle. "Is she not almost Russian! So brave, and so beautiful..."

"What about that waiter," asked Lorraine pointing at the one passing by them.

"He may be Russian, but I doubt it," said Kropotkin with a dismissive gesture, "but I did not come here to talk of waiters. Ladies and gentlemen, I give you our Lorruska!"

The guests applauded and continued to do so as the Russian president continued his praise. Lorraine edged through the swinging door into the serving area; there she saw the mysterious waiter unloading dirty champagne glasses from his tray. When she entered, he stopped what he was doing and looked up at her.

"Well," said Lorraine uncomfortably, as he continued to watch her, "at least you're not applauding."

"It's not that I don't appreciate what you're doing," said the waiter, "because I do."

"Well, then what?" said Lorraine.

"You need to do more."

"More?!" Lorraine stood with her hands on her hips. "Did you see that little gathering out there? I've got everyone from English cowpokes to Russian presidents telling me I'm the greatest thing since the wife of the guy who invented sliced bread. I've got a woman who struggled to put herself through law school and build her own practice telling me I'm an inspiration. Me! I've got a single mother who is holding down a full-time job and raising a daughter, looking at me like I'm the fulfillment of all the silly dreams she ever had but will never achieve. And there's a room full of others who act like it's the highlight of their year just to be breathing the same air as me, and you think I should do more?"

"Yes," he said, "you need to because there's more to do."

"Great, what do I do for an encore? Save the world?"

"No, just my corner of it," said the waiter.

"I hate to disappoint you," laughed Lorraine, "but actually, I was thinking of doing less. This is all too much, and I'm not sure I feel quite right."

The waiter looked deeply into Lorraine's eyes. The look was disconcerting, but at the same time showed a depth of kindness and understanding absent in the adoring mob outside. Finally, after she felt as if he had studied her entire soul, the waiter spoke.

"You won't do less," he said as if it were settled.

"Oh?" she said. She wanted to argue the point, but all she could manage was a feeble, "why is that?"

"Because you can't do any less than you were created to do."

Lorraine nodded. Somehow, this waiter knew her mind better than she did herself, a fact which was both comforting and unsettling.

"How do you know that?" she asked.

"Because," said the waiter, "I made you."

"You?"

"Well, I made you and several loved ones who are no longer with us. There's a bit of Martina, and Verity, and a lot of Elinor in you. And I just helped put it all together. You were made from such lovely people. That's probably why everyone loves you so much."

Lorraine opened her mouth to dispute this last statement but found she had no words with which to respond. She felt light-headed as if she would fall, and then suddenly felt as if she were supported by the waiter's strength, though he was standing an arm's length away.

"You're fine."

"I am." Lorraine wasn't sure whether she was asking a question or making a statement.

"You are," said the waiter. "You are Lorraine Innis, born Lorraine Ammaccapane. You were born in Morristown, New Jersey. You graduated from William Patterson College. And now you're a book editor for Marlton Press..."

As he spoke, Lorraine felt strengthened and warmed by his words, as if they were some sort of healing incantation.

"You live in Colts Neck, New Jersey," he continued, "with your husband..."

The waiter hesitated for a moment, and Lorraine felt a welling up of emotion in her bosom.

"...Martin C. Innis..."

"Yes, yes," said Lorraine, "that's right. That's all exactly right. I know all that, and more. Would you like me to tell you?"

"That isn't necessary," he said. "I think you know your own mind."

The confusion inside her head evaporated.

"Yes," said Lorraine, with a smile, "yes, I think I do." Then the dull throb in the back of her head began anew, bringing with it the confusion. "But sometimes..."

"It'll be all right," said the waiter anticipating her objection. "It's for what you've prepared. Just focus on that. You were made to do. It's the reason for your being. Most people just are. They barely exist their whole lives long. You live to do."

"But I'm not supposed to save the lives of world leaders," Lorraine protested, "or be some kind of a role model."

"That just happened along the way, and so you did that too, but don't let it distract you from what you have to do."

"But how do I do it all?"

The waiter gave Lorraine a wry smile. "Just focus on being yourself. Just exist."

"But you said I was a doer," said Lorraine.

"That's the ironic part," he nodded. "But it's ingrained in you. It's been thought out, and gone over, and rehearsed in your mind a million times. Now all you have to do is be yourself."

"Be myself," said Lorraine. "Lorraine Innis."

"That's right," said the waiter, "be Lorraine. For now, you have to be Lorraine."

Lorraine found herself repeating her first name over and over. As she did, she felt less confused and more self-assured. The ache in her head, though still there, seemed less insistent, and the flurry of facts settled down, each to its proper place.

"Lorraine, Lorraine," she repeated, and as she did so, she felt growing within her the strength she needed to carry on. And as she did so, the man smiled and began to fade into the background like the Cheshire Cat. Soon, even the room faded into darkness, as if the hotel and the universe beyond were gently melting away until there was nothing left but her.

And the tinkling of a cheap bell.

- 2 -
The Cleric and the
Cheesey Cataleptic

A few miles away from the bathroom floor, in St. Francis Hospital, a dark-haired man moved unnoticed through the wards and semi-private rooms. Clad in black, he stopped by each occupied bed, hovering beside it like some dark angel, pondering the fate of each patient. Some he reached out to touch. Some he barely visited. He glanced at each chart, examined the personal effects and gifts nearby, and then moved on.

Walking into one double room, he saw there was just one patient, a woman in the bed nearest the door. As was his routine, he scanned the chart.

Valerie Fierro. Automobile accident. Brought in the previous afternoon.

He shook his head. On the side table was a single flower arrangement. He opened the attached card. Often the cards would tell him more than the charts. He was about to read the note when a shaft of light from the room across the hall pierced through the gray shadows and landed on the face of the woman in bed.

"*Mio Dio,*" he whispered.

Forgetting all else in the room, or that he was even in a hospital, the man in black stood aside the bed studying the woman named Valerie Fierro.

"*Bella, bella,*" he said, almost in supplication to the figure in the bed. After several minutes of admiration, he reached out, to caress her cheek, but froze when the door opened wide, bathing the room in even more light.

"What are you doing there," said a woman's voice.

The man wheeled around and lifted his finger to his mouth.

"Oh, Father Michael, it's only you," said the nurse. "Isn't it a bit late for your visitations? It's nearly two in the morning."

Michael Valvano shrugged his shoulders and smiled.

"We had the annual Parish business meeting tonight," he said. "They can run pretty late...besides, I couldn't sleep."

"You do too much," said the nurse shaking her head.

"An assistant rector's work..." said Father Valvano, trailing off. He was snapped back to reality as the nurse began writing on Valerie's chart.

"She's quite beaut...I mean, she's quite young," said the priest.

"Yes, she's got us a bit worried."

"Oh? Why is that?"

"She was in a car accident, then woke up, and then fainted. Now, she's almost completely unresponsive."

"Almost?"

"Sometimes," said the nurse returning the chart to its holder, "she'll ask for cheese."

"What kind of cheese? A little Provolone, or some Pecorino Romano?"

"No particular kind, just cheese."

Father Valvano rubbed his hand through his short curly hair. "Really? I haven't heard her."

"It seems to happen when...wait, I'll show you..."

The nurse picked up the television remote control and turned on a cable news station. A commercial came on for a toe ointment whose spokesperson was an animated hedgehog. The priest looked at Valerie, then at the nurse, and shrugged his shoulders.

"Wait," advised the nurse.

A few seconds later the animal finished his pitch, and the news resumed.

"Recapping our top story," said the night anchor, "Russian President Nikolai Kropotkin has survived an assassination attempt in Wilmington, Delaware..."

Father Valvano gave a start on hearing the news for the first time. He looked at the nurse, and then at Valerie, who was still lying there motionless.

"Wait."

"...Kropotkin's life was saved by the heroics of this woman," a blurry photograph of a woman leaving the Hotel du Pont popped onto the screen, "whom authorities have identified as Lorraine Innis."

"Cheese," moaned Valerie, though her eyes remained closed, "cheese."

"By all accounts, Ms. Innis..."

"Cheese, cheese," repeated Valerie with increased agitation.

The nurse clicked off the television.

"Hush, Dear, it's all right," whispered the nurse to Valerie before turning to the priest. "See?"

"Amazing," agreed Mike Valvano, "but what does this Lorraine..."

"Cheese," blurted Valerie.

The nurse put her finger to her lips.

"Sorry," he said, "but what does this woman have to do with... anything."

"That's her cousin," said the nurse. "She was with her this afternoon when they had the car accident that put Miss Fierro in here. The cousin wasn't hurt."

"No?" said the priest.

"Not only wasn't she hurt, she went out and saved the life of the president of Russia. She's a hero. That was her on the television."

"The cheese lady," said Valvano, nodding towards Valerie.

"She was here earlier in the evening with Miss Fierro. Then she left. A few hours later we see her on the news saving what-his-name's life. That's when Miss Fierro woke up, saw her cousin, fainted, and since then has been unresponsive."

"Except asking for cheese when she sees or hears mention of her cousin," said the priest.

"Except for that."

"Maybe they were in the cheese exporting business together."

"No, she works for a bank," said the nurse, pointing to Valerie.

"Like half the people in town."

The nurse cocked her head towards the flowers on the bedside table. "Still, she must be pretty important at the bank. The secretary of the president of the bank came in with those flowers."

Mike Valvano nodded and opened the card accompanying the flowers. After reading it, he glanced at Valerie, and then back at the card. He looked up for a moment then rushed for the door.

"Father Michael," said the nurse startled by his abruptness.

"I've got to go," said the priest, halfway out the door.

"The card," said the nurse.

"Yes, the card," he muttered.

"In your hand," said the nurse pointing.

"Oh, yes," he said rushing it back to the table.

A moment later, he was gone.

- 3 -
With Love from Miasma
to Hubris

The three men groped through the darkness of the South Jersey pine forest, walking into low branches, and stumbling over exposed roots as they went. Occasionally, as one would get a branch slapped into his face, he would mutter a profanity which was muffled by the soft carpet of needles beneath their feet.

Finally, after walking for nearly a mile, the man at the rear of the small column spoke.

"This is far enough, Alphonse," he said.

The three men stood in the stillness of the forest for a moment before Alphonse replied.

"Mr. Rosen, ain't the miasma ubiquitous ta'night," he said in a thick South Philadelphia accent.

"What the f**k are you talking about?" snarled Peter Liverot. Liverot was short-tempered over any inconvenience, but tonight even more so. Tonight, his former colleagues had driven him into the wilds of Atlantic County for the express purpose of depositing a bullet in his skull and then dumping his carcass in a shallow grave. In Liverot's estimation, you couldn't inconvenience a person more than that.

"I wuz talkin' about the miasma," said Al in the slow, measured way he voiced all his words. "And it being real ubiquitous."

"Alphonse is taking a correspondence course on improving his vocabulary," explained Julius Rosen.

"Miasma," said Alphonse, "that means like da mist, and ubiquitous, meaning dat dere's a lot of it around."

"I know what it means, you asshole," said Liverot.

"He's only trying to improve himself," said Rosen.

"Isn't it enough, Julie," said Liverot, "that I gotta get offed by this imbecile, without getting a vocabulary lesson from him first?"

"Da guy on the disk says it ain't never too late to improve yourself," said Alphonse.

"I'd say it's just a little too late for me, you friggin' moron," cried Liverot. "You're going to pop me in a minute!"

Julius Rosen put his gloved hand on Liverot's forearm. "Relax, Pete, you're getting yourself all upset. You don't want to go out this way. Al's only doing his job, as we all are; even you, even now. Why not depart this world like the professional you've always been."

"Yeah, okay," said Liverot rolling his shoulders. "You're right, go out with the class I've always had."

"That's it," said Julius, patting the bank president on the back. "You know it makes sense."

"Sure, Mr. Liverot," said the hitman, "show us a modicum of decorum."

Liverot stared at Alphonse for a moment in the moonlight before lunging for his throat. "You f**kin' moron! I'll give you a modicum of strangulation!"

The other two men struggled to break Liverot's grip.

"I'll kill him," cried Liverot as he wrestled with Alphonse. "Let me kill him. He can kill me, but let me kill him first!"

"Stop it, Pete," said Julius, "go out like a man."

"As soon as I strangle the brains out of this shithead's head," gasped Liverot as Alphonse put him in a headlock.

"Mr. Rosen's right, Pete," said Al calmly, "you're resistance is disconcerting."

"He's still doing it," gurgled Liverot, his arms flailing.

"Take it easy, Al," said Julius. "You don't want to hurt him."

Alphonse relaxed his forearm, while still maintaining control over his prey. Liverot took the opportunity to catch his breath, while Julius brushed the pine needles from his cashmere topcoat.

"There," said Julius, "that's better. Has everyone calmed down?"

"Yeah," panted Peter Liverot.

Alphonse started to open his mouth, but Rosen raised a gloved finger to his lips.

"Wisdom would dictate you not talk," he said to the hitman. "Mr. Liverot's upset enough. Besides which, we don't want to be wrestling in Jersey all night."

Alphonse nodded.

"Okay," said Julius, motioning to Alphonse, "let's get this unpleasantness over with. No one is enjoying themselves here."

Alphonse nodded.

"Julius?" said Liverot.

"Yeah, Pete?"

"Anyway," he paused, hoping against hope in the answer, "anyway out of this?"

Julius was silent for a moment giving Liverot a brief swell of optimism.

"You know as well as I do, Pete," said Julius. "There's no way out. You know that."

"The stupid bitch," said Liverot referring to Marcia Laffler.

"It was very clean the way you appropriated her husband's business," said Julius, a trace of regret in his voice. "Stealing his wife, on the other hand, made it very messy. You reached for too much, Petey. You got greedy and lost sight of your goals."

"Hubris," muttered Alphonse.

"What?" said Liverot.

"Hubris, you got too much hubris, it means..." began Alphonse before he noticed Mr. Rosen shaking his head. "Uh, never mind. I don't know what it means."

"Well, no matter," said Julius. "What's done is done."

"Almost," said Alphonse, pulling a pistol from inside his leather jacket.

"Almost," whispered Liverot.

The banker's pulse pounded in his ears followed by the sound of Alphonse sliding back the bolt of his handgun. He held his breath, waiting for the sound of the impact, and then it came, but not with a bang, as he expected, but with a chirp.

"Hold it," said Julius.

Liverot turned his head towards Rosen and wound up with the barrel of Alphonse's gun up his nostril. Beyond that, he saw Julius opening his cell phone.

"What?" snapped Julius. "Oh, sorry, I didn't know it was you. Yes, we're about to complete the exercise. What? Why? Okay. Yeah. We'll be there as soon as we can."

Julius closed his phone. With his free hand, Alphonse turned Liverot's head forward to deliver the first and final bullet to his brain.

"No," said Julius quietly, "forget that."

"Huh?" said Alphonse.

"This evening's exercise has been canceled. It's off. Put away the gun, and let's get going."

"What?" said Liverot, not sure heard correctly. "You mean I can go?"

"You can go with us. He wants to see all of us. Now," said Julius.

Liverot staggered to his feet, his knees still wobbly.

"He's calling off the hit?" asked Liverot.

"Is that legal?" asked Al.

"Are you complaining?" asked Rosen.

"No," blurted Liverot, "I just wanted to be sure. I mean, you know, if it's okay with him, it's okay with me."

"I suppose it's okay with me too," said Al. "I always liked Mr. Liverot."

"Liked me?" said Liverot. "A minute ago you were going to blow my brains out!"

28

"Yeah," said Alphonse, "but I wasn't going to like doin' it. It was not going to be a savory experience."

Liverot slapped him on the side of his head even though Alphonse stood a few inches taller than him, was much stronger, and still was carrying the gun that had almost ended his life. Alphonse took the slap with resignation. The phone call had returned everything to normal. The trio marched silently back to the SUV.

"Let's get outta here," said Liverot, climbing back into the Cadillac. A few minutes ago he was begging on his knees; now he was back to giving orders to no one in particular. "The further away from here, the more I'll like it."

Alphonse climbed into the driver's seat, while Julius Rosen got in the back with Liverot. Despite Liverot's rediscovered hubris, Alphonse waited for Rosen's signal before driving away.

As they pulled away, it finally occurred to Liverot to ask the critical question.

"So," said the banker, trying to be nonchalant, "what's up?"

"What?" said Rosen.

"I mean, why didn't you…you know. I mean, what's he want?"

"Does he have to want something?"

Liverot was silent for a moment.

"Yes," he said, "he never did nothing for nothing."

"I used to like that song," piped up Alphonse.

"What song?" growled Liverot.

"*Nothing From Nothing*," said the hitman.

"Shut the f**k up, and drive!"

Alphonse shut up and drove on.

"So," said Liverot, "who do I have to kill?"

Julius laughed a cold, dry laugh.

"Like you could off somebody," said Rosen. "You'd be worse at that than me."

They drove on in silence for another minute. Finally, Rosen spoke. "He wants you to take care of this woman…"

- 4 -
The Asset Allocations of a
Potato-Headed Bastard

After a night of vivid, often disturbing dreams, Lorraine Innis had finally fallen into a deep, restful slumber. Well, it was almost deep and restful. Once the dreams had pushed through like a storm front, the only impediment to her sleep was that cheap bell that kept sounding every few minutes.

Trying to sleep on a bathroom floor was difficult enough. Doing so with some second-rate Santa jingling his sleigh bells in the next room only aggravated the situation. Still, the sound never lasted long enough to rouse her fully, and Lorraine always drifted back to sleep before the bell's tinny echo faded away. What finally woke her were the rays of the morning sun shining through the bathroom doorway onto Lorraine's eyelids.

Lorraine's eye twitched several times, and in her dozy state, she imagined she was once more being interrogated, as she had been twice the previous day.

"My name is Lorraine Innis," she muttered. "I'm a woman from Colts Neck, New Jersey. I live there with my husband, Martin."

Then the jingle bells began again.

"Stop those bells," she moaned, "I'll tell you anything you want to know, just please stop that noise."

She stirred enough to realize the bell belonged to a cheap phone; Valerie's cheap phone. Springing up from the floor, Lorraine bolted through the door, ran to the bedside table, and picked up the handset just as it stopped ringing.

She listened to the dial tone for a moment.

"I hope it wasn't important," she said. "If it was, I'm sure they'll...oh, my..."

Lorraine looked at herself in the mirror across the room. The reflection was of a woman's head atop a body that was much too masculine. She was narrow of hip and of breasts bereft.

"Oh," she said as she sat on the edge of the bed. It was coming back to her. How the night before she'd encountered the same body while getting undressed. She closed her eyes and tried to concentrate, but when she did, the same thoughts repeated through her mind like some sort of irresistible mantra.

"I am Lorraine Innis, I am Lorraine Innis, Lorraine Innis, be yourself, yourself, you know your own mind."

The thoughts were comforting and reassuring, though less so when she opened her eyes.

"I do know my own mind," agreed Lorraine aloud. "Of course I'm Lorraine Innis. Who else would I be? But what about this?"

She hiked up her long purple T-shirt and looked down at the contradiction between her legs. She was hesitant to touch it, not because she had never touched one before, but because it must belong to someone else.

"That's ridiculous," she said, "it's not like I got another person's order in a restaurant. Still," she reasoned, "if it's not mine I'd rather leave it alone."

Somehow, she thought, she had gotten someone else's body, specifically one belonging to some man. It was evident from the neck up she was who she always had been. Her head and its contents were as female as they had ever been, she thought. Or were they?

She stopped for a moment and recalled the events of her life, her childhood. She had a childhood, of course, it was a girlhood, naturally. She could remember where she went to school, college, and her career as a book editor. All those events were set in her mind like facts chiseled in stone. It was almost as if she had memorized a history book of her own life. Still, she thought, they were facts, indisputably so, even more factual than the body that now confronted her in the mirror. She had, after all, lived with those memories all her life. That body had only appeared last night.

Lorraine's thoughts were interrupted by the sudden need to pee. Entering the bathroom, she saw the clothing she had worn the day before, including some very realistic padding. She shuddered as she recalled her discovery of it the previous night.

Lorraine hesitated, staring at the commode, not sure whether to lift the seat or not. Her upbringing dictated that she should sit, but she didn't know when she'd get the chance to pee standing up again. She lifted the seat, then put it down, then lifted it again, before finally putting it down for good, and sitting. Conditioning had won out over curiosity.

After she was done, she tore off some toilet paper but hesitated. She really didn't want to touch *it*.

"Stop being so ridiculous," she said to herself. "It isn't like you've never touched one before."

"Not one of my own," she answered herself.

"Come on; you're a grown woman with a husband..."

Lorraine gasped.

That's right. She was married. Martin was an indisputable fact, too.

"I'm a grown woman with a husband," she repeated, "a grown woman with a husband and a penis. That can ruin a good marriage if the wife shows up hung like a..." she looked down, "well, like a pony."

At least she wasn't more generously endowed than Martin, or was she? She couldn't remember how big he was. Odd, but she couldn't remember much about his physical appearance or much beyond the significant biographical facts of their life together: how they met, their anniversary, what he did for a living, and so on. She couldn't recall little details, like his smile, or his sense of humor. Still, she reckoned, it didn't matter how big her appendage was in relation to his. At any size, two of those in the family was one too many. It wasn't like his and her towels or two cars in the garage.

She looked down at her bare chest. "And I've no breasts!"

The first was obviously worse, especially being married. Lorraine would only need the boobs if, for example, she were a nursing mother...

"Oh, no," she said aloud, "I'm not a mother, but I will be."

Lorraine remembered telling Valerie yesterday that she was pregnant. For a brief moment, she could recall Valerie saying something in regards to that, but she couldn't remember what. Her internal self-assertion that she was Lorraine Innis, somehow preempted any deeper thought on that subject.

"Valerie!" she cried out. "Valerie's in the hospital. Here I am, worrying about my little problems, well, my problems, while Valerie may be lying there in a coma, or worse. I can worry about all this later. There's got to be some explanation, scientific or otherwise. Right now, though, I've got to suck it up..."

She looked at her crotch in the bathroom mirror.

"...make that tuck it up. I've got to get dressed and go do what I can do for Valerie. After all, I live to do..."

That last statement gave Lorraine pause. Where had that come from?

"Yes, that's right," she said upon reflection, "I live to do, that's what I was made for..."

She stopped again and thought.

"What an odd way to put it," she said with a shake of her head. "No matter, I'm a doer, and now I need to do what I can for Valerie. I'll figure you out later," she said to the torso in the mirror, as if it were some foundling left on her doorstep.

She picked up the false breasts from the floor and cradled one in each hand.

"At least they're the right size," said Lorraine, "no one will realize they're not mine. I just better get mine back before I have that baby." She looked down. "You've got to go too. There's no way I'm delivering a baby through YOU!"

She had donned her underwear and padding and was looking through Valerie's closet for something to wear when the phone rang. She sprang to answer it on the first ring but then paused.

What if it was Martin? What would she say to him? How would she explain what had happened?

The phone rang a second time.

Martin would understand; wouldn't he? Of course, he would, she told herself. He would be as understanding as any man who learned his wife could now accompany him to the steam room at the gym.

The phone rang a third time. There was no putting it off, Lorraine told herself, as she sat on the edge of the bed and lifted the receiver to her ear.

"Hello?" said Lorraine tentatively.

"Hi, honey," replied the voice at the other end.

"Thank goodness it's you, dear!"

Lorraine was relieved to hear the voice of her husband Martin, or at least she thought it sounded like Martin. It was hard to tell.

"You sound odd," said Lorraine.

"I'm on my cell phone. I must be in a bad cell. I'm at the airport."

"Airport?"

"Yes, between planes."

Lorraine laughed in a release of tension. "So you weren't home last night."

"No, of course, not," he said.

"No wonder I couldn't get you. I tried calling all evening."

"I've beem away on business all week. Don't you remember?"

Lorraine thought for a moment. She didn't remember. Still, with so many details jostling for position in her mind that could have easily slipped her mind.

"I guess I remembered to forget," she said.

"What? Are you all right, honey?"

"Well, not exactly," she said looking downward. "A lot has been happening. We were in an accident yesterday and other things..."

"We? Are you okay? Who else was in the accident?"

"My cousin and I. She's in St. Francis Hospital. I don't know her current condition. I was just about to go and see her.

"Oh, but you're okay?"

"I feel fine," Lorraine said. "More or less..."

"What do you mean, more or less?"

"Well," Lorraine ran her hand across her torso, "I mean, in some areas less, and in others...more. Look, darling, I think I'm going to have to stay here until I know how she is."

"I thought you said you were going to the hospital."

"I am," she said, "but I'm going to have to stay here."

"Where?"

"At her house."

"Why don't you go home?"

Lorraine couldn't understand why Martin wasn't grasping the geographical necessities of the situation. Why should she go all the way back to New Jersey every night, especially if he was traveling, rather than stay at Valerie's house? Instead of having a semantic debate, Lorraine settled for a vague answer. "Don't worry, I'll be around."

"Oh, right," he said. "Well, when I get home, do you want me to come over?"

"Where?"

"To the house."

"What's the difference?" When he was home, he would be at the house, she thought.

"Well, where do you want me to go?"

"I know you're trying to be considerate," said Lorraine, "but you're only confusing me, darling, and I don't need any more of that at the moment."

"But, I…"

"Look," she said, "when you get back, just find me. Whether I'm at the house, or the hospital, or at home, just find me. I'll be in one of those three places."

"But that's two places," he said.

"Just find me!" she snapped. "I'm sorry; it's just that everything's going crazy."

"Is there something else wrong?"

"Oh, oh," blubbered Lorraine as she broke down. She was afraid to verbalize her condition, thinking that saying the words would make them irretrievably true.

"You can tell me," he assured her.

"Do you love me?" asked Lorraine tearfully. "I mean really love me?"

There was a hesitation on the other end of the line. As the seconds passed, Lorraine felt her tears run cold.

"Well," she said, "do you love me?"

"What's the matter?" he asked evasively.

"Do you?!"

"Sure, okay," he said with a strange detachment in his voice.

Perhaps, Lorraine thought, he had guessed what she was trying to tell him. No, she thought, that was impossible. How could a man guess that his wife has been retrofitted with his team's equipment?

"Well," she continued, "I'm not so sure you'll love me after I tell you what I have to tell you."

"It can't be all that bad."

"No, it's worse," said Lorraine, her tears flowing once more. "I think, I mean, I'm going to have some difficulty with the baby."

34

"Baby? What baby?" he said.

"The baby...our baby."

"OUR BABY?"

"Yes, our baby," she repeated. "It's going to be, to say the least, a... difficult delivery."

"We don't have a baby," he said with a nervous laugh.

"At the very least, I'll have to deliver caesarian," said Lorraine.

"You can deliver it FedEx for all I care, lady. I'm not having a baby."

"How can you say that about our child?"

"It may be your baby, lady, but it ain't mine!"

"What?"

"I've heard about scheming women..."

"Scheming women?!"

"...scheming women," he continued, "trying to rope a guy into a commitment with a phony story about being pregnant. Then, after the poor sap is signed, sealed, and on his honeymoon, it turns out to be a false alarm. Nice try, but I wasn't born yesterday."

"Well, if it isn't yours," cried Lorraine, "whose is it?"

"I don't know, go ask the milkman! All I know is that I'm careful with my long-term assets. I know where I invest them."

"Assets? Investments? What are you saying?" cried Lorraine.

"Just that if you're pregnant it's not by me! I don't go around making little deductions haphazardly. You ought to know that!"

After everything she had gone through in the last day, now her husband was accusing her of infidelity with a milkman.

"You potato-headed bastard!" she shouted, unable to control her anger any longer.

"Run those figures somewhere else," he said, "I'm not buying it."

"You heartless..." She searched for an epithet low enough for the situation.

"Call me any name you want," he said. "It's not going to work. I'm not the father of your or anybody else's baby."

If this is the kind of cretin she'd married, Lorraine was almost glad she wouldn't give him a child. "I, I, I hate you," she shrieked. "I never want to see you again!"

Lorraine slammed down the receiver with enough force to break it in two. Great, she thought, now, on top of everything else, she had to buy Valerie a new phone. Valerie! Now Valerie was the only person to whom Lorraine could turn. Lorraine sat on the edge of Valerie's bed and reached for another handful of tissues from the box on the nightstand. After a half an hour she calmed down enough to make a plan of attack for the day. She would make herself presentable and go down to the hospital to care for Valerie. After all, her cousin was all she had left. Everyone, including her own body, had betrayed or deserted her. Maybe, she thought, she could go home and see her doctor. But which one: her general practitioner or her gynecologist? She tried, but couldn't recall the names of either.

Never mind, she thought, that can wait. She certainly didn't have to rush for the sake of that Irish ingrate, Martin Innis! No, she'd take care of Valerie, and then the two of them could sort it out together. She returned to Valerie's closet and resumed her search for something to wear.

- 5 -
You Can't Hide Your Lionize

It was already 9:30 as Davis Flemming took his first sip of coffee and his first bite of muffin in his office at Camp David. The coffee was cold, but the row of televisions was hot and had been so since before dawn. Flemming was monitoring the cable and network news outlets trying to gauge how the media was covering the previous evening's assassination attempt on Nikolai Kropotkin. As President Quinton Merton's top advisor, Flemming was kept appraised of the situation in Delaware, but little of that information interested him. He didn't care that Kropotkin was secure in his suite at the Hotel du Pont, or that Yuri Belikov, Kropotkin's nephew and aide, was resting in stable condition after being winged by one of the shots, or even that a gunman was in custody. That was the past, and the past held little interest for Davis Flemming. History was for musty, tweed-clad men. He wanted to know what was going to happen; to anticipate the next event so he could get ahead of the curve. He wanted to guide events to his advantage or at the very least, to be a step or two in front of them.

"Come on, come on," Flemming muttered, as he scanned the monitors, "tell me something. Give me something." After several more minutes of fruitless search, combined with an on-going review of the internet, Flemming turned away.

"Not one damn pundit has gotten their arms around this yet," he sneered. "Facts, just stupid, hollow facts."

In his frustration, Flemming took a bite out of his muffin, and then threw the remainder of it in the wastebasket. Though he hated to admit it, he needed the opinion makers. They were his core constituency, the raw material with which he molded public opinion, the medium of his art. Still, unlike cold lumps of clay, or inert blocks of marble, Flemming needed the input of his medium. Though he doubted the press realized it, he was at his most effective in leading the public after he discerned the subtle direction indicated in their editorials, opinion pieces, and columns. It was then, like an expert forecaster reading an approaching hurricane from a wisp of clouds and a gentle breeze, that he could exploit his talents in ways that almost seemed magical to those witnessing it.

"Come on, you bastards," he said to the screens, "lean, damn it, lean! Lean so I can push you the way you want to go. Tell me..."

A "special report" graphic suddenly popped up on CNN, followed quickly in turn by ones on Fox News, Headline News, and MSNBC. This could be what Flemming was waiting for. Flemming turned up the sound. Maybe, he hoped, this was the start of a juicy new crisis, preferably something away from Delaware and Nikolai Kropotkin, something that would draw away coverage from that assassination attempt.

That would be best. It was Flemming's manipulation of Kropotkin's dim-witted aide that put the Russian leader in Wilmington in the line of fire of two separate assassins. If the story continued to grow in that direction, Flemming's part in it might come to light. As he had most of the previous night, Flemming cursed the assassins for their inaccuracy. If only they had killed Yuri Belikov, instead of just wounding him everything would be fine. Now Kropotkin and Yuri were out of his reach. If Kropotkin started asking questions, and Yuri started answering...

"...we go now," said the CNN anchor, "to our correspondent in Wilmington, Delaware, the site of last night's attempt on the life of Russian president, Kropotkin..."

"Shit!" spat Flemming. "More Wilmington! Why do we even have Delaware? It never does anything to help me! They're not worth their lousy three electoral votes!"

They switched to the reporter, an attractive woman, standing in Wilmington's Rodney Square.

"I'm here at the spot where at least two gunmen made an attempt on the life of visiting Russian president, Nikolai Kropotkin. We've learned that President Kropotkin will address the media to make what is being called a major announcement..."

"Not good, not good!" said Flemming. Major announcements from enraged world leaders were rarely helpful; especially not those he had placed in the assassins' crosshairs.

His secretary buzzed him on the intercom.

"What?!" Flemming snapped.

"Dr. Egonski is here, and..."

"Hold it a minute," he said.

Great, he thought, Kropotkin was poised to ruin his career, and now he had to deal with Dr. Egonski. Flemming reminded himself that the psychiatrist helped save Quinton Merton's presidency following his nervous breakdown the year before. Her methods, a sort of early-childhood regression therapy, were unconventional and would be politically ruinous if they became public, but they had kept Merton's fragile mind from completely going to pieces. All Flemming's one-man spin machine needed was someone who looked good, could deliver his lines, and not realize he was a complete tool.

Flemming brushed the crumbs off his desk and went to the door to welcome Dr. Egonski.

"Doctor," he said, forcing a smile for the forty-something blonde with her hair in a tight bun, "please, come in." Once the door was closed, he lowered his cheery façade. "Okay, how bad is he?"

"The President," said Dr. Egonski, "is comfortable. I've given him a sedative."

"You sedated him, now? I, that is, the country needs the President's hands-on guidance at this critical time, especially with what's going on in Wilmington with Kropotkin."

"That's what precipitated this current episode," she said. "You, that is, the country needn't worry. It's only a mild sedative. He's awake."

"Has he…" Flemming wanted to ask if Merton had been to "Romper Room," but he knew that Egonski took offense to flippant references to her treatment regimen. "Has the President had any…therapy today?"

"I tried to get him to participate in some higher level of his role-playing," said Dr. Egonski.

Flemming nodded. The "higher levels" meant that Merton played with toys appropriate for an eight-year-old.

"Unfortunately," she continued, "the shock of the attempt on President Kropotkin precluded his behavioral functionality on that level."

Flemming almost said, "so he flunked sandbox again," but caught himself.

"Currently he's calmest with a favorite stuffed animal," she said with a clinical detachment.

"Yes," said Flemming, "I brought him his teddy bear last night."

"You served him well, by doing so. I'm a strong believer in allowing the patient to find his or her comfort level as a safe base from which to stage their recovery."

Wonderful, thought Flemming. He needed a propped up, adult Quinton Merton, and Dr. Egonski seemed content to leave him in daycare.

"Where is he now?"

"He's resting comfortably in his office," said the Doctor.

"What's he wearing?" During his therapy sessions, the President had been known to wear cowboy hats, space helmets, or even feathered war bonnets.

"Simple slacks and a cardigan, I believe. That's one of the reasons I came to see you, Mr. Flemming, he's asking for you."

"And his therapy session is over?" With the Kropotkin crisis in full flower, Flemming didn't have time to read him nursery rhymes.

"For the time being, yes," she said. "Of course, I'll check in on him in the afternoon. But for now, he's quite calm, quite adult. When I left the President, he was sitting on the sofa in his office, watching the television..."

"The television," exclaimed Flemming. He looked over his shoulder at the wall-to-wall coverage of Kropotkin's announcement on the monitors. "Damn it, woman, you might as well left him chewing on razor blades, what were you thinking?"

Without waiting for an answer, Flemming dashed down the hall to the President's office, bursting into the room. A startled Quinton Merton looked up from his seat on the sofa and put his finger to his lips.

"Shh," said the President nodding to the large television in front of him.

Flemming's eyes darted to the screen where he saw an oversized pink lizard leading preschoolers in a song about crossing the street.

"Come on in, Davis," said the President once the song ended. "They're doing 'Please and Thank You' next."

"Thank you, sir," said Flemming, "but I really should be going. I'm monitoring a situation back in my office."

"Really," said Merton, sounding more adult, "is it important?"

Of course, it's important you infantile fool, Flemming thought. "Yes, sir, I suppose you could say it was important. I've got to get back. There's something on the news..."

"Well, let's watch it here," said the President picking up the remote.

"No, that's okay, sir," said Flemming backing away towards the door. "You wouldn't like it. It's not much fun."

"Nonsense," said Merton, "besides we have to share, don't we? That's what Ignatius says, isn't it?"

"Ignatius?"

"Ignatius Iguana," he said, nodding to the giant lizard. "Besides, I've seen this one twice already."

The President began flipping through the channels until he came to one of the cable news outlets. Then, he tucked the remote under his thigh, putting it out of Flemming's reach.

"There," he said with an odd mixture of presidential authority and preschool truculence. "Now, sit down."

"Yes, sir," said Flemming sitting on the opposite end of the sofa.

"Where's that?" said the President pointing at the screen.

"Wilmington, Delaware."

"Have I been there?"

"No."

"Did they vote for me?"

"Yes, twice," said Flemming.

"Oh, that's okay then."

"Are you sure you want to watch this, Mr. President? I mean, it's just a boring speech, I doubt if..."

"Look," said the President, "there's Nikolai."

"Yes, sir," said Flemming as Kropotkin exited the hotel. Absent any other new information, the reporter anchoring the coverage was commenting on Kropotkin's new suit, tailored that morning by one of the exclusive shops in the hotel's concourse.

"He's okay then," said the President. "They didn't shoot him?"

"Apparently," said Flemming rolling his eyes. It was like watching with a chatty six-year-old.

"He's about to begin," said the President. "What's it about?"

"No idea. Kropotkin called this one himself…"

Quinton Merton held up his hand signaling for silence and then pointed at the television screen. Nikolai Kropotkin strode up to the podium. He cut a dashing, larger than life figure in his dark blue double-breasted suit, and light gray tie.

"Look at all those TV cameras," said the President.

"That's more than were there last night," said Flemming. He saw many of the media who were at Camp David the night before. That damn Russian was stealing all the coverage. There had to be hundreds of reporters there, including the evening news anchors who usually stayed in New York. These, along with the local curiosity seekers, placed the crowd in the thousands.

"Don't they have anything better to do on a Saturday morning," muttered Flemming.

Kropotkin smiled as he looked into the bank of television cameras, and then removed a sheaf of papers from his breast pocket.

"My friends around the world," began the Russian, "this morning I am speaking to you from a site which a little more than twelve hours ago was intended to be the place of my premature death."

Here it comes, thought Flemming, he's going to blame us for the assassination attempt.

"I would like to thank those individuals, many of whom are here this morning," said Kropotkin as he gestured around at men and women in the crowd that Flemming knew were in the Secret Service, "who worked to prevent this infamous deed."

The agents standing in camera-range shifted uncomfortably at the mention, ruining even their semblance of anonymity. The fact that they all wore dark suits, dark glasses and held one hand to their ear already blew their cover.

"Sadly, the real heroine of the day is not here, however, though I would like to lionize her nonetheless."

"Ooh, lionize," exclaimed Merton. "See if we can have Lyonnais potatoes at lunch. They're very tasty!"

"This young woman," said Kropotkin, "not only saved the insignificant life of a politician, but she also saved the much greater cause of world peace. I am speaking of course of one of the bravest, wisest individuals I have ever met, America's own, Lorraine Innis."

41

The audience applauded.

"Lorraine Innis?" said President Merton.

"Yes, sir," said Flemming through gritted teeth. She had made his life that much more difficult with her heroics.

"Did she vote for me?"

"I don't know. Probably not, sir."

"Oh? Do we like her?"

"No!"

"It is in tribute to this remarkable woman," continued Kropotkin, "that I have crafted this manifesto."

Kropotkin held up several sheets of hotel stationery.

"I have named it 'the Lorraine Accord,' in honor of the remarkable Mrs. Innis. It is a plan for global disarmament that I will first present to President Merton…"

"How nice, presents!" said Merton.

"…and then to the other leaders around the world as a blueprint for a lasting and equitable peace and security for all the world's peoples."

"I anticipate the reaction of many skeptics," said Kropotkin as the photographers clicked their cameras. "I too would view such a bold promise with skepticism. To these individuals I say the Lorraine Accord will lead us into a new era of cooperation between nations, a reality you will see for yourself once the plan is unfolded in the coming days.

"Others may object that this is another ploy in the game of international power politics. I would not criticize anyone for thinking so, after all, that is what the majority of we world leaders are - politicians. I am a politician, first and foremost, normally acting out of my own short-sighted self-interest."

There was an audible gasp from the reporters.

Very clever, thought Flemming, every one of those reporters knows that "statesmen" are only small-time hack politicians but on a bigger stage. However, for one of them to admit it was astonishing. It was just one step above admitting they're all liars.

"I have also lied to you all," said Kropotkin next, evoking an even more audible reaction. "I have allowed rumors that I was an alcoholic to spread unchallenged. I am not an alcoholic, nor have I ever appeared in public drunk. I purposely allowed this impression to go on because I was hiding something of which I was even more ashamed."

The clicks of the photographers' shutters came even more furiously.

"I suffer from a condition called 'candida,'" Kropotkin confessed. "Simply put, this means I cannot properly digest products containing yeast. Doing so converts certain foods to alcohol in my stomach. I apologize for any hurt this deception has caused my country, my friends and my family. I also apologize to the kind ladies who had the misfortune to witness my latest candida-induced episode last night. I beg your forgiveness."

"Wow," said Quinton Merton, "he can't even have a sandwich. How 'bout that! He can't even eat a box of animal crackers."

"I'd like to shove a whole menagerie of them down his windpipe," grumbled Flemming. The media around the podium were almost in a feeding frenzy of news, and why not? Any of Kropotkin's announcements would have made headlines around the world for days. Flemming imagined the editors of the major news magazines throwing their pressrooms into chaos as they scrapped their weekly editions in the light of the unfolding events.

"I admit, this news is also a little hard to digest," said Kropotkin as he humbly folded his hands in front of him. "Again, I must credit this to my dear friend, Lorraine Innis. It was her remarkable act of self-sacrifice that made me take pause and ask: 'why?' Why would this American woman risk her life to save the life of a cynical politician and his only child? Her bravery helped me realize that the pomp and posturing of the international arena is not real life. Real life is the everyday love and kindness of parents towards their children, family for family, friends for friends, and even, on occasion, strangers for other strangers. We politicians can swagger and maneuver, and jostle for advantage among ourselves, but it doesn't matter in the end. What matters ultimately are the seemingly insignificant acts of daily life that make our existence bearable, and the occasional sacrifices that hold out hope for a brighter future. This is a human trait the world over that is too often forgotten in the halls of power. It is the lesson that has been taught to me by my angel of peace, Lorraine Innis."

Kropotkin closed his unscripted remarks by reaching for a handkerchief. Upon finding that he hadn't one in his new suit, he dabbed away a tear from the corner of his eye using the cuff of his new shirt. A majority of the hard-boiled press corps joined him in the misty moment. Indeed, the entire crowd stood in hushed silence for more than a minute, overcome by the sheer momentousness of it all. The more misanthropic ones, Davis Flemming included, were dumbstruck by the realization that, for the first and probably last time, they had witnessed a politician speak with undiluted sincerity. After another minute Nikolai Kropotkin looked up and noticed the media was still in rapt attention.

"Please, excuse me," the statesman said with a shrug of his shoulders, "I must now go and visit my nephew in the hospital."

Kropotkin walked back into the hotel as the crowd of reporters silently watched. Only after he departed did the assembly break into soft, almost reverent applause.

"Well, that was pretty interesting," said President Merton finally. "I'll have to watch the news more often."

"Political grandstanding!" said Flemming.

"Is it?" asked Merton. "Gee, he seems pretty sincere."

"It's all for show! It's not bad enough that he pulled that surprise visit to Delaware, but now this. You know, Sir," added Flemming as he jumped from his chair, "I wouldn't be surprised to find out that the whole assassination thing was a set-up. He's just trying to leverage you out of the spotlight on this summit deal - public relationally. And now this so-called 'Lorraine Accord,' and this mystery illness…all a play for public sympathy. It's just like those false rumors we planted about you after the New Hampshire primary then blamed them on your opponent! That's all it is. Well, we can play this game, can't we, Sir? Sir? Oh, no."

Flemming ended his rant to discover that his boss had a freshly glazed expression on his face. Flemming's cynical reaction to Kropotkin's announcement had been too much for Merton to process. Merton had withdrawn, much as an insecure child would after a parent's outburst. Now, the President of the United States was staring glassy-eyed at the screen, holding the edge of his sweater like a makeshift security blanket.

"Sir, sir?" Flemming waved his arm in front of Merton's face and then let it drop. "Oh, shit! You're gone!"

Flemming switched the television back to the preschool channel. There a hippopotamus hand puppet was teaching about dental hygiene. The President fixed his eyes on the screen, as Davis Flemming went off in search of Dr. Egonski.

- 6 -
Bang, Bang, Twankey's Silver Pacer
Went Racing Down the Hill

While Nikolai Kropotkin was offering to save the world in Lorraine's name, his inspiration for world peace was rummaging through Valerie Fierro's closet trying to find something to wear.

If Lorraine had realized the attention Kropotkin's speech would bring, she would have looked through Valerie's suits. If she knew the media attention that was beginning to focus on her, Lorraine would have climbed inside the closet and hid.

At that moment, however, Lorraine was doing all she could to concentrate on the parts of her life that provided her with some semblance of sanity. She accomplished this by sorting her mind, much as she was currently sorting Valerie's closet. Just as she was categorizing Valerie's clothing as "suitable" and "unsuitable" to wear, so Lorraine was arranging thoughts as "worthy" and "not worthy" to remember.

Orange top? No, she thought, orange isn't my best color.

Martin! How could he say those things? No, I can't think of him right now. If I do, I'll lose my mind.

That skirt is good, but is it too tight across my...

My groin? Does that show? Maybe I should just go to the doctor? But what would I tell them?

The doctor? Yes, I've got to see the doctor, about Valerie. My problems can wait. I've still got my health; my physical health, generally speaking. But I've got to keep focused. I've got to help Valerie get well. After she's well, then she can help me figure this out. Just keep remembering that, and forget the rest.

Hmm, that green top... Green? No, not with my ashy complexion.

Finally, she settled on a mid-length denim skirt that flared enough as not to reveal her less than feminine assets, and a red ribbed turtleneck sweater that accentuated the others. As Lorraine sat at Valerie's vanity to put on her makeup, she felt her focus increase as she applied the cosmetics. Her confidence grew, as each brush stroke seemed to say "Lorraine, Lorraine, Lorraine," covering over any confusion asserting itself in other regions. One final swipe of lipstick and Lorraine was ready to go to the hospital. She looked out the front window, there sitting in the driveway was the bulbous AMC Pacer that Purvis Twankey had provided as a loaner car. The vehicle's shiny silver paint job combined with its unusual shape made it look like a giant blob of mercury from an oversized thermometer. Still, Lorraine sighed, it would get her to the hospital. She walked downstairs and took a light jacket from the hall closet, picked up her purse, and walked out of the house. Parked out on the street was a local TV news van, with two competitor's vans waiting catty-corner from it. All three vans had their microwave relay towers at full mast. Preoccupied with the events of her personal life Lorraine saw the vans, but that they might be waiting for her, failed to register in her mind. The crews of the vans seemed preoccupied as well. Since they didn't seem to be paying her any attention, she ignored them as well.

Lorraine climbed into the Pacer, adjusted the seat, and put the key in the ignition.

"An 8-Track player?" Lorraine exclaimed, noticing the large plastic case sticking out of the car's stereo. "Rubber Soul," she said, reading the label on the tape. It stood to reason that, being from Northern England, Purvis Twankey would be a fan of the Beatles. She turned the key, and the engine groaned to life, as did the 8-Track. Quite appropriately, "Drive My Car," began to play, but soon came to a grinding halt as the antiquated tape machine started to eat the equally ancient tape, bringing the song to a constipated stop. Lorraine pulled the tape out of its player and was treated to a pile of brown plastic fettuccine coated with iron oxide gravy; so much for the 8-Track. She'd drive to the hospital a capella.

Any hope of a peaceful drive was interrupted as Lorraine threw the gear shift into reverse.

The exhaust system rebelled as the tape player had: audibly and with a resounding BANG!

"Oh, great," said Lorraine, backing into the street. When she went to put the car into drive, another loud BANG punctuated the movement.

Lorraine looked in the rearview mirror. If her leaving the house had been noiseless, the performance of the Pacer more than made up for it. The three news vans were now a flurry of activity as engineers scrambled to lower microwave masts, drivers shouted instructions, and reporters frantically hopped up and down.

Lorraine could hear shouts of: "Mrs. Innis, stop," "we want to ask you a few questions," and "she's getting away."

Wanting no part of any interviews, Lorraine drove on as quickly as the speed limit would allow. As she reached the end of the block, she saw in the rear view mirror that the news vans lacked her respect for residential traffic laws. The three vans were following her and burning rubber as they came. Perhaps, she hoped, they weren't after her but had been summoned away to an important story.

Lorraine pulled out of Valerie's development and on to busy Limestone Road when the three vans came tearing around the corner in hot pursuit. In their mad scramble, the vehicle from the CBS affiliate almost sideswiped the NBC affiliate in an attempt to pass the ABC van in the lead. Once out on the main road, Lorraine realized she knew the general direction to Wilmington, but didn't know how to get to the hospital. She was about to turn into a gas station to ask directions when she checked her rearview mirror. There, bearing down on her in a triangular formation, were the three news vans jockeying for position and gaining on the Pacer. Rather than pull over, Lorraine instinctively stepped on the gas. The loaner car responded with several backfires, and then a surprising burst of speed. As the Pacer pulled away, its pursuers also put down their accelerators, closing the gap once more.

The Pike Creek suburb of Wilmington, where Valerie Fierro lived, is heavily populated. Its main artery, Limestone Road, is a busy thoroughfare that wound up and down several steep hills with only strategically placed traffic lights on hand to break up the roller coaster effect of the topography. As Lorraine picked up the pace, gaining on the downslopes and losing up the hills, she was glad that the road had two lanes in each direction - not counting various turning lanes and concrete islands - giving her plenty of room to maneuver. Unfortunately, the wide roadway not only allowed her space to dodge other cars, but it also gave her pursuers plenty of room to do the same. As she passed several strip shopping centers, she was glad that it was early enough that the Saturday morning traffic had not reached its peak, and she'd only had two near collisions.

Nearing the crest of a hill, Lorraine noticed the traffic light atop it was turning yellow. Normally, for prudence sake, she would stop, but Lorraine reasoned, prudence wasn't driving with her today. Flooring the gas pedal, the Pacer emitted another BANG and lurched forward, flying through the yellow just as it turned red, soaring airborne over the crest of the hill, and hitting on the other side with a metallic crunch that gave all the Pacer's, and some of Lorraine's spare parts a good jiggle.

"That'll hold them," Lorraine muttered, as she eased off the gas and looked up into the rearview mirror. "Oh, no!"

The CBS affiliate had run the red light with all four wheels off the ground and was pulling up on her right. The reporter inside was leaning across the driver, blocking his view, sticking her head out the window and thrusting a microphone at Lorraine. In the back window, a cameraman was filming the attempted interview.

"Mrs. Innis," shouted the reporter, "Lorraine! Could you…"

"Go away," shouted Lorraine through the closed window, and pulled ahead.

She could still hear the reporter shouting, but couldn't make out the words. Why couldn't they just leave her alone? Another look in her mirror showed no sight of the other two vans. At least they had sensibly given up, and…

Her thoughts were interrupted by the frantic honking of two horns. Lorraine looked behind her, then to the right, and finally, to the left. There, across a concrete median, driving southbound in the two northbound lanes were the NBC and ABC vans, pulling even with her. Their reporters were similarly hanging out the windows and shouting questions while their cameramen rolled, and their drivers forced on-coming motorists off the road.

In an attempt to stop the vehicular madness, Lorraine pulled far enough ahead of the van on her right to cut across the lane and swerve into a supermarket parking lot. The severity of the turn caused the Pacer to bank on two wheels, but thankfully the squat design of the "world's first wide small car" kept it from flipping over. The CBS van followed her into the lot, while the other two were forced to cut across the highway, back into their proper lanes, where they accessed the parking lot further down the road.

Lorraine dodged in and out of parked cars, around loose shopping carts, and between light posts with the skill of an Olympic skier on the alpine slalom. She was heading for the lot's far exit, when she noticed the ABC and NBC vans converging on either side of her, attempting to cut off her escape in a pincer movement.

With a spirited backfire from the Pacer's exhaust, Lorraine floored the gas pedal and sped for the exit. The vans came on quicker. Someone, Lorraine reasoned, will have to give way. She was banking on the fact that the news vans wouldn't plow into the very person they wanted to interview, or would they?

"You can't hit me," Lorraine shouted, "it's not logical!" But still, the news vans continued on a collision course.

"I can't let them hit me," Lorraine said, "not in a borrowed car." But she kept her foot on the gas.

"I want to get to the hospital, but not as a patient…"

The vans kept coming.

"…I can't get hurt," Lorraine suddenly recalled. "If they examined me …it could be quite embarrassing."

With the thought of her recent "addition" being exposed in an emergency room, with several TV news crews there to cover the revelation, Lorraine lifted her foot off the accelerator and slammed on the brake. The Pacer went into a skid, with Lorraine pulling the steering wheel to the left, bringing the car to a halt, ten yards short of her impact point with the vans. A split second later, both vans also pulled up short, not for Lorraine's sake, but in response to the four brown and white New Castle County police cruisers that injected themselves into the situation, their lights blazing and sirens blaring.

Lorraine breathed a sigh of relief. Baring a strip search, she'd much rather wind up in a police station than an emergency room. As an officer emerged from the cruiser nearest her car, however, Lorraine felt her relief consolidate into a lump in her throat, which then sank into a pitiful feeling in her stomach. What was she going to tell this policeman? What excuse could she give for taking part in such an outrageous display of vehicular mayhem? Take part in it? Lorraine not only joined in the insanity, but she also inspired it, and she drove the pace car.

She fished her New Jersey driver's license from her purse and rolled down the window. Maybe she should cry. Hadn't Valerie told her that a pretty girl crying could always beat a ticket? Was Lorraine pretty enough? Could she cry on cue? Also, she doubted whether the approaching trooper was going to issue her a standard speeding ticket. The real question was: could a reasonably attractive woman crying, beat a charge of motorized lunacy?

The officer with the flat-brimmed Smokey the Bear hat and the reflective sunglasses stooped down and peered into her window. "Lorraine Innis," he asked in a voice that sounded impervious to all tears.

"Yes, officer," squeaked Lorraine as she held out her license. She wondered how she would get to the hospital and ultimately back home after her car had been impounded for her part in the suburban stock car race. "Look, I know I was wrong, but those vans began chasing me and something inside me panicked, and…"

"Mrs. Innis," interrupted the officer, "we've been designated to escort you to St. Francis Hospital. Will you please follow us?"

"…I just naturally…" Lorraine stopped in mid-sentence and just batted her eyelashes. "Escort? To the hospital?"

"Yes, Mrs. Innis, it would be our honor."

"Wow!" said Lorraine, "even Valerie never dodged a ticket like this!"

- 7 -
I've Always Relied on the Kindness of the Insentient

Purvis Twankey had been waiting over four hours for visiting time to begin at St. Francis Hospital. He didn't have anything better to do. He didn't need to address the international media. He didn't need to regress into his childhood. He didn't have a traumatic fight on the telephone, agonize over sudden and unexplained changes in his body, or lead a fleet of news vans in mobile pandemonium. Since the previous evening, his only pressing business, after dropping off the loaner car for Lorraine, had been rinsing out his socks and going to bed. The next morning when he awoke he had even less to do given that his socks were now clean. There was nothing left to do but wait at the hospital for Lorraine Innis to appear. While he waited, Purvis went to work on a love song that he titled: "Lorraine."

Despite having written dozens of songs, mostly about horses and black pudding, Purvis Twankey was having trouble immortalizing his secret love in a ballad. The beginning was easy. It oozed from his overflowing heart like treacle from a treacle tart.

"Oh, Lorraine, Lorraine, Lorraine..." began Purvis riding his initial wave of inspiration. After this crest, however, he stared at his large yellow writing tablet for the better part of an hour while he sat in the hospital lobby.

The difficulty was not in finding a rhyme for "Lorraine," there were plenty of those. His problem was that all the rhymes he could think of were less than complimentary. When you want to sweep a woman off her feet with a heart-wrenching love song, Purvis figured, it was best not to insult her in the process.

"Lorraine, Lorraine," muttered Purvis Twankey as he clamped his eyes shut in thought. "Lorraine...insane. No, that's no good."

"Lorraine...plain. No, she's not plain; she's beautiful."

"Lorraine...pain. Ee, that's worse...can't call her a pain, ye dozy twonk!"

"Lorraine...drain. Nobody thinks 'bout drains, 'less they back up."

"Lorraine...strain. No, don't be daft!"

"Lorraine...brain. Hmm. That might work. Lorraine, Lorraine, Lorraine, you're always on my brain."

Purvis thought about it a moment, then another moment, and finally he wrote it down, studied it, and then finally tore it up.

"It's all right to say a lass is on your mind," he concluded, "but saying she's on your brain sounds like you're calling her a tumor!"

"Lorraine...bane. Bane?" He knew "bane" was a word, but he wasn't sure what it meant. It sounded medieval, however, and that meant knights and damsels in distress, and women loved that kind of romantic thing. Purvis reached in his jeans for the tattered pocket dictionary he carried for composing emergencies.

"A person or thing that ruins or spoils," Purvis read aloud (as he always did when by himself). "A deadly poison."

"Ee, by gum!" he muttered, tossing the dictionary aside. You might, he reasoned, be able to slip over a word like "bane" on a less educated girl, but Lorraine was too smart to be swayed by a sloppy lyric...especially with her being a book editor. You didn't want to compare a pretty book editor to a deadly poison, no matter how well it rhymed.

Purvis paced the waiting area, partially to stir his mind, partially to stir his foot, which had fallen asleep.

Lorraine...inane. He couldn't give a dictionary definition of "inane," but he knew it wasn't very flattering. If only he had met her on a train. Lorraine, Lorraine, Lorraine, I'm so glad we both took that train. That would have been great since country songs and locomotives just naturally went together. Or if they'd met on a plane...on their way to Spain! The possibilities! Too bad the weather had been fair. Lorraine, Lorraine, Lorraine, we met that day in the rain. Rain was another popular component of country songs.

As he continued, Purvis realized that he met the girl of his dreams under terrible circumstances for composing a ballad. They had their accident on a street, not a lane. The pavement had been dry, so his car didn't hydroplane. Though her cousin bled, she hadn't gotten any on Lorraine, thus avoiding a stain.

After hours of effort, Purvis Twankey sat down to rest.

"Ee, but love hurts," he confessed, as he rubbed the sides of his lucky boots. His main impetus for wearing the boots today lay in the fact that they had a two-and-a-half inch heel. Usually, Purvis cared little about his height, but now he hoped this extra lift would allow the woman of his dreams to look up to, rather than down at, him. At the very least, he hoped, they would see eye-to-eye.

Purvis Twankey's brittle concentration was broken when a hospital volunteer turned on the television suspended from the ceiling in the corner of the room. A news station was playing excerpts from Nikolai

Kropotkin's "Lorraine Accord" speech (as it had been tagged) along with commentary by the anchors on its importance and the woman of the hour: Lorraine Innis.

Purvis sat in stunned silence. He didn't have a television at home, long having vandalized his 13" Toshiba for parts that went into his various inventions. Thus, Purvis knew nothing of Lorraine's fame. Hungry for any details on Lorraine, he welcomed the sketchy information being aired. After realizing, however, that the facts were rather incomplete, Purvis became disenchanted with the coverage. He was glad he had stripped his own TV bare if the medium wasn't going to tell him her favorite color, her brand of perfume, or what hobbies she enjoyed in her spare time. Purvis' disillusionment turned to dismay as he realized that the time allotted to Lorraine's part of the story surpassed that given to the Russian president. She was famous, really famous. Words like "inspiring," "brave," and "symbol of hope" were being bandied about with disconcerting ease. Purvis would be the first person to admit that he was a traditional Northern Englishman, with old-fashioned Lancastrian notions, especially when it came to roles of men and women. In his mind, a wife should not be more famous than her husband. His mother hadn't been more famous than his father. True, neither of them was the least bit famous, but at least they were equally inconspicuous. That was the way it should be, Purvis thought. The aspiring inventor and cowboy singer didn't know if he could reach his full potential next to a wife who was both a book editor and an icon of international peace.

"Ee," he muttered to himself as he watched the unfolding coverage, "'ere I am trying to write a song to tell her how special she is, and everyone all over telly is doing a much better job of it! A fellow can't keep up with that sort of competition! I feel a right puddin'!"

He stared down at his yellow pad with its three identical words scribbled on it and felt very foolish. He felt like crying, but couldn't bring himself to do so while wearing his special boots. Instead, he just bit his lip and watched the television as they once again replayed the two extant film clips of Lorraine Innis, the first showing her thwarting of the assassination, the second of her exiting the hotel a few hours later.

Seeing her made Purvis's lips smile, though his eyes felt just as they had back when he was a boy, and his father backed the family's Morris Minor over his tricycle. He sure did love her, but now, apparently, so did everyone else. His heartache eased a minute later when one of the newscasters mentioned the fact that, although they weren't sure of her husband's name, the prevailing belief was that Lorraine Innis was a married woman. A close-up of Lorraine in the second clip confirmed this. It showed her shielding her eyes from the photographers' flashes with her left hand which bore both an engagement and wedding band.

Purvis Twankey crumpled up his abortive love song and tossed it in the nearby wastebasket as if it were an object of shame. Yesterday he had been so enamored of Lorraine that he failed to notice the rings on her finger. Purvis was embarrassed for entertaining the notion of a relationship with another man's wife, even inadvertently. He wasn't that type of cowboy singer, nor that type of inventor; not even that type of auto mechanic. Purvis felt his face glow a bright crimson, before realizing that he hadn't told anyone of his passion for "Miss Lorraine." Fanning himself with his cowboy hat, he breathed a sigh of relief. Just then a gentle bell sounded marking the beginning of visiting hours. Purvis went to the reception desk to get a visitor's pass. Even if he wasn't going to be related to Valerie by marriage, Purvis still felt an obligation to the woman he had put in the hospital.

Exiting the elevator, Purvis walked down the corridor to Valerie's room. He was surprised to find that no one else was there, not even Lorraine. There were no doctors or nurses around either. The double room was still only occupied by Valerie, who lay in the bed nearest the door. Aside from the card and flowers that Patsy Einfalt brought the night before, the only other foreign objects in the room were several plates of cheese. The television was on, but with the sound turned down low. Purvis crossed to the remote control and shut off the set, then picked up a wedge of cheddar and slowly chewed on it while standing over Valerie. It was the first time Purvis had a good look at her.

He examined her face. It sure was pretty, he thought. He hated to seem fickle, but Purvis Twankey admitted Valerie was almost as pretty as her cousin. As much as he liked Lorraine, perhaps she was a bit too flashy. Valerie on the other hand, aside from the tubes running up her nose, had a clean, fresh-scrubbed, natural look about her. Purvis liked that in a woman. He even liked the kink in her nose. It reminded him of an Alsatian he had as a boy.

As he helped himself to another slice of cheese, Purvis began talking to the unconscious young woman in the bed.

"I sure am sorry, Miss Valerie," he began, and then stopped to examine her ring finger. It was bare. Breathing a sigh of relief, he continued. "I would have liked to say all this yesterday, but they wouldn't let me in. Honest, I tried to see you. Your cousin can tell you. She was right upset with me, too. I can't blame her for being upset with me. Ee, but I was a right pillock, rammin' into your car that way, and puttin' you here in hospital. I don't blame her for being mad, but she's been just champion to me. Your friend Patsy was here too. She's nice an' all."

Purvis scanned the room trying to think of something else to talk about.

"Those flowers over there," said Purvis nodding, "your friend, Miss Patsy, brung 'em. I don't know if you've seen them, but they're pretty. Least I think they're pretty. I think you're pretty, too."

That last observation just slipped out. Purvis Twankey didn't make a habit of telling unconscious women they were beautiful.

"Sorry," he said, recovering from his brash compliment, "You'll think me a cheeky fast cat, but I'm not. I don't usually say things like that to girls I hardly know. But, Ee, you are a looker. You're even as pretty as your cousin, and I was a bit daft over her recently, and no mistake."

Purvis Twankey, encouraged by the lack of a negative response, relaxed. He had never talked to a girl who made him feel so at ease. But then, he had never talked to a semi-comatose girl before, either. Sitting on the edge of the bed, Purvis took off his cowboy hat and continued baring his soul to Valerie Fierro.

"Ee, but I had quite a bit of a crush on your cousin," he continued. "She really is champion, that Lorraine."

"Cheese," groaned Valerie, her eyes still closed.

"Thanks, don't mind if I do!" Purvis popped another chunk of cheese into his mouth. "What a woman. Little wonder some lucky chap swept her up. A man would be a fool not to grab a lady like your Lorraine."

"Cheese," repeated Valerie in a barely audible moan.

"Oh, no, I've had three already…well, maybe just one more. It's tasty, but I don't want to eat up all your cheese." He looked around the room. "No crackers? Ee, but they make some champion crackers for cheese back home. I'll have me mum send me some, and we'll have a real do. I'll bring the crackers, and we can invite Miss Patsy and your Lorraine…"

"Cheese," moaned Valerie.

"Yes, and you can bring the cheese, an' all. Ee, I never knew a lass that was so fond of cheese. I never knew one that was so easy to talk to, an' all. You're nowt like other girls. By that, I mean you're better. When you get all woke up an' out of hospital, I sure would, I mean, I'd be honored if…that is…"

Purvis Twankey stopped to muster up his courage as well as to suck a stray wedge of cheese out from behind his molar. The cheddar fragment dislodged with a loud pop.

"What I'm trying to say is, Miss Valerie, you wouldn't want to step out with a great puddin' like me? Would you? I know you can't really answer now but think about it. Rest on it. I guess you've got plenty of time to do that, an' all."

Purvis tensed as he heard a footstep behind him followed by a gentle cough. Turning around, Purvis saw a priest standing just inside the doorway. After staring at the priest for a moment, Purvis realized he was still sitting on the bed and hopped off of it.

"Sorry," said the priest, "didn't mean to disturb you."

"Oh, 'eck, uh, no, I, mean we were just having a bit of a chin wag, your worship, just having a bit of a chat."

"I can come back," offered the priest, "Mr…."

"Twankey, Purvis Twankey," said Purvis extending his hand, and then drew it back to wipe some cheesy residue from his fingers on to his jeans.

"Yes, well, Purvis," said the priest, as he shook Twankey's hand, "nice to meet you. I'm Mike Valvano."

Purvis eyed the priest, who he guessed was around five ten, and like himself, slim. He had curly light brown hair, and a narrow face, which was perfectly divided by a thin, pointy nose. He was in his late twenties or early thirties.

"Are you Miss Fierro's, um, uh, vicar?" asked Purvis, not sure whether this Mike was a father, or padre, or reverend.

"No," said Father Valvano, "nothing as impressive as all that. I'm just the assistant rector at St. Anthony's. It's just up the hill," he gestured over his shoulder. "I was on my usual morning visitation rounds and saw the name outside the door. Is she a Catholic?"

"Who?"

"Miss Fierro," said Father Mike nodding towards Valerie.

"Oh, um, I don't rightly know. We haven't got 'round to discussing religion yet."

"Well, I can come back," said the priest.

"No, I can leave for a minute if you want to sprinkle her with something, or pray, or do them beads, or..." said Purvis trailing off.

"That would be fine," said the priest. "I think I'll just pray today. I left my sprinkler back at the rectory. I won't be long. You don't have to leave."

"No, I'll just go out for a while and...do...something else," said Purvis backing out of the room and closing the door behind him.

Purvis Twankey didn't do something else; instead, he stood opposite Valerie's room and waited for the priest to leave. After a few minutes, he started getting fidgety. How long was this prayer going to take? If this indicative of Mike Valvano's way of doing things, he wouldn't be stopping into St. Anthony's for a quick sermon on a Sunday. Of course, he wasn't a Catholic, but still, long sermons put him to sleep. Another thought struck Purvis. What if Valerie was Catholic? This may be important, for though Purvis Twankey didn't usually act fast in matters of romance, his heart did. What about their children? Would that be a big issue? Oh, well, thought Purvis, he could always get himself some prayer beads. After all, Valerie was awfully pretty and really easy to talk to, at least while she was out cold.

Purvis Twankey's reverie was cut short as a trio of nurses strode up the hall and into Valerie's room. He tried to get a peek into the room, but the last nurse closed the door behind her. Purvis heard some general commotion in the room, and then after a few more minutes, the nurses emerged wheeling Valerie and her bed with them. Father Valvano was the last to exit the room. The priest nodded to Purvis as he started up the hall. Purvis grabbed Father Mike's elbow.

"Ee, what's to do? Where are they taking Miss Valerie?"

"She's going upstairs," informed the priest.

"Upstairs?" Purvis' heart sank. He'd lost another girlfriend. That made two in less than twenty-four hours. And he had no other prospects since they were the only girls in the car he had rammed. He hung his head low. Then he realized that not only was his new girlfriend gone, but he caused her demise. Purvis Twankey felt sick.

"Yes, they're moving her to a private suite," said Father Valvano.

"Private…you mean she's not dead?" asked Purvis.

"Dead? Who said she was dead?"

"Well, you know, I thought maybe 'upstairs' was, like, priest talk for dead, an' all," said Purvis, embarrassed by his lack of fluency in ecclesiastical lingo.

"No, it isn't," said the priest.

"Well, what do you vicar rector chaps say when someone has died?"

"Usually, something like, 'they're dead.'"

"And 'upstairs?'"

"Usually means 'on a higher floor than the one you're currently on,'" said the priest.

"And not heaven?" clarified Purvis.

"No, usually we just refer to that place as 'heaven."

"Ee, you lads have words for everything," said Purvis Twankey with a shake of his head. "No wonder you all have to go to school for so long."

"Yes, so long," said Mike Valvano.

Purvis watched the priest depart down the hall and into one of the elevators before he realized he didn't find out where upstairs Valerie was being moved. He ran towards the elevators, but the door had already closed. To Purvis' surprise, however, the second elevator opened and out stepped Lorraine Innis.

Purvis stopped short as Lorraine exited the elevator, then took a long look at her from head to toe, and gulped involuntarily. In her ribbed sweater, Lorraine looked plenty healthy. He recalled the meeting they had attended the night before on breastfeeding and thought she'd make a dandy model for their recruitment posters. For a split-second, he thought about switching back from Valerie to Lorraine until he remembered the rings on her left hand.

While Purvis was staring at Lorraine, he noticed she was staring at him, as well. It was as if she were taking inventory, or trying to make up her mind about something. He came to her eye level now, thanks to his wearing his best boots.

"How do, Miss Lorraine," he said, then recalled she was married, "I mean, ma'am." He smiled sheepishly.

Then, without warning, Lorraine threw her arms around him and embraced him.

"Uh, Miss Lorraine," stuttered Purvis, "um, I mean, Mrs. Innis…"

"Please, just hold me," said Lorraine. "I just need someone to hold me."

"Yes, ma'am," said Purvis, as he cautiously put his arms around her. She squeezed him more tightly, nearly introducing his front ribs to those around back.

Purvis cursed his bad luck. Why couldn't she have done this yesterday before she was married? Then he reminded himself that Lorraine had been married the day before, only he hadn't known it.

"Did you find the car I left?" He gasped, "I got the address from Miss Patsy…"

"Please, Purvis, don't speak."

"Okay, I won't," said Purvis Twankey being simultaneously agreeable and contrary.

"Hush," she said.

"For how long?" he asked trying to comply precisely with her request for silence.

"Please, Purvis, just hold me. You don't mind, do you?"

Purvis Twankey crooked his chin downward as best as he could in the position he found himself. From his vantage point, he could see Lorraine's healthy bosom neatly filling in the cavity of his own sunken chest. He gulped again.

"No, I don't mind, not at all," he squeaked in a register he hadn't used since the onset of puberty.

"I just need someone who will make me feel like… like a woman."

"Ee, you sure feel like one to me," he gasped.

Resigned to his momentary role as a hugger, Purvis decided to relax as best he could and enjoyed the view while it lasted. Still, he felt a little guilty for his infidelity to Valerie, especially after they'd been getting on so well together. To soothe his conscience, Purvis Twankey closed his eyes, enjoyed the moment, and hoped that bodies ran in the family.

– 8 –
The Steel Cage Mantra

L affler, visitor," said the guard at Gander Hill Prison.

Aaron Laffler looking much the worse for his recent experiences peered through the steel bars. Due to the magnitude of his crime, Laffler had been locked up by himself. He was grateful for this. Otherwise, he had feared that he would have been selected to be the "wife" of some beefy inmate with a name like "Moose." Also, Laffler didn't think he could use the toilet with other people watching him, and the open plan facilities left little room for modesty.

Laffler was stunned to see his wife Marcia bouncing in from the free world. She looked smart in her silk pantsuit, despite her usual vacant expression.

As they faced each other with the bars between them, Laffler thought about the first time they had met. There were bars then, too. He was a senior at Penn; she was Marcia Delneczak working in a go-go club, dancing in a cage. It was the first bar he'd ever been to. He loved the sense of excitement she brought to his life. She had a constant need for outside stimulation that he found vital. Being an Ivy Leaguer, Laffler was tired of women with long thick sweaters who wanted to discuss relevant social issues till dawn. He wanted some vapid irrelevance. He didn't particularly like television, however, so Marcia was the perfect person with whom to turn off his mind and relax. Both had met the other when they'd had their fill of the usual types they had dated.

"Hi, Arri," said Marcia with a smile. "What's new?"

Laffler just stared at her as if the answer to her question were self-evident. Still, he thought, she had never been known for her depth. If had he any fight left in him he would have grabbed Marcia's neck through the bars and screamed: "What do you mean, 'what's new?' I'm in prison for trying to assassinate a world leader, and you drove me to it!"

That he no longer had the urge for even enjoyable violence was probably a good sign. He was adjusting to his situation and beginning to deal with it rationally.

"I came over as soon as I heard what happened."

"What for?" said Aaron Laffler warily.

"To be with my husband in his time of need."

Laffler stared at her. She sounded sincere. Perhaps there was a spark of caring left for him in her heart. Maybe his daring act had rekindled their marriage. Maybe he had overreacted to her leaving. Peter Liverot stealing his business was devastating, but he would have weathered it without resorting to violence if he still had her love. Now, here she was when he needed her. Poor Marcia, she was easy prey to Liverot's money and flashy lifestyle. Now, when it really mattered, she was back where she belonged. The expression of suspicion on Laffler's face relaxed into a soft smile. He could feel his sanity returning to him for the first time since she had walked out two days earlier.

"Thank you," said Laffler as he touched Marcia's manicured fingers through the bars. "I really appreciate it."

"Yeah," agreed Marcia, "Petey said you would."

"Petey?"

"Petey Liverot."

"WHAT!"

"I know, I thought it was pretty corny, too," she said.

"Pretty corny?"

"Yeah, real square." She unwrapped a stick of Juicyfruit and crumpled it into her mouth, "Petey said I should wear black or something. But I thought that was kinda over the top. Don't you? I mean, you're not dead, yet!"

"Yet?" His dalliance with mental health began to flit away.

"Yeah, I mean they got a pretty good case from what the TV is saying. Petey says they got the death penalty in Delaware, too."

Aaron Laffler fought the urge to renew his career as a deranged assassin. He took two deep breaths.

"Marcia," he began, "thank you for coming in this morning. I know this cannot be a pleasant venue in which to meet me."

Marcia Laffler looked down at her ensemble in puzzlement.

"Venue," he sighed, "means the place we're meeting, not what you're wearing."

"Oh," she smiled, "that's a good one. I'll have to remember that."

"I think I've had enough comforting right now…"

"Okay," said Marcia. "I can wear a black dress next time if you like. Well, if you want to be alone, I'll get going. I'll be back at the house if you need me."

"Our home?" he asked. "I'm surprised you'd want to go back there."

"Yeah, well, I really want to be there."

Laffler wavered for a moment, as did his sanity. Marcia never was very bright, he thought. Like a simple-minded child, she was easily swayed by the last person she talked to. He had no doubt that Liverot said all those things, and told her what to do and say, and she, unthinking, repeated everything, including his instructions, verbatim. But perhaps he was jumping to conclusions. Maybe he could still win her back. He still loved her, and she was going home. The home they shared as man and wife. And she wanted to be there. There was still a connection between them, no matter what Liverot said or did.

"You're going back to our home?"

"Yeah," said Marcia with a smile.

"That's nice," said Laffler, returning the smile.

"That makes you happy?"

"Yes, it does," he held her fingers with his index fingers. "Very happy."

"Yeah," she said punctuating her words with a snap of her gum, "Petey said it would. He said it would look better that way, too. At least for a while."

"This is his idea?"

"He said I should come over and calm you down."

"Calm me down? Why should he care if I'm calm?!"

"So's you don't sing," she said matter-of-factly, "you know, blow the whistle. So I said, okay, I'll go home. I was going to go to his bank's apartment, but he changed his mind about that. Besides, he can come over and work out of the house if he needs to. I mean you won't be using the den for a while, will you?"

"My den?"

"Only he doesn't want me to be seen around his place, especially after last night. For some reason he takes off in the middle of the night with his friends, then he comes back this morning all hopped up about something. He had sand all over him, like he's coming back from the beach or something, and saying he's got something going on with some other dame. Can you believe the nerve?"

"MY DEN?"

"Sure," said Marcia, "I mean, only while you're inside, okay? I'll leave if you get out."

"IF I GET OUT?"

"Petey says they have the death penalty in...oh, I already told you that, sorry."

Aaron Laffler stared at the blank expression on his wife's face, then reared his head back and screamed at the top of his lungs.

"GUARD!"

Then, repeating the word like a fakir chanting his mantra, Laffler kept calling for the guard, as he rhythmically rammed his head against the bars of the cell. A guard dashed in and rushed the bemused Marcia Laffler out of the area on her four-inch heels, leaving her estranged husband to continue to get in touch with his surroundings.

– 9 –
Suites to the Cousin
of the Sweet

E xcuse me, who's in charge here?" asked Lorraine Innis as she entered Valerie Fierro's private hospital suite. The three nurses who had just finished moving Valerie stared at Lorraine in silent awe.

Lorraine tried again. "Please, who authorized the moving of my cousin?"

While the relocation of Valerie irked Lorraine, it also refocused her attention. A scant ten minutes earlier she had been reduced to seeking comfort in the arms of Purvis Twankey. Now, caring for Valerie, the last anchor to her normal life, took precedence. It also renewed her self-confidence.

"Why was my cousin moved? I'm responsible for her well-being. Why wasn't I notified?"

One of the nurses, a skinny RN in her late twenties, broke the silence.

"It's her," she whispered to the male nurse at her side, a plump specimen who merely nodded. The third nurse, a woman in her forties who had seen just about everything one can see during a 20-year hospital career, finally answered Lorraine.

"Pardon me, Mrs. Innis," said the nurse, "but the hospital administrator ordered it."

Lorraine's abrupt entrance had prevented her from getting a good look at Valerie's new room. A second glance, however, revealed the room to be more like an upscale hotel suite than a hospital room. It was more than twice the size of a standard room even though there was only one bed. The bed also, was larger than a standard hospital bed, with a headboard and a spread that made it look homier. There were also tasteful pictures on the walls, drapes on the windows, and carpeting on the floor. To the side, closer to the windows, was a sitting area with four comfortable chairs around a coffee table. Beyond this, there was a small kitchen complete with sink, refrigerator, and microwave oven. Even the room's television was different, hidden away in an oak armoire rather than being suspended from the ceiling by a metal bracket.

Lorraine knitted her eyebrows in puzzlement.

"The hospital administrator authorized this?"

"Yes, he was asked to," said the nurse.

"By whom?"

"By President Kropotkin...personally."

Nikki, Lorraine thought, as she nodded her head, how sweet of that big Russian bear. In all her confusion, she almost forgot about her new friend. Too bad she didn't know the Russian leader better. He probably could help her sort out some of the crazy things going through her mind. She wished she could talk to Martin again. There must be some explanation for why he said those cruel things. Never mind, Lorraine reasoned; there was enough time for personal problems later. Things would get sorted out eventually. Right now Valerie was her top priority.

"That was very kind of President Kropotkin," said Lorraine, "but..."

"And he said he would personally take care of all Miss Fierro's hospital bills," added the nurse.

"Thank you," said Lorraine, her indignation deflated. Lorraine crossed to Valerie's bed, as the first nurses wheeled Valerie's original bed out of the suite.

"*Cugina*," said Lorraine, brushing a stray hair from the bandage on Valerie's forehead. "How are you today? Don't worry, I'm here, and you're in a beautiful suite, and we're going to see to it that you get well."

Lorraine studied Valerie's face. It was missing its usual cosmetic embellishments. She didn't look any worse, Lorraine thought, just different. Lorraine noticed the two nurses returning carrying plates of cheese into the room, along with Patsy Einfalt's little mug of flowers.

"Why are you bringing all that cheese in here?" asked Lorraine.

The male nurse, to whom the question had been directed froze in his tracks and swallowed hard, as his eyes grew wide as saucers. The skinny young nurse, sensing her coworker's veneration for Lorraine, answered.

"We're just bringing it up from the other room, Mrs. Innis."

"Your cousin has been asking for it, Mrs. Innis," explained the head nurse.

"You mean Valerie has been awake?"

"Not exactly," said the nurse, "but she had some episodes when she asked for cheese. But her eyes were always closed, and she wasn't conscious."

"Cheese?" said Lorraine. Valerie liked cheese. Most Italians liked cheese, but few stirred themselves from comas to request it. Lorraine crossed to the male nurse who was still frozen in place. She examined the two plates in his hands. There were wedges of cheddar, one or two pieces of Muenster, and even a thin sandwich slice of American.

Lorraine picked up one of the pale yellow cubes, sniffed it then shook her head.

"I'm sorry, but if my cousin asked for cheese, and I'm not doubting you," said Lorraine, "she wouldn't have wanted any of this."

"Please forgive us, Mrs. Innis. What would you suggest?"

"Some Asiago, some Gorgonzola, a little Parmigiana Regiana, or some Montasio, or Grana Padano," said Lorraine.

"We'll get some right away," said the older nurse.

"No, no," said Lorraine, realizing she was being picayune over cheese, "I'm sorry. It's really not necessary. I can get her some later if she wants it. I'd just like to be alone with my cousin now if that's all right."

The nurse nodded and motioned for her two assistants to remove the offending *formaggio*. The head nurse left last, closing the door behind her.

"If you need anything," she said on her way out, "just press the button on the side table."

Lorraine smiled and then turned back to Valerie. She crossed to the side table and toyed with the mums and daisies in Patsy's mug. After several moments of this half-hearted activity, Lorraine sighed and sat down next to her cousin.

"Oh, Valerie," she started, "you really need to get well soon. It's just that so much happened since yesterday. I know it hasn't been long, but it seems as if it's been forever. We really need to talk."

Lorraine rubbed the back of her head. Spending the previous night passed out on Valerie's bathroom floor hadn't done the lump on her head much good. And while she would have welcomed a nice therapeutic massage, it was her emotional state that really needed caressing. She had hoped to receive that support from Martin. Maybe Valerie would have the right words to say. In her current state, however, it seemed Valerie could say little more than "cheese," and that was hardly the encouragement she needed. Lorraine reached out and took Valerie's soft, limp right hand. She felt like crying but fought back the tears when she heard a soft knock at the door.

"Yes?" asked Lorraine in a wavering voice.

She had expected to see a member of the hospital staff, but instead, the door opened a crack and in popped the head of Purvis Twankey.

"How do! I found you," said Purvis with a toothy grin.

"Yes, so you did," said Lorraine with resignation. She no longer wanted his reassuring arms around her. In fact, at the moment she didn't want any of him in her general vicinity. "Look, Purvis, I'm sorry about what happened in the hall, I just, well, I've had a rough time."

Purvis looked down bashfully and then looked up as if he were groping for something to say. "I got these from a nice lass in the coffee shop," said Purvis after an awkward pause. He held out a roll of quarters. "I've got to keep going down to feed that thingumybob parking meter every hour. It'll only take four at a time." Purvis walked to the window and craned his neck sideways and downwards against the glass. "See, there's me car!"

"Thank you, Purvis. I saw it yesterday."

Purvis ignored her reference to their collision and continued to bask in the simple pleasure of seeing his battered Chevette from a height of five stories. After thirty seconds of watching his bliss, Lorraine interrupted.

"You don't have to go on feeding that parking meter, Purvis."

"Aye, I do. Else they clamp this heavy metal gizmo to your tire, and you can't drive. I know. I tried driving with it once. It makes the car go 'cuh-chunk, cuh-chunk, cuh-chuck, fwap!"

"No, you don't understand...fwap?"

"That's the sound the tire makes when it goes flat. Like I said, you can't drive with that thingee on your wheel."

Lorraine sighed once more. "What I meant, was that you didn't need to stay here all day. Valerie's being cared for, and I'll call you if there's any change in the situation."

A look, not unlike that of a puppy who had just been accused of missing the newspaper, spread across Purvis Twankey's face.

"Oh, aye," he said, "well, never let it be said that Purvis Twankey was one of those thickies that couldn't take a hint."

Despite her need to be alone, Lorraine could not bring herself to throw Purvis out of the suite. She marveled at his ability to evoke frustration and sympathy at the same time.

"No, Purvis, wait," said Lorraine rising from the edge of the bed. "I didn't mean that you had to leave. I suppose I just wanted a little more time alone with Valerie."

Purvis nodded. "I understand. You ladies have been through a lot."

"Thank you, that's very nice of you to see it that way," said Lorraine. "You really have been very sweet."

Lorraine gave him a short hug. Purvis blushed and fumbled with his hat.

"Gosh, well, I'll stop in later, in a little while, this afternoon," said Purvis as he backed away toward the door. Just as he was reaching for the handle, the door swung open almost knocking him to the floor. A man in a dark suit and sunglasses entered and scanned the room. Lorraine recognized him as a Secret Service agent. The agent scrutinized Purvis Twankey.

"Excuse me, sir." The government-issue apology sounded routine and insincere.

"That's all right," said Purvis, never anything but sincere. He looked at the door and brightened. "Ee, Miss Lorraine, I mean, Mrs. Innis, that's a grand idea for an invention. A door with a built-in beeper, like they got on trash lorries for when they back up. Put that on a door, and you'll avoid some nasty tumbles, I venture."

The agent ignored Purvis Twankey's latest stroke of genius, turning his attention to Lorraine.

"Mrs. Innis? President Kropotkin would like to pay his respects," said the agent.

Lorraine was surprised. World leaders rarely asked her permission to come into a room. What's gotten into everyone today, she wondered.

"I suppose," she said, "I mean, yes, of course."

The agent eyed Purvis Twankey.

"Oh, this is Mr. Twankey," said Lorraine, "he's a friend of the family."

The agent nodded, but still cast one last wary glance at Purvis as he exited. A moment later, Nikolai Kropotkin entered, crossed to Lorraine and took her hands in his.

"Lorruska," whispered Kropotkin in deference to Valerie. "I have come to see you and your cousin. We must go back to Camp David soon."

"Then your nephew can travel?" asked Lorraine.

"Yes, his arm is in a sling, but he is fine. And your cousin?"

"Not as well," said Lorraine. "But really, Nikki, you shouldn't have gone to all the trouble and expense of this suite. It's too much."

"Pah!" said the Russian. "What good is it being in power if you cannot take good care of those you care about?"

"That's so sweet, and we're grateful Nikki," said Lorraine, "but you shouldn't be ending your sentences with a preposition."

"Forgive a prodigal grammarian," said Kropotkin. "But other than my broken down speaking, everything is well, Lorruska?"

"Not exactly." She motioned for Kropotkin to follow her to the window, out of earshot of the others.

"Lorruska, you are upset," he said placing his hand on her chin. "What can your Nikki do? Is it the suite? We will find a better one. Bigger…"

"No, Nikki, the suite is wonderful," said Lorraine as she looked out the window, "it's just everything is so crazy today. Like the world's been turned upside down. I can understand some things, but others…"

"For instance?"

"Well, everyone's looking at me oddly, as if I had two heads. I understand now about the police escort…"

"I requested that."

"Yes," she said, "but you should have seen the way some of the nurses were treating me; as if they were afraid to speak."

Kropotkin's face turned red. He stopped looking at Lorraine and turned to the side.

He cleared his throat as if to dislodge the words stuck there. "I fear you will be displeased with me, Lorruska."

Kropotkin paused for a moment as if he were waiting for her to contradict him. Instead, Lorraine waited for his explanation.

"Ah, yes," he continued. "It seems I am the cause for your sudden adoration. Have you seen any news reports this morning?"

"No, but I was chased halfway here by three news vans. Why? What's happened?"

Kropotkin took her by the hand and explained his all-night brainstorming session on behalf of world peace. During some of the account, specifically those portions dealing with his plan, the Russian leader spoke hurriedly and with considerable animation. His excitement paled considerably, however, when he described how he had named her as his inspiration. Throughout, Lorraine Innis just stared out the window at the pedestrians on the street below. By the time Kropotkin completed his tale, Lorraine wondered when she could rejoin the ranks of the everyday walking-around folks again, if ever.

"The Lorraine Accord?" mumbled Lorraine when he had finished.

"You are angry with me?" he asked.

"No, I suppose not. I'm very flattered. Not many Jersey girls have a plan for world peace named in their honor.

"But this complicates things, does it not?"

"It surely does," admitted Lorraine with a stiff exhale of breath. Not many women get a peace accord named after them, and new body parts in a single day, she thought. She'd gladly have taken neither.

"You will get used to celebrity," said Kropotkin, "I only regret that I have thrust it on you without your permission."

"I expect it will die down soon, enough," said Lorraine. "I don't see how an average woman like me could hold a prolonged fascination with the public. At least it explains the way people are treating me."

Perhaps, she thought that was why Martin behaved so strangely on the telephone. If Martin saw the news, he might have been upset by it all. After all, being Irish, he wasn't accustomed to America's media circuses, was he? There must be some logical reason for his cruel outburst. He certainly would revert to his old lovable self after having a chance to acclimate to her newfound fame. After that he'd have to absorb the fact that she now had a...no, she'd worry about that later.

"The attention will probably go away, eventually," said Kropotkin as he drew a folded note from his pocket.

"Eventually?"

"Yes." He unfolded the paper, "just before I came up here; I was asked to appear on *Views Behind the News*."

"That's an important program. It will give you a chance to talk about your peace plan."

"And *Front Page Faces*," added Kropotkin mentioning another of the Sunday morning interview shows.

"Two in one week," said Lorraine, "it doesn't get much more impressive than that."

"Well, yes, it does," he said as he handed Lorraine the sheet of paper. "They want you on those programs as well, along with invitations for you alone to appear on *News Grillers*, then other programs after that. Here is a list of the requests."

Lorraine scanned the long list of requests, her jaw dropping as she continued down the double-column page. Kropotkin braced himself for an adverse reaction. Lorraine just shook her head.

"I can't do all this," she muttered.

"You don't have enough time?" asked Kropotkin.

"I don't have enough shoes," said Lorraine.

– 10 –
The Television with the One-Foot Screen

S aturday was like a carnival at the Einfalt home. Patsy Einfalt, single mother, and executive secretary to Peter Liverot, lived in Pike Creek, not far from where Lorraine had squared off against the three news vans in the Skirmish of Limestone Road. Patsy spent the day basking in her minor celebrity status. It was more attention she'd received in her life; even from the man who had fathered her daughter, and whose last name she adopted, even though she never married him. She would have married him, if he asked, or if he even lingered longer than the brief encounter which resulted in her pregnancy. Still, Patsy, ever the cheery optimist, told herself that one day he would return to resume his relationship with her, and begin one with the daughter he didn't know he had.

It was against this backdrop that Patsy Einfalt enthusiastically welcomed the events of Friday evening. Not only was she on television, but she also had a front row seat to a major news event, knew one of the major players in that event and was interviewed on TV because of it. That first interview led to even more media appearances. Happily, Patsy spent Saturday entertaining family and friends replaying the clips of herself on the news dozens of times. Most of the visitors saw the footage when it had first aired, but few minded seeing their Patsy prolonging her fifteen minutes of fame. The visitors kept the party atmosphere going well into the late afternoon. Then, over a dinner of hoagies from the local deli, the gathering received a fresh infusion of life when one of Patsy's interviews was re-edited into a profile of Lorraine Innis for a network newscast. The only one not impressed was Patsy's toddler daughter, Rachel, as the hogging of the television kept her from watching her favorite kiddie programs.

Now, on Sunday morning, as her daughter played nearby, Patsy was curled up on the couch, reading an article entitled: "Lorraine Innis; Her

Local Connection." The writer of the story interviewed Patsy the day before. Patsy's pleasure was tempered, however, when she saw herself identified as: "Patricia Unflatz." Patsy circled the erroneous reference with a red pen and wrote next to it: "really me."

She was just about to cut out the story for her scrapbook when the phone rang. Thinking it might be another interviewer, Patsy checked her appearance in the mirror before answering.

"Hello," said Patsy, using the professional tone she used at work, "Einfalt residence."

"How do..." said the British-accented voice.

Patsy's heart leaped. Maybe it was the London *Times* calling for her observations on Lorraine.

"...it's me, Miss Patsy; Purvis, Purvis Twankey."

"Oh, hellooo, Mr. Twankey, how nice of you to call!"

This was even better than a call from the British media. Though she had been preoccupied with her guests the previous day, Purvis was never far from her mind. In Patsy's estimation, he was the second most talented and handsome man on Earth, right after Donny Osmond, but more available.

"Yes, ma'am," said Purvis. "I hate to call you of a Sunday morning, but I'd like to know if I could stop by and talk to you."

"Certainly, Mr. Twankey," she cooed. She loved calling him Mr. Twankey since it was so close to Mrs. Twankey, a name she might like to adopt, especially since the hoped-for return of Mr. Einfalt seemed indefinitely postponed. "What would you like to talk about?"

"You might say it's a matter of mutual importance, an' no mistake," he said. "You're a woman."

"Thank you," said Patsy. Any recognition was nice.

"And I'm a man, an' all."

"Well, then, come right over," she said. She wondered what the "an' all" entailed, but the man part was quite enough to qualify him.

Patsy gave Purvis directions to her home, hung up, and began frantically preparing for his impending visit. By the time Purvis Twankey knocked on her door, Patsy had showered, done her hair, and gotten dressed in something she hoped would be more flattering than the sweatsuit she had been wearing. She had even put on lipstick. She was fixing Rachel a jelly sandwich when Purvis arrived. Wiping the sticky residue from her hand, Patsy handed her daughter the sandwich on a plate and left her to it.

"Purvis, what a nice surprise," said Patsy as she opened her simulated wood-grain steel-reinforced front door. "Please, come in."

"Thank you, Miss Patsy," said Purvis Twankey with a nod of his cowboy hat. Purvis took a moment to look Patsy over.

"Ee, you're even more dressed up than the other night," he said, "an' then you were coming from work."

Patsy could feel herself blush. Maybe the two-piece suit, complete with heels was a bit overdressed for a casual morning at home.

"Those are nice," he said, pointing to the two barrettes holding back her spiral perm. "Real gold!"

"Well, yes," said Patsy, touching them, "no, that is they're gold-tone."

"Dazzlers, they are," he said. "I'm sorry."

"For what?"

"Well, for dropping in just as you're coming from church."

"Oh, no, it's fine," she said. "We didn't go to church today. My daughter has a little bit of a sniffle, and the TV said it would rain."

"Oh."

"But we usually go," she said. "Besides, how could we just be getting home from church? You only called an hour ago?"

"I don't know," said Purvis. "Maybe they got pew-phones. If they don't, I could invent some."

From the kitchen, Rachel cried for a cup of milk.

"Pew phones? Oh, that's my daughter," said Patsy. "Do make yourself at home. I'll be right back."

Patsy tottered off to the kitchen as fast as her heels would allow her to, while Purvis looked around the living room.

"Nice place yuh got here," shouted Purvis. "Very...country like."

"I like it to look homey," she shouted back. "I think a home should be homey. And it's amazing what you can do with a few dollars at Wal-Mart."

She returned to the living room to see Purvis standing in front of her curio cabinet, filled with her collection of "Happy Memory" resin figurines.

"I see you've found my collection," she noted.

"Ee," he said marveling at the figurines, "Ain't they got big eyes. We had a lad in school with eyes like that. He turned out to be hydrocephalic, an' all."

"Oh?" She stood aside him, admiring her collection. "Most of them were given to me by friends."

"As presents?"

"Certainly as presents!"

"Oh," said Purvis, "so you wanted them."

"Yes," said Patsy blankly. She thought she had just been insulted, but she wasn't quite sure.

"Then they're proper champion," said Purvis with a condescending smile.

"Won't you sit down, Purvis?" said Patsy, suppressing the urge to add, "or would you prefer to shut up where you're standing?"

Purvis sat down on the end of the pilly green sofa and crossed his right leg in a 90-degree angle to his left one. Patsy sat next to him in the armchair.

"You said you had something important to ask me," she said, anticipating some sort of romantic offer.

"Yes'm, Miss Patsy," he began. Patsy sensed his nervousness and put her hand on his knee.

"Please just call me, 'Patsy.' You don't have to worry. I'm your friend, Purvis. I like you very much."

"You do?" Purvis Twankey exhaled and removed his hat. "Ee, that's a relief. You know, it's difficult for a chap like me to talk about, you know, mucky stuff."

"Mucky stuff?"

"Well, like romance, and love, an' all."

There was that tantalizingly mysterious "an' all" again, Patsy thought.

"It's all right," she said, softly. "Women like a degree of gentleness in a man."

"Ee, I was lucky to get out of me fifth year," said Purvis. "That's like your high school, but I've nowt got degrees."

"No," said Patsy, who herself had only a smattering of community college and secretarial school, "I mean, girls like a man to be tender at times."

"Do they?"

"Of course they do. It shows that a man is sensitive."

"That's me, sensitive," said Purvis, rubbing his chest. "Ee, I got the hives just talking about this sort of thing."

At that moment Rachel could be heard in the kitchen calling for her mother. Patsy heaved an annoyed sigh and ran out of the room.

"She only wanted some cookies and her crayons," said Patsy upon her return. "Go, on Purvis, you were saying?"

"Oh, aye, I was...cookies? What kind of cookies?"

"Keebler Sandwich cookies," she said.

"Them tiny elves with the fudge betwixt?"

"Yes, that's right."

"Really," he said with interest before a determined look spread across his face. "No, I'll not be waylaid. I've got to speak me heart."

"Why, Purvis, how forceful. What is it?"

"Miss, uh, I mean, um, Patsy, I think I'm in love," he blurted out.

"Oh, Mr. Twankey!" Patsy blushed. "This is so sudden!"

"I know it," said Purvis as he rose to his feet, "an' maybe I'm being a bit headstrong, but when a heart stays coiled up like a spring it's bound to go ka-boing when it's finally set loose. Do you know what I mean?"

"Ka-boing, oh yes, I do, Mr. Twankey," said Patsy.

"Then, what I need, I mean, it's..." Purvis was starting to sweat and falter.

"Just say what's in your heart, Mr. Twankey," said Patsy. She was afraid he might evaporate before he uttered the words that she longed to hear.

"I'd rather sing it," said Purvis as he rushed to the door.

For a split-second, Patsy thought he was making a break for it, and urged him to stop and reconsider. She relaxed when he merely reached on to the porch and retrieved his guitar. Purvis returned to the sofa and sat down, placing the instrument across his knee.

"I just wrote a little song about what's in me heart. You don't mind me pickin' it out, do you?" he asked.

"No, not at all, Mr. Twankey," she said, trying to suppress a toothy grin. Mind? She'd swap half the figurines in her curio cabinet and chop off her perm for a man who would serenade her.

After a few tentative plucks to get his six-string in tune, Purvis Twankey began a soft ballad. Though she was no music critic beyond the unsurpassed merits of Donny Osmond, to Patsy, it was wonderful. It was filled with tender sentiments of chance meetings, unrequited love humbly expressed, set against falling autumn leaves. Patsy sat transported by the romantic opus. The song perfectly fit Purvis Twankey's flat, nasal voice. He was obviously inspired, she thought, and best of all, she was his inspiration.

As Purvis sang, Patsy slowly rocked on the edge of her chair, her legs crossed, her arms held across her slight bosom, her hands resting delicately upon her chin. She remained transfixed in this blissful state until Purvis reached the last line. It was then he warbled:

"You're the most heavenly creature whatever could be,
Yes, I love you, I love you, my sweet Valerie!"

At this reference, Patsy Einfalt was jerked back to reality. Purvis Twankey hadn't been singing to her, but to someone he had only seen lying insensibly in a hospital bed; a hospital bed in which he had placed her. As if yanked by the cruel hand of fate, Patsy fell off her seat, her crossed-leg shooting out from under her as she fell and driving through the screen of the console television across from her. The tube cracked with a loud bang as acrid-smelling smoke wafted from what had been a glorious 27" Trinitron picture tube. In the kitchen, Rachel began crying in reaction to the sound. Patsy wanted to cry, as well, not from the broken TV screen, or her injured foot, but from her shattered expectations.

Purvis Twankey, a man who apparently had firsthand experience of more than one broken picture tube, stared at the smashed TV set.

"Ee," he said, "hope you don't have any more payments due on that one."

– 11 –
The Triumph of the
Guileless Grammarian

While Patsy Einfalt didn't have any payments left on the shattered remnants of her Sony TV, neither did she have any way of watching what pundits around the nation were calling "a television debut of epochal proportions." For not long after Purvis Twankey was wrapping up his song, and Patsy was wrapping up her injured foot, Lorraine Innis was wrapping up her second interview of the morning on the Sunday talk programs.

Like Patsy Einfalt, Lorraine Innis had taken great care getting ready that morning. Unlike Patsy, however, Lorraine was not getting ready for one man, but millions of them, and women as well, according to the ratings. Laboring under the necessity of clothing herself from Valerie's closet, she tried to piece together something that would look presentable on television. Complicating matters was the fact that Lorraine only had one pair of shoes with her. While she and Valerie wore the same size in clothes, anywhere between a generous 6 and a stingy 10 depending on the garment, they had a two-size difference between them in shoes.

She could have gone shopping on Saturday, but Lorraine spent the day at Valerie's bedside. She hoped her cousin would display another episode of speech if only to say "cheese," once more. For that matter, "Eggs," "butter," or "milk," would have been equally encouraging. Instead, while Lorraine was there, Valerie neither spoke nor stirred. Whatever need inspired her anxious cheesy utterances, it had been satisfied. The only interruptions came via media requests for interviews, quotes, or even the barest facts about Lorraine. Lorraine only spoke with the staffs of the three interview programs on which she was to appear. Initially, she declined the invitations, but when all three programs made arrangements for her to broadcast in an up-link from the small ABC bureau studio less than a mile from the hospital, she agreed as a favor to Nikki Kropotkin.

Her appearance on *Views Behind the News* started the ball rolling. Initially, the show had been set aside for Kropotkin. The show's producers had failed to realize the magnitude of Lorraine's influence on the Russian president, imagining her to be merely a sidebar for human interest. Consequently, the first few questions were condescending in nature. As these softballs were lobbed in Lorraine's direction, she promptly hit each out of the park – metaphorically speaking – with cogent answers. The moderator was caught off guard. As a result, he failed to adjust his line of questioning, continued to talk down to her, and wound up looking foolish.

One half-hour later on *Front Page Faces*, the panelists were better prepared than their colleague on the first program. Still, Lorraine handled herself like a seasoned professional. In this second program, she was given equal time with Kropotkin. This suited the Russian fine since he not only treated Lorraine with the mutual respect usually reserved for a fellow head of state but also helped her tag-team the panel of media veterans into easy submission. Kropotkin also made it clear that not only was Mrs. Innis the heroic inspiration behind his daring peace initiative, but she was, in effect, the intellectual catalyst as well.

Afterward, Kropotkin, who had made his appearances from Washington, telephoned Lorraine.

"Lorruska," he said with an elation that bordered on inebriation, "you were marvelous."

"Thank you," she said. "Are you okay? You haven't been eating bread or anything like that, have you?"

"Lorruska, your performances this morning are all the stimulation I need to feel positively tipsy!"

"So I did well, then?" asked Lorraine. "It's all so new to me."

"Lorruska, if I were speaking to anyone else I would apologize for making you go on those programs," he said. "But in your case, I apologize to the poor people who have to interview you."

"Am I that bad?"

"Nyet," said Kropotkin, "you are that good. I have never seen anyone handle the press as well as you do. By that I mean that not only did you beat them at their own game, but you had them liking it...no, loving it."

"Really?" Lorraine. "All I tried to do was answer their questions truthfully to the best of my ability."

"Da, that is what they are not used to. You gave thoughtful replies without...what is the word? Oh yes, without guile. It is wonderful. I cannot wait to see you on *News Grillers*."

"I'm not very familiar with that program."

"I'm told that it does not feature a moderator as much as a referee."

"Referee?" said Lorraine apprehensively.

"Da, they have two guests on differing sides of an issue and let them gnaw away on each other."

"I'm scheduled to be on with White House Chief of Staff, Davis Flemming," said Lorraine, reading from her schedule. "Do you know him?"

"Very well," said Kropotkin. "Don't worry, it will be fun."

"Oh, is he nice?"

"Not at all. He is a barracuda, but as I said, it will be fun; for me at least," chuckled Kropotkin. "I look forward to you, as a private citizen, doing what I, as the Russian president, could never do, but always wished I could."

"I see," muttered Lorraine with mounting trepidation.

"I would wish you luck," said Kropotkin, "but you don't believe in luck, do you, Lorruska? To you, it's all part of a greater plan. I will be watching."

Lorraine hung up the receiver and looked out the window. There was a heavy overcast to the south hanging over the Wilmington train station. It had been raining off and on since the previous evening, and the warm temperatures that had graced the area on Friday had been replaced with a raw wind that was a harbinger of approaching November. Lorraine tugged at the hem of Valerie's navy blue suit that she had appropriated for the occasion. The studio was damp and chilly, and she wished that the skirt had been longer than its slightly-above-the-knee length.

"Ready for our last round, Mrs. Innis?" asked the director who came to retrieve Lorraine from the break room. "I've got to hand it to you," he said as he escorted her back to the set, "for someone who's never been on television, you're doing great."

"It's all very new to me," she said. Though she didn't say so, Lorraine thought her appearances that morning had been therapeutic as well. The last four hours at the studio had taken her mind off Martin, her pregnancy, and her other issues. She found her immersion in the media spotlight immensely interesting.

As she sat down in the seat from which she made her first two appearances that morning, Lorraine looked behind her.

"This that a new backdrop?" she asked pointing towards the sickly green screen behind her chair.

"Nope, same backdrop, different lighting," explained the director. "It's projected on there. We change it with the flip of a switch."

"Oh, yes, of course," said Lorraine. "Do you think that green is really suitable? I liked the marbleized blue-gray pattern you used earlier. I thought it complimented my ensemble well."

"Yes, ma'am," said the director, "only it isn't up to either of us. The producer of *News Grillers* asked for the switch."

"Oh," said Lorraine sitting down behind the garish backdrop, "I guess that's pretty normal for television."

"No, not really," said the director. "I mean, it's a visual medium, isn't it? It's strange for a producer to ask for such an ugly background..." His voice trailed off, and he went back to review his notes.

Unless, Lorraine thought, you wanted to make someone look bad. But why would some television producer in New York or Washington want her to look bad?

Lorraine looked at the two monitors in front of her. The first, the live network feed, featured a commercial for some mutual fund in which imprudent investors were being mauled in the middle of Wall Street by hyenas in three-piece suits. Next to the on-air monitor was one showing the off-air feed of the *News Grillers'* set in Washington. Lorraine recognized venerable Harlan Dutton, the show's host since Moses had been plucked from the bulrushes. As Dutton shuffled some papers, a much younger man strode on to the set. He had a thick crop of hair, nicely trimmed on the sides, and wore a dark gray blazer, over a blue oxford dress shirt and a red and navy striped tie. The classic look of the upper portion of his outfit clashed with the shabby white Dockers and casual moccasins that he wore below. This mismatch of styles was hidden as the man sat down behind the table. He was speaking with someone off camera. Lorraine could barely hear the men speaking until the sound technician entered the frame and attached the lavaliere microphones.

As the mike was clipped to the younger man, Lorraine caught the tail end of his sentence.

"...adjust that background on the remote?"

"Yes, sir," said the disembodied voice off camera, "but if she's wearing the same outfit she did on the other shows it's not going to look right, in fact..."

"Don't worry about what it looks, like," said the younger man. "This isn't a fashion show. This is the arena of ideas. You're a news producer. You shouldn't care what it looks like."

"Then why do you care?"

The young man shot a withering look off camera but quickly replaced it with a disarming smile. "Because I'm not a news producer."

A makeup woman adjusted the young man's hair and received a wink and a salacious waggle of his eyebrows for her efforts. A moment later Harlan Dutton turned his attention towards the cameras and introduced himself to Lorraine. Next, the elder statesman of journalism introduced Davis Flemming, who flashed a boyish grin at her. Lorraine said hello, without trying to reciprocate his charm.

So, thought Lorraine, the president's assistant asked for the background to be changed. But why would the White House care what she looked like?

Harlan Dutton's explanation of the program's format was cut short as stagehands in both Washington and Wilmington started the countdown to air time. Dutton began the show with an introduction of Flemming and Lorraine and then directed the first question towards the White House aide. Davis Flemming totally ignored the question, which was about Quinton Merton's reaction to Kropotkin's peace plan. Instead, he slid further away from it as he wove ever-lengthening sentences filled with increasingly vague rhetoric. Lorraine wondered if this was his usual method of answering, or not answering a question. Mr. Dutton listened as if he had heard it all before, if not in content, then at least in style.

"Excuse me, Mr. Flemming," said the moderator, breaking Flemming off in mid-sentence, "but I think we need to hear from our other guest. Mrs. Innis, would you care to comment on Mr. Flemming's remarks?"

"I'm sorry," said Lorraine, "but I don't believe I can add anything to what Mr. Flemming has said."

Davis Flemming leaned back in his chair, a confident smirk played around the corners of his mouth.

"Apparently," said Flemming with a patronizing lilt, "our lovely guest agrees with the Administration's comprehensive agenda for world security."

"No, sir, it isn't that," said Lorraine. Flemming's expression drooped slightly and then recovered.

"Then you don't agree with Mr. Flemming's speech, that is, his remarks," asked Harlan Dutton.

"I'm not sure," said Lorraine. "In order to comment on what Mr. Flemming has said," she paused, "he would have actually had to have said something. You'll pardon me, gentlemen. I'm not trying to be flippant, but aside from some…unique grammatical construction, there really isn't much upon which I can comment."

Now it was Harlan Dutton who struggled to suppress a smile. "How refreshing an assessment, Mrs. Innis."

Davis Flemming, on the other hand, appeared far less refreshed.

"Really," said Flemming trying to force a smile through his clenched teeth, "Mrs. Innis, surely you can find some redeeming quality in what I've said?"

Lorraine thought a moment. Although she had taken an instant distrust to Davis Flemming that bordered on dislike, she didn't want to give vent to those emotions. She had always been raised on the maxim that if you didn't have something kind to say it was better not to speak at all. Finally, she said the nicest thing she could think of under the circumstances.

"Well," she said, "it was …creative."

"Creative, how?" asked Flemming, like a circling shark probing for a weakness.

"You said many…imaginative things."

"Like what?" said Flemming. "Come on, Mrs. Innis, you're on a nationally televised opinion forum. Don't be afraid to give your conclusions."

Lorraine felt her face redden. Here she was trying not to stoop to Flemming's ill-mannered level, and he was rubbing her face in it. Sitting up in her chair, Lorraine thrust back her shoulders and braced herself for action.

"Mr. Flemming," began Lorraine, "to begin with, your opening remarks were, to say the least, imaginative. By this, I mean that they were strewn with combinations of letters that can only pass as words in the respect that they contained recognizable phonetic groupings. For example, you showed great initiative in taking it upon yourself to forge new verbs where once only stood nouns. 'Decisioning,' and 'innovationed,' are not words. They are sloppy jargon developed by people who are too lazy to either learn proper usage of the language or take the trouble to find the correct word for a situation."

"Listen, little lady," said Flemming, "everyone I know uses those words."

"Excuse me, Mr. Flemming," said Lorraine, "I believe you cajoled this response from me, please have the courtesy to let me finish it. Despite your contention that you and all your acquaintances reside in grammatical backwaters, that still does not make it correct. It is true that through repeated misuse poor English becomes legitimized. Language has laws, however, just as society has laws. If everyone in Washington began breaking the laws of the nation would we be compelled to legalize murder and bribery? When laws are broken cavalierly, it weakens the system they were enacted to support. In society, this results in chaos. In language, it results in muddled communication. This, in turn, leaves us at the mercy of glib practitioners who may appear to wax eloquent while either saying nothing or worse, hiding their stupidity or duplicity under a torrent of verbal effluence."

At this point, Harlan Dutton looked as if he wanted to stand up and applaud, but he remained seated.

"Very nice words," said Flemming, "what fairy tale do they come from? Sorry, but I have to work in the real world where we use a living language. When I speak, people know what I mean."

"They may think they know what you mean," said Lorraine, "and you may hope they find some meaning in what you say. Unfortunately, if we were to examine your opening remarks this morning, I'm afraid we'd find them lacking in any discernible content germane to Mr. Dutton's question."

"That's libelous!" said Flemming.

"Actually," said Lorraine, "it's slanderous...unless, of course, it's true."

"In the cause of fairness to you, Mr. Flemming," said Harlan Dutton, "perhaps we should let you defend your opening statement. After all, Mrs. Innis has made some serious charges to your qualifications as a professional communicator. Wouldn't you like to prove her wrong?" Dutton grinned as he tossed the gauntlet at Davis Flemming's feet. Rather than being fair, he was actually giving Flemming extra rope with which to tie a better noose.

"I don't know if that's necessary," said Flemming realizing the trap.

"Really?" asked Dutton. "The challenge has been made. Here's a transcript of your opening remarks that the staff has just handed me. Would you care to explain what you said?"

"That's not...germane at this time," he said.

Lorraine saw the anxiety in his eyes, almost like a trapped animal. From his expression, she thought, he rarely, if ever found himself painted into such a corner. It was a no-win situation. He either had to make some sense out of words that were nonsense or admit that he was a charlatan out to deceive the public or confess he was an outright idiot who didn't know how to use English correctly. As he sat, mentally groping for words, she felt bad for him.

"Mr. Flemming," said Dutton, "the ball is in your court."

"Mr. Dutton if I may?" said Lorraine. "I believe that Mr. Flemming is constrained by his sincere desire to serve his country."

"Mrs. Innis?" said the moderator, not quite sure he was hearing correctly. He tapped his earphone.

"Yes," continued Lorraine, "Mr. Flemming was asked here to give an official response on a delicate, and most intricate, matter just hours after it has first been introduced. We are all eager to know the details of President Kropotkin's plan and hope it is equitable and amenable to all nations. Any response from the administration at this time would be ill-advised, though I'm sure President Merton will give it the full and serious attention any such proposal warrants."

In Washington, both Harlan Dutton and Davis Flemming stared for a moment at the in-studio monitor, and then at each other. Dutton finally broke the silence.

"Graciously stated, Mrs. Innis," said the moderator. He turned to Davis Flemming and muttered: "Is that what you meant to say, Mr. Flemming?"

The stage director motioned that it was time for a commercial break signaling the end of the segment. Harlan Dutton thanked his guests on camera, following which the director announced they were safely "in commercial."

"Thank you, again, Mrs. Innis," said Harlan Dutton as Lorraine rose from her seat. "It was a distinct pleasure. I haven't had so much fun since I was a cub reporter back in Des Moines."

"Thank you, Mr. Dutton," said Lorraine as she unclipped the microphone from her lapel.

Davis Flemming rose slowly to make way for the next guest. A stagehand rushed in to wipe the sweat from Flemming's palms from the tabletop.

"Yes, Mrs. Innis, it was...interesting," said Flemming.

"Thank you, Mr. Flemming," she said holding the tiny clipped microphone in her hand.

"Just one thing, Mrs. Innis. You're new to all this, aren't you...I mean, interviews, Washington, television...right?" asked Davis Flemming. An ad for a new pizza-flavored laxative played on the studio's live monitor.

"Yes, Mr. Flemming."

"Well, where did you learn how to spin the media so well?"

"I was the assistant captain of the high school debating team, Mr. Flemming," she said. "Now if you'll excuse me, I have to go shopping. I need a few things, and Macy's is having a sale, you know."

"A sale?" repeated Flemming.

"Yes," said Lorraine as she put down the microphone. "I believe men's dress trousers are on sale, too."

The stage manager began the countdown signaling the end of the commercials as Davis Flemming stood off-camera staring at his threadbare slacks.

– 12 –
The Grapefruit Daiquiri Objects

"S tupid tit!"

"Excuse me?" said the bartender.

"I said, 'Stupid tit,'" repeated Eugenia Bupp. "STUPID TIT!"

"Keep it down, lady," said the bartender. "This is a family place."

"No it's not, it's a shitty bar, in a shitty airport, in shitty Denver," said Bupp. "And three things don't help: that you make a rotten drink; that I've got a wedgie; and, that she's a stupid tit."

The "she" to whom Bupp was referring was on the television screen behind the bar.

"Her?" said the bartender, surprised at the object of his customer's wrath. "I dunno, I think she's pretty brave, and smart too. Did you see her on that news show before? She sure gave it to that snotty little guy from the White House."

"Of course I saw it, jock strap! I watched it with you. I've been sitting here for the last five hours waiting for my connecting flight back home."

"Where's home?" said the bartender reflexively.

"Coeur D'Alene," she said. "That's in the great state of Idaho, which is right next to none-of-your-f**kin'-beeswax."

"Just making conversation," said the bartender, turning his back on her, and turning up the sound on the television.

"...after her remarkable appearances on three of the major Sunday interview programs this morning," the anchor reported, "Lorraine Innis made a surprise appearance at a mall in Delaware. There she quickly attracted a throng of admirers..."

The accompanying footage showed Lorraine struggling through a crowd of department store shoppers. Men and women were pushing forward, waving scraps of paper and articles of merchandise for Lorraine to autograph.

"She's wonderful, a great inspiration," said one woman on camera.

"She's a stupid tit," Bupp shouted at the screen.

"She autographed my innersoles," said a middle-aged man waving the implements.

"I wouldn't let her autograph my ass," countered Bupp.

"We're delighted that a celebrity of Mrs. Innis' stature came into our store," said a woman identified in a graphic as "P. Barlett, Asst. Mgr." "It really has helped sales."

"After mingling with her fans in the shoe department," the reporter continued, though the video revealed the "mingling" to be more like a drowning, "Lorraine did her best to slip away to the relative privacy of the lingerie department, reportedly to buy some underwear..."

"Dumb twat," muttered Eugenia Bupp. The image of Lorraine Innis haunted her on her two-day trek back home, on newspapers, magazines, and the television. The constant reminder of the woman who foiled her hired assassin was bad enough. Now, however, it seemed her popularity was growing. Each new report added to Lorraine's adulation, and Eugenia Bupp's aggravation. She pounded on the bar. "Barkeep, hit me again."

"Haven't you had enough?" said the bartender.

"Apparently not, toerag," said Bupp. "I can still see what's-her-tits, there."

"Come on, that's not a nice way to be. You seem like a nice little old lady..."

"Liar," spat Bupp. "I'm an 88-years-old bitch and a pain in your ass."

"Watch the language. I've told you this is a respectable establishment. If you can't..."

"I've been your only customer for the last hour. Just give me another."

The bartender sighed. "Another grapefruit daiquiri, coming up."

As he turned to mix Eugenia Bupp another drink, the television began yet another feature on Lorraine Innis.

"Dumb twat," growled the old woman. "You're definitely going on the list."

– 13 –
Requiem for a
Concrete Block

It had gotten slightly more bearable, though it had taken years. Still, the smallest remembrance could transport her back causing the wounds to reopen and the tears to flow afresh. At least these episodes were confined to the times when she was alone. Unfortunately, she spent too much time alone.

There were days or at least hours that she almost didn't think about it. Then she turned on the television news. She saw it first on the BBC and watched in shock, the spell only breaking when the story ended. Not believing it, she switched to ITV and saw the same thing. It couldn't be. It was impossible. But there was…what was the name that they kept repeating? Lorraine Innis? Two major news outlets couldn't be so wrong, could they? Or were her eyes deceiving her? Or was she finally losing her mind? She took off her eyeglasses and wiped them as if that would somehow change what she was seeing, or what she was thinking.

She almost called others to verify what her eyes were telling her and her mind couldn't believe. She stopped. What if she were the only one who saw it? What if she had finally gone mad?

She paced around her room in the cottage, wringing her hands, trying to come to grips with it. Her mind raced. There had to be an explanation. Unable to look away she returned to the television and went through all available news channels. This Lorraine Innis was all over them. Lorraine Innis? Lorraine Innis! That wasn't the name. She could think of at least two names, but it couldn't be either of them.

Then one outlet replayed an extended portion of the debate that aired earlier on *News Grillers*. That was when she heard the voice. Different, she thought, but unmistakable. Her heart raced as she hoped against hope that it was true. But how…

Suddenly a thought crossed her mind.

He wouldn't.

He couldn't.

He didn't.

Did he?

How could she ask him? He'd deny it.

She couldn't confront him. She didn't have to.

There was another way.

She looked out the window. The autumn sun was just below the western horizon. Soon it would be dark.

She hurried and changed into her oldest slacks and dug a pair of Wellington boots from the back of the closet. Then, pulling on a heavy woolen pullover and a light coat, she started out. She almost took the car but thought better of it. No, she didn't want to attract attention, not that there were many people about, but still, if she was seen it would only lead to questions that she didn't want to answer. If she were wrong they'd think she were balmy; they'd have her committed. If she were right, well, she didn't want anyone to know that either, not yet.

Stopping by the shed to grab a battery-operated lantern and a spade… oh yes, and she'd need a screwdriver… she then made her way across the property. She took the long way through the forest, avoiding the open fields. It took her nearly half an hour that way, but it was better than being seen. In was almost pitch dark now. A heavy cloud cover had moved in. The wind picked up, whipping her long brown hair around her neck as if it were a scarf.

Coming around from the back she could see the big house in the distance. Not many lights were on, at least not on the side of the house facing her. And that copse of trees shielded her from anyone who might look out. It was only about ten yards from the edge of the wood. She emerged, half crouching as she approached. Just as she neared the stone, she saw car lights coming up the drive. They were over a quarter of a mile away, but she still turned off the lantern and dove behind the stone. The back of the stone was covered with shrubs. In the dark she stumbled and fell through the planting, throwing her hand up against the stone to catch herself. That's when she felt it.

Writing? There was writing chiseled on the back of the stone. She had never been around the back of the stone before. Why would she? She wasn't in the habit of examining the backs of headstones. No one inscribed anything on the backs of headstones, did they? She didn't, and she had ordered this one, or at least she had dictated the inscription.

She had just been to visit the grave the day before yesterday, placing fresh flowers on it as was her ritual. Everything was as it usually was then: she was alone; she spent nearly a half hour; and, of course, she had cried. Oh, yes, and the inscription was on the front, as it always had been. Unless, she thought, unless someone had turned the stone around, but who would do that? Children? There were no children allowed there, and she doubted whether the ones from the nearest village would even know about the grave's location. Besides, the stone was too large to be moved without heavy equipment.

Slowly she lifted her head over the top of the stone. The car that made her duck down was gone. There were no other lights on that side of the house. Confident that she wouldn't be observed, she turned the lantern back on, taking care to keep it behind the stone, just in case. Then she knelt down and pushed aside the shrubbery to read the inscription. What she saw made her gasp. She read it several times trying to make sense of it.

Why did it say that? Why would he do it? Why? She wracked her mind for a logical explanation. Then she reread it, giving special attention to the last line.

"Well, he didn't write that," she said. "Only one person would..."

That made sense, or at least it fit with what she'd seen on the television. She stood up, keeping the lantern well behind the stone. She examined the shrubs to make sure they didn't betray her having been there. But then, she reminded herself that no one but her ever came there any longer. No one but her had ever bothered. Why would they, she thought, especially if...

Not waiting to finish her thought she grabbed the spade and came around the front of the grave marker. The autumn leaves from the adjacent wood had begun to fall covering the gravesite. She could do what was necessary and then conceal her work with the leaves when she was done.

She stepped out a pace from the front of the stone and placed her foot on the back of the blade. She paused for a moment. What if she were wrong? What if she had imagined what she thought she'd seen on the news? She glanced over her shoulder towards the stone. No, she hadn't imagined that.

Still, she whispered "forgive me," in case she was terribly mistaken, and then stepped down on the spade. It was difficult emotionally, but she was driven on by...what? Curiosity? No, it was more than that. She was digging at the very least to learn the truth. She may be digging to retrieve her own life. Recent rains had made the ground more pliant, at least the first several feet. Soon the ground proved harder, and her neck and shoulder and arms began to ache, but she didn't dare stop. A shiver ran through her body when at last she struck the box. She carefully pulled the lantern from the side of the hole and once it was below the surface turned in on and looked at her wristwatch. Not even two hours. Thankfully the old saying of being "six-feet under" was only that. She estimated she was down three feet. Not wanting to damage the coffin, she pushed the remaining soil from the top and then pulled a screwdriver from her pocket and began to unscrew the coffin lid. Five minutes later, and not without some difficulty she removed the final screw. She bowed her head and said a brief prayer against the possibility that she had been wrong. Then she took a deep breath, and steeling herself against what she might see, she lifted the lid.

Aside from some concrete blocks, it was empty. She broke down in tears, tears of joy, tears of relief, and finally bitter tears of anger.

The pieces quickly came together as she recalled brief snatches of conversations that she had hardly considered at the time they were spoken. She was fairly sure she knew *why* he did it. But *how* could he?

She started to screw back down the coffin, but then realized it didn't matter. She climbed out of the grave and began to fill it back in. The threatening storm began to break, and large drops of rain fell, splattering on the lenses of her glasses, running down her face, diluting her tears. She continued working at the same pace. She would soon be soaked to the skin, but it didn't matter. The important thing was now she knew. But no one else must know that she knew, at least for now until she could decide what to do next.

– 14 –
The Nearly Ubiquitous Face of Hope

After the frenzy of the mall, the corridors of the hospital offered blessed sanctuary to Lorraine Innis. It was almost three o'clock by the time she arrived at Valerie's suite on the fifth floor. As she entered the room, shopping bags in hand, Lorraine was surprised to see Patsy Einfalt sitting reading a magazine.

"Hi," said Patsy looking up.

"Patsy, what are you doing here," said Lorraine.

"Well," she began sheepishly, "I was in the neighborhood, out of necessity…"

With that, Patsy swung her right foot on to the coffee table. It was swaddled in bandages and protected by a large cloth boot.

"What happened to your foot?" Lorraine asked putting her bags on the chair.

"Purvis Twankey."

"He broke your foot?"

"It's only badly cut," said Patsy, "and no he didn't exactly do it, the dope!"

"Where's your daughter?"

"She's with Purvis. He drove me to the emergency room. After they fixed me up, I thought I'd stop in to see Valerie. Purvis took Rachel to the zoo. He wanted to come up here, but I had enough of…that is, I didn't think it was a good idea."

Lorraine crossed to Valerie. "How is she?"

"She was talking."

"Really?" said Lorraine turning to Patsy. "What did she say? Did she get up? I need to talk to her. What did she say?"

"She asked for cheese. That's all, just cheese."

"Oh," sighed Lorraine. "She never even says that while I'm here."

"She only said it when I was watching television," said Patsy. "Funny, I don't remember her eating cheese when she watched TV. I saw you on the news. That mob at the mall was crazy. It must be wonderful to be famous like that."

"It's not all it's cracked up to be."

"Why?" Patsy seemed genuinely puzzled.

"It's just not," said Lorraine.

"Oh," said Patsy. A thought brightened her mind. "Did you get your underwear?"

"What?"

"At the mall? They said on TV that you were going to buy underwear. Did you get it?"

"You mean they didn't tell you?" said Lorraine sarcastically. "Didn't give you a complete report? Didn't give the full rundown on hipsters or briefs? The color? Cotton or nylon? The size? Lorraine Innis...36 double-D...film at eleven!"

"No," said Patsy mystified. "They just said you wanted some underwear."

"And they call themselves journalists!"

"Are you really a double-D?" said Patsy staring at Lorraine's breasts. "You don't look..."

"No," said Lorraine, pointing at the TV set, "but that wouldn't stop anyone from saying so! And that, Patsy, that is why it isn't so wonderful to be famous."

"Oh," said Patsy, looking down.

Lorraine stared at her for a moment, then, with her anger subsided, sat down next to her.

"I'm sorry," said Lorraine putting her arm around Patsy's shoulder. "It's been a long couple of days. A lot has gone on..." Lorraine paused and thought about her physical mysteries. "Let me rephrase that. A lot has happened. At least it's all over now. I'm sorry if I got bitchy with you. Hopefully, it will all calm down now."

"I'm sorry," said Patsy.

Lorraine chuckled and squeezed Patsy's shoulder. "Why should you be sorry?"

"Because it's not all over," said Patsy without looking up, "at least not quite."

"What do you mean?"

Patsy slowly pulled a slip of paper from her purse and handed it to Lorraine.

"You're going to be on *Wake Up, America* tomorrow morning. Sorry."

"How?"

"They called here, looking for you, and I answered," blurted Patsy. "I don't know what happened. I never spoke to a television producer before, and she was so nice. And they asked if I were your scheduling secretary, and I said 'yes, I was.' After all, I do that sort of thing all the time at work, but never with television people. And before I knew it, I said 'yes, she'll be there.' I just never thought you wouldn't want to do it, because, after all, I've never been on television, at least not until the other day, and I didn't think anyone would say no, and I'm sorry."

Patsy broke into hysterical-blubbering, and Lorraine patted her head if only to keep from strangling her. After several minutes, Patsy brought her crying jag under control.

"Thank you," she said as Lorraine handed her a handkerchief. "the television report was right."

"Yes," sighed Lorraine, "I did buy underwear."

"No, they called you a 'gentle inspiration.'"

"Great, a gentle inspiration with a change of underwear," Lorraine exhaled. "Well, I suppose I can go back to that little studio one more time."

"No," said Patsy. "You don't have to go there. They're sending a limo to take you to New York."

"New York? I don't want to go to New York."

"But it's in a limo! With coffee, breakfast, a TV, anything you need. You could have a hairstylist or even a secretary."

Lorraine stared at Patsy. Their worldviews had collided. Lorraine's repulsion at going all the way to New York City just to be subjected to another interview had collided with Patsy's fantasy of riding anywhere in a limousine. Though it would take her away from the things that mattered most, Lorraine thought, perhaps she should just go. Besides, maybe she could use the media as much as they were using her. She could make a discreet appeal to Martin over the air.

"Okay," agreed Lorraine, "I'll do it. What time?"

"About 4:15."

"In the morning? Patsy, why would you agree to that?"

"That's when they needed you. Besides, I don't know what came over me. I'm used to talking to bankers and regulators. I've never talked to real TV people before."

"Real TV people? Is that an oxymoron? 4:15! I'll have to get up at two! And I'll have to figure out what else I can borrow from Valerie's closet."

"You just went shopping."

"Yes, that's a relief," said Lorraine dryly, "at least I'll satisfy my mother's admonition to be wearing clean..." Lorraine stopped short. Mother? What did her mother look like? She could remember her mother's name, where she was born, where she went to school, and a dozen other facts, but not what she looked like.

"Are you okay?" asked Patsy.

"Hmm?"

"Are you okay?"

"Oh, sure, don't worry Patsy. I'll find something to wear. It's just one more time."

Patsy was silent for a moment before she whispered. "Three more times."

"What?"

"You're booked on *AM, I Said* right after *Wake Up, America*. The one network will pick you up at the other network, and then take you over to their studio. Then the third network will pick you up at the second network."

"What's the third one for?"

"You're taping the Cookie Babcock prime time special after the two morning shows."

Lorraine glowered at her. It only took four seconds for Patsy's perky smile to evaporate and for her to start squirming. Another three seconds and she vowed: "And I promise to never talk to another TV producer again."

"Good," said Lorraine. "I would hate for the electronic media to lose their credibility."

"How would they do that?"

"By having to report that their gentle inspiration had just disemboweled an executive assistant with her bare hands."

"Oh," said Patsy in a whisper.

By four the next morning, Lorraine had resigned herself to the fact of doing three more television interviews, but only three more. After that, she hoped, the public would have their fill of her, and she could get back to making repairs in her own life. She found a suit in Valerie's closet. It was in a subdued pattern of hunter green and gold with a gold silk shell to go along with it. The fact that the items still had their tags attached made her feel a little guilty, but, she reasoned, Valerie would understand this was an emergency.

The limousine that would take her to New York arrived at 4:25, and was everything Patsy could have imagined and more. Aside from the television and phone one would have expected, the stretch Lincoln also featured a wet bar, microwave, and refrigerator. Lorraine thought of Purvis Twankey and guessed the vehicle was more comfortable than his apartment.

It was one of the least technologically advanced accessories of the limo, however, that caused Lorraine the greatest consternation: the magazine rack. A quick scan of the latest weekly magazines revealed that they all featured Lorraine on their front covers.

Lorraine winced as she saw her face on the cover of *Time* along with the headline: "The Face of Hope." The photo was a digitized adaptation taken from one of her television appearances the previous day. *Newsweek* was next, featuring a blurry enlargement from the video of Lorraine saving Nikolai Kropotkin's life. The caption read: "From New Jersey with Love."

U.S. News and World Report, thanks to the scarcity of available photos of Lorraine, had commissioned an artist to sketch her dressed in diaphanous white robes. In one hand the cartoon Lorraine held a dove, while the other was occupied catching a bullet. In the background, Nikolai Kropotkin was flinching from the gunshot. This last one irked Lorraine most, not only because she felt the headline: "Goddess of Peace," was too extreme in its hyperbole, but the caricature exaggerated her nose.

Lorraine turned the copy of *U.S. News and World Report* face down on the seat and looked back towards the magazine rack. Her eyes grew wide as she saw the masthead of the next periodical peeking out. With great trepidation, Lorraine reached for the glossy cover of the thick magazine. Drawing it upwards until she could fully view the cover, Lorraine heaved a sigh of relief. At least she hadn't made the cover of *Playboy*.

With nothing else to do, Lorraine decided this was as good a time as any to call home. It had been almost 48 hours since she argued with her husband. Surely, that was a long enough time for both of them to cool off. By now Martin would have heard about all the extraordinary events that had happened to her, well, most of the extraordinary events, the public ones, at least. He would be back from his trip by now. She glanced at her watch as she dialed the limo phone. It was a quarter to five. She hated to wake him up, but at least she knew he'd be home.

The phone began ringing. Her mind was in conflict. Part of her wanted to be held and comforted by him, while, oddly, something nauseated her at the same prospect. She let it ring at least a dozen times with no answer. For several minutes, Lorraine sat there, the receiver cradled limply in her hand as it continued to ring.

The glass barrier separating her from the driver lowered.

"You okay, ma'am," said the driver in a robust New York accent.

"I suppose," Lorraine said.

"Don't be nervous," said the driver. "This happens every day."

"Really?"

"Sure, I pick up guests for the show five days a week."

"Oh, of course," said Lorraine. A thought occurred to her. "Say, driver…"

"Dominick," he said.

"Dominick, you're going to drive me back, aren't you?"

"Sure, I drive everyone back. Otherwise, we'd have a lot of spare people piling up around the studio."

"Do you think we could make a side trip on the way back? It wouldn't be very far out of the way."

"Well, normally, I'd say that was against the rules," said the driver, "but seeing as it's you, Mrs. Innis, it'd be no problem."

Lorraine smiled. Perhaps Patsy Einfalt wasn't entirely wrong. Maybe fame did have some privileges.

– 15 –
Ingratitude for a
Kissed Boo-Boo

An object of pity!

Davis Flemming seethed as he scanned the Monday morning newspapers. It was unanimous. He was an object of pity. He didn't know which was worse, that he, Washington's top powerbroker was portrayed as a thing of sympathy, or that he only appeared as such in sidebars to the stories on Lorraine Innis.

With Kropotkin back at the Camp David summit, and the details of his peace plan still unknown – Flemming couldn't bring himself to refer to it as the "Lorraine Accord" – the press had little else to do but write story after story about the heroics of Lorraine Innis. Lorraine Innis! How he hated every television report, every magazine article, every reference, every photograph. The photographs, they were the most galling to Flemming. In every photo, she appeared so serene, so calm, so together. She was handling the media feeding frenzy so effortlessly, even Flemming was impressed, or at least he would be if he didn't hate her so. Seamless, graceful, so placid, like some icon that had existed for a thousand years, and as such was unaffected by all around her. She was perfect, and she knew it, thought Flemming, and how he despised her. The one consolation, he told himself, was that while everyone in the media reported in great detail on how she bested him in their debate, no one picked up on how he felt about her, or more importantly, why.

This solitary scrap of comfort for Davis Flemming's tortured soul was snatched away from him as he turned to the editorial page of the *Washington Post*. There, at the top of the page, not in the text, but in an editorial cartoon, was the truth behind Flemming's torment. It was a two-panel cartoon, the first of which portrayed Flemming as a bratty child… that metaphor was nothing new. What was new was that instead of being drawn as a precocious kid getting his way, Flemming was being spanked over the knees of a woman...Lorraine Innis. The cartoon Flemming was bawling and struggling, while Lorraine calmly administered parental justice. As bad as that was, it was the second panel which nearly drove him mad. There, nursing a sore backside, was Flemming, receiving a compassionate kiss on the forehead from Lorraine. The caption read: "Mother Knows Best!"

Though he was rarely on the receiving end of a political beating, Flemming could handle it. Usually, he would plot his next move, one which, given the vicious atmosphere of Washington, would be justified, expected, and even welcomed by the press. This, however, this was something he couldn't fight. He squinted at Lorraine's photo on the front page. There she was, tranquil in the midst of an adoring mob at some shopping center. He slowly mangled the photograph in his hands as if he were strangling the genuine article. No, he couldn't fight her in the usual way. She was too "virtuous." The media wouldn't accept it, yet. A new strategy was in order. Davis Flemming took mercy from no man or woman - especially a girl from New Jersey - without exacting revenge.

As Flemming weighed his options, a summons came from the President's office. Flemming looked at his watch. It was a little early for Merton to be ready for business. For one thing, his favorite cartoon program was still on. He really didn't want to hear the President's commentary on crime-fighting turtles or mighty morphing space monkeys today. Still, it was one of his responsibilities. If only the idiot who had drawn that political cartoon could see who was the country's real responsible adult. He, Davis Flemming, was the nation's daddy.

"Good morning, Mr. President," said Davis Flemming entering the President's office. Oddly enough, cartoons weren't playing. The television wasn't even turned on, nor was there any evidence of Quinton Merton's unorthodox therapy.

"There's the boy," smiled Quinton Merton.

Flemming took his usual seat in front of the President. "You look well-rested sir," he said. "Had a good night's sleep?"

"Practically none," said Merton. "What I did have were some excellent talks with Nikolai, President Kropotkin, last night. Did I say last night? They were practically all night."

"Alone?" said Flemming anxiously.

"Yes, just he and I."

"Do you think that's wise, Sir?"

"Why not? He's a president, and I'm a president. We had a meeting of the presidents' club."

"Yes, but without even a political advisor..." Like me, thought Flemming.

Quinton Merton brushed Flemming's objection aside with a dismissive wave. The gesture couldn't have stung more if it had been a slap across the face. Who suddenly gave Quinton Merton a mind of his own?

Kropotkin? And who helped Kropotkin develope a generous nature? The evil influence from New Jersey: Lorraine Innis.

"As I was saying," continued Merton, "I spoke with Nikolai until very early in the morning. After I left him, I took a walk."

"Alone?"

"Yes, why?"

"No reason." Flemming was astounded that Merton could find the door by himself, and then function alone on the other side of it.

"Standing there in the chill morning air, just before dawn, made me think," continued the President. "These are exciting times we're living in right now. The chances for disarmament are better than ever, thanks to the Lorraine Accord."

Davis Flemming winced at the mention of the name.

"Yes, that Lorraine Accord really has some merit to it," noted the President. "I wasn't sure it would. But it really is something, that Lorraine Accord!"

"Yes, Mr. President," Flemming agreed as he gritted his teeth. As galling as it was to keep hearing that name, it was doubly painful having it come from the mouth he usually programmed.

"So you like the Lorraine Accord, too?" said Merton. "Maybe we should have her down to the White House soon, you know, Lorraine. But then you've already met Lorraine. What's her last name?"

"Innis," said Flemming through clenched teeth.

"That's it. Innis, Lorraine Innis. Has a nice ring to it. Very American. I like that. Unfortunately, I didn't get a chance to see you and Mrs. Innis. Is she nice?"

"Delightful," muttered Flemming.

"But what?" said Merton. "Is something bothering you, Davis?"

"It's only that referring to the plan under that name is counterproductive to your goals, and frankly, a personal affront to you."

"It is?"

"Certainly, Mr. President. After all, you've been the major proponent of world peace since your earliest days in the Senate. If any name is attached to the plan, it should be yours."

"It should? But it's not my plan; it's President Kropotkin's. Shouldn't he call it whatever he wants?"

"Well, maybe, technically, yes," said Flemming, "but really, he wouldn't be here if you hadn't invited him, would he? After all, he's your guest. This is your summit."

"I suppose that's true."

"And everything that's happened to him here is thanks to you, isn't it?"

"Is it?"

"President Kropotkin wouldn't have come to America if you hadn't invited him. He wouldn't have gone to Delaware, either. He should thank you for everything that's happened since he came to America. You're his host, after all."

"That's right," said Merton proudly before his expression drooped. "But wait, they tried to kill him in Delaware, didn't they?"

"But they didn't succeed, thanks to your excellent public safety programs and anti-crime initiatives."

"That's true."

"So, in effect, you saved his life, Sir. Didn't you?"

"I guess I did...didn't I?" said Merton.

"Just as you say, Mr. President." Flemming breathed more easily. If Quinton Merton started talking to people and thinking on his own where would it all end?

"And now he wants to give the credit to someone else," said Merton taking the bit in his mouth.

"After all," said Flemming, "what did that woman do?"

"Well, she did jump in front of that assassin's bullet."

"Right, but who put him in front of that assassin's bullet?"

"Uh, who?"

"You!"

"Me?"

"Yes, Sir," said Flemming as Merton arrived back where he belonged.

"Thank you, Davis," said the President rising to shake his aide's hand. "This little talk has been invaluable. I always have a clearer picture of the situation after I've discussed things with you."

"That's why I'm here," said Flemming. "I'm just a servant."

"I think I'd better go tell Kropotkin, don't you think?"

"No," said Flemming, thinking the Russian would change Merton's mind again. "No, Sir, why not wait until your joint press conference later today. After all, much of negotiation lies in posturing for position. You don't want to give up your advantage by tipping your hand."

"Yes, I suppose you're right. Thank you again, Davis." Merton shook his head. "And to think, I was going to sign on to that plan. World peace? Maybe, but at what price?"

Flemming quietly backed out of the office as Quinton Merton began rambling to himself. In the outer office, he punched a number from his cell phone's speed dial. As he waited for an answer, he saw a copy of *USA Today* sitting on a nearby table with Lorraine Innis's picture smiling up at him.

"Yes," said Flemming into the phone. "Give me Rocher."

"Well," he said to himself as he waited, "Welcome to the big leagues, Mrs. Innis."

- 16 -
The Guest of the Cosmetically Destitute Millionaire

By the time the limo deposited Lorraine Innis amidst the concrete canyons of Manhattan, the first rays of dawn were edging over the eastern horizon back in Wilmington. The cold front, which had brought the raw showers of Sunday, had now moved through, bringing in its wake an invigorating atmosphere. Soft diffused light began to filter into the hospital room as Valerie Fierro's eyelids began to flutter, and then, for the first time in three days, she opened her eyes.

Immediately, Valerie realized she was in unfamiliar surroundings. After a few more moments, discovering the monitors and IVs attached to her, she reasoned she must be in the hospital. She vaguely recalled being in a hospital a few days before, or had she dreamt that? Still, the room she was in now didn't look like a hospital room. It was more like an upscale hotel. She particularly admired the oak armoire. She wondered if they had room service since she was very hungry. Maybe she wasn't in a hospital or a hotel but in the guest room of some millionaire. She dimly remembered the car crash; a blue car heading straight for her. Maybe the blue car had been driven by a millionaire, a young, handsome millionaire, who, after seeing her beauty, insisted on caring for Valerie in his own private hospital wing back in his mansion. That would be nice, she thought. Her perfect explanation was derailed by the further recollection that the blue car was old and junky. A millionaire wouldn't drive anything like that, she reasoned, not at least any millionaire she'd want to know. Wait, she thought, it could have been the millionaire's reckless son. No, that was unlikely, since millionaire's sons usually drove nicer cars than their fathers. Or maybe the millionaire was forcing his son to work as a construction worker to teach him the value of hard work. Yes, that was good. Valerie smiled as she thought of the hunky muscles and great tan the millionaire's son would have from working bare-chested outdoors all day.

Valerie stretched out and writhed with kittenish pleasure, anticipating the millionaire's son entering the room at any moment, on his way to work, stripped to the waist, wearing only blue jeans, work boots, and a bright yellow hardhat. He would tell her that this was his last day of working in construction. He would receive his full inheritance tomorrow, and then they would be off in his private jet to the Caribbean.

Touching her face, Valerie was thrown into a state of panic as she realized she wasn't wearing any makeup. She couldn't meet the millionaire's son - soon to be a millionaire in his own right - cosmetically naked. What if the millionaire's son had already seen her without her makeup? What if he had looked at her spotty chin and her slightly bent nose without the benefit of a good foundation or some corrective contouring? Maybe he had already seen her and was out looking for a more attractive girl to run into. Valerie looked over to the bedside stand in hopes of finding a mirror with which to survey the damage. Failing this, she hoped she could find some makeup. Nothing extensive, just the bare necessities: foundation, powder, blush, eye-liner, shadow, mascara, lip-liner, eyebrow pencil, and concealer – all preferably in her shades though, Valerie conceded, beggars couldn't be choosers. She opened the drawer. Instead of anything useful, all she saw was a bedpan. It was a plastic one, at that, not even gold plated. What sort of cheap millionaire would have a common plastic bedpan in his private hospital wing?

Valerie Fierro was interrupted in mid-speculation when a nurse entered the room. The nurse glanced at Valerie awake in bed and did a double take.

"Hello," said Valerie.

"Good morning, Miss Fierro."

"Has the millionaire's son left for work, yet?" She asked, believing this was the core question that would provide the answers to all others.

She stared at Valerie with a puzzled look on her face. "The millionaire's son?" She asked.

"Yes," said Valerie impatiently. "Your employer, has he gone to work, yet?"

The nurse opened her mouth to reply, and then just stood there, with her jaw hanging open.

You would think, Valerie thought, that a millionaire would hire a smarter staff. First the cheap bedpan, now a slow-witted nurse. There would be some changes around here after she was in charge. Growing weary of having the nurse staring at her, trying to answer the simplest of questions, Valerie decided to move on to more practical matters.

"Look, forget about that. Please get me a set of makeup brushes."

"Makeup brushes?"

"Yes, sable hair brushes would be nice, but anything. As long as they're clean. Oh, and some foundation. Something to match my complexion."

"I'd better get Dr. Lester."

"Dr. Lester?"

"She'll answer any questions you may have."

"I know how to use makeup brushes," snapped Valerie.

As the nurse started to exit Valerie asked a simpler question, one even this dim-witted nurse could answer: "What day is it?"

"Monday," said the nurse as she rushed out the door.

The clock said it was 7:15. On a typical Monday morning at this time, Valerie would be eating breakfast while watching *Wake Up, America* on the portable TV in her kitchen. Hopefully, that stupid nurse would return quickly with some serviceable makeup. She reasoned any millionaire who could afford a private hospital room in his mansion, must stock at least a supply of essential cosmetics. After making herself presentable, she would order breakfast.

Valerie propped herself up on the pillows. Her head ached a little at the movement, but at least she could now reach the television remote control on the table. She picked up the remote, pointed it towards the set nestled in the armoire, and turned on *Wake Up America*.

As she watched an ad for a woman's underarm deodorant that insisted it was potent enough for a warthog but designed for a ballerina, Valerie regretted not seeing the news summary that began the show. She couldn't help feeling that she had missed something by being unconscious since Friday, that is, of course, if today was the Monday after the accident. The nurse had only indicated it was a Monday. It could have been more than a week since the crash. Or two. Or a month. Her anxiety was relieved as the commercial ended (with the ballerina hugging a non-malodorous wildebeest), and one of the show's anchors, the perky Pepper Parissi appeared and announced the date. Valerie sighed in relief. It had only been three days. Pepper began the introduction of her first guest.

"It is our honor, this morning," began Ms. Parissi, even bubblier than her usual effervescent self, "to have as our guest the woman who single-handedly has saved, among others things, the international peace process. After the events of Friday evening and the following days, I doubt there is a person in the world who isn't at least a little familiar with our guest." The close-up of Pepper showed that she was having trouble remaining calm. "You'd almost have to be living in a cave without cable not to know her," ad-libbed Pepper as her hair bobbed back and forth across her forehead.

"Or out cold for the weekend, Pep," said Valerie to the TV.

The screen switched to a long-shot showing Pepper Parissi with her guest sitting across from her. Valerie's eyes immediately went to the guest to critique her clothing. This woman was wearing, in Valerie's opinion, a stylish looking suit that blended dark greens and golds with understated refinement. It was further enhanced by a rich-looking gold silk top and perfectly matched accessories. The only flaw in the entire presentation, Valerie thought, was that the woman was wearing one necklace too many.

"Ha," muttered Valerie, "must be a Jersey girl." Valerie firmly believed females from the Garden State were prone to over-accessorizing. "Who taught her how to dress?"

A moment later, Valerie realized that the reason she so admired the outfit was that she had just purchased the same ensemble. Another moment after that first moment, Valerie got around to scrutinizing the guest's cosmetic skills. It was then that it dawned on her that the woman whose face had a pretty good makeup job was very familiar... uncomfortably so. Pepper Parissi confirmed Valerie's suspicions as she finished her introduction, and a cameraman reconfirmed it with a close-up of the special guest.

"I am speaking of course," concluded Pepper Parissi, "of Lorraine Innis who has kindly consented to speak with me this morning..."

◆

Down the corridor, the nurse was hurrying back to Valerie Fierro's room with Dr. Janet Lester keeping pace by her side. Both women stopped dead in their tracks by the sound of a piercing scream coming from Valerie's room. Dr. Lester and the nurse broke into a full run for the final twenty feet. Dr. Lester was the first one in the suite where she found Valerie passed out on the bed.

Janet Lester opened her patient's eyelids and shone a penlight into Valerie's pupils.

"I thought you said she was awake," said the doctor.

"She was," said the nurse, "she was talking just as plain as day."

"What did she say?"

"She asked what day it was, and..." The nurse trailed off.

"And what?"

"Well, she wanted brushes."

"Brushes?" asked Dr. Lester. "What kind of brushes?"

"Makeup brushes," said the nurse. "She really said it. I'm not making it up."

"Yes," said the doctor, "well, she's out again. That must have been her screaming. Evidently, something traumatized her."

In the background, Lorraine Innis' smiling face could be seen on the television screen in close-up.

"Well, yes, Pepper," said Lorraine in reply to Ms. Parissi's latest question, "I believe we have an inherent responsibility towards others..."

Dr. Lester was making a notation on Valerie's chart when the patient began muttering once more for cheese.

– 17 –
The Cleanest Home
on Jutland Drive

"Take the second left, please, Dominic," said Lorraine Innis as the limousine driver turned down the residential street.

The vehicle glided along past two-story colonials and rambling ranchers, none of which seemed to be more than fifteen years old. All of them were on such large pieces of land that the area hardly seemed qualified to be labeled a "development."

Following her appearance on two network morning shows Lorraine had been scheduled to tape an interview for that evening's Cookie Babcock special. A leaky roof in a Toronto stadium had forced Sunday night's World Series game to Monday. As a result, the Babcock special was moved back a day to Tuesday. In light of these schedule changes, Babcock and her producer decided to bring their crew down to Wilmington on Tuesday to capture Lorraine in the surroundings in which she became famous.

"This next right," said Lorraine. As she had done on the way to Manhattan, Lorraine rode with the partition between her and Dominic lowered. Not only because it made it easier to give directions but also, because her sudden rise to fame was starting to make her feel quite isolated from her fellow man. This particular fellow man, Dominic, put her at ease. From his name and appearance, she surmised he was Italian-American, and vaguely reminded her of numerous distant uncles and cousins, though she couldn't actually recall what any of them looked like. He also treated Lorraine like a regular person, which now, more than ever, she appreciated.

"Jutland Drive?" he asked reading the street sign.

"Yes, that's right."

"Funny name," he said.

"It's a region in Denmark," said Lorraine, "off of which was fought the largest naval battle of the First World War."

"Is that right," muttered Dominic.

"Yes, Admiral Jellico commanded the British and..." Lorraine cut short her history lesson as she saw the house on its secluded lot. "There it is! Number 27, the federal blue one on the right! That's my house! Just pull in the driveway. I just need to pick up a few things, and we'll soon be on our way."

Actually, Lorraine hoped they wouldn't soon be on their way, not at least if she found Martin at home. He should be back from his trip and at work, but then he hadn't been doing anything according to his usual routine in the last few days. Even if he weren't home, perhaps she'd find some clue to why he had acted so cruelly on the phone the other morning. At the very least, she could pick up some clothes.

As Dominic pulled into the driveway, Lorraine looked at the house and smiled. It was her dream house, wasn't it? Lorraine thought of the hopes and aspirations invested in those walls. She imagined the family she and Martin would raise there, and then, as she grew older, baking cookies with grandchildren on snowy days, Christmases, Thanksgivings; it all said home to her. And although they had only moved in a few months before, she couldn't help but feel a vague sense of her past was there as well as her future.

Lorraine hopped out and ran to the front door. With all the upheaval in her life, it seemed as if she'd been away for years, rather than just since Friday morning.

"Hey, wait, Mrs. Innis," said the driver walking towards the street.

Upon reaching the front step, Lorraine reached into her purse to retrieve her key. As she grabbed the doorknob, however, she noticed that the door was unlocked. That's odd, she thought, Martin wouldn't leave the door wide open like that. Even more curious was the fact that, upon entering the foyer she noticed the house was empty. They had been robbed, and not just robbed. The house had been completely cleaned out. She turned left into the living room – totally bare. Lorraine moved across to the dining room – devoid of everything but the carpet on the floor.

"I don't believe it," said Lorraine in a soft voice, which, due to the barren state of the rooms, resounded in a hollow echo. As she walked into the kitchen, her heels tapped out even louder reverberations. They had taken everything. Lorraine felt as empty inside as the house. She staggered back to the foyer and sat down on the stairs. The chauffeur entered.

"You okay, Mrs. Innis?" asked Dominic. "You don't look so good; like you're in shock."

"It's gone," she said. "All of it. How could someone totally clean out a house? Burglars don't usually take everything, do they? Even the artwork on the walls...gone."

"Burglars don't," he said, "but movers do."

He pushed the door wide open and held up the sign he had removed from the front lawn: *For Sale - Colts Neck Realty*.

"Martin," said Lorraine as she broke into tears. "Why?"

– 18 –
The Private Files
of Beverly Marlton

S everal miles to the north, in the town of Piscataway, Dennis Ullmer was asking the same question: "why?" For Ullmer, the director of human resources at Marlton Press, the nagging question first popped up while he was reading the Sunday paper. At the time he thought there must be a logical explanation for what he was reading, a case of misinformation, or a misprint. This morning, however, he watched the interviews Lorraine Innis gave on the morning shows. Rather than clarify the situation, her appearances only heightened his suspicions. When he arrived at the office, he double-checked his files to make sure he wasn't mistaken. He wasn't.

Now, the bespectacled Ullmer was entering the office of his boss, Beverly Marlton, publisher, and owner of the mid-sized publishing house.

"What is it, Dennis?" asked Beverly Marlton, not bothering to look up from her desk, which was strewn with proofs, photos, and contracts. "I've got an editorial meeting in ten minutes."

"It's about this Lorraine Innis woman." Ullmer delivered his words as if they were tiny bits of gristle wedged between his teeth.

The mention of Lorraine caused the publisher to pause, and glance up at him over her reading glasses.

"What about Lorraine?" asked Beverly Marlton.

"It has been widely reported in the press, both the local papers and the national news services, as well as on various television reports, first on those talk shows yesterday, then this morning on *Wake Up, America*, and next on *A.M. I Said…*"

Beverly Marlton sighed and ran her hand through her shoulder length red hair.

"Sometimes I wish, Dennis," she interrupted, "that you were made of paper rather than flesh and bone so I could take a blue pencil to you and edit your rambling down to a more digestible length. Get to the point. What about her?"

"Um...she doesn't work here," said Ullmer.

"What? You didn't fire her, did you?"

"No."

"Did she quit? If she did, I wouldn't blame her, having to deal with the likes of you. I'm often tempted to resign, but I own the place."

"No, she never worked here."

"What do you mean?"

"Well," he said, "when her name began cropping up in the news this weekend, I, as much as anyone, admired her for her contribution to world peace."

"So?" said Beverly Marlton, as she tapped her pencil on the desk.

"So, I was genuinely interested in her story. Especially since she's from New Jersey, too; just up the road from me, in fact, in Colts Neck. I live in Tinton Falls," said Dennis Ullmer.

"I know," said Beverly, "I go to that open house that you and your wife have every Christmas." She said this with a sigh that made Ullmer wonder if his annual gala was growing stale.

"Well," he continued, "it was reported that she was one of our editors. I first thought: that couldn't be right. I know all of our editors, all our employees, in fact. I thought: they're mistaking us for Merlin Press. But they kept reporting it as Marlton Press. Marlton Press! Finally, this morning, this Innis woman said it herself on television, that she works for us, that is, for you."

"And?"

"And she doesn't. I went through all my files with a fine-toothed comb, metaphorically speaking, of course," Ullmer smoothed back his own thinning brown hair.

"Did you go through my desk as well?" asked Beverly Marlton.

"Of course not," gasped Ullmer.

"Too bad," said Marlton as she opened her drawer, pulled out a single yellow file and dropped it on her desk. "'Cause that's where her file is."

The H.R. director leaned over to examine the file, which was clearly labeled: "Innis, Lorraine E."

"Lorraine has been reporting to me directly the last few months," said the publisher, "or don't you recall she's working on a special project for me?"

"Uh, I...I could have sworn I knew everyone in the company. I'll put the file back for you then," he said as he reached for Lorraine's file.

"Leave it," she said, flattening her palm atop the folder. "I'm not done with it."

"Just as you say," he smiled. "You're the boss."

"Yes, I am," agreed Marlton. "Oh, and Dennis, I don't want Lorraine disturbed in any way. Do you understand? I don't want anything, or anyone to bother her, contact her, or root through her records."

"But, why would…"

"She is suddenly a very famous young woman," continued the publisher. "I'm sure there are some unscrupulous types even here in our little family who would share some of the confidential information on her for their own profit or glorification."

"Yes, Ms. Marlton."

"And if that happened it would be unfortunate for that person; wouldn't it?" She stared into Ullmer's eyes as if to say: "This means you!"

"Understood," muttered Ullmer as he turned towards the door.

"Oh, and Dennis, don't feel too bad. As the company grows, we can't remember everyone that works here; can we?"

"I guess not, but I could have sworn…"

"Dennis, you've been working too hard. Take the rest of the day off. I insist," said Beverly Marlton as she pressed the intercom button on her desk phone.

"Shirley," the publisher said to her secretary. "Bring in today's clippings on Lorraine Innis when you're done compiling them. Oh, and will you try and get her on the phone. She won't be at home. Call one of those TV shows she was on, they'll know how to contact her. Tell them it's her boss calling."

She hit the button again and looked up at Dennis Ullmer.

"Are you still here, Dennis? You really look terrible. Go home."

– 19 –
The Ecclesiastical Monty Hall

It was noon as Father Mike Valvano finished his rounds at St. Francis Hospital. He ended just where he had begun: on the fifth floor. Usually, he would have started on the top floor and worked his way down. Though it wasn't efficient, starting and ending on the fifth floor afforded the priest two opportunities to visit Valerie Fierro.

"Oh, hello Father," said a nurse checking Valerie's vital signs. "Making an extra visit today?"

"No," said Father Mike with a smile, "I seem to have lost my rosary. I'm just retracing my steps."

The priest pretended to look around the room.

"Oh? Well, if I see it, I'll set it aside for you," said the nurse.

"Thank you. Oh, how's the patient…Miss Fierro, isn't it?"

"She's calmed down a little since this morning. She's not asking for as much cheese."

"Cheese, huh?" he said to himself looking at a plate of Gorgonzola.

"Well, I'll tell the other girls to be on the lookout," said the nurse as she started to leave.

"For what?"

"Your rosary."

"Oh, yes, thanks a million," said the priest. "I mean, bless you… millions of blessings. I'll just stay for a moment, as long as I'm here, and give Miss Fierro an extra prayer."

After the nurse left, Mike Valvano crept to the door and closed it, then turned to admire Valerie's form laying in the bed. He couldn't decide what to do, and for the first time since he'd become a priest he couldn't even figure out what to pray. His seminary training had omitted special benedictions for unconscious women with whom you'd like to commit cardinal sins. After another moment of indecision, he approached the head of the bed, bowed down, and kissed Valerie Fierro hard on her lips.

Coming up for air, Father Valvano, made a sign of the cross.

"In Nomine Patri et Filio et Spiritui Sancto. Amen," he recited, before looking upwards and saying: "Okay, let's make a deal."

- 20 -
The Home That
Ran Away from the Girl

"Take a belt of this," said Dominic the chauffeur handing Lorraine Innis a crystal tumbler.

"What is it?" said Lorraine as she wiped her eyes with her handkerchief.

"Just a little brandy," he said. "I stock a full bar in the limo."

"I usually don't," said Lorraine before tossing back the drink like a professional guzzler. "And now I know why," she coughed.

Lorraine was seated at the bottom of the staircase of her home. At least she thought it was still her home. Wasn't it? Following the realization that the downstairs was bare, she had gone upstairs to get some of her clothes to take back to Valerie's. The upstairs was as empty as the downstairs. For some reason, Martin had taken everything, even her clothes.

"You'll be okay, it's just a shock, that's all." He offered her his hand, and she stood up.

"You've been very kind, Dominic," she said as she looked around at the empty rooms. "How could he empty the house so quickly? I just spoke to him Saturday. He said he was on a business trip, but I don't recall that in his schedule. Maybe that was just an excuse while he was doing this. Could he move the contents of a two-story colonial in that space of time?"

"Sure," said Dominic. "My cousin's a mover. They could clear out a joint, I mean, a home like this in a day...six hours tops. Of course, that takes planning."

"Planning? So it couldn't be done on the spur of the moment?"

"Naw! The movers would need to know how many boxes they need, what size trucks, stuff like that. Like I said: planning."

"Planning," said Lorraine.

Had Martin been planning to run away even before she became famous? If so, why? What had happened before Friday night? She found out she was pregnant. But Martin wanted a family. Didn't he? It was all so mysterious. The more she thought about it, the more confused Lorraine became. Of course in her present physical state, she couldn't have a baby. Could she? Did she still have a womb under...well, down there? No, she had to get out of here. It had been a mistake to come home. She had to go back to Valerie's. That's it. She'd go back to Delaware, retrace her steps, and perhaps then she would find her sanity, her body, her baby, her husband, her home...she stopped. One step at a time, she told herself. She'd go back and wait for Valerie to get better. Valerie would help her sort it out.

"Well," said Lorraine, walking towards the door, "I guess there's no use staying here any longer. It's obvious that my husband isn't returning." She stopped and turned to the driver. "Dominic, you're a man."

"That's what my proctologist says."

"What would cause a man to abandon his wife without any warning?"

"I dunno," said Dominic. "A guy doesn't bail except for two reasons. Either he's running to something or away from something."

"To something...as in another woman," said Lorraine. She paused to think. No, Martin was always very attentive. Wasn't he? "Or away...from what?"

"Pressure?" guessed the chauffeur.

Lorraine stared at the sugar maple in the front yard. Its leaves were at their peak of color. Pressure, she thought. Financial pressure? It couldn't be that. They weren't rich, but they were comfortable. The pressure of finding that you're suddenly married to a celebrity? That didn't make sense. Martin wouldn't care about me being famous. Besides, he couldn't have emptied out the house so quickly if her fame were the motivation. She hadn't been in the spotlight more than a day or so. So what would he have to be afraid of...unless...

"Would you be unnerved, Dominic, if your wife became famous?"

"My wife?" laughed the driver, "not likely. What would I care if my old lady got famous? Unless I was on the lam from the cops, you know?"

Lorraine looked back at the dangling wires in the middle of the ceiling, all that remained of the lighting fixture that had once hung there. That was it, she thought. Martin had some secret in his past from which he was running. Of course! And he wouldn't have told me until it was time to leave. Now, though, he couldn't take me along because my fame would draw attention to him. And he took all our furniture and possessions to sell for getaway money.

She had never suspected Martin to be the type to have secrets. He had always seemed so happy-go-lucky. Hadn't he? If only he had confided in her, she could have helped him with his problem, whatever it was. Or could she? It must be something terrible to make Martin put the house on the market and take all their belongings. She could understand him selling the house if he needed money, but all their things including her clothes? Lorraine suddenly realized the implication. She had no clothes, aside from the dress she had worn on Friday, some shoes and underwear she had bought at the mall, and whatever she had borrowed from Valerie. The notion of all her things being sold in some secondhand shop or online made her feel violated.

"Well," said Lorraine, purposely breaking off her train of thought, "There's nothing to keep us here. I suppose we ought to be on our way."

"Whatever you say, Mrs. Innis." Dominic was just about to grab the knob when the door swung open and a woman wearing a bright mustard-colored blazer entered.

"Hi," said the woman who was carrying a clipboard, "sorry I'm late. I had a minor emergency back at the office. That's why I left the door unlocked for you. I just knew once you saw the house you'd want to look inside. It's everything I told you on the phone, isn't it?"

Lorraine and Dominic just stared at the woman.

"You're not the Watkins, are you?" asked the woman.

"The Watkins?" repeated Lorraine.

"I was supposed to meet them here this morning, to show the house. I left the door open, oh, I already explained that."

"We ain't the What'sises," said Dominic as he put his arm around Lorraine's shoulder.

"Well, if you're interested," said the woman as she handed Lorraine a fact sheet on the listing. "Between you, me, and the wallpaper, you can get a terrific deal if you act quickly. The owner is very eager to turn this over and fast."

Lorraine looked at the piece of paper then buried her face in Dominic's shoulder as she burst into tears.

The realtor just stared as Dominic took the flyer from Lorraine and handed it back to her.

"Oh," said the woman, "was it something I said?"

"She's had a rough morning," said Dominic.

"Oh, dear, is there anything I can do?" asked the Realtor.

"Naw," he said, "did you ever think of running away from home?"

"I suppose," said the woman, "when I was little."

"Yeah, well, in her case home beat her to it and ran away from her."

– 21 –
Secretary's Day Comes But Twice a Year

Roses!" cried Patsy Einfalt as she limped into the office. As a rule, Patsy didn't start her work week by exclaiming "roses," or "chrysanthemums," or even "aspidistras." This morning, however, she broke with tradition because a vase full of them was on her desk. Purvis Twankey, she hoped, as she grabbed for the card, let them be from Purvis Twankey. Maybe, on reflection, the Lancashire cowboy realized that she adored him and that Valerie Fierro was out of his league. Beyond the obvious reason that he had put Valerie in a coma, Patsy couldn't see Valerie appreciating Purvis' simple sweetness. Valerie was more sophisticated than her. Whereas Patsy was flea markets and chain restaurants, Valerie liked upscale boutiques and bistros. If she didn't like her, Patsy would have called Valerie snooty, but since she liked Valerie very much, she just concluded that Valerie had more expensive tastes than her. The unassuming Purvis belonged in Patsy's world, not Valerie's upwardly-mobile atmosphere.

Patsy fumbled with the envelope, imagining the clever verse Purvis Twankey would have composed just for her. When she read it, the card actually said: "To Patty, Happy Secretary's Day, Mr. Liverot." Her shoulders drooped as she slumped into her chair.

Peter Liverot peeked out of his office.

"Good morning, Patty," said Liverot, "surprised?"

Liverot usually called her "Patricia," but shortened that to "Patty" for special occasions, though no one else ever called her by either name.

"Good morning, Mr. Liverot. Sorry, I'm late."

Liverot looked at his Rolex.

"Think nothing of it," said Liverot. Most days she was a half-hour early. "You can stay late tonight."

111

"It won't happen again," said Patsy. She glanced at the roses again and thought she would have swapped them for a kind smile, as long as it came from Purvis Twankey. "My friend was on television this morning, and I had to go over to my parent's house to see it. My set's broken. Then I had a doctor's appointment. Oh, and thank you for the roses, they're very nice."

"Really? You don't seem so thrilled with them. Those are top notch blooms," he said. "I got a guy in Jersey gives me a great deal."

"Yes, sir."

"So what's the problem?"

"It's not Secretary's Day," said Patsy.

"It's not?" he said feigning surprise.

"No, that's in April."

"Are you sure?"

"Yes, sir, I'm sure." She should be. Each year, Patsy had to remind him and then order her own flowers, and never anything as pricey as roses.

"Oh, well, two in one year won't hurt, will it?" said Liverot, "especially when you've got the best secretary in the world."

Patsy looked at her boss sideways. Though she regularly came in early, stayed late, and skipped lunches and breaks, Peter Liverot rarely threw a word of praise in her direction. Oh, he was okay as a boss, Patsy told herself, but she wondered what he wanted. Whatever it was, she assured herself, she'd find out soon enough, and it would likely involve more work.

"Come on into my office," said Liverot. Patsy started picking up her steno book. "No, book," he added while rubbing his hands together, "just for a little...chat."

She shrugged her shoulders and hobbled into Liverot's office. As was her custom, Patsy started towards the chair to the right of Liverot's desk, where she sat for dictation. Liverot cleared his throat to attract her attention and then motioned towards the cushioned chairs around his coffee table. On the table were two china cups and a matching pot, along with an assortment of pastries.

"I thought we'd have coffee and cake together," said Liverot, "after all, I thought it was Secretary's Day."

Patsy moved back towards one of the comfortable chairs and plopped down as gracefully as she could with her ankle heavily bandaged. Patsy fidgeted in her seat, smoothed out her dress and started reaching for the coffeepot.

"Allow me," said Liverot, smiling broadly. "Milk? Sugar?"

Patsy indicated two sugars. Her boss prepared her cup and handed it to her. Whether or not he had thought it was Secretary's Day didn't matter. He never acted like this. She had never been invited to join him for coffee and pastries. Patsy figured she had better enjoy it while she could. She grabbed a cinnamon bun and took a bite.

"You've had quite a weekend, haven't you?" said Liverot.

"Sir?"

"I mean what with all the excitement of Friday night."

"Oh, I didn't know you knew about all that."

"It's in all the papers," smiled Liverot.

"On TV, too," said Patsy. "I was on television, as well!"

"Yeah, I know. I mean, yes, that's what someone told me."

Patsy squirmed. She was wondering if Mr. Liverot was angry with her for performing poorly on TV. Maybe he thought it reflected poorly on the bank. Or worse yet, she realized, she hadn't mentioned the bank at all.

"I guess I didn't do very well on TV," said Patsy.

"No, no," Liverot, "you were fine. I was very proud of you."

"Thank you," said Patsy. She relaxed and took another bite of the bun.

"And poor Miss Fierro," said Liverot, "having that nasty accident on Friday afternoon."

"Yes, she's still in the hospital."

"Yeah...I mean, is she? I wonder if there's anything I can do for her."

"I took her those papers to work on like you asked me," said Patsy, "but she was too unconscious to get to them."

Peter Liverot turned red. "Yes, that was silly of me, wasn't it?" he chuckled. "I don't know what I was thinking. You should have said something."

Usually, when an employee disagreed with Peter Liverot, the only thing they could say in objection was: "I quit." Otherwise, you just had to go along with it.

"Yes, sir," said Patsy.

"And wasn't that something about Miss Fierro's cousin, rushing in and saving that Russian big shot? A remarkable dame, uh, broad, that is, er, lady."

"Yes, I like her a lot," said Patsy.

"I've been thinking about poor Miss Fierro, there in the hospital, and all the excitement surrounding her cousin, and I've come to a conclusion. We here at the bank need to help out our employees in their times of need."

"We do?" This was a novel idea. Up until now, Peter Liverot had always complained about employees private lives interfering with his business' bottom line. Collections for things like wedding and baby gifts had to be done behind his back.

"We should see to it that Miss Fierro and her cousin have no worries while she's incapacitated. Maybe see to it that she gets a private room."

"She's already in the nicest suite in the hospital," said Patsy.

"She is?" said Liverot. "Well, then I can help with those bills."

"The Russian president is already paying them."

"He's got his f...riggin' nerve!" said Liverot, barely restraining himself. "Coming over here, turning our town into a shooting gallery, and then trying to horn in on my..."

Liverot stopped himself short and took a swig of coffee.

"I mean," he said, "I think we should explore every opportunity to help out Miss Fierro and her cousin...especially her cousin."

"Yes, sir."

"Get her on the phone and ask her to come in for a nice little chat."

"She's still unconscious, I think," said Patsy.

"I meant her cousin...besides I'm sure that she'd like to see where Miss Fierro works."

"I suppose," said Patsy, substituting those two words the first two that came to mind: "What for?"

"I can see her whenever she's available. Okay?"

Patsy rightly concluded that their convivial coffee break was over. She lifted herself up, and favoring her bandage foot, started shuffling back to her desk. Liverot finally noticed her foot as she exited.

"Cut your ankle?"

"Yes, sir," said Patsy.

"Too bad, you should get a doctor to look at it," he said ignoring that she had already explained that was why she had been late.

"Thank you, Mr. Liverot."

"On your own time," said this year's version of the kinder, gentler bank president.

– 22 –
Advance and
Be Recognized

"Ms. Marlton will be with you in a moment, Mrs. Innis."

"Thank you, Shirley," said Lorraine.

As she sat outside of Beverly Marlton's office, Lorraine couldn't help but be unnerved by the reaction of her co-workers. Shirley had never been so formal before, had she? She certainly hadn't called her "Mrs. Innis." The others were the same. Lorraine had greeted most everyone she had met on her way in by name. In return, most had merely nodded, or worst of all just stared. Could they all be so affected by what had happened to her since she left work the previous Thursday? She couldn't help but notice that they all looked horribly overworked as if they had aged years in just a few days. She didn't know how they could be so overburdened, especially since there were several new staff members whom she did not recognize.

"That's an attractive new hairstyle, Shirley," said Lorraine trying to engage the secretary in conversation.

The woman stared at her as if she had two heads, before confessing she'd been wearing it that way for years.

Lorraine decided small talk was futile given the odd mood that had descended upon Marlton Press. She continued her wait in silence. It was almost noon. She had hoped that by now she would have been back at Valerie's side. She shouldn't have stopped in Colts Neck. It had only made her more upset, though it did help explain Martin's irrational behavior when she spoke to him on Saturday. The more Lorraine pondered it, the more she was sure that her husband was running from the attention generated by her sudden fame. He must be involved in something secret that would be exposed by her celebrity. She also reasoned that he was on the run to protect her. That's why he had acted so belligerently the last time they spoke. Martin was hoping that by seeming to be so callous, she

115

wouldn't try to find him. Now that she had deduced his motive, she was even more determined to find him and help him. If nothing else, Lorraine told herself, she was the type of a woman who stood by her man. Wasn't she?

Under these circumstances, Lorraine welcomed the call from her boss, Beverly Marlton. The publisher had reached her in the limo, just as they were leaving Colts Neck. Lorraine knew Beverly to be a demanding but fair boss and was confident that the publisher would help her, if only by allowing her a leave of absence.

"So, Shirley," said Lorraine, attempting once more to break the ice, "have I missed anything?"

"Uh, no," said Shirley slowly, "I suppose not."

"Everyone's acting so...formal around me," said Lorraine. "I know I've been in the news the last few days, but I'm still the same person."

The secretary stared at Lorraine. A moment later, the intercom buzzed. The secretary answered it, and then announced: "Ms. Marlton will see you now."

"Thank you, Shirley," said Lorraine rising. "Well, we'll have to have lunch, sometime soon."

The secretary gave her an odd look that Lorraine tried to ignore. She had enough to worry about without adding the strange reactions of her coworkers.

"Hello, Ms. Marlton," said Lorraine as she entered the publisher's office. "It's nice to be back in familiar surroundings after all that's been happening."

"Thank you for coming in...Lorraine." The publisher rose from her desk and shook Lorraine's hand firmly while scrutinizing her. Despite trying to ignore such behavior, Lorraine noticed it immediately. She tried to dismiss the look by blaming it on her clothes.

"It's my cousin Valerie's suit," she said, though Beverly Marlton was studying her face, not her outfit. "I borrowed it."

"Very nice," said Beverly, still not taking her eyes off Lorraine's face. After another moment, the publisher realized she had been staring. "I'm sorry, won't you sit down? I appreciate you coming in today. I imagine you must have a lot on your mind."

"You don't know the half of it, Ms. Marlton."

"How long have you worked here, Lorraine?"

"A little over five years. Six next spring."

"I see. Then why don't you call me 'Beverly?' I'd prefer it if you did. After all, I feel our working relationship will be entering a new phase, one that will be closer than before."

"I'd like that, Ms. Marlton...Beverly," said Lorraine. "I mean, I'd like to call you by your first name, as well as working more closely with you."

"Good. What have you been working on lately, Lorraine?"

"Actually, I'm between assignments," said Lorraine.

"Right," said Beverly slowly. "Well, I'm sure you'll want some time off to sort out some work-life issues."

"Yes, thank you," said Lorraine. "It's very kind of you to understand."

"Not at all. When you come back to work, I'd like to put you on a special project. A very personal project...if you agree, of course."

"Personal? How personal?"

"That's up to you. I'd like to publish your autobiography."

"My what?" Of course, Lorraine knew what an autobiography was. She'd written other people's autobiographies as a ghostwriter. While Marlton Press was a very respectable publisher, they didn't have the clout to attract top celebrities for their memoirs. Consequently, most were authored by cable TV personalities or supporting players from old sitcoms.

"The public is eager to know more about you. You're the woman of the hour. They want to know your inner thoughts, your motivations, the woman beneath the skin," said Beverly Marlton.

"I don't know," said Lorraine. "Right now, I'm not sure that even I want to explore what's beneath my skin, let alone lay it bare for the world to see."

"Of course, if it's money," said Beverly, "we would continue your salary, while still giving you a generous advance on sales. You'd be getting paid twice. Once for writing your story, and once for editing it. You are an editor, after all, aren't you?"

Lorraine did a double take. That was an odd question.

"That's what you've been paying me to do all these years, isn't it?" said Lorraine. "If you have any doubts about my past work..."

"No, no, please," said Beverly. "I didn't mean to question your qualifications. I just...that is, I didn't know if you'd feel up to editing your own life story. You're my best editor, of course. You've always been like the little sister I never had."

"But you have a younger sister," said Lorraine.

"She doesn't count," said the publisher. "What I'm saying is that you'd want to keep your biography in the family. It would be the book that puts our little company in the big time."

"It is tempting," said Lorraine. Writing her autobiography would allow her to tell her story, in her own way with a heavy emphasis on her relationship with Martin. She could not only use such a book to help find him, but also send him a message reaffirming her love, and thus coax him back to her side. Besides, the money might help, not only to search for Martin but also to help him out of whatever trouble he was in. "Do you really think my autobiography would be a best seller?"

"I guarantee it! In fact, I'll write you out a six-figure advance right now. Of course, the sooner we get the book in the stores, the more we can cash in on your current notoriety."

"How soon would you need it?"

"As soon as possible. I understand you're quite involved with caring for your cousin..." said Beverly Marlton.

"Not to mention all the interviews."

"Yes, well, we wouldn't want too many more of those before we could get your book on the street. We'll keep you in front of the public just enough to whet their appetite for more. Don't worry. I'll handle all that."

"That would be a relief," said Lorraine. "It's been quite overwhelming. Oh, but I'm supposed to do the Cookie Babcock special tomorrow night."

"Certainly, do that one!" said Beverly, "that's quite a coup. Aside from that, though we'll taper off for the time being. I've had legal draw up a contract, and here's a portion of that advance."

Short of cash, Lorraine nearly leaped at the check and put it in her purse.

"All I want you to do is write...at your own pace, of course," said Beverly. "Just get it done as rapidly as possible."

"Take my time, just be quick about it?"

Beverly Marlton smiled. "You're a clever girl, Lorraine. I'm going to enjoy working with you."

"Still," added Lorraine.

"Oh, yes, still," the publisher agreed, "I've always enjoyed working with you."

- 23 -
Patricia Arranges
a Surprise

Patsy Einfalt had been trying to contact Lorraine Innis all morning, per Peter Liverot's orders. First, she called the hospital, then Valerie's house, to no avail. She even spoke to a mystified attaché at the Russian embassy before she remembered the list of television producers from the previous day.

"Hello? Is Mrs. Innis still there?" Patsy asked the first producer she called. "Well, when did she leave? All the way back then, huh?... Oh, this is...Mrs. Innis' appointment secretary...No, she hasn't gotten back yet, at least nowhere where I'd expect her to be... Yes, that is a good idea. Do you have the phone number for the limousine? ... Right, got it. Thank you... Wait a moment, may I ask you a question? ...Well, aside from being Mrs. Innis' scheduling secretary, I'm also one of her closest confidants. I was wondering, would you be interested in interviewing somebody close to Lorraine who had an interesting story of their own?... You would? ... Well, I think I've got something you'd be very interested in... It would give your viewers a whole new perspective on Lorraine... No, thank you... Yes, I have to check on a few things, but I'll call back as soon as I can... Me? I'm Patsy, that is, Patricia Einfalt... Yes, goodbye."

Patsy hung up the phone and clapped her hands. Her moment of self-congratulation over, she pulled out the Wilmington telephone directory and started flipping through it furiously. There was so much to do, and so little time.

"Lorraine will be so surprised," she said, as she dialed.

– 24 –
Eugenia and the
Clay Commodity

Well, Mrs. Bupp," said the registrar at Coeur de Lane Community College, "back for some more courses, are we?"

"Not we, just me," said Eugenia Bupp as she handed the woman her registration card. "I ain't got a giraffe up my ass, you know!"

"That's not what I meant, oh, never mind," said the woman taking the card. "Let's see what class you'd like to take this time…oh, 'Modeling in Clay.'" That sounds like fun!"

"Ain't doin' it for fun, Judy Jetson!"

"My grandmother took that class," said the woman ignoring the last comment. "She made an ashtray. Of course, no one in the family smokes…"

"Then what the hell did the stupid old twat make an ashtray for?"

"Granny just took the class to keep busy," said the registrar as she entered Eugenia Bupp's information in the computer.

"She must have lost her marbles," said Ma Bupp. "Life's too short to be slappin' your clay around just to keep busy. Tell her to get a real job."

"But she's almost 85!"

"She don't have to work the swing shift at Lockheed," said Mrs. Bupp. "She could be wiping tables at Burger King, or picking up trash at the mall."

The woman gave her a patronizing smile. "Oh, my," she said, "you are a caution!"

"Or if she's gotta take up space in a community college, tell her to make something useful like a…"

"A nice flower vase?" suggested the registrar.

"Have it your own way. I was gonna say a bedpan," said Mrs. Bupp.

"I think I'd rather have a pretty flower vase."

"Yeah, well, you try squatting on a pretty flower vase," mocked Bupp, "in the middle of a cold night when you gotta pee in a hurry. You'll wish she'd made that bedpan."

The registrar handed back a confirmation slip. "You're all set. You got the last open spot in the class. That will be $50."

"$35," said Eugenia Bupp, shoving some rumpled bills over the counter, "I get the senior citizen discount."

"Oh, of course, forgive me,"

"And it's just lucky for you I got in, or we'd have to make room, see?" said Bupp.

"My, you must be looking forward to that class," said the woman. "It will be fun. A lot of ladies around your age take that course."

"I ain't paying 35 samolians to sit around with a bunch of dried up old snatches! This is business!" She grabbed her receipt.

"Well, you have a good time," said the registrar with a smile. "You're not going to be making a bedpan, are you?"

"If you must know, nosy-Parker," said Eugenia Bupp as she exited, "I'm making myself a new set of teeth!"

- 25 -
Friend of the Bribe?
Friend of the Goon?

"Your lawyer's here!"

Aaron Laffler sat up on his bunk in solitary confinement at Wilmington's Gander Hill prison. The guard escorted Laffler down to the visitor's area, a narrow room separated by a plexiglass barrier. There were chairs, tables and phone sets on either side of the barrier. The room was empty except for a man wearing a topcoat, and holding a homburg. Laffler glanced back at the guard in puzzlement. This wasn't his lawyer. His lawyer, whom he met briefly on Saturday, was a public defender fresh out of law school. This man had a more prosperous look about him and was at least 20 years older than his attorney. He was about to tell the guard there'd been a mistake, but decided to find out who this visitor was.

Laffler and the man approached opposing chairs and sat down. He studied the man's face while the man stared into Laffler's eyes. The visitor appeared impeccably groomed, from his slicked-down salt and pepper hair to the clear coat of polish on his manicured fingernails.

"Good morning, Mr. Laffler. I'm Julius Rosen, I've been asked to advise you."

"You don't look like you're from the public defender's office."

"Hardly," laughed the lawyer without displaying any humor in the process, "I've been sent by a friend."

"A friend? What friend? Whose friend?"

"May we just suffice it to say, your friend. A family friend."

"I've got no real family, other than my wife," said Laffler before realizing that his visitor looked like a character out of a mob movie. A lump hardened in Laffer's throat. "The Family?"

"A family," said the lawyer, looking sternly in Laffler's eyes. After a moment the icy stare thawed, and Mr. Rosen seemed less threatening. "You know, Mr. Laffler, or may I call you 'Aaron?' Aaron, a family can be of great help in times of need, can't it?" said Rosen

"But what do they have to do with me?"

"There are many ways to come in contact with a family. May we say through marriage, or friendship, or...business."

Liverot, thought Laffler, as a shiver ran up his spine. "I see."

"I thought you would," said Rosen with a satisfied nod. "You see, the family I represent would hate to see something happen to a friend of theirs."

"They would?" They were trying to secure his silence, thought Laffler.

"Naturally," said Rosen. "We all like to take care of our friends."

After a moment's thought, he asked, "Am I a friend of your family?"

"Are you? You would know your own friends better than I, Aaron."

Laffler pondered the question carefully. Over the last few days, Laffler had been able to sort out quite a bit. He realized he would be going to prison for a while. Now, this visitor came with an offer of help, he assumed, in return for keeping any mention of Peter Liverot out of the whole affair. He had looked forward to exposing Liverot as the man who had driven him over the edge. Now, however, it seemed that might not be such a good idea.

"It's good to have friends, isn't it?" asked Laffler.

"It's very good," observed the lawyer.

"How good?"

"We can safely conclude," noted Rosen, "that friends can be at your side to advise you on things like plea bargains, and the intricacies of establishing temporary insanity. Then, when one finds oneself in a confining situation for what is hopefully a brief hiatus from freedom, one's friends can make sure one is secure and comfortable. Mostly secure."

"I see."

"Of course, without friends that same environment can be very inhospitable and even dangerous."

"Dangerous," repeated the prisoner.

"One could imagine it becoming very dangerous. Without friends to point the way, one could be exposed to a plethora of unfortunate accidents."

"It is good to have friends," said Laffler.

"May we say it's also very wise as well," agreed Julius Rosen as the grim corners of his mouth turned slightly upwards.

– 26 –
Harnessing the Power of Nikolai Kropotkin

C an I get you a drink, Uncle?" asked Yuri Bellikov as Nikolai Kropotkin sat in the living room of his guest lodge at Camp David. "Vodka? Bourbon? Cherries Cokes?"

Kropotkin did not even stir at the mention of the Cherry Coke. Yuri was worried. He had seen Kropotkin in furious rages countless times before, but the leader's present mood was even more frightening than those legendary outbursts. From the looks of it, a pressure was building beneath Kropotkin's stoic exterior that would make Vesuvius' eruption seem like a popped boil by comparison.

"Have you talked with Mrs. Innis, today," asked Yuri, trying to change the subject.

At first, Kropotkin smiled at the mention of her name, but then a scowl crossed his face.

"Do not blame her," said Yuri, fumbling with the sling that supported his injured arm.

"Blame her?" said Kropotkin, his eyes blazing. "She is the only one not to blame in this idiot's country."

"Who is an idiot?" asked Yuri, relieved that for a change he was not his Uncle's fool of choice.

"Merton," snapped Kropotkin, "Merton is an idiot...you idiot."

Yuri hung his head.

"I am sorry, my boy. You are not an idiot," said Kropotkin quietly.

Yuri did a double take.

"Uh, thank you, Uncle," said Yuri, cautiously.

Kropotkin brooded for a minute before breaking his silence.

"Imagine," said Kropotkin, softly, but still with an edge to his voice, "imagine rejecting a peace proposal out of hand for the lone reason that he didn't like the name!"

"Who?" asked Yuri.

"That idiot, Quinton Merton! You were there at the press conference. You heard him!"

Yuri nodded. He had been at the joint press conference an hour ago when Merton had dismissed the Lorraine Accord as unacceptable. At first, his objections sounded reasonable, though vague. As he spoke, however, the American President seemed to ramble and started attacking, not the proposal, but its inspiration. The assembled media seemed astounded. They had expected the two men to announce an agreement, or at least an agreement to seek an agreement. Yuri was also astonished, not only because Merton had tossed aside a serious proposal for nuclear disarmament; but because Kropotkin hadn't wheeled around and punched Merton in the nose. Instead, and much to his nephew's surprise, Kropotkin had given a restrained response to the press before excusing himself and his staff. It was only as the Russian entourage walked away from the journalists that Kropotkin ordered Yuri to begin preparations for their immediate departure from Camp David. Since then, he had remained anchored to the overstuffed armchair making sporadic outbursts of disbelief surrounded by long, ominous silences, while his staff bustled around him arranging for his departure.

Fifteen minutes later, one of the staff whispered in Yuri's ear.

"We are ready to go," said Yuri, turning to Kropotkin.

"Thank you, Yuri," whispered Kropotkin.

"Is there nothing else I can do for you, Uncle?"

"I require nothing."

"You will feel better once we get back to Moscow," said Yuri.

"We are not going back to Moscow."

"Uncle?"

"We are going to Paris next," said Kropotkin. "Then to London, then to Beijing, and on to all the other nations in the nuclear club."

"Do they know we are coming?"

"I shall call them personally," said Kropotkin. "Once we are in the air. I do not trust the security of these lines. I will take Lorruska's Accord on to the other nations. Just because this foolish American behaves like an irrational child, that is no reason not to go forward with our plans. If the Accord is fair, as I believe it is, other nations will agree and stand with us. But to reject it all just because it is named after its inspiration, a young lady who…"

Kropotkin's voice grew more passionate as he referred to Lorraine Innis, and Yuri thought the anticipated tirade was about to break with the force of a tidal wave. Instead, all that issued forth was a gentle shower, as Kropotkin stopped in mid-sentence to wipe a tear from his eye.

Yuri edged backward. "I will see to the final preparations, Mr. President," said Yuri as he tiptoed away, wondering what power this American woman held to sway such a potent force of nature as Nikolai Kropotkin.

- 27 -
The Spy Who Came In for a Mint Mocha Frappe

Thanks for meeting me on such short notice, R.R.," said Senior Agent Paul Rocher, as he ground out his half-smoked Camel on the pavement outside the coffee bar, and held out his hand. "Should we go inside?"

The man known as the Roto-Rooter squeezed Rocher's outstretched palm.

"Yeah, I guess so," said the Rooter, curling his lip disdainfully at the franchise shop's façade. "They're really moving in, aren't they? Here we are two blocks from the White House, and you can't get a decent cup of coffee for under ten bucks."

"That's what we're fighting for," said Rocher holding the door for his friend.

The other patrons in the establishment, mostly young government lawyers grabbing a late lunch of trendy concoctions slapped between overpriced baguettes, ignored the more seasoned men as they each purchased a cup of coffee and then secured a small table in the corner.

"How are things going since your..." Rocher groped for a gentler phrase than "termination," and after a brief pause selected: "retirement."

"They're going," said the man with a grunt. "Whatcha got?"

"Hazelnut mint blend," said Rocher swirling his recycled paper cup emblazoned with the shop's logo.

"I wasn't talkin' about the coffee," said the Rooter squirming on the iron and teak stool. "Man, these seats play hell with a guy's boxers."

"It's a job; if you're interested," said Rocher. He took out another cigarette before recalling the indoor smoking ban. "I just started these up again the other day. A lot's changed since I gave 'em up."

"A lot's changed," said the Rooter. "But I'm still interested in an honest day's work. What's the budget?"

"Unlimited," said Rocher. He had almost added: "if we get the results," but didn't. You don't question the qualifications of an ex-CIA operative who had gotten kicked out of the agency for being too good at his job.

"Out of the neighborhood or local?" asked Root.

"Local. East coast. Mostly Jersey."

The former agent winced. "Sure they ain't got any real coffee here? If I have to go to New Jersey, I want something stronger than Mint Mocha Frappe."

"That's all they got here, V.L."

The operative shot a hostile look at Rocher. He had accidentally used the Rooter's real initials, a dangerous error. The Rooter had killed men for using his full given name.

"Sorry," muttered, Rocher, "I mean, R.R."

The Rooter stared at him for an uncomfortable moment, before continuing with business.

"What's the target?"

"It's not a removal," answered Rocher. "Strictly information: wires, records, surveillance, background. Do anything you want, discreetly."

"Enemies foreign or domestic?"

"I don't know. Between you and me I think it's a political set-up."

"What isn't 'round here?" said the Rooter wiping his nose and looking out the large plate glass window. "Politics," he spat, "it'll damn well ruin us all."

"You don't want to do it then?"

"I didn't say that. Just making a minor philosophical observation. We all gotta live. So it's a smear job, eh?"

"No, nothing like that," said Rocher. "At least, I don't think it is. Do what you do best. Just get the info. Report back to me with the findings. Right up your alley. They don't call you the Roto-Rooter for nothing..."

He nodded. "I cut through the clogged-up shit. I'm sure they'll be plenty of it. You ever spend much time in Jersey? Look, old friend, it's not that I'm not grateful for the job, but if that's the kind of places you're going to send me, next time we'll have to meet in a bar...a real bar."

Rocher laughed.

"So who's the unlucky subject of this political, bipartisan, innocent smear job?" asked the Rooter.

Rocher sighed wistfully and shook his head.

"What'sa matter?" said the Rooter.

"Nothing, nothing," said Rocher. "It's just, well, did you ever meet someone who you thought was someone, but you knew that it couldn't be them?"

The Roto-Rooter parsed the question and then shrugged his shoulders. "Yeah, I guess. What about it?"

Rocher shook his head again, this time as if to try and dislodge a nagging thought. "Nothing, skip it, it's not important."

"Okay. So, anyway, who's the target?"

Rocher glanced down at his coffee cup and tapped it against a copy of the *Washington Post* that lay on the table. He moved the cup to one side to reveal a front-page photograph of Lorraine Innis.

"Really," said the former operative. "I was wondering how long that would take. And she used to be such a nice lady, too."

– 28 –
The Way That
Cookie Crumbles

Lorraine Innis rarely overslept, but given the dizzying events of the last few days, one could hardly blame her for a few extra moments of slumber. Not that she found any release in sleep. The thoughts she tried so hard to repress during her waking hours came rushing out in odd, vivid dreams. Though they were varied in location and situation, all the dreams had the themes of searching and loss running through them. They all were also liberally laced with phallic symbols, a fact that was not lost on Lorraine, even in the midst of them.

It was the last dream of the morning, one in which a giant boa constrictor ate Martin, and then tried to attach himself to her, that finally woke Lorraine.

Sitting up with a start, she looked at the clock and then jumped out of bed. As she had the previous two mornings, Lorraine hiked up her nightshirt and checked to see if her unexpected anatomical visitor had vanished in her sleep. She sighed. It hadn't.

"I'll worry about you later," she muttered to herself, as she pulled on Valerie Fierro's fuzzy magenta robe. "I should have been up an hour ago. Those television people will be here in ninety minutes."

Cookie Babcock and her crew were due at 10:00 to begin what Lorraine hoped would be her final interview for a while. With any luck, the taping would be over by lunchtime so she could return to Valerie's bedside. Lorraine had spent most of the previous evening at the hospital, with only one interruption. Patsy had called asking that she meet later in the week with Valerie's boss. Purvis Twankey had been conspicuously absent over the last 36 hours. With no other interruptions, Lorraine began her autobiography, using the laptop computer Beverly Marlton had given her.

Lorraine was both encouraged and disappointed over the news that Valerie had woken up Monday morning, but had lapsed back into unconsciousness. As she had before Valerie seemed to rest more comfortable when Lorraine was there; when she wasn't, Valerie was agitated and prone to calling out for cheese at almost anytime. This subconscious yearning was as much a mystery to Lorraine as it was to the medical staff - especially since it continued no matter how much cheese was rushed to her bedside. The only time she wouldn't ask for it was when Lorraine was there, further deepening the riddle.

As she descended the stairs, Lorraine heard a thump against the aluminum storm door. The paper's late, Lorraine thought, as she opened the door. As expected, she found the morning newspaper. What she didn't expect, however, that it was handed to her by the legendary newswoman, Cookie Babcock. Standing behind Ms. Babcock, their lights blazing, and cameras rolling, were her crew.

Lorraine let out a scream, grabbed the paper from the reporter's hand, and then shut the door putting her back to it.

She heard a gentle knock on the door.

"Good morning, Mrs. Innis," said the voice from the other side of the door. "It's Cookie Babcock."

"I thought you were going to get here at 10:00," Lorraine called out.

"We like to show up early," said the woman, "often we get some of our more interesting footage that way."

Lorraine looked down. Her robe was hanging open revealing her purple nightshirt and her bare legs from mid-thigh down. Fortunately, the shirt was loose enough and long enough as not to betray any personal secrets from the absence of her false breasts to the addition to her groin.

"I saw lights," said Lorraine. "Were you filming?"

"Filming? Not much, really," said Babcock, "just a little bit. It's what we call 'B roll.' Please, open the door."

Lorraine cinched the robe around her and double knotted the cord around it. She reached for the knob and then stopped.

"No," she called out.

"No? No what?"

"No," said Lorraine, "I'm not letting you in. Not until you destroy that film."

"It's videotape," called out a voice she assumed belonged to the cameraman.

"Then erase it," said Lorraine.

She heard a low murmur of discussion on the other side of the door.

"Mrs. Innis, you agreed to appear," said Cookie Babcock.

"And you said you'd be here at ten," said Lorraine. "I'm not talking until you agree not to show me in my…robe."

"Okay, you win."

"I want it in writing," said Lorraine.

While Cookie Babcock and her producer drafted an agreement that would gain them access to the house, Lorraine threw the safety bolt and went back upstairs to get dressed. She was half-dressed, sitting on the edge of the bed donning a pair of black tights when she noticed the headline on the front page of the morning paper: PREZ SEZ "NO" TO LORRAINE ACCORD.

Lorraine sat with her mouth agape, and her hose stopped halfway up her thighs as she read the details of the story, which essentially said that President Merton had rejected Kropotkin's peace plan because it was named after her. In the article, Davis Flemming was quoted calling her "a glory-seeking private citizen.'

"That's crazy," muttered Lorraine. "What sort of man would reject a peace plan solely on the basis of its name?"

Lorraine noticed her tights stuck at half-mast and hiked them up around to her waist as she stood to examine the rest of the front page. A companion story's headline read: MOST AMERICANS SAY "YES LORRAINE," "NO MERTON."

Overnight polling data revealed that a majority of Americans, a full 68 percent, thought President Merton acted rashly in rejecting the Lorraine Accord. Only 15 percent agreed with their leader. In addition, the President's approval rating had plummeted after the announcement, from 57 percent to an embarrassing 22 percent. The public's perception of Lorraine Innis, on the other hand, was overwhelmingly favorable. 88 percent of Americans knew and approved of Lorraine, while only 4 percent disliked her. 5 percent hadn't heard of her, and 3 percent confused her with a new instant soft drink called "Lemonade in a Minute."

As she finished pulling on Valerie's vibrant ruby chenille sweater, another story caught Lorraine's eye: "New Jersey Man Missing." Her heart beat faster. Perhaps the authorities were looking for Martin. Maybe they were the ones her husband was fleeing.

"A Southern New Jersey man has officially been classified as a missing person after being absent from his apartment for the last four days, his landlady reported yesterday…"

Lorraine stopped reading. Colts Neck was in Central Jersey, and besides Martin didn't have a landlady, he had a wife. A very anxious wife. And, when she had time to think about it, a very confused wife. After slipping into a knee-length black wool skirt, and applying her makeup, Lorraine checked her appearance in the mirror. Not bad. A reinforcing dab of Valerie's "Five Alarm Rendezvous" lipstick, and Lorraine was ready to face Cookie Babcock and her crew.

Before leaving the bedroom, Lorraine looked out the front window. They were still down there. She was amused to see that there were also two local news vans filming the presence of the network van. Completing the sideshow atmosphere were a dozen or so neighbors enjoying the inconveniences of having a celebrity on their street. Indeed, the only individual unaffected by the media circus was a telephone repair worker who was calmly fiddling with the insides of the green junction box on the lawn next door.

Back downstairs, Lorraine put the chain on the door, unbolted it, and opened it enough to allow a piece of paper to pass through. Examining the pledge to destroy the unauthorized footage, Lorraine counted the signatures at the bottom, and then, through the door, counted the number of crew members waiting outside. Satisfied that her modesty was secure, she undid the chain, letting Babcock and her crew inside.

Cookie Babcock looked like she did on television, while at the same time looking quite different. For one thing, she looked shorter and much frailer. Lorraine guessed the interviewer wasn't much more than 5'0" and would have to do some serious carbo-loading to hit 100 pounds. Her smile seemed permanent, and nearly painful, thanks, Lorraine guessed, to one facelift too many.

"Hello, I'm Cookie Babcock," said the woman, shaking Lorraine's hand.

"Yes, I recognize you from television," said Lorraine. "I'm Lorraine Innis."

"And I recognize your face from practically everywhere," laughed Babcock. "I'm sorry about that little incident with the crew. They get a little trigger happy, you see. They're accustomed to covering movie stars and media celebrities, so they tend to shoot first..."

"...and edit later?" said Lorraine.

"Yes," said Babcock, "in fact, we bumped an interview with Hollywood's sexiest new starlet to be with you."

As the crew hauled their equipment into the house, Lorraine glanced at her appearance in the hallway mirror.

"Maybe you should have done that interview," said Lorraine. "I'm no starlet. I'm just an average woman."

"I'd hardly classify you as an average woman," said Babcock.

"But I am," said Lorraine closing the door, "usually."

"Maybe you were a week ago," said the journalist as she wandered around Valerie's living room. "But since then you've foiled an assassination attempt, advised an international leader, inspired a peace plan, charmed the better part of the electronic media, bested a presidential spin doctor in a verbal jousting match, and became one of the most popular figures in the Western World. I'd say you may have looked average before, but you were just lying dormant waiting to burst on to the international stage." Babcock stopped in front of the sofa. "Alex, we'll set up here. I'll be in the wing chair, Mrs. Innis will be on the settee."

Lorraine edged past the crew as they unpacked, working her way to the sofa.

"Oh, not yet, dear," said Babcock. "We don't need you, yet."

"Cookie," said a man setting up lights, "Can we move the picture from that wall to directly behind you?"

"Sure," said Babcock, before turning to Lorraine, "it's okay with you, isn't it dear?"

Lorraine nodded. They had overrun Valerie's living room with the irresistible force of a colony of army ants. She edged her way back towards the kitchen, and with nothing else to do, put on a pot of coffee.

Within ten minutes the downstairs of the townhouse had been transformed into a television studio. Lorraine, wound her way through a jungle of electronic equipment, lights, cameras, and microphones, carrying a tray, and handing out mugs of coffee to the preoccupied crew. She delivered the final mug to Cookie Babcock, who was sitting in the wing chair, studying her notes through tiny reading glasses. Babcock took the coffee without looking up, had a sip, and muttered a thank you. Another moment later Babcock looked up at the man who Lorraine guessed was the producer.

"About set, Alex?" she asked. "Where's Mrs. Innis?"

"I'm right here," said Lorraine, standing at her side, still holding the tray.

"You shouldn't be doing that," cooed Cookie Babcock in a tone tinged with condescension. She patted the sofa cushion. "Have a seat, right here. You're the heroine of the hour."

"If only it had been just an hour," muttered Lorraine as she smoothed her skirt beneath her, sat down and crossed her legs. She wondered when her moment of fame was over if Cookie Babcock would be so pleasant.

"Would you like some coffee, dear?" asked Cookie as if Lorraine were her guest which, in a way, she was.

"No thank you," said Lorraine, "I could use a glass of water. It's rather warm under these lights."

Lorraine began to rise when Cookie gently pushed her back down.

"Alex, water for Mrs. Innis," she said.

"I could have gotten it."

"You're a star, dear," said Babcock, "you've got to let others do for you now, or you'll never get done all the other things you need to do."

"Like what?"

"Like chatting with me," said the reporter, "and all the millions of people around the world who want to know about the real Lorraine Innis."

Alex slithered through the cables and placed a glass of water in front of Lorraine.

"Now, let's get started, shall we?" said Cookie Babcock. "We'll use the regular format. You've seen my specials, haven't you?" she asked rhetorically.

"No, I haven't," said Lorraine.

"Oh," said Babcock momentarily nonplussed by Lorraine's honesty. "Well, then, we'll just start."

"Glasses, Cookie," said the producer.

Lorraine looked down at the water, while Cookie Babcock whipped off her reading glasses, threw her shoulders back and seemed to double in size as the cameras started rolling.

"What does Lorraine Innis want?" began Babcock. "And don't give us the peace and understanding, Miss America response. What do you really want out of life?"

Lorraine thought a moment. "I suppose I want to get back to being me. I want to restore the parts of my life that I've lost the last few days."

"The simple things, like going shopping?"

"No, I miss the people that make life worthwhile. All the events of the last few days have been a little intrusive on my normal relationships."

"What do your parents think about your sudden fame?"

"They're both deceased," said Lorraine quietly.

"Family?"

"Just my cousin and my husband."

"What do they think of your notoriety?"

"Well, my cousin's unconscious in the hospital, and my husband…he's dealing with it in his own way. We'll work that out as soon as we can."

Lorraine was beginning to prefer the questions the Secret Service had asked her while she was under suspicion for attempted-assassination. Those were less invasive and much less painful. And besides that, their lights weren't as hot. After a moment's silence, Lorraine added: "I just wish things would get back to the way they were."

"But, don't you see? You belong to the world now," said Cookie, "you're a great symbol to women everywhere."

"That's ridiculous. Not that I doubt your assertion that I'm a symbol," said Lorraine. "I just think saying someone is a symbol for women is silly. Why can't someone who does something that is worthy of emulation be a symbol for everyone regardless of their sex, or race, or whatever segment of the population into which they get fragmented?"

"Then you reject the notion of being an inspiration to your gender?"

"I don't have gender!"

"Pardon?"

"I have sex. You have sex. Human beings have sex. Words have gender," said Lorraine pedantically. "'Gender' is a word that, through almost relentless misuse, has come to be synonymous with 'sex.'"

"You seem almost obsessed with words at times," said Cookie.

"Because words have meaning. Misuse them, and you abuse the intellectual process that enables us to function honestly as a society."

"Do you think words are abused today?"

"Flagrantly," said Lorraine. "And like anything we abuse, the more we do it, the easier it becomes to commit greater abuses. It all started, as far as I can tell, with advertisers who manipulated the language to sell things."

"What's wrong with that?" Cookie Babcock. "We, I mean, our economy relies on sponsors, that is, advertisers and marketers. It helps keep the economy going, doesn't it?

"I suppose," said Lorraine, "but at what price? I mean if a little exaggeration helps sell a little more soap, is that justifiable? Perhaps, but then our politicians adopted the same tactics. Now, it's so pervasive that we're all segmented into our own little portions of society to the point when someone can only be a symbol to white, middle-class, women of New Jersey."

"Do you want to be a symbol for everyone?"

"I don't want to be a symbol for anyone, but if I do something that makes someone else want to emulate me, they should be able to do it without regard to what sex I am, or where I live, or anything. We're all just people."

"So you think we're too segregated as a society?"

"We've all been broken into our own special interest groups by clever advertisers and slick politicians. We're not a nation anymore; we're market segments and voting blocks. Instead of pulling together like a team, we're being divided and conquered, and we're doing it to ourselves. We're no longer a country but a three thousand mile nursery of overgrown, selfish babies, each wanting to be fed before any of the others."

Cookie Babcock shifted in her seat as she changed the topic. Lorraine leaned over to take a sip of water.

"So is that the core of your philosophy?" asked Cookie.

Lorraine laughed. "Certainly not. That's the core of the problem. The answer is the opposite."

"And what is the answer?"

Lorraine shrugged her shoulders as if it were evident. "Instead of saying 'what about me,' we need to start asking 'what can I do for you?'"

"Is that what you live by?"

"That's what I try to live by, though I don't know how well I succeed."

"Help out the other person," reiterated Cookie.

"Before we help ourselves," added Lorraine.

"That's marvelously profound in its simplicity. Why hasn't anyone said that before?"

"Someone did," said Lorraine, "in the Sermon on the Mount. 'Do unto others, as you would have them do unto you.'"

"Are you a Christian?"

"Yes."

"Exclusively?"

"One would have to be to follow Christ's teachings," said Lorraine.

"Isn't that being a little narrow-minded?" asked Cookie. "I mean do you think Christianity is right and everything else is wrong."

"If we're really serious about our philosophical choices we must believe that what we choose is the best, or else why would we choose it?

That's not to say I don't respect other's opinions on politics, or religion, or whatever. I'm nothing special, but I do have a logical brain in my head, just like everybody else. I try to make logical decisions, as I hope we all do."

"So you don't think everyone has to share your opinions?"

"I should hope not," laughed Lorraine. "It would make buying shoes very difficult."

– 29 –
More Fun Than
a Paternal Ferret

My husband, Martin Chuzzlewit Innis, is a native of Ireland, though we met in New Jersey, lost each other in Manhattan, and found each other, and our love, in London. And while it may seem uninteresting to most, for Martin and I it was the start of a romantic banquet on which our souls will feast for the rest of our days.

Lorraine Innis stared at the words on her laptop computer as she sat beside Valerie's bed. She had hurried through the details of her childhood to bring her to this place. This, after all, was why Lorraine had agreed to write her autobiography. More than her own story, this would be a romance, the story of how she and Martin had met, fallen in love, fought, lost each other, and then in what could only be destiny, had found each other again halfway across the world.

This was more like it, Lorraine thought. For the first time since she began writing, she found an emotional attachment to her own life. The rest of it seemed as dry as ancient history. Had she been editing someone else's story, Lorraine would have criticized them for making it just cold dates and places. It wasn't that she didn't recall her upbringing. She did, but it was just so many facts, like the Magna Carta or the Battle of Bosworth Field. Now, thankfully she was writing something that seemed real. A few hours ago Cookie Babcock, famous for her probing interviews, had never even touched on her courtship with Martin. All Babcock's questions had centered on Lorraine's heroics, which were accidental, her inspiration of Kropotkin's peace plan, which was unintentional, and her fame, which, Lorraine was sure would be fleeting.

Still, thought Lorraine, Babcock and her crew were more than satisfied with their version of her story. She, on the other hand, was just warming up on her own. Though Beverly Marlton assured her it would sell millions, Lorraine was writing it for an audience of one.

"It was a stormy night in New Jersey," wrote Lorraine, "and not surprisingly at a shopping mall. There, inside a bookstore…"

Lorraine was just about to write about the night she met Martin when the phone rang. With Valerie's room being her main base of operations, and requests for interviews streaming in from around the world, the hospital had hired several temporary operators to screen her calls.

"Hello, Mrs. Innis," said the hospital operator, "sorry to bother you, but you have a call from your work, and it sounded important."

"Thank you. I'll take it," said Lorraine, and then heard several clicks as they transferred the call. "Hello? Mrs. Marlton? I mean, Beverly."

"No, Mrs. Innis," said the voice on the other end. "This is Dennis Ullmer. I'm the director of Human Resources at Marlton Press."

Lorraine laughed. "Dennis, of course, you are! I've been through a lot, but I don't have amnesia!"

"Yes," said Ullmer slowly, "well, I'm sorry to bother you, Mrs. Innis, and I wouldn't dare to unless it was imperative."

"I don't doubt that, Dennis. Don't let all that's happened to me change anything. I'm still the same. I'm still Lorraine…not Mrs. Innis." Though Lorraine wondered just how much she was Mrs. Innis given the mysterious absence of Mr. Innis. "What can I do for you, Dennis?"

"In light of your new role with the company," said Ullmer, "that is, your added responsibilities as an author as well as an editor, I need you to complete a new W-2 form before I can release any more checks to you."

"Can you fax the forms to me?"

"Actually I need to witness you signing them."

"Really?" That sounded strange, but she didn't doubt him. Dennis Ullmer was nothing if not thorough. "I suppose I'll have to come into the office then," she sighed.

"No, don't come here! I mean, there's no need to come all the way up here," said Ullmer. "I can meet you half way. I just need to see you sign the forms. It doesn't matter where."

After making arrangements to meet Dennis Ullmer the following noon at a diner in Mount Laurel, New Jersey, Lorraine hung up the receiver and went back to work.

It was nearly 8:30 that evening when she finally stopped writing. Though exhausting, writing the story of her romance with Martin was also therapeutic. It helped her to focus on the things that mattered most to her. Working at Valerie's bedside was also helpful. If she could just get both of them back into her life somehow everything else would fall into place. She opened her purse and took a photograph of Martin from her wallet. It wasn't a particularly sharp picture, but since he emptied their home, this was the only photo of Martin she had. Lorraine stared at the picture of Martin standing in a pub in his native Ireland. It was odd, she thought, writing their story made her heart swell inside with emotion, but looking at his photo had a neutralizing effect that she couldn't quite describe as if he wasn't quite real even though she knew otherwise. Maybe it was what he did to their home, or perhaps what was now their former home in Colts Neck. Maybe, she reasoned, Martin couldn't sell it without her. How could he? That hadn't occurred to her. She was the co-owner of the house. Wasn't she? At worst, she could always buy the house back from herself. She could even overpay for the house, thus giving Martin the money he needed. Of course, even if Martin was "on the lam," the Realtor must know how to get in contact with him. She would look into that tomorrow after she met with Dennis Ullmer. Yes, she would do that tomorrow afternoon, and rush back for her appointment with Valerie's boss.

Lorraine's train of thought was interrupted by a soft knock on the door, and around the corner peeked Purvis Twankey.

"How do," he said bashfully.

"Purvis," said Lorraine, "where have you been? And just look at you!"

Indeed, Purvis Twankey was a sight to behold, at least by singing cowboy standards. He was wearing matching powder blue denim jeans and jacket with white stitching, over a white shirt and bolo tie. The string tie was held in place by a large silver disk with the initials "P.T." engraved in the center. The engraving was duplicated on Purvis' belt-buckle, as well as on a disk on the crown of his new dark blue cowboy hat. Although a little country gauche, Lorraine had to admit that the ensemble looked tailor-made to its owner's body and personality.

"Do you like it, Miss Lorraine?" he asked sheepishly.

"Oh, Purvis, it's you, and I like you, so, yes, I like it very much."

"Ee, that's a load off me mind. I was afraid I looked like some great backwoods puddin'."

"You look like you belong on the stage of the Grand Ol' Opry."

"You never can tell," he said with a cryptic grin.

"What is it, Purvis?" said Lorraine. "Are you hiding something? You had better have a pretty good reason for leaving me alone here these last few days."

Purvis missed her facetiousness and took the complaint to heart.

"I wouldn't leave you, nor your cousin unless it was real important!"

"Well?"

"I can't say nowt, but I'll show you…" Purvis looked at his watch, "… in ten more minutes. Can I turn on the telly? That woman is going to be interviewing you."

"You don't really want to see that, do you? It's nothing special. I know, I was there."

"Now, you're just being modest," said Purvis switching on the television. "Let's just see the start, then. I'd like to see you on telly, while I'm sitting next to you. It'll be like stereo."

They waited while the lead-in program, the premiere episode of a sit-com finished. The show's premise for hi-jinx was that a middle-aged guru living in the San Fernando Valley got hit by a low-emission carpool van and came back to inhabit the body of his son's pet ferret. Lorraine concluded that *My Father, My Ferret* was not half as amusing as the show's laugh track purported it to be. Purvis wasn't very impressed either, even though he had a cousin who claimed he could commune with stoats.

Next, they sat through a lunchmeat commercial in which a husband complained to his wife in song that she had substituted an inferior brand of meat for the one advertised. Lorraine thought the refrain, in which the burly hubby pleaded for his spouse to "Slip Me My Old Salami," was vulgar. Purvis, however, thought it very inventive. He missed the point of the ad completely, however, when he said, "I gotta buy me some of that mustard," at the commercial's conclusion.

Finally, the network logo appeared, after which the screen went dark for a second, then slow-motion footage of the attempt on Nikolai Kropotkin's life lit up the screen as a voice could be heard singing:

You came into our lives, at just the right moment...

Lorraine's mouth dropped open. Purvis Twankey glanced over at her, and then looked down at the carpet.

You brought us love; you brought us hope...

As it had hundreds of times in televised replays, the footage showed Lorraine leaping out to save the Russian leader's life. Then the picture faded to various candid shots of Lorraine over the last few days as she entered or exited the hospital, interspersed with footage from her numerous network interviews. The song, a delicate melody softly strummed on an acoustical steel guitar, continued on till it reached the chorus.

And you're here when we need you, Lorraine,
And thank heaven we're glad that you came,
Yes, you're here now we need you, Lorraine,
And don't you ever leave us again.

As Lorraine Innis began to cry softly, the video dissolved to the singer as he performed in a dimly lit studio. The picture confirmed Lorraine's suspicion: it was Purvis Twankey.

At the song's conclusion white letters in the corner of the screen revealed: "*The Ballad of Lorraine*; Purvis Twankey; Parvo Slouch, producer."

"Oh, Purvis," sobbed Lorraine, "thank you, that was beautiful."

"Ee, do you really mean it?"

"It was…it was proper champion," she confessed using one of his native phrases. "Really, it was lovely," she confessed; as she reached over to pat his hand. "But how?"

"Miss Patsy called up the producer of the special to ask if they wanted to talk to any of your friends," said Purvis. "They said 'sure,' and she gave 'em my name."

"I'm glad she did," said Lorraine with a smile.

- 30 -
The Nut Case and
the Nut Smasher

Lorraine Innis' appearance on *The Cookie Babcock Special* was also being watched in the Oval Office. There they sat in the dark: Davis Flemming on the sofa, Quinton Merton in an armchair, both viewing in silence, their somber faces illuminated by the glow of the television. The atmosphere was gloomy all day thanks to the precipitous drop in the President's poll numbers. During the first commercial break, an ad for cocktail prunes, President Merton spoke.

"There's little doubt why she's so popular," said the President. "Maybe we could invite her down here. You know, bask in her popularity like we do with athletes."

"I doubt she'd come," muttered Flemming.

"No? Why not?"

"Gee," said Flemming, daring to be sarcastic, "I don't know. Maybe because someone just rejected Kropotkin's plan because they didn't like her name!"

"That's what we agreed upon," said Merton defensively.

"But you don't say it in those words. You say that you have been working towards a disarmament plan. You mention that the negotiations had been going on long before the assassination attempt. That's what you had to say...subtly. You can't attack a person solely on the basis of their name. You might as well have said she has a big nose."

"She does," said the president. "Not unattractive, but it is larger than average..."

"But you can't say that in public!"

Merton scowled.

The President had been difficult to manage the last two days; even more difficult than usual, thought Flemming. Throughout their relationship, Merton had had his times of assertiveness, his more manic episodes. The main difference now was that for the first time he was aggressive, and his aggressiveness was directed at his top aide. In the past, Flemming had been able to keep him focused, mainly because the outcomes had been positive. Now, for the first time, however, Flemming's advice, albeit poorly executed, had been disastrous. The unthinkable had come to pass. Quinton Merton's approval ratings were in the toilet, making him question anything Flemming said or did. He had never before mistrusted Flemming's counsel, and the aide was hoping he could keep Merton under control until the poll numbers rebounded.

As the vivacious hostess on the screen offered her guests another cocktail prune for their martinis, the President continued.

"Yes, she's very popular, that Mrs. Innis. She comes across as very intelligent, brave, and, uh…"

"Sincere," mumbled Flemming.

"That's it, sincere. Maybe we could have Mrs. Innis come down here and advise me on sincerity. She could teach me how she does it."

"She's wouldn't tell you."

"Why not?" asked the President.

"It's like a magician's trick. If she's not sincere, she's not going to tell you how she looks sincere, because then she wouldn't seem sincere anymore."

"What if it's not a trick?"

Flemming chortled. "If she really is that way, which I doubt, she couldn't teach you how to be that way, since that's just the way she is."

Merton's eyebrows knitted together in a perplexed expression. "Do you think she's a phony?"

"Undoubtedly," said Flemming. Actually, he thought Lorraine Innis was genuine, but he couldn't admit as much. In his economy, while it was humiliating to be bested by someone slicker than yourself, it was devastating to be beaten by a guileless amateur whose only weapon was their innate goodness.

"Really? She's not on the level?"

"Sir, you've been in politics your whole life," said Flemming. "You've seen every calculating charlatan." The President nodded. "Well, this woman makes them all look like cub scouts. Not a word comes out of her mouth that she hasn't crafted and honed and examined from every angle. Look at the con job she pulled on Kropotkin."

"That's right!" exclaimed the President.

"And she tried it with you, but you saw through it."

Merton sat up a little taller. "I did," he said, before slumping down again. "But the poll numbers?"

"She can't last," said Flemming with a dismissive wave of his hand. "When she's exposed, you'll be on top higher than before, because you were the only one who wasn't fooled. Just sit tight, and wait. She can't touch you. In fact, I've got some good news…"

143

The President held his finger to his lips and pointed at the television. The interview was continuing.

"Tell me, Lorraine," began Cookie Babcock, "it must be flattering, to say the least, to have a peace accord named after you."

"Yes, it is," said Lorraine. "And it's very humbling as well."

"Humility," said Merton.

"Phony," assured Fleming.

"It must be disturbing," said Cookie, "to learn that President Merton has rejected the plan just because it has your name attached to it."

"Uh, oh," intoned the President.

"I was stunned," said Lorraine.

"How would you categorize this sort of behavior by the White House?" asked Cookie.

Lorraine thought for a moment as the camera pulled in for a close-up. Then, after careful deliberation, she said the magic word: "Infantile."

Quinton Merton nearly fell out of his chair, and then sprang to his feet.

"Did she just say what I think she just said?"

"Infantile?" repeated Cookie Babcock.

"Infantile," reiterated Lorraine. "What would you call it?"

"Infantile," agreed Cookie.

"She knows, she knows!" screamed the President grabbing his skinny aide by the collar, and then dropping him on the floor. "She knows it all!"

"She couldn't," cried Flemming, "calm down, Sir."

It was of no use. Merton was beside himself with fear.

"She knows about the whole therapy thing...Dr. Egonski...the toys! She knows it all!"

"It was just a coincidence. It had to be," cried Flemming.

"No! No! You said she's sharp, she's clever, she's slick. Nothing comes out of her mouth by accident. And she kept saying it. Infantile! Infantile! She knows! How could she find out? How? How? You! You told her! You told her!"

The President began to hyperventilate. He then jumped on top of Flemming, wrapped his fingers around Flemming's neck, and started pounding his aide's head against the floor.

"You told her! You told her!" gasped Quinton Merton as he continued hammering Davis Flemming's skull into the carpet. Fortunately for the aide, it had double padding.

"You're choking me, Sir," croaked Flemming.

The President relaxed his grip on Flemming's scrawny neck. Flemming massaged his Adam's apple as he sat up.

"Calm yourself, sir," said Flemming trying to raise his voice above a hoarse rasp. "She couldn't know."

"No?" Merton panted.

"Of course not, she's just a stupid woman from New Jersey, who got lucky."

"But you said she was smart," said Merton genuinely confused.

"She's smart in some ways," said Flemming, "but she isn't omniscient. She couldn't know about the therapy, and I certainly didn't tell her. It was just luck. Just like she was lucky to save Kropotkin's life. She was lucky in her interviews, and she was lucky right now with the choice of that word."

"Are you sure?"

"Absolutely," said Flemming. "You'll see. I've been on top of this entire Innis matter. We'll soon have the upper hand."

"Upper hand?"

"Yes," said Flemming, "she'll soon be neutralized, after which we can use her to our advantage."

"That would be nice," said Merton. After a deep breath, a cautious smile overspread his lips. "Is it secret?"

"Absolutely," nodded Flemming. "We've got the best agents on it."

"Good. Good. That's good," said the President before his attention was drawn back to the two women on television. "Unless, of course, I'm ruined before then!"

"Really, Mr. President, I didn't utter a word to that woman about anything. I wasn't even in the same studio with her, remember? It was all done via satellite."

"Oh, oh, yes, yes," said the President. "That's right."

"Yes," said Flemming, "we did all our talking on the air."

"Right, over the air…where you just talked, and, and, you antagonized her, and flushed my presidency down the hopper! And you told! You told!"

President Merton resumed his beating of his closest advisor by the soft, warm glow of Lorraine Innis' ruby chenille sweater as televised on *The Cookie Babcock Special*.

◆

Like the President of the United States, Peter Liverot, the President of Fourth Fiduciary Trust was also watching the program in his darkened lair. Liverot wasn't the least bit threatened by Lorraine's popularity or her choice of words. Instead, the banker just sat with his feet propped up on his desk, drinking bourbon and smashing peanuts on his desk blotter. Soon, the area was strewn with pulverized shells. As he munched and gulped, Liverot never took his eyes off Lorraine, as if by staring intently at her might be able to peer into her soul.

"What motivates you? I mean: what is your philosophy summed up in a sentence?" asked Cookie Babcock.

"What can I do for you?" replied Lorraine.

145

Sucker, Liverot thought. This dame obviously hadn't spent much time in the real world. If he had made "What can I do for you" his motto, he'd probably be dead by now. The banker slid open his desk drawer, scooped out another pile of peanuts, and dropped them on the desk. The interview broke for a commercial for disposable toupees. Liverot got up to splash more bourbon into his glass.

What had he learned about this Innis broad? He asked himself. She seemed to be pretty brainy. So was her cousin. That made it harder. Luckily, Valerie Fierro was still out cold in the hospital. He didn't know how long he could count on that stroke of luck, however, so he had to move fast. But he still needed his angle. The commercials came to an end, and Liverot resumed his nut-smashing from his swivel chair.

"Lorraine," asked Cookie Babcock, "How do you view fame?"

"Well," said Lorraine after a moment's reflection, "Francis Bacon compared fame to a river that lifts up the light and swollen and drowns everything weighty and solid."

"So you don't think your fame will last?"

"I hope not," Lorraine laughed. "Hopefully there's life after fame."

"I see, so, where do you want to go from here?"

"I've often thought about going into business someday," said Lorraine. "Charitable work would be nice."

"Charity? How exciting!"

"Yes," said Lorraine, "as Addison said: 'to content ourselves to be obscurely good.'"

Peter Liverot sat bolt upright in his chair and slammed his open palm on the desktop with a resounding slap that sent peanut hulls flying everywhere.

"That's it," he said as he clenched his fist, "I've got her!"

– 31 –
The Hospital Bed
Stand-Off

As the first rays of dawn broke across the keyboard of her laptop computer, Lorraine Innis looked up, surprised to learn that she had been writing all night at Valerie's bedside. Rather than fatigue, however, Lorraine felt more alive than she had in days. Reliving the story of her courtship had been a reaffirmation of all that she loved and believed. It made her feel more vital than any interview or a thousand television cameras. In brief, she felt more like herself.

Lorraine was just saving her work and powering down the computer when the door opened, and a nurse entered.

"Oh, sorry," whispered the nurse, "I didn't know you were still here Mrs. Innis."

"Yes, I guess I stayed overnight. I didn't break any hospital rule, did I? I wouldn't want to get anyone in trouble."

"You, Mrs. Innis?"

"Please, call me Lorraine."

"Lorraine," she gasped as if she had been given the password into some secret society, "thank you. Yes, I'll do that. I'll be out of your way in a moment. I just have to check on Ms. Fierro." The nurse began to jot down Valerie's vital signs, as Lorraine put away her computer.

"Oh, Mrs. Innis," said the nurse holding up an envelope from a side table, "a letter came for you. I guess you didn't see it over here."

Lorraine took the envelope. It was square in shape and was ecru in color. The address was handwritten in a gentle script that looked strangely familiar.

"Who would be writing me here?" Lorraine asked aloud. She ran her fingernail down the side and removed a matching card with a raised border, upon which in the same hand was written:

"Wait for me. I love you."

147

And that was all.

Lorraine looked at the front of the envelope again. The stamps and the markings indicated it had been posted from England. Was it from Martin? It must be. The writing seemed familiar. But what was Martin doing in England, and why hadn't he signed his name? Perhaps it was a legal technicality. Maybe he didn't sign his name so she couldn't definitively say where Martin was if she was asked by the authorities...or whoever was chasing Martin.

"I'll be out of your way in a moment," said the nurse interrupting her train of thought.

Lorraine glanced up.

"It's usually pretty quiet in here," said the nurse. "The only regular visitors are you and Father Valvano."

"Father Valvano?"

"The assistant up at St. Anthony. He's in here quite a lot. Funny that you haven't met him before."

The nurse finished, and then stood awkwardly in front of Lorraine.

"Was there something else?" asked Lorraine.

"No," said the nurse, lowering her voice, "well, yes. It's against policy, but...could I have your autograph?"

"My autograph?"

The nurse motioned for Lorraine to be discreet.

"Sorry," said Lorraine more quietly. "But, I'm not famous, not really."

"I don't want it because you're famous," explained the nurse. "It's more because you're, well, an inspiration."

"I don't understand."

The nurse pointed to a small pin in the shape of a double-barred cross on her lapel.

"The Cross of Lorraine? Is that a family heirloom?" Lorraine asked.

"No, ma'am," said the nurse. "I just got it yesterday. A group of us on the floor started wearing them...because of you."

"But that's from a province in France," said Lorraine. "I'm not French."

"Yes, ma'am, we know. It's just that we were talking on break about all you've done, and the peace plan, and we just thought it was terrific."

"But I'm just an ordinary person," protested Lorraine.

"Yes," said the nurse, her eyes filled with admiration, "and that's what we admire about you. And we just decided to wear these, as a show of support, and a reminder of what an ordinary person can do."

"But, you've got to understand," said Lorraine holding the nurse by the shoulders, "I didn't really do anything, not intentionally. You nurses are much more heroic. You care for the sick and dying every day. That's real heroism."

"But you did what needed to be done," she said. "And you're so modest. You're so real. You're really real. You're the type of woman we all aspire to be."

"Thank you," said Lorraine, more than a little embarrassed.

The nurse produced a pen and piece of paper from her pocket and handed it to Lorraine.

"Whom should I make it out to?" asked Lorraine.

"Nancy, please," said the nurse.

Lorraine autographed the paper and handed it back to the nurse, who thanked her. She then thanked her again and left as excited as if Lorraine had just given her a hundred dollar bill.

Lorraine watched the nurse leave, then turned and looked at Valerie in bed. She half expected Valerie to wake up laughing at the notion that she had become an object of veneration. Shaking her head, Lorraine crossed to the refrigerator in the corner. When she turned back around, she saw a priest had entered silently and was standing, almost hovering over Valerie's face.

"Can I help you," asked Lorraine. "Father Valvano, is it?"

The young priest straightened up with a jump and turned to Lorraine.

"Oh, yes, hello," said the priest, "yes, I'm Mike Valvano, Father Valvano."

Lorraine crossed to the side of the bed opposite the priest and placed her hand on Valerie's forehead in an almost territorial way.

"Lose something Father?" she asked. "Or are Catholic priests doubling as vampires?"

"Vampires?"

"Well, the way you were hanging over my cousin's face," said Lorraine, "you either dropped your rosary, or you were getting ready to bite her neck."

"Actually, yes," said the priest, regaining his composure, "I did lose my rosary. I thought maybe it slipped..."

"Down my cousin's neck?"

"On to the bed," he said placing his hand on Valerie's pillow as if he were staking a rival claim.

So, thought Lorraine, that was the way it was going to be; was it? She stared him in the eye, and to her surprise, he stared right back. She smiled sweetly at him, and he returned the smile even more broadly. There would be a fight, she told herself, for Valerie's soul.

"She was awake," said Lorraine, her eyes locked with his.

"Yes, on Monday morning," countered the priest, "but only briefly. I was here right after it."

Drat, thought Lorraine, this priest knew too many details to be just a disinterested spiritual advisor. She blamed herself. She should have been there Monday morning. She should have been there the whole time. In fact, if she hadn't left Friday night none of what had happened would have happened. Maybe somebody else would have saved Nikolai Kropotkin's life. Perhaps somebody else would have inspired a peace plan and had nurses forming admiration societies around them. If she had only stayed, she'd still be an obscure nobody, with a husband, and probably her normal body. In any event, if she'd been around more this liturgical lothario wouldn't have moved in on Valerie.

"Why aren't you in Mass?" challenged Lorraine.

"What?"

"Don't you have a seven o'clock at St. Anthony's?"

"No, we don't."

"What a shame," said Lorraine. "What are those little old Italian ladies in their long black dresses supposed to do for their early morning spiritual guidance? Well, at least you're here, ministering to my cousin."

"Yes, among others."

"What? You mean other priests are sneaking in here when I'm not looking?"

"No," said the priest, "I meant that I minister to all the Catholics in the hospital. It keeps me busy. We have a shortage of little old ladies in the parish."

"I see," said Lorraine forcing an even sweeter smile. "You know Ms. Fierro will be a little old Italian lady someday. I just hope there aren't too many pretty young accident victims lying around when she puts on her black dress and goes to morning mass."

"I'll say a novena that your cousin will be well-cared for in her old age," said the priest. "Oh, and you too, Mrs. Innis. You are Mrs. Innis, aren't you?"

"You bet I am," said Lorraine. "Who else would I be?"

The pair stared each other down for another minute before the priest broke it off giving Lorraine at least a momentary victory.

"Well, I guess I'd better be going," he said.

"To find your rosary?"

"On my rounds, yes," said the priest. "It was...lovely to meet you. I hope we'll meet again."

"Yes," said Lorraine as he left, "I'll be looking out for you."

She turned to Valerie and sighed.

"I don't trust that man," she told the unconscious Valerie. "His collar might be back to front, but his eyes were certainly the right way around. Or does that guy just go around picking up unconscious girlfriends? And speaking of that, how come your boyfriend, Boden what-his-name, hasn't been around? Or has he? Well, never mind. From now on, I'm going to be here, keeping an eye on things."

Lorraine looked at her watch. "Just as soon as I drive to Jersey, and then come back and see what your boss wants."

– 32 –
The Delusional Advances
of Dennis Ullmer

By the time she pulled off at Exit 4 of the New Jersey Turnpike, Lorraine Innis had wished she had gotten some sleep the previous night. As exhilarating as writing the story of her courtship had been, at the moment she'd trade half of those precious memories for twelve uninterrupted hours in a nice soft bed. For now, however, she'd have to settle for a booth at the Eat-Em Up Diner, a quick bite to eat, and a short meeting with Dennis Ullmer. Through her fatigue, the dizzying parade of events jockeyed for attention in her cluttered mind. It was enough for a lifetime, and that had all occurred since the previous Friday afternoon.

Not helping matters in the least, she thought, was the subtle reminder that every time she changed her clothes, or visited the restroom, she had mysteriously acquired the body of a man from the neck down. She wondered if somewhere some man had gotten her torso as the part of some alien experiment. If so, she hoped he was treating it with the same courtesy, respect, and most of all restraint she was affording his.

She steered Purvis Twankey's AMC Pacer into the diner parking lot and spotted Dennis Ullmer standing by the entrance of the restaurant.

"Hello, Dennis," she said with a smile as she walked up the diner steps. "It's so good to see a familiar face again."

"Again?" said Ullmer, as he held the door for her.

"Yes," said Lorraine, "so much has been going on. It seems like years since I've seen you. Thanks for meeting me half-way. It really was a help, what with everything happening."

"Not at all," muttered Ullmer.

Lorraine couldn't help but notice the suspicious way he was eyeing her, much as many of her other co-workers had done on Monday. It must be all the media attention she was getting, she reasoned.

151

After being directed by a waitress in a shiny black polyester uniform to an equally shiny black vinyl booth, they sat down. Lorraine patted the seat before sitting down to make sure that the tacky feeling was only the vinyl and not the residue of a previous patron's meal. The waitress, Estelle, according to her plastic nametag, handed them two large menus also covered with sticky plastic.

"So, how's everything at the office?" asked Lorraine flipping through the menu.

"The office," repeated Dennis.

She glanced up. He was scrutinizing her face.

"Is my lipstick smudged?" asked Lorraine.

"No," said Dennis, looking away.

Lorraine returned to her menu. "The tuna salad platter looks good, but you've got to watch out for tuna in a strange diner. Still, it's tempting, but I don't know..."

"I don't know either," said Ullmer.

Over the top of the menu, Lorraine could see he was studying her again. What was his problem?

"Of course," she continued, trying to ignore his rude behavior, "take it from a lifelong Jersey resident, the safest bet in any diner is a good old-fashioned burger. Don't you agree?"

She looked up to find his scrutinizing had grown into a piercing stare.

"Really, Dennis," she said, fidgeting in her seat, "don't tell me you're at all phased by what's happened. You're in human resources for goodness sake. You deal with people every day. You should know I'm the same Lorraine Innis that I was the day you hired me."

"I never hired any Lorraine Innis," he blurted out.

His assertion hit her like a slap across the face. Then she thought about it for a moment and relaxed into a smile.

"No, of course, you didn't."

"Ah, ha!" said Ullmer jabbing his index finger in the air.

"You always love to do that," said Lorraine, "catching the editors in some technical inaccuracy. You're probably a frustrated editor yourself."

"Inaccuracy?"

"Yes, you're right, you didn't hire Lorraine Innis," she said reaching across the table and patting his hand. "You hired Lorraine Ammaccapane. I started at Marlton Press before I got married. Now, what are you going to order?"

"Ammaccapane?"

"Do you think the chicken croquettes are good?"

"Croquettes?"

"Diners often make a good chicken croquette, unless they're mushy. There's nothing worse than when they're mushy, unless if they're dried out. Still, there is the hamburger, you can't..."

Lorraine stopped in mid-sentence as Dennis Ullmer reached across the table and grabbed her by the wrist.

"Dennis, what are you doing..."

"Stop it," he cried. "Stop this charade."

"What? Dennis, what are you talking about? Control yourself," she said pulling her hand free. "I'm a married woman, and you're a married man. Think of Imogene!"

"Imogene?"

"Yes, Imogene! Your wife, you know!"

"Yes," he said, "I know. I know. The question is how the hell do you know?"

"I've met your wife. I've been to your house."

"Never!" said Dennis.

"I've been there for your holiday open house. It's a lovely little Cape Cod done in natural cedar shakes..."

"Anyone could know that," he said. "My address is in the phone book."

"And your wife," continued Lorraine, "is a lovely lady. Medium height, slim build, brunette, with a... lilting laugh. Actually, Imogene Ullmer was a thin, shapeless tube of a woman, and her laugh sounded like a pot-bellied pig with its tail caught in an electric fan. Lorraine was trying to flatter the woman, especially since Dennis seemed to be suddenly smitten with her.

Ullmer looked at her again with a simmering expression, as he leaned over the table. Lorraine spotted a ketchup bottle over to the side. If he tried to kiss her, she would have to bop him on the sconce with it. Instead of trying to kiss her, however, he stopped just short of her face.

"Who are you?" he growled.

"Dennis! What a question!"

"I don't care if I lose my job. I don't care if you tell Beverly Marlton. But I've got to know..."

At that moment the waitress returned.

"We'll need another moment," said Lorraine with a polite smile, and then turned back to face Dennis.

"I've got to know, who are you?"

"I'm Lorraine Innis," she said with a shake of her head. She said it with the same assurance that she would have said, you're wearing a yellow tie, we're sitting in a diner, or I'm afraid you're losing your mind, Dennis. She repeated herself. "I'm Lorraine Innis. Who else would I be?"

Their eyes remained locked for a moment, and then as if he had exhausted his last nerve, Dennis put his head down on the tabletop and began to sob. Cautiously, since he seemed to be infatuated with her, Lorraine reached out and patted his shoulder.

"It's all right, Dennis," she said. "I know it's very confusing, but you've got to think of Imogene." Poor Dennis, she thought. Poor Imogene. Poor Martin.

153

He looked up at her and wiped his eyes with a paper napkin.

"Don't worry," said Lorraine. "We won't mention this ever again. I won't tell Beverly."

The waitress returned.

"We're still trying to decide," Lorraine told the waitress, who left in a huff.

"You don't understand," said Dennis.

"You must have been under a tremendous strain," said Lorraine.

"It's not about me," he said, "it's about you!"

Apparently, Lorraine thought, he had a deep infatuation with her that her sudden media attention had brought rushing to the surface. "Look, Dennis, if I've ever given you any reason to think that I was interested in anything outside of my marriage, I'm sorry. I don't know if it was a look you misunderstood, or if I wore something too provocative, or whatever it was, you got the wrong message."

"I couldn't have," he said with a renewed frustration. "I've never met you before in all my life."

She just looked at him. First the scrutiny, then the passion, and now totally denying he knew her. He was losing his mind. It was always the case, Lorraine thought. No matter how bad your own problems may be, there's always someone worse off than yourself.

"Yes," she said looking down with a sigh, "maybe that is the best way to deal with it, Dennis. Just act as if we had never met."

"Because," he insisted, "we have never met!"

"Yes, it's better that way."

"It's not better that way," he insisted, "that's the way it is."

Lorraine shook her head. "Yes, whatever. Have it your way, Dennis. Look I have to get going. Say hello to Imogene for me."

She started to get up, but he grabbed her wrist, pulling her back down. "Dennis!"

"I don't know," he said with a maniacal grimace, "I don't know how you know all the things you know. But we have never met. I work at Marlton Press, you don't. I am married to Imogene, but you've never been to our house. I don't know what you're trying to pull, but I do know for a certainty that I don't know you! I've collected every scrap of information I could find about you…"

"And?" said Lorraine trying not to appear too patronizing.

"And there's nothing," he said. "Well, nothing until the other day. You say you were born in New Jersey…"

"I was…"

"I couldn't find any birth record…"

"That's silly, of course, I was born. I'm here, aren't I?"

"You went to school here, too, eh?" He said, his deluded confidence growing.

"Elementary through college," she said matching his assurance.

"No record."

"Ridiculous," she said.

"You're good," said Dennis nodding his head. "You run a good con, you've even got Mrs. Marlton fooled, but whatever you're up to, I'm not going to be the fall guy."

"You've been reading too many cheap detective novels, Dennis," said Lorraine. "You really should take some time off and get some rest."

"That's what Mrs. Marlton told me."

"Well, that makes two of us, then," said Lorraine. "Really, if I was trying to pull some sort of scam why would I be saving people's lives, and giving interviews on television?"

"You tell me," said Dennis sitting back. His face now wore a wide-eyed, crazed expression.

"Okay, Dennis, that's fine," she said standing up. "Think whatever you want to think. I've got to get back to Delaware. Now, please just give me that form you need me to sign, and I'll be on my way."

He stared at her. "There was no form," he said.

"And I'm the one with some sort of silly secret agenda?"

Lorraine paused a moment, expecting either an apology, a renewed declaration of love, or a plea that she wouldn't tell Beverly Marlton about the fool's errand he'd sent her on. Instead, he just sat there, as confident in his delusion, as she was in her reality.

Having nothing else to say, Lorraine exited the Eat-Em Up Diner for her return trip to Delaware, and her appointment with Peter Liverot.

– 33 –
The Rat I Never Knew

I t's me," said Peter Liverot in a low voice into the phone. "I've got the next piece lined up."

The banker walked to the mirror on the back of his office door and straightened his blood red tie. He was wearing his black double-breasted suit, the one he always wore when he wanted a psychological edge. The silk suit made him feel like a shark.

"Gibraltar? No problems there; it's locked up tight. Albrecht's not family, but he's a good soldier just the same, obedient, ambitious, but not quite in the big leagues. Did Julie tell you, Laffler's all set? Yeah, his prelim hearing is starting any minute."

The banker checked his watch.

"He'll open his mouth long enough to plead guilty, and that's it. What? I'm about to take care of her right now. It'll be perfect, don't worry."

Liverot hung up the phone. Then he smoothed his hair in the mirror, opened the door and stepped into the outer office.

"Miss Einfalt," he said, "do I have any appointments this afternoon? If not, I thought I'd go over to the club for a rub down."

A look of confusion crossed Patsy Einfalt's face. "Why, yes sir, Mrs. Innis is here to see you. Don't you remember?"

"Mrs. Innis?" He looked at Lorraine sitting in the chair across from his secretary's desk. "Oh, yes, that's right, Miss Fierro's relative. I'm sorry, Mrs. Innis. How forgetful of me, won't you please come in?"

Lorraine Innis said goodbye to Patsy and walked past Liverot's outstretched arm and into his office. As she passed Liverot scrutinized her body. Not bad, he thought, good ass, really good tits. Face? No knockout, but not a deal-breaker either.

"Won't you sit down," he said closing the door. Lorraine sat down on the sofa and crossed her legs. Nice pins, too, thought the banker as he imagined them all the way to their tops. She looked up at him. He smiled.

"How is your cousin, Miss Fierro," he asked sitting in the chair opposite Lorraine.

"Still unconscious," said Lorraine.

"What a shame," said Liverot. Good, he thought, let her stay that way, at least a little while longer. Divide and conquer, and they won't know what hit them. "We miss her. Not just her business acumen, but her warm personality. You're probably wondering why I asked you here today."

"Yes, I was," said Lorraine stifling a yawn. "Oh, excuse me, I didn't get any sleep last night."

Good, Liverot thought; and decided not to offer her any coffee. Keep her groggy.

"What a shame," said Liverot. "Your cousin's condition must keep you awake."

"That and other things," said Lorraine trailing off. "But then, you didn't ask me in to discuss my sleeping habits."

"True," said Liverot with a chortle. "You're just like your cousin. Right to the point. I always admired that in her." Valerie Fierro was a pushy bitch, he thought, and so are you. "We here at Fourth Fiduciary Trust," said Liverot trying to sound avuncular, "are really more a family than a business."

"Oh?"

"Absolutely! When one of our employees is injured, or in trouble, we pull together like a family. That's why I sent my secretary over to the hospital as soon as I heard your cousin was injured."

"Yes, I recall," said Lorraine. "I'm sorry, but she hasn't gotten to that work you sent over. I'm sure she'll work on it when she regains consciousness."

Liverot could feel his face redden. "Oh, that. That was just a little misunderstanding between my secretary and myself. I asked if there was anything we could take to Miss Fierro, and Mrs. Einfalt thought I meant work. I was thinking more along the lines of flowers or candy."

"Still thinking about it?" asked Lorraine.

"What?"

"Well, we haven't seen any flowers or candy from your...family."

This broad was getting on Peter Liverot's nerves. Still, like all good executives he had a standard excuse.

"Really? I asked Mrs. Einfalt to send fresh flowers daily. I'll have to inquire about that, personally. Probably a screw up at the florist."

"Or the hospital," said Lorraine.

"Yes," said Liverot. He looked at her sideways. She didn't believe his excuse. Clever little bitch. "That's probably what happened."

"We just had to think of it," smiled Lorraine as she began to stand. "Well, now that all that's cleared up, I'll thank you for the flowers that were sent but never arrived, and I'll be on my way..."

"Hold it, hold it," said Liverot waving her down. "I mean, don't go. What I really wanted to talk to you about was your cousin's future."

Lorraine sat back down. "Shouldn't you be discussing that with Valerie?"

"Well, it is something we've had talks about in the past," said Liverot, "but this concerns you as well."

"Me? I have a job Mr. Liverot, and it's nothing to do with banking."

"Neither does this," he said, "not exactly. Has your cousin ever told you what she does here?"

"Something about regulations and compliance..."

"Yeah," said the banker, "but we're thinking about moving her up, promoting her into a new area, something more interesting. Have you ever heard of Community Reinvestment?"

Lorraine thought for a moment. "No, I don't believe so."

Liverot smiled. Good, something the little smart ass doesn't know.

"By law, banks have to give back to the community, that is, do things to foster growth and development in the area we serve. We do it through investments, grants, donations..."

"Like a charity?"

"Not exactly," said Liverot, "but that's the general idea. It's called CRA, or the Community Reinvestment Act."

"What a good idea," said Lorraine.

"Isn't it?" said Liverot. No, he thought, it was just another example of the Feds sticking their nose in his business and their hands in his pocket.

"How does this concern Valerie and me?" asked Lorraine.

"Well, I've been considering making Miss Fierro our new director for Community Reinvestment. You understand, our discussions were all very preliminary. But I've decided against giving her that job."

"Oh," said Lorraine, "she probably would have been excellent in that position."

"Don't worry. I've got something better in mind. You see, I've long thought that the law didn't go far enough. I mean, banks owe their very existence to the community. You take away the people, you take away the deposits and pretty soon...no bank. It's simple. We owe the community much more than the measly little grants the government says we have to give out."

Liverot stood and crossed to the window overlooking downtown Wilmington. "We need to do more. It's always been my dream to start something that would really make a difference, a foundation that would help the little people down there. Not just in the city, and not just in the state, but all around the country, and all around the world. We do have subsidiaries in other countries, you know."

"Oh?"

"Well, one country," he clarified. "Gibraltar. That's near Spain."

"Yes, I know," said Lorraine.

"We do our international business out of there. So as you can see, we do business around the world. The world is our community. We should be helping the world. And that's where you come in."

"Me?" said Lorraine.

"You and your cousin," said the banker, sidling up to her on the sofa. "You see," he said in hushed tones, "I don't think charity should be a showy type of thing. It's like this guy Addison said, you do good, so no one knows about it. Do you understand what I mean?"

Lorraine looked at him with genuine surprise.

"Yes, I do," she said, "in fact, I was just saying that the other day."

"Were you? Then you know what I'm talking about. And I want you, and your cousin to run that foundation."

"Us? But why?"

"Simple. I want to exploit you."

"What?"

"Look, Mrs. Innis," said the banker, "I didn't even know Miss Fierro had a cousin until the other day. Then that whole thing happens down at the hotel, and you're suddenly famous."

"Yes," sighed Lorraine.

"But that sort of stuff doesn't last."

"It doesn't?"

"Naw," he said, with a wave of his hand. "Trust me, you're a flash in the pan; the flavor of the month. That's why you've got to exploit it while you got it. Now, if I didn't know what an upstanding woman your cousin was, and figured that you came from the same stock, I'd say go out, make your deals, and grab your bundle while you could. Cash in. That's okay for the average jerk who stumbles into something like this, but you're different. To begin with, you've got brains, and now you've got the influence and a chance to make a real difference. You could parlay this fame into something bigger. You could be an international ambassador of goodwill and charity. That's a tough job, but with your cousin at your side, the two of you could change the world."

Lorraine was silent. Come on, thought Liverot, bite, bite.

"Exactly what kind of charity work would we be overseeing?" she finally asked.

"Whatever kind you think needs doing. I trust you to do what's right."

"I can't imagine Valerie not being interested in something like this. If she recovers, of course."

"When, when she recovers," said Liverot. "And you're right, she'll be nuts about it."

Lorraine looked as if she were sorting out something in her mind, while at the same time scrutinizing his face. Liverot didn't like her look.

"What's your part in this whole scheme?" she asked.

The banker winced inwardly at her use of the word "scheme." Outwardly, however, he just smiled. "I'm the bankroll. The guy with the cash. I'll help get the foundation going with a nice little grant, say, one or two million dollars. Plus, I have connections with other corporate executives around the world who are always looking to make a contribution, some for charitable reasons, others for tax purposes. That's my part. So, how about it? Sound good?"

"It does," said Lorraine suppressing a yawn, "even if you are a rat."

"What?"

"Excuse me?" said Lorraine.

"You just called me a rat!"

"Did I?" Lorraine thought for a moment. "No, I couldn't have. I'm not supposed to know that, am I?"

"Look, if you don't trust me…"

Lorraine looked at him with genuine puzzlement and shook her head.

"No, it's not you, Mr. Liverot," she said shaking her head. "Every once in a while I get these thoughts that come flying in sideways into my mind. I can't explain it. I need to remember to forget about it, I suppose."

"Yeah, whatever," said Liverot wondering if she didn't have a screw loose somewhere. "But, it's good, right? I mean, our little organization. You run it. You make the decisions. I'll set it up and supply the funding. Right?"

He extended his hand to her. Lorraine looked at it hesitantly and then shook it.

"Great," said the banker leading her to the door. "Just leave everything to me. You go back to your cousin, and don't worry." As he reached for the knob, the door swung open, almost hitting him in the face. "Who the fu…" he began, before catching himself.

"Oops, sorry," said Marcia Laffler, as she barged into the office.

Liverot rolled his eyes upward. His mistress not only had shown up at his office during business hours, but she had also done so in a dress that screamed: BIMBO! The blonde was wearing a tight fuchsia dress with huge black polka dots. Its skirt came in so tightly at the hem as to make it's wearer knock-kneed, while its bodice was so low as to be an advertisement for the milk marketing board. The only thing that possibly drew attention away from the dress was the matching broad-brimmed hat that overhung the whole monstrosity like the flight deck of a polka-dotted aircraft carrier.

"Hi, like it?" said Marcia, indicating her ensemble. "This is my court outfit. I just got back."

"I think you've got the wrong office," said Liverot.

The blonde lifted her large round sunglasses. "Petey, it's me. See?"

Liverot glanced over at Lorraine who didn't seem to be registering any emotion beyond fatigue.

"Oh, yeah," said Liverot, "I didn't recognize you at first. This is Miss, uh, Miss Capicola…"

"Capicola?" repeated Marcia.

"Like the lunchmeat?" asked Lorraine.

"Yeah, that's right," said Liverot. He couldn't very well introduce her as Mrs. Laffler. That name was too much in the news at the moment, and if anyone would recognize it and make a connection, it would be the woman who helped foil the assassination attempt in which Aaron Laffler had been a principal player. "Miss, uh, Miss Capicola's grandfather invented that delectable deli meat we all know and love."

"Ew, I hate it," said Marcia.

"Shut up and like it," Liverot muttered in her ear.

"Okay," she shrugged, "I got used to lots of names, once you're a Laf..."

Liverot interrupted her just in time. "Where are my manners? Miss Capicola, this is Mrs. Innis."

"My pleasure," said Lorraine.

"Innis?" said Marcia, her face lighting up. "Like Lorraine Innis? You were on TV, weren't you? You saved that foreign guy, didn't you?"

Lorraine blushed. "Yes."

"What a small world. You saved the guy, and my..."

Liverot kept Marcia's small world from getting any smaller by grabbing her by the elbow and rushing her out the door.

"Well, thank you for stopping by, Miss Capicola," he said. "Too bad you have to run. Stop up any time from the secretarial pool." He turned to Lorraine who was following them into the outer office. "Miss Capicola is one of our secretaries. I encourage all our employees to stop by anytime at all. That's the kind of company we are. Stop by any time, Miss Capicola."

After he herded Marcia Laffler out of the executive suite, Liverot threw a hard look towards Patsy Einfalt, who was watching from her desk with her mouth agape.

"Well," continued Liverot returning to Lorraine, "like I said, I'll get everything done up and send you the papers in a few days. I assume that you can be reached..."

Liverot was cut short as Marcia Laffler stuck her head in from around the corner.

"I'll see you back at the house," she whispered loudly. She added a provocative wink and ducked out of sight.

"She also cooks," fumbled Liverot. "That is, she makes up gourmet meals for busy executives, for bachelors such as myself."

"Very convenient," said Lorraine.

"Yes," said Patsy Einfalt eyeing the doorway, "isn't it?"

- 34 -
One Size Fits
and Starts

"Wouldn't you know it?" muttered Lorraine Innis as she stared at the ceiling of Valerie Fierro's bedroom. "Too exhausted to sleep."

She sighed. She had come back to Valerie's house after her meeting with Peter Liverot in hopes of catching a nap before heading back to the hospital. Instead of enveloping her weary body, the soft bed that had been beckoning to her throughout the day now was as uncomfortable as a slab of concrete. She punched the pillow, trying to get comfortable.

It wasn't the pillow or the bed that denied her sleep, Lorraine conceded. It was the torrent of thoughts rushing through her head that kept her awake. As if she didn't have enough going on, she had just agreed to lead a global organization.

Am I crazy, thought Lorraine, or just tired?

Maybe things will look brighter after a few hours sleep. If only I could get a few hours, even one hour. If only my brain would shut off.

At least, she thought, running the charity would keep her busy. Yes, that was a good point.

Busy? Don't I have enough to do? To start with, I've got to find out what happened to my husband. But maybe the publicity the foundation generates will help me find Martin.

Or it will drive him further away.

If nothing else the foundation will give me a job.

But I already have a job, or do I?

Of course, I do, she thought, in fact, I have two jobs at Marlton Press.

But what about Dennis Ullmer? What if in his recent delusional state he accuses me of sexually harassing him? Would he do that? Why not? He's an HR director. They're the most anal-retentive people on earth.

Her conversation with Dennis replayed in her mind.

Imagine, she thought, not being able to find any proof of her existence. Dennis had all the information in her personnel file. All he had to do was verify it. Insisting that she didn't exist, ridiculous; while she was sitting right in front of him. Verification would be easy, especially in the information age. Even the most backward internet search engine would confirm anything in her file. Wouldn't it?

Of course, it would, she told herself. You could find anything online, from a Yorkshire Pudding recipe to show times for a Malaysian cineplex. Lorraine unconsciously scratched her groin, bringing to the surface the most troubling question she faced, the one that she had tried to bury under all the others: her baby.

"The internet," she said sitting up. "That's it."

Lorraine leaped out of bed, hurried into Valerie's home office, and turned on the computer. Why hadn't she thought of this before?

As soon as she logged on, Lorraine went to one of the major search engines, typed in her own name and pressed "enter." She was both relieved and disturbed to find over 800,000 hits on her name, relieved because it was overwhelming proof that she was right and Dennis Ullmer was wrong and disturbed because it was evidence of the notoriety that had practically obliterated her private life. Wading through the entries, Lorraine was dismayed to find that they all seemed to be only a few days old, and all were references to either saving Kropotkin's life or inspiring his peace plan. She decided to refine the search and entered her name along with the college from which she had graduated. The only hit was a mention by a student who attended her alma mater and wrote about Lorraine in his blog. There was no reference to Lorraine actually attending there. She tried similar searches with other schools she had attended, places she had worked, and professional associations to which she belonged. Again, the few references only mentioned what she had done in the last few days, and then in a detached sort of way. There was no evidence that she had gone to, worked at, or belonged to any of them.

"This is crazy," said Lorraine aloud, "there's got to be some mention of me more than a few days old, something that mentions the real me."

As she continued to search, Lorraine was frustrated to learn that as far as cyberspace was concerned, she was incredibly famous and about five days old. She began to wish that someone, somewhere, had cared enough to invade her privacy by posting something about her before last Friday. There had to be a public record of her somewhere.

"That's it," she said, "the public record." She should have looked there first. After a little searching, she found an online record of births for the hospital where she had been born. They had her birth year. They had her birth date. They had seven babies born that day. None were her. She searched the days surrounding it, thinking there must be a clerical error. Then she searched the months, and finally the years. There was no mention of her.

Next Lorraine searched for a record of her wedding, the result was similarly fruitless. Could it be, she thought, that someone had purposely erased her life. But who would want to do that? She was almost universally admired, much to her embarrassment. Wasn't she? The only person who had been less than kind to her was Davis Flemming, the presidential aide. He had been quite nasty with her on that program. But she had been kind to him, kinder than his rudeness deserved. And they had ended their appearance on cordial terms. At least she thought they had. It was one thing to give a girl a backdrop that clashed with her outfit. It was another thing altogether to try to eradicate her past.

"My past," said Lorraine, her face brightening. "Whoever did this might be able to wipe me off the public record, but they can't erase everyone else in my past."

With renewed hope Lorraine did extensive searches on Martin, her parents, and her family. The only queries that bore any fruit were of Valerie and her side of the family. Why had they been spared, Lorraine wondered, and everyone else disappeared?

Martin, she thought. Maybe Martin didn't run away, maybe he was involved with something so top secret that they were destroying all mention of him. Martin: a spy? That was far-fetched. He was just her sweet Irish potato head. He couldn't be a spy. He was in the fruit import business. Import business? That would give him an excuse to travel around the world, supposedly trading bananas and kumquats, but in reality, gathering secret information and toppling foreign governments. Toppling governments: that made Lorraine think of Kropotkin. Perhaps, she reasoned Martin's disappearance had something to do with her accidental heroics. Or, perhaps, she ventured further, her accidental heroics hadn't been an accident. What if she were the unwitting dupe of some international plot? What if Martin had been trying to prevent the assassination of Nikolai Kropotkin? What if Purvis Twankey was a British agent working for MI5 and had given her that rigged up cellphone so she would jump out and save Nikki?

It was only the notion of Purvis Twankey as an international espionage agent that made Lorraine realize she was diving head first into the whirlpool of delusion. She knew that she was too tired and too upset to think straight, but she'd have to be awake for a year and have a complete nervous breakdown to mistake Purvis for James Bond.

Still, she thought, if Martin were involved in some covert business it would explain everything, wouldn't it? Lorraine thought a moment. No, it wouldn't. It would explain some things, perhaps, but not everything. For example, it wouldn't explain what had mysteriously happened to her body. No, that would take more than the simple explanation that she was married to a spy.

Lorraine stared at the computer screen for a moment. No, she thought, if Martin were involved in some mysterious business it wouldn't explain everything. It wasn't a one-size-fits-all solution.

"One-size-fits-all," she muttered, repeating her own thought. One size rarely fits anyone, she told herself, no matter what the marketing people said. "But you could explain it with two things that just happened to occur at the same time. Martin could be some sort of secret operative. That would have forced him to disassociate with... Wait, of course! I've read about that. That would explain the rest of it!"

As if a light suddenly shone in the dark corners of her mind revealing all, Lorraine Innis began to type rapidly as she scoured various websites. Within seconds the answers started falling into place. It was so obvious, she thought.

Ten minutes later, with the greatest mystery of her life put to rest, Lorraine Innis fell asleep at the keyboard and dreamt happily of babies and motherhood.

– 35 –
Erickson, Steeplejack, and Bleistift

ational security?" repeated Dennis Ullmer as he slowly sat down behind his desk at Marlton Press.

Ullmer's eyes were riveted on the government ID badge held a few inches in front of his face. It was 8:05, in the morning, and his visitor had been waiting for him when he arrived at work.

"Yes sir," said the compact, middle-aged man whose badge identified him as Special Agent Len Erickson of the Justice Department. "May I shut the door?"

Ullmer nodded, his mouth agape.

The agent smiled inwardly. Ullmer obviously saw himself as an upstanding, law-abiding citizen. These types were usually cooperative, and very easy to deal with. As he closed the door, Agent Erickson glanced around Ullmer's office, it was neat and organized to the point of obsession. That was good, too. Cooperative, orderly, easily led, Erickson concluded as he sat down across the desk from Dennis Ullmer.

"What we are about to discuss is to be kept confidential," began Erickson. "Do you understand?"

Ullmer swallowed hard and nodded again.

"Good," said Erickson. "It concerns a woman posing as one of your employees: a Lorraine Elizabeth Innis."

Ullmer's power of speech returned. "I knew it!"

"Yes sir, of course, you did," said Erickson.

"Really, I did," said Ullmer. "I even confronted her on it, but she denied it and even pretended to work here. She even said she knew my wife and that she had been to my house!"

"Of course."

"No, she did," insisted Ullmer. "I don't know how she knew all that… she even had a work ID that looked like the ones we issue here! I suppose you've got the goods on her, eh?"

"Sir?"

"The goods: the evidence on whatever she was up to," said Ullmer. "What was it? Fraud, embezzlement, some sort of confidence scheme?"

"You don't understand, Mr. Ullmer," said Erickson, leaning forward and lowering his voice. "This woman isn't under any suspicion."

"She's not? Then who is she?"

Erickson rose and crossed to the window. He looked through the mini-blinds at the cloudy Jersey sky and then spoke with his back to his host. "Mr. Ullmer, Lorraine Innis is a government agent."

"Holy shit!" muttered Ullmer as he slumped in his chair. "Is she Secret Service?"

"*A* secret service, though not *the* Secret Service, it's even more secret than the Secret Service."

"What about her saving the Russian President?" asked Ullmer.

"What about it?"

"Did she?"

"Did you see her do it?"

"On television," said Ullmer.

"Then we can safely assume she did," said Erickson turning around.

"I think I get it," said Ullmer with the trace of a smile.

"What is that, sir?"

"This whole thing, the life-saving, getting into the Russian's confidence, lowering their guard, all of it," concluded Dennis Ullmer, "it's a setup."

"A setup, Mr. Ullmer?"

"She's working her way into the Russian's inner circle...hey, I bet that whole assassination thing was a fake. Just part of the plan. Right?"

Erickson stared intently at Ullmer until beads of perspiration began to form on the human resources director's forehead, and he started squirming in his seat. This took about five-and-a-half seconds.

"I suppose you couldn't tell me that, though, huh?" said Ullmer.

Erickson stared another ten seconds before continuing as if hadn't heard Ullmer's question.

"As I was saying, Mr. Ullmer, this is a matter of the highest levels of national security. There are powers that would torture or kill to learn what you have discovered by your clever reasoning."

"They w-would?"

"Without hesitation," said Erickson as he examined some framed book jackets on the office walls. "I read this one," Erickson nodded towards a spy novel: *The Blood-Caked Dossier*. "Enjoyable, engaging...totally unrealistic."

"But why does she say that she works here?" said Ullmer.

"Cover."

"Why didn't she tell me this yesterday when I talked to her?"

"You wouldn't expect her to blow her own cover, would you, Mr. Ullmer."

Ullmer nodded. "No wonder Mrs. Marlton had insisted on keeping it quiet. This operation, whatever it was, had gotten more public than they, whoever they were, had anticipated. Right?"

Erickson merely cleared his throat.

"So what do you want me to do?" asked Ullmer.

"Do?" said Erickson. "You don't have to do anything, Mr. Ullmer."

"Except keep my mouth shut, right?"

"Your mouth shut? Why would you have to do that?"

"I mean about Lorraine Innis, right?"

Ullmer wasn't picking up on his vague instructions. Typical of the slow-witted, myopic thinking of an HR director, thought Erickson.

"Lorraine Innis?" repeated Erickson. "Who would that be?"

"Your agent."

"Agent? We have an agent named Lorraine Innis?" said Erickson, with a hard stare. Ullmer finally got the point.

"Oh, no, I mean," said Ullmer, "I just have to keep quiet about Lorraine Innis…our, our employee?"

"I suppose," said Erickson, "you, as the personnel director of the company, would afford your employee, this Mrs. Innis, the same degree of confidentiality as any of your employees. But then it's not my job to tell you how to handle your employees, is it?"

This time it only took Dennis Ullmer a second to catch on.

"Oh, right," he grinned. "No, Mrs. Innis is one of our most loyal employees. She's been here for a number of…"

"Five," interjected Erickson.

"…Five years," said Ullmer. "Yes, my wife and I have always found her quite a charming and personable young woman."

"Thank you for your cooperation, Mr. Ullmer," said Erickson reaching for the doorknob, "it's men like you that help keep the world secure." The agent opened the door and announced in a loud voice: "Yes, well, if you need any more temporary staffing, just get in touch with us, Dennis. Oh, my card."

Agent Erickson shook Dennis Ullmer's hand and presented a brightly colored business card. Ullmer looked at the card. It read: "Ralph Steeplejack, Regional Recruiter and Placement Specialist, Temporary Staffing, Inc."

Out in the parking lot, Agent Erickson opened the trunk of his late model Ford and stored all the documents referring to him as either Len Erickson or Ralph Steeplejack. Then he climbed behind the wheel, took out his cell phone and dialed a number. After four rings, the person on the other end picked up.

"Hello," said a groggy woman's voice.

"Mrs. Innis," he said.

"Yes?"

"I'm Boden, Boden Bleistift, your cousin's boyfriend."

"Boden?"

"I know we've never met, have we?"

"Hmm? No, we haven't," said Lorraine. "Where have you been? Did you know Valerie's in the hospital?"

"I just found out. I've been out of town on business. Can I see you this afternoon?"

"I'll be at the hospital. Valerie's room is on the fifth floor…"

"I'd, I'd rather not see her that way, just yet," he said, affecting a tremor to his voice.

"Oh, yes, I understand," said Lorraine. "I'm sorry. Well, I could meet you at Valerie's house? About four?"

"Three would be better," said Boden Bleistift, alias Len Erickson, alias Ralph Steeplejack.

"Oh, yes, well then, I'll see you at three."

"Thank you, Mrs. Innis, I really appreciate it," said the free-lance operative known as "The Roto-Rooter." He hung up the phone and smiled to himself. Life was fun again.

– 36 –
Cousin Boden and the Loquacious Lemonade

In the few hours it took him to travel south to Delaware, The Roto-Rooter had reinvented himself yet again, this time in the men's room of the Cherry Hill rest stop on the New Jersey Turnpike. In the space of fifteen minutes, the man with the dour expression and the close-cropped hair entered carrying nothing but a briefcase and emerged a different individual. This new man looked ten years younger with more stylish, longer hair in a lighter shade. He was at least two inches taller and appeared five pounds lighter in his imitation designer suit. He also had wire-rimmed glasses on his nose, a raft of new identification in his wallet, and a tan on every part of his body that showed. Even his "natural" expression, which had been deadly serious, was now friendly, harmless and even somewhat obtuse.

Whistling the latest chart-topping pop tune (he had hummed a Sousa march on the way in), he returned to his car and drove away, but not before placing an "Accountants do it by the numbers" sticker on his car's rear bumper.

He pulled up to Valerie Fierro's townhouse at precisely 2:42. The Pacer he had seen in the driveway the other day while he tapped the phone wasn't there. She must not be back yet. It would have been child's play to pick the lock and let himself in, but out of character for his current incarnation: Boden, the dorky accountant. He just sat there, looking harmless, checking the tiny vials in his pocket, when the silver Pacer came around the corner and pulled into the driveway. The driver, a harried Lorraine Innis, jumped out of the car without unbuckling her shoulder harness and almost choked herself in the process.

"Are you okay?" asked the man in a voice that was now closer to a tenor than the low baritone he had used on Dennis Ullmer.

"Oh, yes, thank you," said Lorraine unbuckling herself. "I seem to do that a lot lately. I suppose I've got too much on my mind. Thank you."

She got out of the car and shut the door on her mid-calf length skirt. Taking a half-a-step away, Lorraine realized she was caught and fumbled for her car keys which were already back in her purse. This operation was complicated by the fact that she was holding a bag of groceries.

"Allow me," said the man, coming to her aid.

"That's really not..." before she could utter the word "necessary," he had retrieved the keys and released Lorraine. "Oh, thank you. I'm in such a hurry. I'm meeting someone, and I've been running late. Then I had to go to the store, and, well, thank you again."

"Not at all," he said with a disarming flash of his now bucked teeth. "You must be Lorraine. I'm Boden Bleistift."

"Yes, how did you know who I was meeting...oh, you're Boden. I'm Lorraine Innis, Valerie's cousin."

"I recognize you from the pictures Valerie showed me," he said, "and I recognize your voice."

"My voice?" She juggled her package to unlock the front door.

"From when I spoke to you on the phone earlier. You sound just like yourself."

"Yes," she said, "It's a relief lately to do anything that's like myself."

"Contralto," he said, "isn't it?"

"I suppose," she said as she entered the house. He followed her.

"I listen to a lot of opera," he said as he pushed his eyeglasses back up the bridge of his nose. "Have you ever sung opera?"

"No, my tastes run toward symphonies. I enjoy Mendelssohn, and sometimes Handel," she said as she unpacked the groceries. "Could you close the door, please? The storm window isn't up yet, and it's a little breezy for the screen."

"Which do you prefer?" he asked as she unpacked the groceries.

"Well," she said looking at the objects in her hands, "if I'm eating breakfast, I prefer the cereal, at other times, I prefer the toilet paper."

"No," he said laughing through his nose, as nerdishly as possible, "I meant who do you like better? Mendelssohn or Handel?"

"Oh, Mendelssohn," she replied, "more of a romantic, isn't he?"

They chatted amiably about music and groceries as Lorraine put away the packages and he watched.

"So, Boden," she said, as she finished, "you're an accountant."

"Yes, that's right," he said.

She stared at him as if she expected more elaboration, but he purposely kept his answers brief.

"And," she continued, "you and Valerie are dating."

"Yes," he nodded, "we're trying to actualize an on-going interface."

Lorraine nodded in return while seeming to suppress a smile. Perfect, he thought. She believed he was an accountant, a boring accountant.

"And you're Valerie's cousin Lorraine," he said with a grin that accentuated his prosthetic overbite.

"Yes, I'm Lorraine," she sighed.

"I hope you don't mind me saying so, but you look tired."

"Well, Boden," she said, "between you and me, I'm exhausted; physically and mentally."

"Golly," he said, "and here you are getting groceries and putting them away, and I've just been watching without offering a bit of help. Here, you come and sit down on the couch and put your feet up or something."

"That's the best offer I've had in days, thank you," said Lorraine as she crossed to the far end of the sofa and sat down. He sat across from her on the ottoman.

"It must be tiring having your cousin in the hospital."

"If that were the only thing I had to worry about,," said Lorraine. "All these other things don't help matters."

"What other things?"

"The television appearances, and the fame, and how it has obliterated my normal life," she said as she massaged her temple.

He stared at her for several moments and then allowed a look of awe to spread over his face.

"You're...you're that Lorraine!" he said as Lorraine smiled weakly. "You're Lorraine Innis...I mean *the* Lorraine Innis! I read all about you on the plane. I saw you on TV. Wow! If that doesn't snap the point off of my Number 2 pencil! You're really *the* Lorraine Innis!"

"That's me," she muttered.

He leaped off the ottoman. "You're *the* Lorraine Innis, and here I am letting you put away groceries. Heck! You might be the lady that saves the world, and I'm letting you put away the groceries!"

"Well, I am multi-talented."

"Golly, Mrs. Innis..."

"Please, I'm just Valerie's Cousin Lorraine."

"Cousin Lorraine," he said reverentially. "Holy smokes! Let me get you something to drink! It's the least I can do after all you've done!"

"That's fine," she said, "if you'll call us even after that."

"Let me get you that drink," he said rushing into the kitchen and looking through the cabinet for where Valerie kept her liquor. "What'll it be? Wine? Something a little stronger?"

"Oh, I'm not much of a drinker," said Lorraine, "especially not so early."

"Are you sure?" he said.

"It's not that unusual," she said. "33 percent of American adults don't drink alcohol. I'll just take a Diet Coke, there's some in the refrigerator."

Soda pop? That wouldn't do, he thought. The carbonation in the soda might make his other flavors a little too obvious. Opening the fridge, he saw what he needed.

"Hey!" he said, "Valerie's got some great lemons."

"Excuse me?"

"Lemons!" he repeated holding up the fruit. "I make a real mean glass of lemonade. It's a Boden Bleistift special."

"Really, Boden," said Lorraine, "the soda will be fine. Don't go to any trouble on my account."

"No trouble at all," he said waving the lemons over the counter that separated the kitchen from the living room, "I've got them right here. Hey, can I let you in on a little secret? I'm going to be your Cousin Boden!"

Lorraine squinted at him as if she found it hard to believe. "Cousin Boden?"

"I'm going to ask Valerie to marry me," he whispered.

"Congratulations," she said, though with little enthusiasm.

"Now that I've let you in on my secret," he said, "and since I'm almost family; you've got to have some of my special lemonade."

"Sure, fine," said Lorraine. "Whoa!"

This last cry came as he grabbed her ankles and then swung her legs onto the couch.

"You relax," he said, "and I'll make you that lemonade."

With Lorraine lying down and thus unable to observe his movements over the counter, "Cousin Boden" started preparing his special recipe. He made it a point to slice the lemons and crack the ice as noisily as possible. He was as quiet as could be, however, when sliding the tiny vial out of his pocket, and slipping its contents into her drink.

"Here it is, a Boden Special," he said, handing Lorraine the glass.

Lorraine sat up so as not to spill it.

"Thank you," she said. "Aren't you having one?"

"I'm not thirsty," he smiled. "Sorry, I usually put a little paper umbrella in it too. Valerie must be out of those little umbrellas."

"And I thought I'd gotten all the essentials at the store," said Lorraine taking a sip. "I'll put it on the shopping list: little paper umbrellas. That's nice," she noted lowering the glass from her mouth. An imprint of her lipstick stayed on the rim. "What's that unusual odor? It smells a bit like…garlic."

"Ah, ah, ah," he cautioned with a wag of his index finger. "I may be almost family, but there have to be some secrets. Drink up!"

Lorraine smiled and took a deep draft of the lemonade.

He smiled back, though his grin was now less genial. Garlic, he thought as Lorraine continued to drink, of course, it has a slight smell of garlic. Don't you know, Mrs. Innis, that that's one of the properties of thiopental sodium or, by trademark, Sodium Pentothal, or by popular misconception 'truth serum?'

The yellow liquid was well disguised in the lemonade, though alcohol was usually the preferred mixer whenever The Rooter served his professional cocktail. He was proud of his own delicate blend of thiopental sodium and scopolamine, a naturally occurring herb root. The drug, while not literally a "truth serum," gently depressed the central nervous system making the subject very communicative. And while one could choose to lie if strongly motivated to do so, the overall result would be a loosening of the restraints that kept one's thoughts in one's head.

By the time she finished the drink, Lorraine Innis looked as if she would melt into the sofa.

"Why don't you stretch out and make yourself more comfortable?" said The Roto-Rooter in a firmer, deeper voice than the one that he had used for his impersonation of Boden Bleistift.

"Okay," said Lorraine, as she wiggled her hips into the cushions.

"There! Isn't that better?" he asked pulling up the ottoman beside her and sitting down.

She smiled broadly, pressed her head into a throw cushion, and closed her eyes. "I think I could go to sleep."

"Oh, don't do that. Let's chat," he said as he discreetly took a digital voice recorder from his pocket and placed it on the table.

"What about?" she said dreamily.

"Oh, nothing in particular," he said in a firm but soothing tone, "just things."

Lorraine nodded. "Did you know," she said softly, "that approximately one-third of the world's population eats with a knife and fork, while a third eat with chopsticks, and the rest use their fingers?"

"No, I didn't know that," he said.

"And did you know the average elephant can hold over six quarts of water in his trunk at a time?"

"No, but…"

"And did you know a sneeze travels out of your mouth at over 100 miles per hour?"

"Yes, I knew that," he said.

"Oh," said Lorraine opening her eyes and looking at him. "I wish I'd known you knew that. I wouldn't have brought it up."

"That's enough talk about 'things,'" he said gently pressing her back down on the sofa. Evidentially, he thought, her mind wasn't suited to general questions that offered room for interpretation. He would have to be very specific with his questions. "Let's talk about you. Tell me about yourself. What's your name?"

"Lorraine Elizabeth Innis."

"Marital status?"

"Married."

"To who?"

"To whom, please," she said. "Martin Chuzzlewit Innis."

"Maiden name?"

"He didn't have one."

"*Your* maiden name?"

"Lorraine Elizabeth Ammaccapane."

"Parents?"

"Two."

"Their names," sighed the ex-agent.

"Pascal Anthony Ammaccapane and Pamela Jane Tracy Ammaccapane."

"Any siblings?"

"No."

"Your address?

Lorraine furrowed her brow above her closed eyes. "I'm not sure. It was 27 Jutland Drive, Colts Neck, New Jersey, but that was last week."

"Place of employment?"

"Marlton Press."

"Highest level of education?"

"BA in Literature, William Paterson College. Summa Cum Laude."

"Summa Cum Laude," repeated the Rooter.

"Yes," said Lorraine, breaking into a giggle, "Valerie says 'if summa cum loudly they should keep the door shut when they're doing...well, that sort of thing. Sorry..."

"Place of Birth?"

"Morristown Memorial Hospital, Morristown, New Jersey..."

Three hours later, in a convenience store parking lot, a mile away from where he had left Lorraine Innis fast asleep, The Rooter was talking on his cell phone.

"I just left her," he said as two boys rumbled by on their skateboards. Through the store's window, he could see a clerk making hoagie sandwiches. "She's sleeping it off. Went off without a hitch, after I got used to how she organizes her mind." A fat woman walked to her late model Oldsmobile inhaling a pack of cupcakes on the way.

"No, she didn't suspect a thing. It was just like I learned from the phone taps. She never met this accountant. What? Oh, yeah, what I told you yesterday? My suspicions were correct. So, do we do what we discussed, or do you have to wait for orders from higher up? No problem. I'll get to work on it right away."

He shut the phone and looked to the right and the left. "As soon as I get myself a hoagie."

– 37 –
I Only Autograph
Pads of Paper

"Mrs. Innis," said the flight attendant, "there's a telephone call for you."

"For me?" said Lorraine, "up here?"

She had never taken a phone call at 30,000 feet before, but then, Lorraine had experienced a lot of firsts in the last eight days.

"Hello," said Lorraine picking up the receiver from the console between the seats.

"Lorruska," boomed the voice of Nikolai Kropotkin.

"Nikki," said Lorraine.

"Do you know you are a difficult lady to find?"

"Yes," she agreed, "even I have trouble finding myself lately."

"You have such a delightfully droll sense of humor," laughed the Russian, though Lorraine hadn't meant it as a joke. "Here I am, in Paris, as they say cooling my feet..."

"Cooling your heels?"

"Da," he said, "the French always keep you waiting, whether it be for a meeting or a table. This is my fourth capital since I left you. Anyway, since we were waiting, I said to Yuri, get me Lorruska on the telephone. And like magic, he tracked you down in a mere five hours. So now I am talking to you, and now the French are waiting for me. But that is not why I called. Lorruska, you must come to visit me, in Moscow, at Christmas."

"I'd love to, but I wouldn't want to leave my cousin, and..." she almost said "my husband," but she still had no clue to the whereabouts of Martin Innis.

"Perhaps she will be well by then," said Kropotkin.

"I hope."

"Then let us say that if she can travel you both can come for a visit, no?"

"Yes," she said, "that would be very nice."

"Good, now I must go Lorruska. I will give your love to the President of France. Goodbye, my dear."

Lorraine hung up the phone and glanced around the cabin of the jet that Peter Liverot chartered for the flight to Canada. Sitting toward the rear of the plane was Liverot, immersed in paperwork, with Patsy Einfalt across the aisle assisting him. True to his promise, Liverot had indeed taken care of everything. In regards to setting up the charity, he had arranged it all down to the tiniest detail. In fact, the banker was so well organized, Lorraine had trouble keeping track of the unfolding events. By Thursday afternoon, Liverot had the papers drawn up establishing the foundation with Lorraine as its chair. He had taken the liberty of calling the new charity "The Cross of Lorraine," after reading about the nurses' grassroots movement in the local newspaper.

The Cross of Lorraine was established as a Gibraltar corporation, Liverot explained, for tax purposes, as well as making it easier to distribute the funds to the needy around the world. As well as Lorraine could understand it, this had something to do with U.S. laws regarding international charities, and the red tape involved in sending donations overseas. The banker put in millions of his own money, along with five million dollars-worth of contributions from friends – all similarly modest donors who wished to keep their well-doing obscure. In addition, Liverot outlined an aggressive marketing plan not only to publicize the charity but also to capitalize on the growing requests for licensing and merchandising of Lorraine Innis products. Although these sponsorship deals made Lorraine uncomfortable, Liverot promised that only the most tasteful, highest quality items would be considered for her endorsement. Also, no product or service would be given the Cross of Lorraine seal of approval without the manufacturer first agreeing to donate at least 15% of sales to the charity. Despite this hefty fee, advertisers and manufacturers soon were queuing up in bunches to associate themselves with the remarkable popularity of Lorraine. Media experts noted that there had not been such an overnight sensation since the Beatles.

By Friday morning, as Lorraine was finishing the rough draft of her autobiography, Liverot was putting the final touches on the unveiling of the Cross of Lorraine foundation. He had planned on holding a Friday evening news conference with Lorraine from the Hotel DuPont. The timing, exactly one week after the Kropotkin assassination attempt, seemed good, but an irresistible opportunity arose from the most unlikely source: Major League Baseball.

Lorraine's popularity had inspired the Commissioner of Baseball to make the seventh game of the World Series "Lorraine Innis Night." Purvis Twankey was also invited to sing the National Anthems of both the United States and Canada, even though he was British. Usually, a World Series needed little outside promotion. This year, however, the fall classic was a ratings nightmare because the two participating teams were from Toronto and Pittsburgh – not exactly powerhouse media markets. Consequently, Major League Baseball turned to Lorraine to share in her popularity. Liverot jumped at the chance to use the deciding game of the World Series to unveil the Cross of Lorraine, agreeing to deliver Lorraine for a special tribute before the game, followed by the announcement of the new charity on network television during the fifth inning.

With so much extra work, Lorraine hardly thought it odd that Liverot would bring Patsy along with them. She did think it puzzling, however, that the banker also brought along Marcia Capicola from the secretarial pool, especially since Marcia spent most of the flight filing her nails, reading fashion magazines, and perfecting her bubble gum blowing technique.

Lorraine looked up a few rows where Purvis Twankey sat with his guitar, laboring to master the chords of *O'Canada*. Thanks to his appearance on *The Cookie Babcock Special* Purvis had become something of a sensation himself. His *Ballad of Lorraine* was rocketing up the pop, country and easy listening charts, and there was talk of him doing an entire album of original songs. Putting down the manuscript of her book that she was reviewing, Lorraine walked up the aisle.

"I haven't seen you around the hospital lately, Purvis," said Lorraine.

"No, ma'am," said Purvis, as he practiced his chords. "And don't think I've forgotten you or your cousin."

"I didn't think that."

"Ee, because you're the nicest ladies I know," said Purvis looking down. "And your cousin..."

"What?"

"You'll think I'm daft, but..."

"But what Purvis," said Lorraine placing her hand on his knee.

"I think your cousin is champion," he said with a bashful grin. "I'd do anything for Miss Valerie. She's the most beautiful girl I've ever seen. I even wrote a song about her, and me producer, Mr. Slouch, wants me to record it, an' all."

"I see," said Lorraine. She couldn't imagine Purvis and Valerie together, and she would hate to see him hurt, but she couldn't think about that at the moment. "You play very well," she said changing the subject. "Bar chords are always so difficult to master."

"Aye," said Purvis looking up. "Do you play guitar, Miss Lorraine?"

"No," she said distractedly, "only the banjulele."

"Ee, the banjo uke! I didn't know anyone outside of Lancs knew about that, let alone played one. Have you played it long?"

Lorraine suddenly drew a blank. "I'm sorry. What did you say?"

"How long have you played the uke?"

"I don't know," she said vacantly. "Do I?" Lorraine gazed out the window at the passing clouds trying to remember when she had ever seen a banjulele, let alone played one. It was the first bout of disorientation she had experienced in days. She thought that her mind was finally settled and at rest. Even the odd visit from Valerie's boyfriend hadn't bothered her, or the fact that she must have fallen asleep while they were talking. In any event, Boden must have let himself out, for she awoke the next morning feeling better than she had in years, but with a strange craving for spaghetti which she attributed to her being pregnant. But now she had this odd mental fugue about, of all things, ukuleles. Was the confusion of the previous week creeping back to cloud her thoughts?

Lorraine forced herself out of this disturbing frame of mind with a shake of her head and a determination to stay as far away from there as possible.

"I missed you at the hospital," said Lorraine, changing the subject. "You haven't been there since Tuesday night when we watched our TV appearance."

"It was proper champion of them to let me be on that show with you," said Purvis. "You helped me reach one of my lifelong dreams of being a singing cowboy."

"How do you like fame, Purvis?"

"It's nowt all bad," he said self-consciously fingering the lapel of his two-tone country-style suit. "If that's what a bloke has to do to do what a bloke wants to do, then I guess I'm the bloke to do it."

Lorraine slowly parsed Purvis' statement, and then smiled.

"I'm very happy for you, then, Purvis," said Lorraine placing her hand on his forearm. "Only please do me one favor?"

"You know I'd do anything for you or Miss Valerie."

"Yes, I know," said Lorraine. "Please don't let success change you."

"No fear there! I still put me trousers on two legs at a time."

"I believe the expression is 'one leg at a time,'" she said.

"Aye," said Purvis, "only I got this invention, 'the Twankey Trouser Horn.' You can jump right in two legs at a time…"

Purvis was interrupted by a tap on the shoulder.

"'Scuse me, buddy," said Peter Liverot, "but I need to speak to Mrs. Innis for a minute."

"Oh, that's all right," said Purvis nodding towards the acoustical guitar across his lap, "I was just brushing up on my picking."

"Yeah, great," said Liverot, motioning for Lorraine to join him towards the back of the cabin. "I got a few contracts for your approval, Mrs. Innis."

The relationship between Peter Liverot and Lorraine Innis had never progressed to a first name basis. As they sat down, Mr. Liverot handed Mrs. Innis a thick legal-sized manila folder.

"You have been busy, Mr. Liverot," said Lorraine weighing the dossier in her hands.

"Yeah, well, you're a pretty popular lady," he said. "This is the fastest I've ever collected money."

Lorraine examined the file offer by offer, nodding her head in agreement to the first five or six proposals. Peter Liverot had done an exemplary job of weeding out those offers that were not up to the standard she had set for the foundation.

"Yes, these look good," said Lorraine until she reached one about halfway through the pile. "No, I couldn't do this one."

Liverot's expression, which had been smug, drooped as he leaned over to see the offending offer.

"What? Why not," said Liverot.

"I'm sorry, Mr. Liverot," said Lorraine, "I just can't."

"Why the hell not?"

"Language, Mr. Liverot."

"Sorry, but why?"

"Because I don't drink that brand of soft drink," said Lorraine.

"You don't have to drink it."

"Only say I do?"

"Right," nodded Liverot.

"That's dishonest. I won't recommend a product to the public when I prefer their competition!"

"But I got them up to 18% with bottles and cans with your picture on them. That's millions for your charity."

"I appreciate your efforts, but I'm sorry. I don't care if it's billions. If I sacrifice my credibility, what good will ultimately come from it?" Lorraine ripped the proposal in half and handed it to the banker. "Sorry."

Peter Liverot grumbled a bit, as she continued through the folder.

"Yes…okay…yes, I like that…yes…" As she reached the final offer in the stack, Lorraine stopped short. "What? No, I'm sorry, never!"

"Which one?"

Lorraine held up the offending proposal between her thumb and forefinger.

"What's wrong with that? That's not some soda," he said. "I mean, you're a woman. You use 'em, don't you?"

"None of your business, Mr. Liverot."

"Stosh Potoski, the guy that pitched this gimmick, is going to pay big bucks to produce these beauties."

"Who else would suggest such a private and personal endorsement? I never," said Lorraine icily, "I never want to have anything to do with Half-Sack again."

"What'd ya mean 'again'? I thought I'm fielding all the offers, and besides, who's 'Half-Sack?'"

"Excuse me?"

"You said you never wanted to do business with Half-Sack again. Who's Half-Sack? And when did you do business with him before?"

"I haven't," said Lorraine, though for a moment the name seemed vaguely, even disturbingly, familiar to her. Where she had picked up the odd name was equally as mystifying. First the banjulele, now this strange name. She was lost for a moment. Maybe she couldn't control her thoughts. Was she going mad? Liverot jarred her back to the matter at hand.

"So what's the big deal?" asked Liverot. "Potoski's one of the biggest novelty manufacturers in the business. I don't get it."

"No, you wouldn't!"

"What? It's high class," argued the banker, "look they made a prototype." Liverot pulled one of the slim, lightly scented items from his breast pocket. "See? They embossed your signature into the pad. Pretty neat, huh? I bet if we held out they could get your face on it."

Lorraine just stared at Liverot in disbelief, and then shuddered.

"I just don't get it," he said. "You're supposed to be a symbol to millions of women?"

"Be that as it may," said Lorraine, "I would prefer to be a positive role model every day of the month, not just at certain times of it."

"Oh, all right," said Liverot. "Here," he added offering Lorraine the prototype of the rejected pad, "do you want it as a souvenir?"

Lorraine shook her head and then handed back the file to Liverot indicating their business was concluded.

"Well, what am I supposed to do with it?" muttered the banker as he walked away. A few rows later, he handed it to Marcia Capicola who smiled and tucked it into her purse.

"Lorraine," said Patsy as she sat down, "Here's the research you asked me to find."

"What did you come up with?"

"All of it," said Patsy matter-of-factly.

"You didn't have any trouble."

"Why would I? It only took a few minutes."

Lorraine opened the large envelope. Inside lay her life, or at least documentation of it: copies of her birth certificate, her complete educational record, the mortgage papers on her home in Colts Neck, credit reports, and bank accounts, among other items. Lorraine sighed with relief at having written confirmation of what she knew to be true. It was especially comforting in light of the mental lapses of the last few minutes.

"Thank you," she said. "How did you get this all so quickly?"

"I'm not only an executive assistant," said Patsy, "I'm a darn good secretary, too!"

– 38 –
The Prettiest Gold-Glover
I Know

They arrived in Toronto two hours before game time and were escorted to the stadium. There the Commissioner of Baseball reviewed the agenda for the evening.

"At 8:15," said the Commissioner, "Mrs. Innis will be introduced, proceed on to the field, and throw out the ceremonial first pitch."

"Is that from the mound or the sidelines?" asked Lorraine.

"Maybe you should do it from the sidelines," said the Commissioner, "just in case you can't throw it 60 feet. We wouldn't want you to be embarrassed, Mrs. Innis."

The assumption that she couldn't reach home plate from the pitcher's mound just because she was a woman irked Lorraine, but she said nothing.

"After the first pitch, the catcher will present you with the ball, and you'll be escorted to the VIP box next to the dugout. There you'll be introduced to the Prime Minister of Canada, and Vice-President Ottinger, and watch the game with them."

Lorraine smiled. She had always admired Quinton Merton's Vice-President.

"Will we be with the Vice-President too?" asked Patsy.

"No," said the Commissioner, "Mr. Liverot and the rest of the party will watch the game from the owner's suite on the press level."

"What about her interview in the middle of the game?" asked Liverot. "The network said they'd interview her after the fifth inning. That's what we came here for."

"That's between you and the network," said the Commissioner. "I can have one of their representatives stop by to discuss it. After Mrs. Innis is seated, Mr. Twankey will be introduced and will sing the anthems. Mr. Twankey you've learned *O, Canada*, haven't you?"

"*Oui, mon-sewer*," said Purvis in Lancashire-laced French accent.

The Commissioner stared at him. "This isn't the French-speaking part of Canada, Mr. Twankey. As we're in Toronto, you'll sing *O, Canada*, in English, second. You'll start with the American anthem."

"I'll sing that in English, an' all," said Purvis.

"*Oui*. I mean, yes," sighed the Commissioner. "After you finish, you'll leave the field and join the others in the owner's suite."

"Can I watch the game with the ground crew?"

"The ground crew?"

"It's me favorite part of baseball. I like the way they smooth out the dirt and draw them lines in white chalk," said Purvis.

"I'll have to check with the crew chief, but I imagine it will be okay."

"Champion!" said Purvis.

At a quarter-to-eight, an usherette escorted Lorraine and Purvis to the field level. On the way down, Lorraine couldn't help but think about how much Valerie would have enjoyed this night. She was sure the nurses back at the hospital would tune in the game for her. Maybe it would help stir Valerie out of her coma. She only wished Martin was a baseball fan. Perhaps if he were watching he would try and contact her again, as he had in that brief, unsigned note.

A few minutes later, in the concrete tunnel leading to the field, Lorraine stood with Purvis. Above the hum of the crowd, Lorraine could hear *The Ballad of Lorraine* being played over the public address system. It all seemed rather unbelievable.

"Are you nervous?" asked Lorraine.

"No," he said. "I've stood in cement tunnels a'fore…plenty of times."

As the starting lineups were being introduced, the team public relations director stopped by to ask Lorraine if she was right- or left-handed. When she indicated she was a righty, he presented her with a brand new fielder's glove. Lorraine smelled the fresh leather and pounded her fist into the glove's pocket while taking care not to break a nail.

After the last player was introduced, the stadium lights were dimmed, and the public address announcer began his introduction of the guest of honor. As the tribute neared its end, a single spotlight illuminated the tunnel entrance. The usherette guided Lorraine to the entrance, and she walked out to an almost deafening roar, drowning out the final sentence of the introduction. Despite everything she had experienced over the last week, the spontaneous outpouring of affection from so many strangers overwhelmed Lorraine, causing her knees to buckle briefly. The Blue Jays catcher steadied her as she reached home plate.

"I'm going to the mound," she shouted in the catcher's ear to be heard over the din. "I'll give you my curve."

The catcher seemed surprised but nodded in agreement.

After a five-minute standing ovation, the crowd settled down for the ceremonial first pitch, and Lorraine strode to the pitcher's mound. There, Lorraine clambered to the top of the small hill, despite encountering some difficulty when her heels sunk into the dirt. Rather than have her delivery hampered, she kicked off her pumps and straddled the pitching rubber in her stocking feet. Once set, Lorraine stared in at the catcher behind home plate. Despite wearing a mid-calf-length skirt, Lorraine wound up and let fly a curveball that hit the catcher's mitt with a resounding slap. Delighted by the effort, the catcher beamed as he trotted out towards the mound to present Lorraine with the ball. The fans cheered wildly. Lorraine was disappointed. She had missed the strike zone.

As Lorraine made her way to the VIP box where the P.M. and Vice-President awaited her, Purvis Twankey walked out of the tunnel and up to the microphone just behind home plate. There, the cowboy singer crooned a serviceable rendition of *O, Canada*. It was when he began singing the more challenging *Star Spangled Banner*, however, that the crowd really took notice. From the opening bars to the final line the crowd listened in hushed appreciation. The difficult melody had finally met its perfect mate in Purvis' unique voice. Veterans wept openly. Aging hippies who had once fled north to avoid the draft sobbed with a newfound appreciation for the song. When he had finished crooning about the land of the free and the home of the brave, the mostly Canadian crowd stood in awed silence for a full ten seconds before bursting into cheers. By the time he made his way back to the tunnel, it was clear that Purvis Twankey would have another hit recording.

Only after Lorraine was seated next to Thomas Ottinger, and Purvis joined the ground crew, did most of the fans remember they were here to witness the most important baseball game of the season. Fittingly, since it was her night, the crowd also witnessed another slice of the growing legend of Lorraine Innis.

It was in the bottom half of the third inning, with the score knotted at two apiece, that it happened. Lorraine and the Vice-President were chatting about a variety of subjects, not the least of which was the Vice-President's grandson sitting in the VIP box with them. Learning that Ottinger's six-year-old grandson was going to be starting Little League the following spring, Lorraine decided to give him the new glove that she had used earlier. She had the glove on her hand and was reaching back to give it to the little boy when a sharp crack of the bat hitting the ball was heard. Instinctively, Lorraine turned towards the sound while extending her gloved hand upwards. In the next instant, Lorraine was rocketed backward and to her right. Her right shoulder was slammed against the seat, and her right wrist was snapped back. When she straightened up a second later, Lorraine found that she had speared a wicked foul ball in mid-flight. The crowd cheered as she stood, still somewhat bewildered, displaying the ball in the mitt. The feat was much more dramatic to the millions of viewers around the world since the replay showed that, had Lorraine not stopped it, the ball would have smashed into the face of the Vice-President traveling at 100 miles-per-hour. A minute later when the giant video screen on the scoreboard confirmed this fact, the fans gave Lorraine her third standing ovation of the night. She had saved another world leader, albeit just a Vice-President, but a popular one, from serious injury.

The game was momentarily halted as Lorraine accompanied Ottinger and his grandchildren into the dugout where a team physician confirmed that they all were unharmed. Rather than return to their seats, they went upstairs to the press level. There Thomas Ottinger and Lorraine viewed the video of her dramatic foul ball rescue. And while her new feat of heroism was unsettling to Lorraine, the Vice-President expressed his deepest gratitude over network television to "the prettiest gold-glover I know."

– 39 –
Up the Cocoa Puff Creek
Without a Paddle

This is too much!" Quinton Merton slammed his fist on the desk. The force of the blow upset his Sunday morning bowl of Cocoa Puffs, sending a rivulet of chocolatey milk running over a legislative draft and onto the morning newspapers.

"Yes sir," said Davis Flemming. Despite Flemming's assurances that the "Innis Situation" was "being handled," the President was growing impatient, and belligerent.

"Well, hotshot," said Merton, "what should we do now?"

"It's not as if she's done anything bad," said Flemming "I mean you can't insist that a private citizen stop saving people's lives."

Merton scowled as he scanned the front pages of the morning papers.

"Look at that," ranted Merton, "she's hogging all the coverage. Look here she is saving Ottinger's life. Over here's a story on how she started some charity. Did you know about that? Well, did you?"

"Yes, sir," said Flemming, wondering if they'd have to sedate the President.

"It says that in the fifth inning she announced her charity, and by the ninth inning they'd had over a million hits on her website, and the toll-free number was jammed."

"Yes, sir," agreed the aide. "It overwhelmed some of the circuits."

"Why can't we do that?"

"Jam the circuits, Sir?" Flemming never knew what odd strategies the President would concoct when agitated.

"No, why don't we have a charity. I could go on TV and save people's lives and look like a big hero, too."

"You don't have a charity, Sir," sighed Flemming, delivering yet another civics lesson to the head of government. "You're the president of the United States. If you want the people to do something nice, you don't solicit contributions, you just go and raise their taxes."

"Well, let's do that!"

"Sir, raising taxes capriciously tends to lower a president's popularity, rather than boost it. The public can feel very benevolent if they're asked nicely to do something, but they can get very aggravated if you force them to do it."

"Let's do the other thing, then. Couldn't I save someone's life?

"It would seem just a little contrived, Sir," said Flemming, "especially after she's saved two prominent lives in a little over a week."

Merton stared at his aide and grimaced.

"Are you slipping?" asked the President. "I mean, you usually have plenty of good ideas on how to get things done."

"Patience, Sir. I have the best intelligence people working on it."

The President's eyebrows shot up. "Digging up something?"

"I wouldn't be a bit surprised."

"Dirt? A smear?"

"At this point, Sir, Mrs. Innis is far too beloved in the public eye to be smeared. Look at the papers. Every move she makes is praised, every action is lauded. The public idolizes her, and the only reason the public ever idolizes any human being is for one reason."

"The person is really nice?"

"The public doesn't really know them. Familiarity breeds contempt," said Flemming.

"Yes," muttered the President. He looked down at the story on the bottom of the front page comparing his dismal poll numbers to the astronomical ones of Lorraine Innis.

Lorraine Innis continued to hold a favorable rating over 90%, while Merton barely made 25%. The story also reported that if it were constitutionally possible, both Nikolai Kropotkin and Lorraine Innis could beat Merton in a race for the White House. Such a contest was pure conjecture since Merton could not run for a third term, Kropotkin wasn't a native born citizen, and Lorraine Innis may be too young to be president, though no one knew for sure.

"Look at that," said the President pointing at the newspaper, "even that old idiot Ottinger has higher numbers than me!"

"He usually does, Mr. President."

"Is that legal?"

"If you recall, Sir, that's why I picked him to be your running mate. He was one of the more popular members of Congress, he's a selfless public servant, and he is perfectly satisfied to go no higher than his current office. In fact," Flemming laughed, "he thinks it's an honor to be vice president!"

"I still don't like it," said the President. "Now he's been saved by that Innis woman. He'll probably be even more popular."

"Quite likely," said Flemming as he watched the puddle of milk from the Cocoa Puffs soak into the desk blotter.

Deep in thought, Merton rose from his chair and put his hand in the soppy mess. He looked down at the puddle, licked his palm, and then wiped it on his cardigan.

"I've got an idea," said Merton. "Why don't we have this woman rescue me?"

"Sir?"

"Well, I could be on the presidential yacht, and fall overboard and she could dive in and save me."

"No, Mr. President, such a stunt would only make you appear reckless or clumsy – not a particularly good trait for a man with control of the world's largest nuclear arsenal."

"Hmm, you're probably right," said Merton. "So, what are we supposed to do about this whole Innis mess?"

"Directly, Sir, there is nothing you can do about her without risking more ill-feelings from the public. While I share your frustration, I suggest you let her be and try to get back into the peace process that is quickly passing us by. Her tremendous popularity has to die down soon. The public will soon tire of her, and she'll once again be a non-factor."

"What if they don't get tired of her? What if she goes to Europe and starts saving politicians over there."

"Highly unlikely," said Flemming. "But if her popularity has legs we can court her in a month or two, so as not to appear as if we're jumping on any bandwagon."

"So, you don't think she's a threat as far as the…you know," asked the President pulling a small toy monkey out of his pocket and waving it in the air.

"Hmm? Oh, no, I don't believe so. I think her use of the word 'infantile' in that interview was only a coincidence. Even if she does know something, she seems content to keep her mouth shut. Another reason to stay on the good side of Lorraine Innis, for the time being, at least until we've got something concrete to exploit."

"You're probably right," said the President. "Glad to see you're getting your wits back about you, Davis. I was worried about you. Thought you may have been cracking up on me."

Davis Flemming resisted the urge to say: "takes one to know one," and merely nodded.

"Oh, and get me some more milk, will you? Hey, who won the World Series anyway? In all that hullabaloo it escaped me."

"Toronto did, Sir," said Flemming as he left the leader of the free world to his soggy breakfast, "5 to 4 in twelve innings."

"Stupid Canadians," muttered the President.

– 40 –
The Nutter Butter Revival

It took her less than two hours after the charter flight landed for Lorraine Innis to shower, change, and resume her vigil at Valerie Fierro's bedside. As pleased as she was with the overwhelming response to the Cross of Lorraine Foundation, Lorraine reminded herself that for the sake of her own sanity her real life was wrapped up in her husband and her cousin. Since her husband was still missing, running, or hiding, Valerie remained her last best link to a normal life.

Upon her return, Lorraine noticed little change in Valerie. She remained comfortably unconscious, or at least almost unconscious. Extra samples of cheese bore testament to the fact that Valerie had once again been calling for it, this time during the World Series telecast, specifically those portions that either featured or mentioned Lorraine. While the nurses fulfilled Valerie's requests, and the cheese offered was a delectable assortment, nothing convinced her to open her eyes and actually eat any of it.

Lorraine nibbled on a morsel of mozzarella, glanced at her watch and sighed. It was ten thirty in the morning. She had hardly slept on the flight back from Canada and was feeling the strain. Despite being asked back to all the Sunday morning interview programs to discuss the new charity, she had declined. In her worn out state, Lorraine reasoned, she was apt to say anything. She feared that she might beg on camera for Martin to come back home, or let slip that she was pregnant, or even divulge her recent delusions concerning her own body. With these thoughts running through her mind, she drifted off to sleep in the comfy chair at Valerie's bedside.

◆

Martin Innis' face leaned over that of his wife's, and despite blocking the sun, his features radiated their own warmth to Lorraine. He kissed her, as she lay on her back in the field of clover.

"Wait for me," he said. "I love you."

"I'd wait forever," said Lorraine.

Martin rested on his elbow at her side. He looked so good, she thought, with his wavy hair, his delicate features, and his soft, smooth, accented voice.

"The baby," said Lorraine, lifting her head.

"Right here," said Martin lifting an infant carrier containing a sleeping baby.

Lorraine smiled.

"He'll be hungry soon," said Martin.

"I need to change him first," said Lorraine.

"You don't need to change him," said Martin gravely. "There's no change."

"No change?" repeated Lorraine.

"No change, no change, no change," repeated Martin, his voice growing deeper as he spoke.

◆

"No change," mumbled Lorraine as she opened her eyes.

It had only been a dream.

The words that she first ascribed to her husband had actually been spoken by Father Mike Valvano who was standing on the other side of Valerie's bed talking to a nurse.

"The baby," said Lorraine, not yet fully awake.

"Baby?" said the nurse turning towards Lorraine.

"What baby?" asked Valvano.

Lorraine sat up. "Oh, no, there's no change, I mean, there's no baby."

The nurse said something quietly to the priest and excused herself. Valvano and Lorraine eyed each other silently.

"Hi," said the priest finally. "I saw you on the World Series last night. Starting a charity is a big undertaking. If I can help…"

Lorraine's eyes narrowed. That sounded sincere enough. Perhaps she had overreacted during their first encounter. Maybe he was just a nice young priest, a handsome young priest, who wasn't necessarily trying to make love to Valerie while she slept.

"You saw it?"

"Yes, I watched it here, with your cousin."

Then again, maybe he was a just a prowling hound in a clerical collar.

"With Valerie," said Lorraine sitting up.

"Yes. It was quite a catch."

"What?" You bet she's quite a catch, Lorraine thought, and twice as easy to get when she's unconscious.

"Your catch," said the priest smiling, "the foul ball. Your first pitch had some nice movement on it, too. Did you play softball?"

"No, I play hardball," said Lorraine looking him in the eye. "By the way, it's Sunday. Why aren't you in Mass?"

"It's three in the afternoon."

"Oh."

They may have stood there all day in their face-off, had not a tall stranger knocked on the open door to the suite.

"Sorry," said the stranger, as Lorraine and priest turned towards him. "I must have the wrong room."

He started to leave, but then opened the door a little wider and reexamined the plate attached to it.

"This is Valerie Fierro's room, isn't it?" he asked.

"This is a private suite," said Lorraine. "If you're a reporter looking for a story please contact either Beverly Marlton, at Marlton Press, or Mr. Peter…"

"I'm not a reporter," said the man, "My name is Boden Bleistift. I'm Valerie's boyfriend, or at least I think I am, her boyfriend, that is."

"You're not Boden," said Lorraine. "I've met Boden Bleistift."

The man took out his wallet, pulled out his driver's license and a few credit cards and handed them to Lorraine.

"Boden W. Bleistift," she read.

Lorraine shook her head and wondered who the other Boden Bleistift had been. The other Boden Bleistift had been odd, not that this one didn't have his own quirkiness. Still, thought Lorraine as she looked him over, she could see Valerie dating this Boden Bleistift. His face was angular in a Teutonic sort of way, though his dirty blonde hair was thinning in the front. Still, he was taller, younger and better looking than the other Boden Bleistift. Given Valerie's tastes, Lorraine knew she would always pick taller, younger, more handsome men over shorter, older, uglier ones.

"I'm sorry," she said handing back the identification, "I'm Valerie's cousin, Lorraine."

"And I'm Father Mike Valvano," said the priest shaking Boden's hand, "from Saint Anthony's."

"Where is Valerie," asked Boden.

Lorraine glanced at her cousin lying in bed, and then looked back at Boden.

"She's right there."

"Where?"

"In the bed, of course," said Lorraine.

"That's not Valerie," stated Boden. A moment later he added an apprehensive: "Is it?"

"Yes," she said annoyed at his reaction. "I think I know my own cousin."

"Perhaps," interjected Mike Valvano, "you're thinking of another Valerie Fierro. Though how many pairs of Valeries and Bodens could there be in a state as small as Delaware?"

"I don't know, I'm from Pennsylvania," said Boden blankly.

"Just how long have you been dating Valerie?" asked Lorraine.

"I guess about five months," said Boden studying the figure in the bed. "I guess that could be her, but Valerie's got different eyes...and bolder... more expressive. And her lips are redder. And her nose isn't so crooked, and her cheeks aren't so round, they're more, more..."

"More defined," added Lorraine.

"That's it," said Boden, "not so...washed out."

Lorraine nodded. "Well Boden, you've never seen Valerie Fierro as nature intended."

"Wow, she sure looks..." Boden paused, "...different."

Lorraine could feel the hairs on the back of her neck bristle. On the one hand, there was Mike Valvano, lecherous cleric, on the other, Boden Bleistift, dense accountant. If these were the sort of men that were available to single women, Lorraine was happy to be married...now if she could only find her husband.

"If you're her boyfriend," asked Mike Valvano, "where have you been for the last week or so?"

"We had a terrible fight on the phone, just after the accident."

"How could you have had a fight after the accident?" asked Lorraine. "She's been unconscious since then."

"I don't know," said Boden, "I spoke with Valerie a week ago Saturday morning. She was at her house, and we were talking, then she started calling me names and told me she never wanted to see me again, and she hated me. Then I read in the paper about you, and they mentioned she was in the hospital. I figured Valerie must have gone into the hospital after that."

Lorraine's mouth opened wide. "That...it...last Saturday she wasn't..." she struggled for the right question, finally finding it. "What sort of name did she call you?"

"She called me a...'potato-headed bastard,'" said Boden. "I thought it odd since people have always told me I had a nicely shaped head, actually."

Lorraine sat on the edge of the bed. That had been Boden Bleistift on the phone, not Martin. She hadn't had a fight with Martin. Martin hadn't disowned their baby and accused her of being unfaithful. He hadn't run away and sold everything they owned... oh, wait, yes, Lorraine thought, he still did do that last bit. For whatever reason, her husband was still running, but at least he wasn't cruel and heartless, at least not in the way she had thought he had been. Lorraine smiled in relief, totally ignoring Boden.

"Oh, that Potato Head," she sighed.

"Is that some sort of Italian thing," said Boden, "calling people a 'potato head?'"

"Of course not," said Mike Valvano. "Don't be a dumb *googoots!*"

"A what?"

"A *cucuzza*," said Lorraine, "it's an Italian squash."

Look," said Boden to Lorraine, "if that wasn't Valerie on the phone who was it?"

"Me," said Lorraine.

"But you've never met me," said Boden self-consciously touching his head. "Why would you call me a potato head?"

"I thought you were someone else," said Lorraine.

"We can't all have nice heads," said Father Valvano. "I'm sure you'll find someone, someday who appreciates your looks."

"I thought I had," said Boden craning his neck to look at himself in the mirror.

"Don't pay attention to him," said Lorraine. "I'm sure Valerie thinks your looks are fine."

"Yes," said the priest, "you've got a fine face. You don't have to cover it up with a lot of those messy cosmetics."

Mike Valvano rolled his eyes in Valerie's direction, and a look of concern darkened Boden's face. Apparently, Lorraine thought, the priest was trying to sour Boden on Valerie so he could make his move.

"Don't listen to him," said Lorraine.

"But he's a priest," said Boden.

"Yes, but not a cosmetologist," said Lorraine. "Valerie is the same beautiful girl you remembered. She just needs a little lipstick and mascara…"

A groan arose from Valerie, and the three of them froze and looked at her.

"Valerie?" said Lorraine. "Did you hear that?"

"Yes," said both men.

"She groaned," said Lorraine.

"Maybe she responded to something you said," said Boden.

"What did I say?"

"Something about me not being a cosmetologist," said Valvano.

"I said she needed lipstick and mascara," said Lorraine.

Valerie moaned.

"That's it," said Lorraine.

"I've read," said Boden, "that people in comas will snap out of it in response to some off-hand comment. One man woke up when someone asked him if he wanted a beer."

"Maybe she doesn't like beer," said the priest sarcastically.

"I think," said Lorraine, "he means the person responds to some deeply perceived need or desire."

"That's right," said Boden. "What do you think she wants?"

"Maybe she wants makeup," said Mike Valvano

"What do you want, Honey," said Lorraine.

Suddenly Purvis Twankey loped in the door, munching a pack of cookies from one of the hospital vending machines.

"Anybody fancy a Nutter Butter?" said Purvis.

Lorraine and the two men turned in Purvis' direction.

"I'd like a Nutter Butter, please," croaked a voice from the bed.

They all spun back around to see Valerie Fierro awake and trying to sit up.

Purvis, his mouth agape, held out the packet of cookies. Valerie accepted one and took a bite. Her eyes scanned the room, first at the man who had given her the cookie, then at the priest, and finally at her boyfriend.

"Hi, Boden," said Valerie, before she self-consciously touched her cheek. Realizing she was cosmetically bare, she blushed as she turned to her last visitor. It was upon seeing Lorraine that her eyes grew wide, and her mouth dropped open.

"Hi, Honey," said Lorraine patting Valerie's hand. "You can't know how happy I am that you're finally awake."

Valerie stared at her, and then looked at the three men at her bedside, and then back at Lorraine.

"What the hell are you doing?" she asked Lorraine, in a whisper that everyone in the room could hear.

"You've had an accident," said Lorraine. "I've just been waiting for you to wake up. You've been here over a week."

"And you've been sitting here, like that?" said Valerie in disbelief.

Lorraine looked down at the sweater and slacks she was wearing. "Oh, this? Well, I had to borrow your clothes. It's a long story."

Two nurses entered the room and gave a start at seeing Valerie alert and sitting up.

"And you've been sitting here for a week wearing my clothes?"

"Not exactly," said Lorraine.

"That's a relief," said Valerie.

"No, I wasn't here the whole time," said Lorraine.

"No, she saved the President of Russia from an assassination attempt," said the first nurse.

"And she inspired an international peace plan and started a charity," added the second nurse."

Valerie looked at the nurses, and then at Boden and the priest before turning back to the man who had handed her the cookie.

"Another biscuit?" asked Purvis Twankey.

"You don't happen to have a belt of Scotch, do you?" asked Valerie.

– 41 –
You Can't Beat 'Em
Until You Join 'Em

I wanna join up," cackled Eugenia Bupp, "I wanna be one of those Crock of Loretta dames."

"I think you mean the Cross of Lorraine, don't you?" said the woman on the other end of the phone.

"Yeah, right, the big-nosed broad with the nice rack," said Bupp from the pay phone in the Kootenai Lodge Bar and Grill just outside of Coeur d'Alene. "Good thing you got a toll-free number, else ways I wouldn't be calling on my dime."

"You can also volunteer online," said the woman trying to be helpful.

"Yeah, 'cept I don't go for that internet crap. I ain't no dot-communist! You're lucky I can use the phone. I'm 104, you know!"

With great difficulty, the volunteer representative signed up Eugenia Bupp as the founding member of their Northern Idaho chapter of the Cross of Lorraine.

"What was that all about, Ma?" asked the bartender, a genially overweight man. He poured a double shot of rye into her glass.

"Gonna send me a membership packet," sneered Bupp as she threw back the liquor then banged the glass twice on the oak bar indicating another hit was in order.

"Membership packet for what?"

Bupp nodded to the television, which was showing that day's coverage of Lorraine Innis on the nightly news. She belched and reached for the bowl of rancid mixed nuts while squinting at the moose head hanging behind the bar.

"Lorraine Innis?" said the barkeep incredulously. "I never figured you to go in for that sort of thing, Ma. Is she right-wing?"

"Naw," said Bupp spraying some cashew particles out from between her false teeth.

"Left-wing?"

"She ain't no-wing. And that's worse. Doesn't know where she stands on anything. Just wants to spread peace and love." Ma Bupp said these last two words in a mocking tone that she washed down with another swig of rye. "Stupid do-gooder. Gets in everybody's way; wastes a lot of time and money. Just another broad with her head up her ass waiting to be exploited by the pinkos and commies."

"So why did you want to go and join the Cross of Lorraine."

"Don't you stock any brains behind that bar, Cogswell," she laughed. "If you want to bust up a joint you got get inside it first."

– 42 –
O' Brave New World
That Has Such Lorraine Innis

In the absence of scotch, the nurses brought Valerie Fierro a plastic tumbler of ginger ale, which she now sipped through a straw as she eyed the trio of men standing around her bed. Two of them were total strangers, and she wondered what they were doing there gawking at her.

The first one, the one who had given her the Nutter-Butter, looked like some trailer park refugee who had just made a small killing on the slots. The clergyman standing in the middle appeared too young and too much of a hunk to be a priest. The last one, Boden, well, he was just Boden, reasonably handsome, somewhat successful, and rather dull.

Then there was the real surprise: Lorraine, sitting there on the edge of her bed, holding her hand, and wearing her clothes. Out of the four of them, she thought, the sight of Lorraine was the most disturbing. It wasn't just that Lorraine was there, it was that Lorraine was acting more "Lorraine" than she had ever done before.

"You've got some explaining to do," muttered Valerie out of the side of her mouth.

"You don't know the half of it," whispered Lorraine.

"What's with them?" asked Valerie from behind the flexible straw.

"I'll tell you after they leave," said Lorraine.

"Well, then get rid of them!"

"Purvis," Lorraine asked the first one, "could you go get me all the latest magazines? It will help Valerie catch up on what she's missed in the last week."

"Ee," said Purvis, "I'd do anything for you ladies."

Lorraine opened her purse and pulled out a wad of cash that made Valerie gag on her ginger ale. There must have been over a thousand dollars.

"Here's a fifty," said Lorraine handing it to the cowboy. "Sorry, it's the smallest I have."

"I'll nowt take it," said Purvis pulling out his own impressive cash roll. "Parvo, that is, Mr. Slouch, my producer, gave me an advance on me royalties."

"Thank you, that's very sweet," said Lorraine as he exited. She turned to the priest. "Thank you, Father Valvano, for spending so much time with us on your rounds. We must be holding up your other visitations."

"No, not really," he said.

Valerie watched as Lorraine and the priest, and the priest and Boden exchanged distrustful looks. It was almost as if they were playing a high-stakes poker game without the cards.

Valerie broke the deadlock.

"Boden," she said, "I'm a little tired. I'll see you later."

"Oh, yes, of course," said the accountant. "I guess I'll be going."

"Don't you have to go, Father?" said Lorraine.

The priest eyed Boden. "Yes, I guess I can go, I mean, I really must be moving on."

After a flurry of goodbyes, the two men left leaving Lorraine alone with Valerie.

"Okay, what the hell are you up to" began Valerie, "and where'd you get all that money? And why are you wearing my clothes?"

"I told you, I've had to since the accident!"

"This ought to be good," said Valerie, folding her arms. "And who was that priest, the hospital chaplain or something?"

"I think so, but I don't trust him. I think he's been putting the moves on you while you were unconscious."

Valerie ran her tongue over her lips. "There are worse things that could happen."

"And what about that half-assed cowboy?"

"His name is Purvis Twankey, he's the one who hit your car. He also has the biggest hit song in the country."

"Twankey? I've never heard of him."

"He's only become a singing star since the accident," said Lorraine as she walked over to the coffee table and picked up an armful of magazines. "Oh, yes, and he's secretly in love with you, as well."

"Another one? How did he get a hit song?"

"That was mostly my doing, along with Patsy," said Lorraine sitting next to the bed.

"You saw Patsy?"

"Yes, we met the night of the accident," said Lorraine.

"You mean, you saw her that night. You know Patsy."

"I knew she looked familiar," said Lorraine. "That's been running through the back of my mind since I met her."

"So you and Patsy made this guy a star?" asked Valerie.

"I suppose we did, inadvertently, you see he sang his song on *The Cookie Babcock Special* last week."

"How did he get on *Cookie Babcock*?" asked Valerie. This was getting more confusing by the minute.

"Patsy managed that one. You see, I was the subject of the show. The hit song is about me, as well."

"Is that where you got all that cash?"

"Oh, that's nothing," said Lorraine. "That's just an advance on the royalties from my autobiography."

"Wait a minute," said Valerie raising her hands. "Wait just a minute! I started out by asking why you're wearing my clothes, and now you're on TV and doing your life story. I think you've strayed a little from the plan."

"What plan?"

"*The* plan. *Your* plan! The whole Liverot thing!"

"Your boss, Mr. Liverot?" said Lorraine. "I met him last week. But how could you know about that?"

"No, your Liverot scheme."

Lorraine stared at Valerie with a concerned look. "It'll be okay," said Lorraine in soothing tones. "After all you've been in a coma for ten days. There's a lot you have to get used to."

"Don't patronize me," warned Valerie, "and don't talk to me like I'm some naïve nitwit! I'm not Patsy Einfalt. I helped you set this all up, remember?"

"Set what up?" asked Lorraine.

"Damnit! What the hell's the matter with you?" Valerie shouted. "Why are you talking like this? Don't you..." Her tirade stopped as she looked into Lorraine's eyes and realized that it wasn't an act.

"What?" said Lorraine.

It was like waking a sleepwalker, Valerie thought. She'd have to be careful, or there'd be a real mess. Still, maybe if she went slowly.

Still looking in Lorraine's eyes, Valerie leaned forward and said quietly: "Chesney."

Lorraine stared back, batted her long dark lashes, knitted her perfectly sculpted brows, and replied: "What?"

It wasn't a "what" as in "what do you want," rather, it was a "what" as in "what are you talking about." Valerie's worst fears were confirmed. He'd gone round the bend, not just round the bend, but round the bend smack into fame and fortune. Still, she reasoned, if you had to go crazy, you might as well go first class.

"Wait," said Lorraine, as if a light bulb had come on, "Chesney?"

"Yes," said Valerie, hopefully.

"That's what you must have been saying while you were unconscious. You said it whenever I was on television."

"Did I? Yes, that would make sense."

Lorraine began to laugh. Valerie began to laugh.

"That explains it all," said Lorraine. "You were saying 'Chesney,' and the staff thought you were saying 'cheese!' That's why all this cheese is sitting around. They thought you wanted cheese! They kept trying all different types of cheese, and you were actually saying 'Chesney.'"

"Yes, that's right," said Valerie. "So you get it?"

"Yes," said Lorraine, "all except one thing. Who's Chesney?"

"Nobody," muttered Valerie as she slumped back onto the pillows.

"It's all right, Honey," said Lorraine. "We'll call Chesney for you. Just relax. A lot has happened since the accident. Don't worry, it'll be okay. I'm just glad you're awake, that's one major problem solved, and one to go."

"What's the other?"

A concerned look crossed Lorraine's face. "Martin is missing."

"Martin who?"

"Martin Innis, my husband," said Lorraine. "Do you have amnesia, as well? Martin emptied out our house, put it on the market and disappeared. He took everything. That's why I've been borrowing from you. I don't have a stitch of clothing aside from my underwear."

"Well, at least you weren't wearing mine," said Valerie.

"I know this has got to be a shock, but here." Lorraine handed Valerie the pile of magazines from the previous week. "This will explain how most of this all started."

Valerie sifted through the weekly newsmagazines, all of which had Lorraine on their covers. She picked up *Newsweek* and began reading the cover story on how Lorraine had saved the life of Nikolai Kropotkin thus setting into motion the incredible sequence of events. Ten minutes later, Valerie put down the magazine and shook her head.

"Are the others like this?" She asked nodding at the pile of magazines.

"Essentially."

"You must have been pretty busy," said Valerie.

"That's only what happened last weekend," said Lorraine. She told Valerie about her book deal, the World Series, and the strange disappearance of Martin Innis. When she started talking about Martin, Lorraine's voice began to break.

"But you can't get upset about Martin," said Valerie.

"Why not? He's my husband, and I love him!" cried Lorraine bursting into tears.

Valerie sighed and put her arm around Lorraine's shoulder. "Yeah, right, of course, you do."

After five minutes of unrelenting sobbing, Lorraine raised her head and took a tissue from Valerie. She then wiped her eyes and blew her nose.

"Sorry about that," she said. "I've been holding all that in since the accident. With all that's been going on, I just wanted you to be okay."

"I'm okay, I'm okay," said Valerie. "Thanks for taking care of things. Oh, and I'm sorry I said that about…Martin."

"I really need you, *Cucina*," said Lorraine.

"*Cugina*," corrected Valerie, "I'm not a kitchen."

"Sorry, *Cugina*," said Lorraine.

The tender scene was interrupted by a knock on the door, followed by the return of Purvis Twankey with a fresh armful of magazines.

"Ee, you did it again, Miss Lorraine," said Purvis. "You made the cover of all those news magazines, plus *TV Guide* and *Sports Illustrated*. And look, at who's on the cover of *Entertainment Weekly*." He held up this last periodical which featured a photo of himself along with the caption: "The Man Who Can Sing the National Anthem: Purvis Twankey and Cowboy Wave."

"Ee, but I'm a pillock, you've been crying," said Purvis. "Are you all right?"

"It's okay," said Valerie. "She's just a little overwhelmed by everything that's happened lately."

"I understand," said Purvis as he placed the magazines on the foot of the bed and started backing out. "I'll be going, now. If you need anything, just give a tinkle."

"A tinkle?" said Valerie after he'd gone.

"On the phone," said Lorraine. "I know he seems goofy at first, but he really is very sweet."

"Yeah, well, I'll have to take your word for it," said Valerie. "Are you feeling any better?"

"Yes, thank you," said Lorraine as she reached for another tissue. "It's just such a relief having you back. All this time I've been holding on with every shred of strength I had, just telling myself: 'It'll all be okay when Valerie wakes up.' I hate to admit it, but I think I needed you more than Martin. You two are the only family I've got."

You poor jerk, Valerie thought. Some family; a cousin who isn't a cousin and an imaginary spouse of the same sex.

"Speaking of families," continued Lorraine, "when do your Mom and your sister get back from that cruise?"

"Mom?" It was a two-week cruise. She should be home in a few days."

"Do you think they've read about any of this mess? I'd hate for her to worry." She pointed at the copy of *Time* Valerie had opened on her lap.

"Mom? I doubt it," said Valerie. "She doesn't usually read on vacation. And Rose doesn't read magazines even when she's not on vacation."

"That's good," said Lorraine glancing at her watch. "You wouldn't mind if I left for a while, would you? I've got to get the draft of my autobiography up to the publisher. They're sending a special courier to pick it up at the house. Beverly Marlton is anxious to get it into production as soon as possible. She's putting every other book aside in favor of mine. It seems I'm hot."

"Are you sure that's such a good idea?" said Valerie. "I mean, would you like me to have a look at it first? You know, for accuracy?"

Lorraine laughed. "Ah, you're afraid I'll say something embarrassing about you. Don't worry. I won't give away any family secrets. I'll be back in a bit." She pointed to the magazines. "You can catch up on everything that's happened. It's funny," said Lorraine putting on her coat and heading out the door, "somehow it doesn't seem as overwhelming now that you're okay. It might even be fun. Bye!"

"Fun?" Valerie muttered as she watched Lorraine disappear down the hall. "I don't know how you pulled it off, but somehow you did. Now, how the f**k am I going to get you out of all this...fun?"

– 43 –
The Discerning Snouts
of Highly-Strung Poodles

So this crap is safe, eh? I mean it won't blow my ass off, will it?"
Eugenia Bupp shoved her thumb into the mound of plastic explosive.
"Not until you want it to; if you want it to," said the man with the scar on his chin. His other features were barely distinguishable in the dimly lit basement.

"I don't want to blow my ass off, Dickwad! Who'd be so crazy as to want to blow their own ass to Kingdom Come?" said Bupp. "I told you, I need the stuff to take out some stumps in my backyard."

"Whatever," said the man in a way that indicated that he neither believed her nor cared.

"And you can mold it into any shape you want?"

"Right."

Bupp sniffed it. "What about the odor?"

"Do you smell any?"

"No, but then I ain't no dog."

"You hired a dog to take out your stumps?"

Eugenia Bupp squinted at him with murderous intensity.

"Yeah, that's right," she sneered. "It's a Cocker Spaniel, and he's got a couple of high-strung poodles on the crew who don't like nasty odors. That okay with you, Jockstrap?"

"The odor can be masked…for your poodles, or any other dogs."

"Give me a couple of pounds of it, Smart Ass."

"Whatever," said the man with the scar on his chin.

– 44 –
Dr. Lester and the Lesser Woman

"Miss Fierro," said the woman in the white coat, "I'm Dr. Lester, I've been overseeing your case. How are you feeling?"

"Pretty good," said Valerie, "considering. I want to ask you about, uh, my cousin."

"Mrs. Innis?" said the doctor. "She really is a remarkable lady. You're a fortunate young woman to have such a dedicated relative."

"Yes. Dr. Lester, I'm afraid that Lorraine is acting a little bit peculiar."

"Well, she's been under a tremendous strain since your accident. Not to mention becoming a celebrity."

"Was she...okay...when I was brought in here?"

"In what way, Miss Fierro?"

"Well, was she injured, as well?"

"No. I spoke to Mrs. Innis within an hour or so after you were brought in and she seemed fine under the circumstances."

"Well, then did someone hit her on the head with a bedpan or something after she got here?"

"If I recall, Dr. Brandon examined her," said Dr. Lester. "She walked in on her own, and after overcoming some mild disorientation, Mrs. Innis has been fine. In fact, she's been more than fine. She's been an inspiration to most of the staff." Dr. Lester pointed to the pin attached to her lab coat. "Myself included."

"What's that?" asked Valerie. "It looks like a telephone pole."

"It's the Cross of Lorraine," said the doctor. "It's the symbol of the charity your cousin founded."

Valerie made a slow whistle. "This thing has really gotten out of control, hasn't it?"

"You've missed a lot while you were unconscious, but I think Mrs. Innis has a pretty firm grip on the situation," said Dr. Lester. "A lesser woman might have fallen to pieces in the light of all that's gone on. As I said, she's an inspiration to us all."

"A lesser woman," muttered Valerie.

"Are there any other concerns I can address?"

"No, it's just that..." began Valerie before hesitating. "It's just that I think she's been rattled pretty hard by this accident. It's like she's not quite... herself...as if she's really preoccupied. It's almost like a sleepwalker if you understand what I'm saying."

"Would you like me to do a full examination?"

"No, no, that wouldn't...I mean...it's not physical. She just seems... different."

"Again, she's been through stressful, life-changing events. She's not the person you knew ten days ago. I suggest you just give each other time to adjust. Everything should be fine."

"Adjust," repeated Valerie.

"You two really are very fortunate to have each other," said the doctor as she started to leave.

"Hmm? How's that?" asked Valerie.

"Well, all the while your cousin was out saving lives, inspiring world peace, and founding charities, her main concern was for you. And now your primary concern is for her. You haven't even asked the simplest of questions about your own health."

"Oh, I'm sorry, what did you want me to ask you?" asked Valerie.

Dr. Lester laughed. "You don't have to ask anything. I just thought you might wonder how you were, or when you can go home."

"Oh, sorry. How am I and when can I go home?"

"You seem to be fine," said Dr. Lester, "but we'd like to keep you under observation for at least another 48 hours. You haven't really eaten for more than a week. We need to reintroduce you to solids gradually. Oh, and despite their obvious medicinal effect, I would keep away from the Nutter Butters for a day or two. If I can answer any more questions," said Dr. Lester, walking towards the door, "please let me know."

"Thank you, Doctor," said Valerie as she reached forward to pick up several magazines. They all featured Lorraine on the cover. *Sports Illustrated*, used the photo of Lorraine snagging the foul ball just inches in front of the Vice-President's face. "Lorraine: The Real Fall Classic," was the headline.

"You're a classic, all right, Lorraine," muttered Valerie staring at the cover. "I doubt there's another woman in the world who's got a dick and doesn't seem to know it!"

– 45 –
Fixing the Hole
Where Lorraine Got In

D o you want any of your flowers or cards?"

"Nope," said Valerie, "chuck 'em all."

Lorraine looked through the cards and notes that Valerie received during her stay in the hospital. Most were from strangers. Some were from Hollywood stars and world leaders. Almost all had been sent, Lorraine guessed, from her own admirers or people who wanted to curry favor with her.

"Even these flowers," said Lorraine holding up an arrangement, "the ones from Purvis?"

"Throw them out first," said Valerie. "That's the most unbelievable part of this whole thing. I could believe you saved the life of that Russian. I could believe you inspired him to write a peace plan. I could even believe you're the most popular woman in the world. But I can't believe you turned that English peabrain into a pop star."

"He's really very sweet."

"I can get sweet out of the candy machine," said Valerie looking off into space. "The man I marry will have it all: money, a Fortune 500 career, and more money. Not only that, he'll have the little things. He'll know how to put a snotty waiter in his place, how to negotiate with a coy BMW salesman, how not to wear brown shoes with his gray Brooks Brothers suit..."

"Not exactly Purvis Twankey, is it?" said Lorraine.

"To your pal, Purvis, going upscale is springing for the double-wide model down at the trailer park. Too bad I couldn't mix Boden's refinement with Twankey's earning potential. Then I'd have something. Throw in the physique of that hottie Father Valvano, and it'd be perfect."

Lorraine grimaced but continued sorting through the flowers. "What about this arrangement from Nikki?"

"Who? Oh, Kropotkin?" said Valerie. "That's up to you. He's your little friend."

"He paid for your suite," said Lorraine.

"Because of you," said Valerie, "he's your boyfriend, not mine."

"It's not like that," said Lorraine. "He knows I'm married."

Valerie gave her a pointed stare. "It's nice that some people know some things…"

Lorraine looked at Valerie quizzically. Ever since she awoke three days ago, Valerie had been making cryptic remarks implying that Lorraine was out of touch, or missing the obvious. Lorraine didn't even bother to ask what it was anymore since Valerie always retreated on the subject when pressed.

"What about the ones from work?" asked Lorraine holding up the smallest arrangement.

"Whose work?"

"Yours," said Lorraine. "Though mine too, now that I work with Peter Liverot."

"Don't remind me," said Valerie. "I still can't believe you made a deal to go into business with that bastard. Didn't you realize anything when he said it was going to be set up in Gibraltar? Gibraltar, that's where Albrecht Eckner is now."

"How was I to know?"

"You more than anyone should have…" Valerie stopped herself. "Never mind."

"What?"

"You'll understand it sooner or later."

"I don't know what you're talking about," said Lorraine, "but I know you'll straighten it out for us, after all, you're working for the Foundation now, too."

"Yeah, thanks."

Lorraine couldn't tell if Valerie was expressing gratitude or complaining since her remarks contained elements of both.

An hour later, after running a gauntlet of media representatives at the hospital entrance, Lorraine was driving Valerie back home. After more than a week of pleasant weather, a cold soaking rain had moved into the area. It was the sort of autumn rain that strips the last reluctant leaves from the trees, clogs the storm drains, and floods the streets.

"When," said Lorraine after several minute's silence, "does Aunt Connie get back?"

"Who?"

"Your mother, my aunt," said Lorraine, wondering if perhaps Valerie had lost part of her memory. "Remember? She and your sister Rose are on that cruise?"

"Oh, them," said Valerie. "They'll be back this weekend."

"Do you want me to pick them up at the airport?"

Valerie stared at Lorraine for a moment with an expression that seemed torn between amusement and horror. "No, that won't be necessary."

"Do you think she's heard all about what's happened?"

"I called her last night, to prepare her," said Valerie. "She'd heard about it, but didn't realize it was you."

"That's odd. I mean how many nieces does she have that are named 'Lorraine Innis?'"

"She didn't make the connection," said Valerie.

Lorraine was beginning to wonder whether all the women on Valerie's side of the family had congenital amnesia.

A smaller and wetter cadre of news vans was parked outside Valerie's house awaiting their return.

"This is getting old," said Valerie. "Look at them standing there in the pouring rain."

"They're not that bad. You just don't want to make any sudden moves," said Lorraine recalling her high-speed chase with the three TV vans.

"You make them sound like wild animals," said Valerie as they climbed out of the Pacer.

"You just wave and smile," said Lorraine, doing just that. "Sometimes it helps when you tell them that you're in for the night. That way they don't have to hang around waiting for you to do something. After all, they just want to get their pictures and leave."

Lorraine unlocked the front door, held it for Valerie, called out a "goodnight, everybody," to the encamped media, and went inside herself.

"Speaking of pictures," said Lorraine as she hung their coats in the closet, "Beverly Marlton wants some pictures for the book."

"So," said Valerie, "that shouldn't be a problem. I'm sure they've got thousands of them from the last week."

"No, she wants some photos from my childhood."

"Your childhood?" said Valerie, moving into the kitchen.

"Yes, but I don't have any."

"Oh?" said Valerie, eyeing Lorraine carefully.

"No, everything I had was in the house. Who knows where they are now that Martin's cleared the place out."

"Right, Martin cleared it out," said Valerie.

"But I was thinking, you probably have lots of pictures of me that we could use, don't you?"

"How would..." Valerie stopped in mid-sentence. Her expression brightened. "Yes, I do. You know me. I have plenty of pictures of you. In fact, let's look at them right away."

"We don't have to do it right away. You must be tired."

"Nonsense, I've been sleeping for more than a week," said Valerie. "Besides it'll be fun. We'll relax, sit on the sofa and look at old photo albums. Okay?"

"Sure," said Lorraine. She was surprised by Valerie's sudden desire to look at old photos. "We can do whatever you want to do, but there's no hurry."

"That's exactly what I want to do," said Valerie.

"Don't you want to change?" asked Lorraine following her cousin into the living room. "I mean, don't you want to get into something dry?"

"Who's wet?" replied Valerie as she rooted through the bottom cabinet of her china cupboard.

"Well," said Lorraine, "my feet are wet."

"Take your shoes off then," said Valerie with her head deep inside the cupboard. She pulled out several albums and scrambled up on to the sofa. "Here we go. This should be interesting."

Lorraine tucked her feet under her thighs, as Valerie opened to the first page of the album. "Those look like recent pictures," said Lorraine. "I thought we were going to look at ones from when I was little. I hope you have a good picture of Martin, as well. I gave the one from my wallet to People magazine. They're doing a special story about the premiere of the book."

"After they print it you'll have dozens of copies," said Valerie, as she flipped through the album. "Besides, after you see these I think you'll have all you need. Where, is it, where…ah, here, this is the one!"

Valerie pulled a snapshot from out of the album and handed it to Lorraine.

"I'm going to need more than just one," said Lorraine taking the photo and looking at it. She froze. There in the picture were a man and a woman.

"Well?" asked Valerie.

Lorraine opened her mouth to speak but found the words stuck in her throat. Her mind was a blur. It was as if all the facts of her life that she had worked so hard to organize over the last week had been tossed into the air and somehow reorganized into a different, clearer picture than the one she had been laboring to build.

There she was in the picture. But she was heavier and dressed like a man. Her hair was short and neat and next to her was Martin, looking much different than the photo she had given *People* magazine. In fact, it was an entirely different person, but obviously Martin, only he was dressed as a woman. For a split second, Lorraine tried to concoct that the photo was them at some Halloween costume party, but even she couldn't deny the truth.

"Martin, it's Martin," Lorraine whispered, before correcting herself. "I mean, Martina."

Lorraine flipped the photograph over. There on the back was written: "Martina and Chesney's engagement party.

"Martina and Chesney," said Lorraine, tears welling up in her eyes. "Chesney. Chesney Potts."

"Sorry to break it to you this way," said Valerie, "but I had to do…"

"No!" wailed Lorraine, jumping off the sofa. "It isn't…that explains… but…it can't be!"

"Yes," said Valerie.

"No, no, no!" Lorraine paced around the room like a caged beast.

"It's okay," said Valerie in deliberate tones, as she stood.

Lorraine snatched the photo album from Valerie's hands and flung it against the wall knocking a picture to the floor with a crash.

"Hey, calm down," said Valerie. "Take it easy."

"No, no," ranted Lorraine as she began tearing at her hair. Valerie rushed to her side and tried to restrain her. At first, Valerie managed to grab Lorraine's arms and hold her in a clutch, but her control was short-lived. After being in the coma, she was no match for the possessed Lorraine who broke free, pushed her aside, and ran straight for the sliding glass door at the back of the house. Expecting Lorraine to run straight through it, Valerie shielded her face, but at the last second Lorraine reached out, flung the door open, and ran into the dark backyard.

"NO! NO!" screamed Lorraine as she looked upwards into the driving rain. The deluge ran down her face. She howled as she furiously ran her hands through her hair and over her face, smearing her make-up into a collage of smudges. Despite being in the middle of a row of houses, Lorraine's shouts were muffled in the downpour. After another moment, Lorraine paused, panting, as she tried to grasp the whirlpool of thoughts spinning out of control inside her head. Finally, she raised her fists to the skies and screamed in a rich baritone.

"MARTINA! MARTINA! I LOVE YOU!" After gulping down a deep breath, she cried: "LIVEROT, YOU BASTARD!"

Then, as if the outburst had exorcised a deeply ensconced demon, Lorraine Innis collapsed in the mud as the rain poured down.

– 46 –
The Geriatric Porn Queen and the Popsicle Stick

Yes, madam," said the middle-aged saleslady, "may I help you?"

"Yeah, I want to apply for a job as one of your mannequins. I've been glued to this spot for ten minutes," said Eugenia Bupp. "I might as well make a career out of standing around this joint."

The saleslady offered a cool apology.

"Never mind any more soft soap, Popsicle," said Bupp, "just sell me one of them brassiere contraptions and let me get out of here. Department stores give me the creeps. Never stepped foot in one these joints 'til they stopped printing the Sears catalog. That was a communist plot, y' know. Where do you think farmers and backwoodsmen used to buy their ammo?"

"What size, madam?" asked the woman.

"Any size, from BB's to elephant gun shells," said Bupp. "Sears carried any ammo you wanted. You could outfit a South American revolution from them. Don't think it's a coincidence that this country's gone limp in the shorts since they got rid of the Sears catalog…"

"Certainly, madam, but I was inquiring as to the size bra that madam requires?"

"Big! Real Big! As big as you got, Popsicle! At least a double D!"

The saleswoman raised the glasses that hung from the chain around her neck and peered at Eugenia Bupp's emaciated body.

"I think madam would be better suited to a 30-A," she said with a polite, but officious air.

"That's where you're wrong, Popsicle. I told you, I need it big, really big; as big as you carry in this overpriced general store."

"What size does madam wear now?"

Eugenia Bupp snorted. "Like I wear one of them rigs. Look, Popsicle, Do you think my girls would be swingin' round my ankles if I did. Look what's the biggest thing you got?"

The woman exhaled and looked heavenward as if she were hoping for divine intervention from the patron saint of harried shop assistants. "In your band size we have a 30-DD, but…"

"Sold!" said Bupp slapping her palm on the counter. "Wrap it up, Popsicle, in fact, give me two, I never know when I might spring a leak!"

She smiled obsequiously. "Certainly, madam must prepare for every contingency. Will that be cash or charge?"

"Ha! The only charging you'd find me doing is up San Juan Hill with Teddy Roosevelt. I'm over 110, y' know!"

"Fascinating," said the woman.

Bupp pulled some crumpled bills from her handbag and put them on the counter. The saleswoman sorted through them to find the amount needed and handed the rest back to Bupp along with her change. All the while, Eugenia Bupp kept up a colorful dialog on how she was going to have massive breast implants and begin making granny porn with the help of her twenty-year-old video producer boyfriend.

"There," said the woman, "I'm sure madam will find complete satisfaction with the garments. If not…well, never mind."

"Thanks, Popsicle," said Bupp snatching the bag from the saleswoman's outstretched hand. She began to shuffle away.

"I assume," sniffed the woman, "that you refer to me as 'Popsicle' since you found my manner formal to the point of being cold."

"Naw," said Eugenia Bupp with a smile and a dismissive wave, "that's not it."

"Oh?" said the woman relaxing somewhat.

"It's 'cause you act like you got a stick up your ass!"

– 47 –
Chesney in Disguise with Diamonds

S tand still," said Valerie Fierro, "or you're going to get stuck!"
"I already am stuck," moaned Lorraine Innis as Valerie applied another pin to the blue sequin cocktail dress Lorraine was wearing. "I'm stuck being someone I'm not. I'm stuck heading up an international charity with a man I was trying to bring to justice. I'm stuck as the most popular woman in the world. Stuck in this stupid photo shoot…"

"Being on the cover of *Vogue* is not a stupid photo shoot," said Valerie. "I would have loved to do it."

"Be my guest."

"Sorry," she said with a mocking smile, "but I'm not the most popular woman in the world. I'm only her cousin!"

"You're not my cousin," muttered Lorraine.

"That's what I always said. Hold still, and don't cross your arms like that. You'll ruin your cleavage!"

"This duct tape is sadistic."

"Welcome to my world," said Valerie with another sardonic smile. "Quit your complaining. At least the money is good."

"The money belongs to the charity!"

"Yeah, well, it's perfectly legal to take 20 or 30 percent off the top for administrative fees. And remember, there are all those endorsement deals."

"Don't remind me of those," said Lorraine. "I must have been out of my mind."

"You've got no one to blame but yourself," said Valerie. "You're the one who couldn't figure out that a woman without boobs and with a penis is what is commonly known as a man. If you had come to that simple conclusion, you would have saved yourself a lot of problems."

Lorraine sighed. "I've been through this before. Everything was happening so quickly. I couldn't think straight, and then I remembered that article on Dissociative Identity Disorder."

"Where people believe something other than what they see," said Valerie placing another pin in Lorraine's dress.

"Something like that," said Lorraine.

"But you got it backward," said Valerie. "Rather than thinking your mind was wrong, you figured your body was. How did the remarkable goddess of peace figure that one?"

"I've told you, the mind leads the rest of the body. If the mind believes something, that's it. If you woke up tomorrow with a man's body, you wouldn't say: 'what's happened to my mind? I'm really a man.' You'd say: 'what's happened to my body? I'm really a woman.'"

"But you were really a man," said Valerie.

"But I thought I was a woman," said Lorraine. "It's all that training and mental conditioning I was going through so I could fool Liverot."

"Too bad you fooled yourself, first."

"And then the accident shocked my mind into forgetting everything but Lorraine."

"You should have figured it out when you kept calling your own phone number and never got an answer," said Valerie.

"I couldn't have gotten an answer," said Lorraine, "because I wasn't there to answer it because I was someplace else calling myself."

Valerie rolled her eyes.

"Then after I saw the Colts Neck house was empty I stopped calling even though the number I was calling was really my apartment," continued Lorraine, "but I had to remember to forget that."

"You're giving me a headache," moaned Valerie.

"It's just a good thing my mother moved a few months before and they hadn't sold her house yet. It would have been very embarrassing to confront the new owners."

"It would have been better than introducing your mother to her new daughter," snorted Valerie. "And you didn't even figure it out when you saw the story about your landlady reporting you missing?"

"I didn't see the name, just the location, so I didn't read any further. When I came back to my senses..."

"I'm still waiting for that," muttered Valerie.

"When I remembered my real self," said Lorraine, "I called my landlady to explain I was on an extended business trip and would be away for at least a month. I called my mother and told her the same thing, so she wouldn't worry if she didn't hear from me."

"I hope that you told them you were going to Mars," said Valerie, "because the way you're going you'll be away a few years."

"Don't say that, not even as a joke!" said Lorraine. "Still, I guess it's proof that all my preparations were correct."

"It's proof that now you're stuck!"

"Yes, and I'm stuck," said Lorraine. "Granted, this is a good chance to get at Liverot from the inside for Martina's death, but being famous does make it a little difficult to make a clean getaway."

"Just slightly," said Valerie, "turn around and let me see how that looks."

Lorraine rotated slowly atop the low pedestal.

"Try to be a little more graceful," said Valerie. "You used to be so much more feminine."

"I used to think I was a woman."

"Well do it again. You can't hide out forever. You haven't made a public appearance in almost a month. Not ever since you had your freak-out in the backyard."

"That's why I agreed to do this photo shoot, though how I'm going to get away with it…"

"I could always hit you on the head," said Valerie, adding, "not hard, just enough to make you more Lorraine than Chesney."

"No thank you," said Lorraine. "I'll get it. After all, I've done it before. I just have to concentrate and then forget I'm concentrating."

"If you say so. Here, let's see it with the diamonds…" Valerie draped a diamond necklace around Lorraine's neck and sighed wistfully. "Some girls have all the luck. You get to wear incredible jewelry, including shoes covered with real diamond, and you can stand to pee."

"Maybe I can stand for that, but I won't stand for this pretentious thing," said Lorraine pulling the tiara from her hair.

"But the tiara completes the look," said Valerie.

"Not my look," said Lorraine. "It makes me look like a cross between the Queen of England and a three-year-old Halloween princess; both images I'm trying very hard to avoid."

Valerie reached for the tiara, but Lorraine tightened her grip on the accessory.

"Fine," said Valerie, "be that way…plain Lorraine!"

"And if all this weren't bad enough, there's that ridiculous publicity stunt by Beverly Marlton."

Valerie suppressed a giggle.

"It's not funny," said Lorraine. "I know I wasn't in my right mind when I let her give an exclusive to *People* to promote the book, and I wasn't all there when I wrote my fictional autobiography as a way to lure back my non-existent husband, but now half the world is out looking for Martin Innis."

"Anything to ease the heartache of their beloved Lorraine," snickered Valerie.

"That and trying to cash in on that $100,000 reward that Marlton set up anonymously for information leading to Martin's return. I still can't figure out why Beverly Marlton went along with the charade. I, that is

Chesney, worked there years ago, but I, Lorraine never did. Why would she cover for me?"

"You really are naïve as ever, aren't you?" said Valerie. "I would have thought being a woman would have smartened you up. She wants to sell books, and Lorraine was a hot property. And since then, you've only gotten hotter. Hold on, I'll be right back."

As Valerie exited the private dressing room at the designer's salon, Lorraine teetered off the pedestal on her three-inch diamond studded heels and crossed to the side table. There was a pile of magazines and newspapers, the majority of which still featured her on the cover. Instead of cooling the public's fascination with Lorraine, her retreat from the spotlight had only increased the demand. The release of her autobiography would probably start a new wave of adulation since she was contractually obligated to a series of promotional interviews and book signings. This trip to New York was the first time she'd ventured out of Valerie's townhouse in weeks, and no one had been allowed inside aside from Valerie's mother and sister. Though neither knew Lorraine's secret, they did know that they didn't have any relatives named "Lorraine." Despite this, they agreed not to talk to the media.

Lorraine's hermitage hadn't hurt contributions to the Cross of Lorraine Foundation which was being overseen by Valerie. A team of administrative assistants from the bank's secretarial pool processed the millions of dollars in donations before forwarding them electronically to the charity's account in Gibraltar.

Neither had Lorraine's absence hurt the career of Purvis Twankey. *The Ballad of Lorraine* had become the number one song in the country and stayed there for over a month. It was soon joined atop the charts by Twankey's next song, *Accidental Love* (which Lorraine suspected was about Valerie and the car crash) and his version of *The Star Spangled Banner*. Purvis was particularly popular in his native country, as testified to by the fact that his *Star Spangled Banner* went gold in England, despite being banned by the BBC for reasons that they didn't want to confuse their listeners by repeatedly playing a foreign anthem.

Aside from Purvis Twankey, a number of singers had hits jumping on the Lorraine bandwagon. These included several versions of the old Nat King Cole song, *Sweet Lorraine*, a country tune entitled: *The Pursuit of Martin Innis*, and a children's chorus singing *I Saw Lorraine Kissing Santa Claus*. The most interesting of these efforts was a Gangsta Rap offering: *Lorraine Cracker Assassin Attacker*.

As for others whom the media dubbed "POLs" (Pals of Lorraine), Patsy Einfalt, despite her initial eagerness to appear on television, stopped giving interviews once she realized that the camera made her hips look enormous. She joined a gym in an attempt to slim down to more Lorraine-like proportions with hopes of attracting Purvis Twankey.

The Girl in the Diamond Studded Heels

Peter Liverot, though not technically one of Lorraine's pals, was nevertheless the man to contact to arrange a Lorraine endorsement deal. According to Valerie, Lorraine's seclusion and her refusal to speak with him on the phone made Liverot nervous: especially as it followed close on the heels of Valerie's recovery. Other than that, the banker couldn't be happier as the endorsements he negotiated were bringing in money faster than he could count it. In addition to product endorsements, Liverot was working furiously to copyright Lorraine's name and likeness. This came in response to her being the hottest subject during that year's Halloween celebrations. Millions of little girls wanted to be Lorraine for trick or treating. Costume and wig shops quickly ran out of light brown shag hairpieces for girls not fortunate enough to already have a style close to Lorraine's. Adults also got into the spirit of that October, and no costume party was complete without at least three or four Lorraines, a few Purvis Twankeys, and even a smattering of Valeries (pretending to be comatose). Wags who couldn't attend parties to which they'd been invited explained that they'd be absent as Martin Innis.

Liverot was angry with himself for not having anticipated the demand for Lorraine costumes. He wasn't going to be caught off-guard for Christmas, however, and negotiated a deal with Mattel for a Lorraine Innis doll. Despite not being the same unrealistic proportions as Barbie, the toy maker was retrofitting millions of the classic dolls with new heads of the even more popular human heroine. Thousands of workers in the Far East were frantically sewing tiny gray jumpers and white turtleneck sweaters. The demand was definitely there as children throughout the world had begun asking their parents for Lorraine dolls before the toymakers and Liverot had even thought to produce them. There was also a full line of Lorraine Innis toys including board and video games, coloring books, lunchboxes, and even an electric road racing set featuring her AMC Pacer along with three news vans.

Additionally, the name "Lorraine," usually towards the bottom of the most popular names for girls, jumped to number one, as new mothers sought to give their daughters a name to live up to. "Lawrence," while not actually the male counterpart to "Lorraine," also saw a rise in popularity, along with the obscure male name "Enos."

Hairdressers were also cashing in on what the media had labeled "Lorraine-a-Mania," by offering special coiffures they called either the "Lorraine Cut," or the "Innis Do." Fashion experts began imitating the Lorraine style, though, in reality, they were copying the tastes of Valerie Fierro. Darker colors were "in," especially hunter green, charcoal gray, ruby, burgundy, and black. Tweeds were also hot, as were skirts of all lengths – since Lorraine rarely wore slacks in public. The Lorraine craze was especially encouraging to women with larger noses since, thanks to Mrs. Innis, they were, for the first time in their lives, in vogue. Some plastic surgeons even reported patients asking for implants to augment tinier beaks to more "Innisesque" proportions. Seemingly overnight, everything was judged through a Lorraine-colored filter. Five foot seven was now seen as the preferred height for women, 130 pounds the ideal weight, 36-28-37 the perfect measurements.

Lorraine shook her head as she scanned the trade journal reports on her success as both a profit and non-profit entity. Her disturbed reverie was interrupted as Valerie returned with a small tray of various bottles and tubes.

"The courier just brought it over," said Valerie, "just in time, too."

"What is all that stuff?"

"This isn't stuff. This is another goldmine...the Lorraine Innis line of cosmetics. Remember? You made us take the third lowest bidder."

"That's because they made the makeup I was already using."

"Your scruples are costing us millions," said Valerie uncapping a tube of lipstick. "I still can't believe you turned down that one ad!"

"You've got to be joking," said Lorraine.

"Three million bucks for a day's work in the fresh air, and you said 'no!'"

Lorraine placed her hands on her hips. "I was not going to stand half-naked in front of the Hotel DuPont next to a double for Nikolai Kropotkin and say: 'I dreamed I saved the world in my Maidenform Bra! I don't even wear that brand!'"

"Fame is wasted on the wrong people," said Valerie, "now, hold still, I've got to do your lips. This shade is perfect. It's called *Burgundy Lorraine Wine.*"

"Don't these marketing geniuses realize that 'Burgundy' and 'Lorraine' are two separate regions of France?" noted Lorraine. "It's as ridiculous as saying 'California Jersey tomatoes!'"

"Just loosen up, will you? You're the girl in the diamond studded heels! Just have fun with it."

Fun? Lorraine thought. This wasn't about fun. It was about the man responsible for Martina's death. If, because of her fame, Lorraine could no longer spy on Peter Liverot, she would have to find another mole to do her digging. Fortunately, she had.

– 48 –
The Fondu Pot of
a Grateful Nation

Two hundred miles to the south, Quinton Merton was feeling light-hearted as he dismissed his National Security team from the Oval Office. They had just smoothed out the final wrinkles paving the way for his embracing of the Lorraine Accord. Although Kropotkin had lined up every other nuclear power, the Accord was virtually worthless without the participation of the United States.

As the last of the advisors left the room, Davis Flemming entered.

"Davis, beautiful day isn't it?" said the President.

"Yes, Sir," said Flemming. "Dr. Egonski is here for your session."

"I don't think I'll need that today."

"Are you sure? Usually, after a National Security briefing, you have the full treatment."

"Not today. I'm in the pink. Never been better!"

"Shall I ask Dr. Egonski to stand at the ready, Mr. President? Perhaps with some Legos or the Etch-a-Sketch?"

"I don't think so," said Merton leaning back in his swivel chair and clenching his fists. "I've got the ol' firm grip back again. Don't you think so?"

Davis Flemming nodded. He wasn't patronizing his boss. Quinton Merton did look the picture of mental alertness and physical vigor. In his dark blue suit, the President could have easily modeled for the cover of a men's fashion magazine.

"Oh, you may want to be in on this next thing," said the President. "I'm calling Kropotkin to tell him we're accepting his plan. Take notes. It'll be good for my memoirs." He picked up the direct line to the Kremlin. "Are you there Nikolai?" Merton motioned for Flemming to sit down across from him.

"They're going to get him," whispered the President, "must be in the bathroom… Nikolai! Yes, it's me, Quinton… Yes, I know we had scheduled to talk later on, but I couldn't wait… I've smoothed out the last few bumps and we're all set to come on board with your plan… Yes, the Lorraine Accord… No, no, I think it's a fine name… I admire your humility in naming it after her. After all, it is your idea, Nikolai… Yes, yes, okay, I suppose she was your inspiration… After all, you'd know that better than me…. What's that? …Me? Well, I think she's one of our finest citizens."

"Of course I'm sincere when I say that Nikolai… In whose eye? … Oh, a pig's … Now, Nikolai, how can you say… No, no, you're right, I've never actually invited her to the White House, not yet that is. But, I've been meaning to. In fact, I think we'll have her down here for Christmas. …She can't? Why not? …You've invited her to Moscow? … Yes, that was very nice of you, Nikolai… Yes, very nice."

Flemming watched as the President's jaw tightened. It was just Merton's luck. He couldn't even sign on to a peace agreement without putting his foot through it first. Flemming wondered if Dr. Egonski had left yet.

"Well, I can be a pretty nice guy too, you know…" continued Quinton Merton. "You're not the only nice guy running a country… Never you mind. Just be assured we're planning something nice for Mrs. Innis, as well… What do you mean you saw her first?… Yeah? Well, she happens to be a citizen of the United States… Oh, don't give me that citizen of the world crap, Nikolai… She still gets her mail here, she still votes here… What?… You don't know that for a fact, she could have voted for me… Well, what of it? Okay, okay, I'm sorry I brought it up… Yes, well, I know you saw her first… Yes, you're right. She should spend the holidays with you."

Quinton Merton rolled his eyes.

"Well, then Nikolai, I guess we'll all be getting together to sign this thing… Okay, the Lorraine Accord. Say, would you like to have it at the White House?… Don't get so touchy, it was just a suggestion… Where do you want to have it then?… Colts Neck, New Jersey?… What the hell is in… Oh, that's where she lived… Well, anywhere you want… Sure, you can have it in the United States, I just offered you the White House didn't I?… Anywhere in the whole damn country… Okay, I'm sorry, sure. It would be an honor… Of course, I'd be happy to co-host with Mrs. Innis… It will be a pleasure… Now, when…Oh, yes, I understand all the details have to be worked out with the other countries…Well, when you're ready, let me know… Thank you… Okay, Nikolai, yes, my people will iron it all out with your people… Goodbye."

"That cheap chiseler," snapped Merton as he hung up the phone. "He's trying to steal that Innis woman from us!"

"Well, Mr. President," said Flemming, "they do have a relationship. You've never even spoken to her."

"Is that my fault?"

"Do you want me to get Dr. Egonski?"

"No," said Merton. "That's not necessary. It's just a little frustrating. Here I am trying to get in on some of this…what are they calling it?"

"Lorraine-a-Mania," sighed Flemming.

"Right, here we are trying to cash in on the most popular public figure since Elvis, and that Russian upstages us again."

"He's inviting Mrs. Innis to Russia for Christmas?"

"That's not the half of it," said Merton "He's bought her house for her."

"From whom?"

"Her cockamamie husband put it on the market and skipped town, and now Kropotkin bought it back for her. It's a surprise. He's going to give it to her for Christmas! Why didn't we think of that?"

"Get her something else."

"Like what?" said Merton as he began pacing. "What can I get her to top a house? A housewarming present? That'll get my poll numbers up! Kropotkin hands her the keys to her house, and I come along and say, 'Please accept this lovely fondue pot as a gift from your grateful nation.'"

"Give her something money can't buy," said Flemming, "like her husband."

"Her husband?"

"According to the media, Martin Innis ran away from a wife to whom he was devoted because of her sudden fame. The rumor is that Innis, an Irish national, is running from some secret in his past that even his wife doesn't know about."

"Yeah? What?" asked the President.

"One can only guess. Innis was a former merchant seaman working in fruit-exporting. But if you put it all together with a little imagination, it could be that he was running guns for the IRA."

"Individual Retirement Accounts?" asked Merton who used to serve on the Senate Banking Committee.

"The Irish Republican Army," said Flemming.

"But that's illegal."

"Exactly. At the very least, Martin Innis could be involved with international weapons smuggling. Who knows? Maybe he was tied up with some terrorist acts or assassinations. Wouldn't that be ironic? An international hitman, with a wife famous for foiling an assassination."

"Can't we get the low-down from the boys at the Bureau or the CIA?"

"They're working on it, Mr. President. So far neither the FBI nor the CIA has any record on Martin Innis. Nor does Interpol or Scotland Yard."

"Probably Innis is an alias," said the President.

"Precisely," said Flemming. "That's why we need to expand our probe of Lorraine Innis to include what her husband is wanted for and where he is."

"Then we get him and lock him up, right?"

"No, we get him, and return him to the bosom of his wife…"

"Bosom," repeated the President.

Flemming looked at Merton. He wasn't sure if the President was behaving lecherously or merely being infantile over Lorraine's breasts.

"…the bosom of his wife," continued the aide, "metaphorically speaking – along with a complete pardon for any crimes committed in the past by Martin Innis."

"What if he didn't commit these crimes against us?"

"Most likely he didn't, or else he wouldn't have been using this country as his hideout. Flex your international influence," said Flemming. "Promise some foreign aid, buy the pardon. What he did doesn't have to be publicized, only forgiven. And you'll be seen as the hero."

"The man who brought peace to the peacemaker," said Merton. "I like the sound of that. It'll play in the polls."

"Precisely," said Flemming with a smile.

– 49 –
The Hot Flashes of
Hogan's Last Hero

Luckily, Patsy Einfalt's favorite TV show was *Hogan Heroes*; lucky for Lorraine Innis, that is. When Lorraine needed someone to ferret out what Peter Liverot was up to, the perfect candidate was an executive assistant who thought covert operations were fun, low-risk, and over in a half-hour.

Patsy never imagined that her boss was up to anything crooked. For that matter, she never thought anyone was up to anything devious. In fact, when Lorraine first approached her to provide a glimpse into Liverot's private files, Patsy was shocked that the woman she most admired, the woman who looked so good on television, would ask her to do something even remotely sneaky. While he was often crude, and always less than considerate, that didn't mean Peter Liverot was dishonest.

It was only after she inadvertently learned from payroll records that Marcia Capicola was actually a married woman named Marcia Laffler, that Patsy realized that her boss was capable of the worse kind of falsehood. As a single mother who desperately longed for a husband, Patsy believed the marriage vow was the most sacred a person could make. Break that, and anything was possible. Besides, Patsy reasoned, Lorraine wouldn't ask her to do something dishonest, or if she did, the ends must justify the means. She would see what she could find out, hoping against hope that she would find nothing, and then everyone could go back to being trusting, honest people.

Deciding to become a corporate spy was one thing. How to obtain Liverot's private files was a little more difficult, especially as she wasn't a devious person herself, her knowledge of *Hogan's Heroes* notwithstanding. She knew he kept certain drawers of his desk locked at all times, and he kept his key ring in his pants pocket. Patsy reasoned that if he had anything secret, it would probably be inside that drawer. This neat bit of deduction was the easy part. How to get into her boss' drawers was another matter.

Using Hogan as her role model, Patsy envisioned a number of clever diversions to separate Liverot from both his keys and his desk. Unfortunately, these all involved elaborate schemes that included such elements as clay impressions, smoke bombs, and the cooperation of at least half a dozen Allied prisoners of war. She was about to call Lorraine and admit she was stumped when the solution came to Patsy via a bottle of pills at the bottom of her purse. There she saw her prescription for the combination pain reliever and muscle relaxant her gynecologist had given her for cramps. Recalling their effectiveness, Patsy uncapped the bottle and crushed one of the pills with the base of her tape dispenser. She then dipped her finger in the resulting dust. It had no taste. The secretary's hands shook as she counted out three more of the oval pills and pulverized them inside a piece of paper, all the while watching and listening for any sign that Liverot was coming. Luckily, the bank president was on the phone with his door closed. Within 90 seconds Patsy had the prescription dust waiting at the bottom of Peter Liverot's coffee mug. Ten minutes later, after he finished his phone call, Patsy took her boss his mid-morning coffee. Ten minutes after that Patsy was summoned back into Liverot's office.

"Hey, Patty," asked Peter Liverot, "Is it hot in here?"

"No, sir, not particularly. I'm comfortable." Welcome to the club, she thought, you're having a hot flash.

"Yeah, well, could you turn on the air?"

"Maintenance has already shut it off for the season, Mr. Liverot," said Patsy, "but I'm sure they could start it up again if you'd like."

"No, that's not necessary," said the banker with an odd silly grin. "It just must be me. I think maybe…"

Liverot froze in mid-sentence as his eyes glazed over. All Liverot would have needed was a slice of pineapple on his head, and he could have done a fair imitation of an Easter ham. Patsy craned her neck sideways as she examined her boss' face. Liverot slid down in his desk chair and almost fell out of it all together.

Patsy lurched forward to catch the hefty executive, but his skid was halted when his feet hit the corner of the desk wedging him into a semi-upright position. Since his eyes were still open, Patsy wondered if Liverot was conscious. A few waves of her hand in front of his eyes confirmed he was out cold. Gingerly, she shut his eyelids and then reached into his coat pocket for the keys.

Next Patsy tried the key in the lock. It worked. Inside there were several files, including ones labeled "INNIS," and "GIBRALTAR," in Liverot's handwriting. She took the files into the outer office, where she copied them on her desktop Xerox machine. Within five minutes the two dossiers were safely tucked back in the drawer, and the keys were returned to

Liverot's pocket. Patsy tiptoed out of his office, closing the door behind her. At her desk, she began reading the documents from the folio on Lorraine. On the second page of the file, Patsy let out a faint scream as she read what was written there.

"Holy Moly!" She whispered. "Lorraine was right! Mr. Liverot isn't very nice."

She picked up the phone and called Lorraine. Valerie answered.

"Valerie, this is Patsy."

"Yes?"

"I just copied those files."

"What files?"

"Mr. Liverot's private files, the ones that Lorraine asked me to get."

"What?" said Valerie. "Oh, wait, yes, those files."

"It's dynamite," said Patsy. "Is Lorraine there?"

"No, she's... she's taking a nap. I'll tell her about it. What did you find out?"

Patsy proceeded to read Liverot's notes over the phone, quickly, and in hushed tones, not knowing when her boss would awake.

"Well, that's it," said Patsy. "Do you want me to send you the copy?"

"Yes, no wait," said Valerie. "On second thought, you'd better destroy the copies."

"Destroy them? But I don't have that much of the prescription left, and it's almost that time."

There was a long silence on the other end.

"Okay..." said Valerie slowly, "whatever. Just destroy those copies. You don't want him finding you with any evidence. And don't mention it again, not to anyone, not even to me, you wouldn't want to risk being overheard. Just leave everything to me."

"Thanks," said Patsy, "and don't forget to tell Lorraine."

"Don't worry." said Valerie, "I'll take care of everything."

– 50 –
A Family Business
Minus the Family

Father Mike Valvano strolled past the collection of aspiring goons lounging around the gravel driveway. He showed them less notice then he had to similar gargoyles at Notre Dame Cathedral. The only difference he could see was that the French sculptures had been erected to ward off evil spirits, while this current collection nestled in the rolling hills of southern Pennsylvania were there to protect them.

They all looked young, thought the priest, as he walked by, too young. Still, playing at being hired muscle was the next logical step for young men raised on gangster movies and violent video games.

It was only as he reached the front door of the large house that Mike Valvano saw a familiar face, though hardly less intimidating.

"Hello, Alphonse," said the priest with a smile, extending his arms to the chief gargoyle.

The threatening features of the man at the door melted into a mixture of surprise and delight.

"Mikey," cried the man, embracing Valvano in a hug that was potentially lethal. "Mikey, what are you doing here? We ain't seen you since I don't know."

The two men held each other at arm's length.

"It's good to see you, Alphonse."

"I view it in a similarly fortuitous light," smiled the gargoyle.

"Still taking your vocabulary course, I see," said Mike.

"Indubitably and incontrovertibly," said Alphonse. "But what brings you here? We didn't know you were arriving."

"I didn't tell anyone," said the priest with a shrug.

"That's ill-advised."

"Really? When do you need to make an appointment to come to your own home?"

"You ain't resided here for years, Mikey," said Alphonse, "not since you went away to cemetery…"

"Seminary…"

"Anyways, there's lots of new employees in our junior executive program," said Alphonse, nodding towards the young men. "They don't know you."

"I always thought this…" Mike pointed to his clerical collar.

"You forget when we wuz kids? Like how Joey Screwdriver was offed by a guy dressed like a bishop?"

Mike Valvano nodded. "You're right, Alphonse. I'll keep that in mind. Is my brother around?"

"No," said Alphonse, "but your grandmother's here. She don't go out much anymore."

Mike Valvano thought a moment. "No, that's okay. I don't want to bother her, especially not dressed like this. She never quite got over my vocational choice. Besides, this is business."

"Mr. Rosen's inside," said Alphonse. "Come, let me escort you…"

The erudite gargoyle nodded for one of his lieutenants to take his place, and then led Mike Valvano through the carved oak door into the stone tiled foyer. He walked over to a telephone, dialed two numbers, spoke in hushed tones, and then hung up.

"He'll see you in the liberry," said Alphonse. "Right this way…"

"I know where the library is," laughed Valvano. "Unless you're rebuilt the house since last Christmas."

"Oh right," said Alphonse. "Then I'll see ya upon your egress."

With that, Alphonse returned to his post.

The library hadn't been moved since last Christmas, nor even redecorated in Mike Valvano's lifetime. Containing more paintings and photographs than books, still, it was a record of his family's history from their roots in Sicily to their recent prosperity in America. As he scanned the faces on the walls, all of them familiar, some through family stories, some through personal contact, Mike Valvano couldn't help but feel a bittersweet attachment to them all, despite his past efforts to separate from them.

"Michael," said voice from behind. "I wish you'd called ahead. I could have given you a better welcome."

Valvano wheeled around to see the impressive figure of Julius Rosen standing in the doorway. The lawyer closed the door. Both men simultaneously motioned for the other to have a seat, as if they both were the rightful host in the home that neither really owned.

"Julie," said Valvano, sitting opposite him on the leather sofa. "It seems that the law continues to agree with you."

Rosen tilted his head to one side. "Jews shouldn't eat too much Italian cooking," he said.

"You could always convert," said the priest, "I can get you in wholesale."

"That's an old stereotype," said the lawyer. "I often pay retail. Do you realize all we need is a Protestant here and we could start a joke?"

"True," said Valvano with a smile, "but not for much longer. That's why I'm here. I had hoped to talk to Robert about it."

"Well, your brother is off pursuing his private...hobby," said Rosen. "He seems to do a lot of that lately. I don't know where he goes."

"I can guess," said Michael with a disapproving shake of his head as he thought of Robert's wife and children. "Still, I may as well bounce it off you first since you'll do most of the legwork on it. I need to go into business."

"Business? You mean the family's business?" said Rosen genuinely surprised. "Michael, you never wanted anything to do with it. Isn't that why you became a priest?"

"Yeah, well," said Valvano evasively. "I'd like to be set up in something legitimate, if possible. I don't want to get involved in family affairs, per se."

"You got involved a few months ago."

"In what way?"

"Your brother told me," said the lawyer, "that it was you who saved Peter Liverot's life."

"Liverot," sneered Valvano. "I didn't know that's what I was doing. God forgive me, but I wouldn't have shed any tears if he'd gotten what he deserved."

"Still, it was your call that made your brother reconsider his decision. Fortunately, for Liverot and for all of us, your call turned out to be a very shrewd and profitable move."

Valvano almost responded, but kept silent. Julius Rosen was himself too shrewd and had too keen an eye for profit to reveal any more information beyond the basic facts.

"But," continued the lawyer, "you said you want to set up a business. I assume this would be in connection with your work for the church."

"No," said Valvano, "I'm going to be leaving the priesthood. I want to establish a business so I can make a living. I want to get married."

– 51 –
Finding a Husband
Where You Least Expect Him

L orraine Innis stared out of the window of the British Airways jet as it began its descent into the dawn over southern England. Sitting beside her, Valerie Fierro looked up from her copy of Lorraine's autobiography. "You know," she said, "this really isn't bad, though you did shovel it on pretty thick in spots."

"At the time I was strongly motivated to find the elusive Martin Innis, remember?"

"And now they found him for you in Ireland," chortled Valerie. "Merry Christmas!"

Lorraine moaned and rested her head in her hand. They were on the first leg of a trip that would include spending Christmas as guests of Nikolai Kropotkin. Before reaching Moscow, however, they would spend a week in London promoting the British release of Lorraine's memoirs. There were scheduled stops at Harrods, and the Waterstones on Trafalgar Square. In addition, the numerous book retailers up and down Charing Cross Road arranged to block off the street for a Lorraine Innis street fair. She would also appear at Hamley's, the giant Regent Street toy emporium to unveil the Lorraine Innis fashion-adventure doll. As if all this weren't enough, the Lord Mayor was to honor Lorraine during a ceremony in Berkeley Square, the locale where she and Martin had supposedly gotten engaged. There had been talk of Lorraine being presented to the Queen, though this never materialized due to scheduling conflicts. She would, however, meet with the Prime Minister in a special afternoon tea at Number 10 Downing Street.

All these gala plans were upstaged, however, just as they were boarding their flight to England. There, as Lorraine approached the security checkpoint, a flock of reporters rushed up to get her reaction to the news that two middle-aged tourists from Rhode Island had discovered

Martin Innis working in a Dublin Pub. One reporter handed Lorraine his cell phone with a downloaded snapshot of a bewildered Martin. He had been working there under the name of Seamus Gynwittie. Another reporter gave her a special edition of *USA Today* with the headline: "MARTIN FOUND!" in a type size usually reserved for declarations of war. The subheading announced: "Lorraine En Route for Early Holiday Present." Lorraine grabbed the paper, declined comment, and hurried into the relative privacy of airport security.

Once on board the airplane, Lorraine read the story, including the barman's denial of ever hearing the name of Martin Innis, let alone using it. The pub's owner admitted that "Seamus" had only started working there six weeks earlier. Reluctantly, Seamus/Martin agreed to accompany the American tourists to London for a rendezvous with Lorraine Innis. To induce Martin to go, the Americans agreed to pay his way, a small price to pay in light of the $100,000 reward they hoped to receive as the first prize in the worldwide scavenger hunt.

Now as the airplane touched down, Lorraine's apprehension grew.

"What am I going to say to this man?" she asked Valerie. "What am I going to say to those people from Rhode Island?"

"I try not to talk to people from Rhode Island," said Valerie not bothering to look up from her reading.

"I'm not kidding," said Lorraine. "I've sicced the world on that poor man. He's been dragged from his place of work, been thrust into the media spotlight and had his life turned upside down all because of me."

Valerie looked at her. "Gee, I can't imagine what that's like!"

"Please, going back to England is difficult enough after what happened the last time I was here."

"Oh, yeah," said Valerie, "that girl..."

Lorraine looked away, fought back a tear, took a deep breath, and then turned back. "Yeah, well, you seem to be doing okay. First class flights, the best hotels…"

"Look," said Valerie, "don't let it get to you, any of it. You've been doing great. You almost have me convinced again, and I know."

"Keep your voice down, nobody else knows."

"That's what I mean," said Valerie. "No one suspects. As for Martin, or whatever his name is, it's not like this guy is really married to you. Just say he's not the guy, and keep going. It's not like you have to give him conjugal rights or anything, as interesting as that would be."

"Very funny."

"You only have to worry about one guy. I've got three men to sort out: Boden, and the two you saddled me with, one with a clerical collar and one who needs a dog collar. I'm sure you've heard that Twankey's album went double platinum."

"*The Music Inside Me Head*," said Lorraine citing the album's title.

"More like the mucus inside his head," said Valerie. "I suspect that one love song is about me."

"I think that's sweet, you should be honored."

"Oh, really? Most of the other songs are about horses," muttered Valerie.

A few minutes later they were being whisked directly through the fast track customs process reserved for VIPs. Lorraine's passport, obtained at the last minute by special arrangement with the State Department, bore a diplomatic designation at the insistence of the Secretary of State.

Upon exiting customs, they were greeted by a barrage of flashes from the army of photographers and reporters waiting for them. The airport's VIP handler was at Lorraine's side and led her to a nearby podium to address the press. The reporters began shouting her name. Lorraine pointed towards a tall man in the second row for the first question.

"Mrs. Innis," began a man with the British accent, "have you spoken with your husband yet?"

"No," said Lorraine. "We've only just gone through customs."

"He's here, you know," added the reporter, "in the airport."

The VIP hostess confirmed this with a whisper in Lorraine's ear.

"Yes," said Lorraine, "he's waiting in a nearby lounge, and I'll be seeing him directly to find out if it really is Martin, but I don't want to get my hopes too high." She nodded towards a woman in the front row.

"Lorraine," said a woman in a thick French accent, "seence you 'av borrowed your name and zat of your fondation from a reegion of la belle France, weel you be deeseminating any of the proceeds zere?"

"I didn't take my name from your country," said Lorraine. She was annoyed at the suggestion that she would be nameless without the generosity of "la belle France." "As for the Foundation, though we share a common name, it was not my decision to dub it the 'Cross of Lorraine.' As for whether or not any of our charity has gone to your country..."

Lorraine was about to accuse the French of trying to extort money from a charitable organization for the use of her name. Sensing this, Valerie jumped in front on the microphone.

"I think I'm a little more familiar with the day to day accounting processes," interrupted Valerie. "In the two months since its inception, the Cross of Lorraine has received more than 1.8 billion dollars from a variety of sources including corporate contributions and individual donations from around the world."

"And precious little of that from France," grumbled Lorraine to herself.

"Also," continued Valerie, "Mrs. Innis has earned the foundation another 900 million through the proceeds of her autobiography and commercial endorsements. Of that combined total of 2.7 billion, more than 2.4 billion has already been donated to charities throughout the world, including hospitals, schools, churches, and homes for the aged. The foundation's grant board has tried as best they could to distribute the funds proportionally to the regions from which the contributions were received. In light of this policy, I can confidently say that your nation has received their fair part of funds from the Cross of Lorraine."

"Will you be giving out any cheques in London?" asked another man.

"We've received great support," said Lorraine, "not only from the people of Great Britain but from their corporations." She glanced at the French reporter. "And we'll be making several presentations throughout our stay here, including one to the Prime Minister tomorrow afternoon."

The roomful of reporters broke into applause.

"Now if you'll excuse my cousin and me," said Lorraine, taking advantage of the applause to make their exit, "we have a rather tight schedule. I'm sure we'll see you again over the next few days."

Led by the airport representative, Lorraine and Valerie stepped off the platform and left the room. As they exited, however, Lorraine heard one reporter at the back shouting a question about Gibraltar. The reference caused a look of concern to cloud Valerie's face as she quickened her pace out of the room.

– 52 –
Turning Putty into Platinum with Parvo Slouch

L ook, son," said Parvo Slouch, "I wouldn't steer you wrong, would I? Hey, you got enough hot sauce on that burrito? It ain't easy getting that brand here in the middle of Manhattan, you know?"

"Ee, no, Mr. Slouch," said Purvis Twankey, wiping a jalapeno-induced tear from his eye, "the sauce is proper champion."

"I'm not talking about the food," said the record producer. "That was an aside. I'm talking about your career."

While Purvis sweated down the remainder of his lunch, Parvo Slouch began to pace up and down the midtown recording studio, pausing only to avoid a microphone boom, or to adjust his shorts beneath his tight blue jeans.

"I mean, don't get me wrong, Purvis, you're like a son to me, if I had a limey for a son. That's why I helped you clean up your songs, and your style."

Purvis looked down at his expensively tacky western duds, which were identical to those Parvo Slouch wore, albeit about six sizes smaller.

"You lucked into me, the best country producer outside of Nashville, and I lucked into you, one of the freshest raw talents in the last ten years. It's just that I hate to see you waste your talent."

"But I've got three songs top of the pops," said Purvis with a mouthful of burrito.

Parvo wheeled around and pointed his finger at the skinny Englishman. "Right, and that's all you got from that session. The rest are all non-starters. Folks don't want to hear you croon about what a nice horse you've got, or how much you'd like to a have a nice horse, or how you miss your dead horse. Once in a while? Okay, but not on half your tracks. Look at your three hits: *The Ballad of Lorraine*, beautiful, touching, inspirational; *The Star Spangled Banner*, patriotic, even if it is 'bout somebody else's country;

Accidental Love, a love song, and not a damn equine quadruped in the batch. Coincidence? I don't think so."

"Ee, but I want to be a cowboy singer, like Roy Rogers or Gene Autry," said Purvis.

"Fine, fine," said Parvo, "but just diversify your portfolio, and get your priorities straight. You saddle the horse, sing about the girl, not the other way around. You got a girl?"

Purvis thought about Valerie and sighed. "Aye, I do, an' all…"

"But?"

"I don't think she thinks much of me."

Parvo Slouch stopped pacing and knocked Purvis' cowboy hat off his head, then vigorously rubbed the singer's sandy hair.

"That's great, that's perfect," said the producer.

"It is?"

"You bet your snakeskin boots it is, son! Nothing makes a good country song like unrequited love. Pulls right on the old heartstrings it does. There's gold in them there heartaches…gold albums, that is."

The producer grabbed a pile of paper from a nearby console and slapped it down on the music stand in front of Purvis.

"That's what I want you to do, write about the girl, nothing but the girl. Let the horses go out to pasture for a while. You're going to do a theme album!"

"A theme album?" Purvis scratched his head. "Ee, I dunno, Mr. Slouch. I sung about her once in *Accidental Love*. I had her name in the song at first, but I took it out."

"That was about her? Perfect. Well, what's her name?"

"Miss Valerie…"

"Use it, sing about it. Sing about how you love her, how you'd like to love her, how you're sad because she doesn't love you."

"What if she doesn't like it?"

"Like it? How could she not like it? It shows you really care. Say it with music. Not many women get even one song written about them. She's going to get a whole best-selling platinum hit album about her. She'll be putty in your hands."

"Aye?"

"I guarantee it," said Parvo, "now wipe that hot sauce off your face. You got a theme album to write, and the theme is Miss Valerie!"

– 53 –
The Failed Audition of Seamus Gynwittie

"You almost lost it with that French reporter," whispered Valerie, as the airport's VIP handler led her and Lorraine through the back corridors to the private reception room where Lorraine would be "reunited" with her husband.

"You've got to watch what you say," continued Valerie. "Remember, the media loves you, so don't blow it. Try to be a little more, well…"

"Lorraine-like?" said Lorraine

"Exactly."

"Or maybe the phrase is 'Lorrainish,' or 'Lorrainesque.'"

"You know what I mean, smart-ass," said Valerie. "You're the world's sweetheart, act like it."

"It was easier then, remember?" muttered Lorraine, as she watched the airport representative three yards ahead of them. "Besides, isn't it a woman's prerogative to act bitchy now and then?"

"Yes, but not until you've actually had PMS; until then behave yourself especially in front of reporters. They can make or break you."

"I still can't understand why no one has seen through it yet, especially with all the coverage I've been getting. And I'd still like to know who's been fooling around with my records? The only fake ID I ever made was the one I carried in my wallet. I never created a birth certificate, college transcripts, marriage license records, or any of it, but somehow it's all showed up. That and…"

"And what?" said Valerie.

"Nothing," said Lorraine, though she wondered who was sending her the anonymous notes. She had thought, in her self-delusion, that the first had been from Martin. Since awakening to her true identity, Lorraine had received two more notes, both expressing undying love. She would have ascribed them to some crank, but there was something unsettling about them, so much so that she hadn't even shared them with Valerie. Perhaps, Lorraine thought, the writer would come forward now that she was in England. She would have preferred meeting that person, whoever they were, instead of the replacement Martin Innis awaiting her down the corridor.

Their guide stopped in front of a door marked: "VIP Lounge."

"This is it," sighed Lorraine.

"Do you want to go in alone?" asked Valerie, "I can go have a drink."

"Are you kidding? Don't you dare leave me."

Their escort opened the door. "If you need anything, there's a hostess in the adjoining suite."

Both Lorraine and Valerie thanked her and entered the room. There, inside the plush lounge were a man and woman sitting on a leather sofa. Lorraine saw no trace of the man who was supposed to be Martin Innis.

"I'm Valerie Fierro, and this is my cousin, Lorraine Innis," said Valerie to the couple.

"We know," said the man, who was dressed in a blue polyester suit. He had a hollow sort of voice that seemed to emanate from a few inches above his head even though his lips were moving. This, combined with his bulging eyes, gave him the appearance of benign insanity.

"We recognize your picture from the cover of *Ladies Home Journal*, at least I do," admitted the woman, who was dressed in a cheap copy of the designer suit Valerie was wearing. "You look just like your picture."

"Only you're much prettier in person, Miss Fierro," he said. He then looked at Lorraine. "And you look exactly like your picture."

Lorraine smirked.

"That's very kind of you," said Valerie, "and you are…"

"We're the Whirleys, Edwin, and Eloise. I'm Edwin," confessed the man. "We found Mrs. Innis' husband for her."

"And where is he?" asked Valerie.

"Oh, he's in the bathroom," said Eloise.

"Or the 'loo,' like you folks say over here," said Edwin.

"We're Americans, too," Lorraine reminded him.

"He's had a couple of beers while we were waiting."

"Good heavens, he isn't drunk, is he?" asked Lorraine.

"I don't think so. I had one too, but you folks like your beer warm," said Edwin Whirley, apparently still assuming that he and his wife were the only Americans in England.

Valerie herded the Whirleys towards the door opposite from the one through which she and Lorraine had entered.

"Could you excuse the Innises?" Valerie asked with a smile as she shoved them out of the room. "It's a family moment. You understand."

"Certainly," said Eloise, "we can wait with the hostess."

"That's where we got the beer," added Edwin. "They got food too, we'll have a sandwich, or maybe we'll try some of your fish and chips."

"That's fine," said Valerie, almost shutting the couple's heads in the door as she closed it.

"Don't forget our reward. We'll be right here," called Edwin as the door clicked shut.

"Thanks," said Lorraine, sitting down. "I didn't want to face this guy with them in the room."

"That's what I thought," said Valerie. "After all, who knows how…"

Before Valerie could complete her sentence, a third door opened and into the room stepped a tall, good-looking man with red hair and green eyes. The man glanced at Valerie, who was standing to his right and then to Lorraine who was seated across from him. After looking at them both, he decided to approach Valerie.

"How d'ya do," said the man offering his right hand to Valerie. "Seamus Gynwittie, at yer service."

"Valerie Fierro."

"Ah," nodded Seamus, "da famous cousin." He then turned to Lorraine who shifted uncomfortably in her seat. "And den you must be the woman who's been looking all over da wurld for me."

As he approached her, Lorraine stood up.

"Lorraine Innis," she croaked in a wavering voice, as she shook his hand then sat back down.

"Well," said Seamus Gynwittie as he sunk down onto the sofa, "what's dis all about, den? Somethin' about me being yer hoosband."

"No, no," said Valerie; "you're definitely not Martin Innis."

"No," agreed Lorraine, "no, you're definitely not my husband."

Seamus Gynwittie laughed, putting both women further on the defensive. "Now ladies, I didn't have ta come all da way from Dublin, and ya both didn't have ta come all da way from America ta say what da tree of us already knew. Did ya?"

"We were coming over anyway," said Lorraine.

"Oh, well, I'm glad fur dat. I'm glad ta see it didn't put ya out any."

"So it's obvious that you're not Martin Innis," said Valerie.

"Never even hurd of da man before yesterday," said Seamus.

"Well, sorry if you were inconvenienced," said Lorraine as she rose.

"Yes, if there's anything we can do for you before you go back to Ireland…" said Valerie as gestured towards the door.

"Well, ya could tell me one ting," said Seamus as he stood.

"Anything," said Lorraine.

"Just where did ya get me picture, and why did ya have it printed in all da newspapers as dat of yer long-lost hoosband?"

Lorraine and Valerie stared at each other.

"Cuz I know dat dis is me," he said taking a clipping of the photo from his pocket. "Dat's me own shirt, wid me own head sticking out the top of it. And dat dere behind me is da pub where once I worked."

The two cousins sat side by side on the sofa in awkward silence, both hoping the other would speak first.

"Well, you see…" began Lorraine before tailing off.

"What my cousin means…" added Valerie.

After their clumsy start, the women just looked at each other again for at least 60 seconds, before Valerie turned to Lorraine and spoke.

"Yeah," she asked, "why did you use Mr. Gynwittie's picture?"

"I didn't know it was Mr. Gynwittie," said Lorraine to Valerie before turning to Seamus. "I didn't know it was you. I found it in an Irish travel brochure. I didn't mean to cause you any inconvenience, really!"

"I see," nodded Gynwittie rubbing his chin, "but ya taut I looked like yer hoosband, Martin Innis?"

"Oh, very much," said Lorraine. "The resemblance is frightening."

"Ah ha," muttered Gynwittie. "So dese folks who drug me here, dey don't get der reward."

"I suppose not," said Lorraine.

"How could they?" said Valerie. "You're not Martin Innis."

"Ah ha," repeated Gynwittie as he slowly walked back and forth across the plush carpet. "And ya want me to tell everybody dat?"

"Who?" asked Lorraine.

"All dese reporters who have been houndin' me fur da last day and a half."

"That you're not my husband? Why not? After all, it's the truth."

"And dat ya clipped me picture outta sum travel book?"

"Why not? Like I said…" Lorraine stopped and looked at Valerie.

"He's got a point," said Valerie. "It's obviously his photograph."

"Yes," said Lorraine, "and he's obviously not Martin Innis, are you?"

"No ma'am, dat I am not," said Seamus Gynwittie. He paused a moment, allowing a coy smile to play across his lips. "Of, course, if ya'd like me ta be Martin Innis…"

Lorraine grimaced while Valerie nodded her head.

"If he were your husband it would be an easy way out," noted Valerie.

"Me? Marry him?" cried Lorraine, before adding for Seamus' benefit, "No offense. Valerie, how could you suggest that?"

"I don't know," said Valerie, "it might be funny, I mean, fun."

"Forget it. It would only be a temporary solution," said Lorraine.

"Not necessarily," said Valerie. "It could tie up the whole Martin thing very neatly."

"But what if someone found out?" asked Lorraine.

"How could they?" You wouldn't tell, would you Mr. Gynwittie?"

"Gynwittie?" said Seamus. "Who would dat be, den? Me name's Innis, Martin Innis."

"See?" said Valerie.

"That's all well and good," said Lorraine, "but what does he get out of it? I mean he's not going to become Martin Innis for a lark. Are you?"

"No, not for a lark," said Seamus. "But I'm not an unreasonable man, either. I'm happy with da simple tings. I joost want to be a little more comfortable."

"How much more comfortable?" asked Valerie.

"Joost a wee bit, say a hundred pounds a week."

"About one hundred and seventy dollars, huh?" said Valerie.

"I tink it's very reasonable. Besides, da paper says yer foundation has plenty of money."

"Not from the Foundation!" said Lorraine. "I'll pay it myself, out of my own pocket, but I will not pay bribe money from the foundation!"

"Please, Mrs. Innis," said Seamus with a hurt expression, "I won't take anyting if ya call it a bribe. I would merely call it a service rendered. For a hundred pounds a week, I'll tell any and all I'm yer hoosband. Dat's reasonable - seein' as I'm piling yer lie on top o' me own soul."

"He's right. I did start it," Lorraine said to Valerie.

"Der's joost one more ting," said Seamus with a nod towards Lorraine's engagement and wedding bands, "what if de actual Mr. Innis objects to dis arrangement?"

"There's little chance of that," said Lorraine.

"Why? Uh, wait, tis none of me business. Dat's yer own affair. I'm joost da hired help. If'n ya say it's all right wid himself, and it's okay wid you, den it's all right wid me. I can't be too nosy for a hundred pound a week."

"Wait, what about you?" asked Valerie. "Won't your family talk?"

"Ah, dat's da beauty of it t'all. Yer lookin' at da only son, of an only son, of an only son. I'm what ye call a loner. I've got no family, and fewer friends to muck up da deal."

"Does this mean he's got to go back to America with us and live with me?" asked Lorraine.

"Ye could say, I've decided to return to me ancestral home, while me wife is off busy savin' da wurld," suggested Seamus.

"Yes, something like that would work," said Valerie pulling her copy of Lorraine's autobiography from her flight bag. "Here you'd better read this. In fact, memorize it. It will tell you everything you need to know about the real Martin Innis."

"I'll stoody it wid all alacrity," he vowed.

"Do you have any money on you?" Valerie asked.

Lorraine fished through her purse and came up with three one-hundred-dollar bills and a fifty, and handed it to Valerie who placed it in Seamus Gynwittie's waiting palm.

"There," noted Valerie, "that should take care of your first two weeks. Lorraine can send you a check every month after that. Where do you live?"

"Well, I was livin' joost outside o' Dublin, but I tink wid this little nest egg I'll be lookin' for that ancestral home, wherever dat might be."

"Martin came from Ennistimon," said Lorraine. "It's in the book."

"Wait," said Valerie. "You can't go back there, the locals might spot you for a phony. Where would you like to live, Mr. Gynwittie?"

"Da name's Innis," winked Seamus as he tucked his first two week's wages into his breast pocket. "I've always been partial to da Northwest, around Donegal. Don't worry, I won't give it away."

"Are you sure about this?" Lorraine whispered to Valerie, trying to avoid any long-term entanglement with Seamus. "I mean we could just as easily pay off Mr. Gynwittie in one lump sum to say that isn't him in the photo. He seems willing to lie for money."

"What about the Whirleys?" said Valerie. "They'll put up a stink about the photo matching Seamus, here, and there will still be an international manhunt for your husband. I say wrap him up now at bargain prices, while you can."

Lorraine thought about it for a moment, and then reluctantly agreed.

"It's all set Mr. Innis," said Valerie, "or should I say, Martin?"

"Martin it tis!"

"Now, of course, you'll be staying with your wife while she's here in London, before you two part company later in the week and you return home to Ireland," said Valerie.

"It'll be like a second honeymoon," said Seamus putting his arm around Lorraine. "Won't it, me dearest?"

"Not at all like it," said Lorraine as she removed his hand. "Not even like a first honeymoon...especially not like a first honeymoon! We'll have separate bedrooms."

"Sorry, I was joost practicin' me role."

"Just let Valerie or me do most of the talking when we have to meet the media."

"Right," said Valerie, "and whatever you do, never, never give any interviews. Refer any inquiries to me or Mrs. Innis."

"Who's dat? Me alleged mother?" asked Seamus.

"Your wife!" said Valerie nodding towards Lorraine.

"Oh, herself, right!"

Valerie reached for the door.

"Wait!" said Lorraine. "Why did he run away and take an alias?"

The trio thought a moment.

"Ya could say I ran away ta surprise ya," said Seamus.

"How about he's shy?" suggested Valerie.

"The rumor was that he was running from the police," said Lorraine.

"Amnesia," said Valerie. "He got amnesia, forgot he was married, sold the house and moved back to the land of his birth."

"Sounds pretty farfetched," said Lorraine.

"How 'bout I sold the house to buy ya a houseboat, den me and it got drug away in a terrible storm, and I washed up on de shores of Galway Bay?" said Seamus.

"I'll just say it was a personal matter between the two of us," said Lorraine.

"Okay, now here we go," said Valerie, "remember, you have just been reunited with the man you love…look radiantly happy!"

Lorraine forced a grin on to her face. "Like this?" she asked.

"That looks more like you've got gas," said Valerie.

Valerie opened the door to the adjoining room and informed the Whirleys that they had indeed found Martin Innis and were thus entitled to the reward. The couple was ecstatic and ran off to phone their daughter back in Woonsocket. Valerie then arranged for Lorraine, Martin, and herself to be taken to their waiting limousine for the drive into London. Along the way, they were blocked by the press. Lorraine stopped to answer a few questions. She tried her best to look happy as Valerie had advised, but as the video replay on that evening's news would confirm, Lorraine looked more like a woman who had a wedgie in her underwear and couldn't decide whether or not she found the experience pleasurable. Seamus, performed his part well, in fact too well for Lorraine's liking. The majority of his act was confined to smiling, waving and holding Lorraine's hand, at which he proved to be quite adept. The difficulty began, however, when Seamus improvised after being coaxed to do so by the photographers. At this point, the Irishman dipped his bride over backward and planted a firm kiss on Lorraine's lips while the shutters clicked and the flashes blazed. The photos made the front pages of newspapers around the world the next day, much to Lorraine Innis' chagrin. Luckily her expression, which was actually mortification, was mistaken for one of delight. This helped sell the ruse that Seamus was Martin, a fact which not even the most skeptical of reporters contested – especially after witnessing what was quickly dubbed: "the feel-good kiss of the century."

As soon as they were alone in the privacy of the limo, however, Lorraine had more than a few choice words for her substitute groom. In his defense, Seamus apologized and explained that he knew he would have to kiss Lorraine sooner or later to see if there were any romantic sparks between them. The Irishman also confessed that much to his disappointment, she did little to excite him.

"'Tis more the pity," confessed Seamus, "for yer sure to bein' a fine figur' of a woman, Mrs. Innis. And I'm not joost sayin' dat 'cuz yer payin' me to be yer hoosband."

- 54 -
The Ersatz Egg and the Genuine Sable

A week after being reunited with her "husband" Lorraine found herself in the arms of another man. Or rather, she felt as if she were being buried alive in the overpowering embrace of Nikolai Kropotkin.

"Lorruska," the Russian President kept repeating as he alternated between holding Lorraine at arm's length and then crushing her against himself. "Lorruska, how I have missed you!"

Lorraine tried to recall if she had found his affection as disquieting before she remembered she was really a man. Ultimately, Lorraine decided it didn't matter. She didn't enjoy it now, but she was in no position to voice her objection, not only because to do so might uncover her disguise, but also because whenever she tried to speak, she got a mouthful of worsted wool from Kropotkin's suit jacket.

"Lorruska," said Kropotkin, letting her up for a prolonged sojourn in the atmosphere. "So you want to be a real lady, do you?"

"What?" Lorraine looked off to the side where Valerie was standing in Kropotkin's office. Valerie's eyes widened at Kropotkin's remark. "You don't think that...I mean, what are you talking about...Nikki?"

"Do you want to be a lady?"

Lorraine looked in the mirror on the opposite wall. What, she wondered, had given her away?

"It is a great honor, I suppose," continued Kropotkin, "not only them making you a citizen, but a peer as well."

Lorraine breathed a sigh of relief. "Yes," she agreed, "it was very nice of the Prime Minister to suggest they make me a British subject by an Act of Parliament."

"So they could make you a lady," said Kropotkin.

"Actually," said Lorraine, "They'd make me a Dame first."

"That's progress," muttered Valerie, "and all this time you've just been shooting for an average broad."

Kropotkin looked at Valerie, taking notice of her for the first time.

"Oh," said Lorraine, "this is my, my cousin, Valerie. You remember her, don't you?"

"Yes, the one in the bed...who didn't talk," said the Russian. He scrutinized Valerie up and down, and then returned to Lorraine. As he did so a broad smile broke across his lips. "Ah, but Lorruska, how you charmed the English! I saw the crowds, autographing books, handing out dolls, meeting with London's leading couturiers."

Valerie giggled. Lorraine thought it absurd that fashion designers would want to copy her "look," but found it more upsetting than amusing.

"But where is your husband?" asked Kropotkin with an avuncular frown. "He hasn't abandoned you again?"

"No, nothing like that," said Lorraine. "He went home to Ireland. He's going to buy us a home there."

"If you wanted to move to Europe, you could have lived here in Russia. Ah, but if I must share you, I will. As it was, I almost had to go to war with old Merton to have you to myself for Christmas."

"Actually," said Lorraine, "the Russian Orthodox Christmas is celebrated in January. We could have come then."

"December, January, your Christmas, our Christmas," said Kropotkin. "What does it matter? As long as you are here with me now, that makes it holiday enough, Lorruska! If I had to send out the troops to get you here, it would not be the first time in history. You would be like that, that Greek...Helen of Troy...the face that launched a thousand ships!"

"Lorraine of New Jersey," cracked Valerie, "the face that launched a thousand missiles!"

Kropotkin cast a puzzled glance towards Valerie. "You know your Greeks?" Kropotkin asked Valerie warily.

"Only that they have the best diners," said Valerie.

"You are making a joke," smiled Kropotkin. "I know it must be difficult for you to think of someone who is so close to you, being so special. But young lady, this cousin of yours saved my life. Not just from the bullet of an assassin, but from years of foolish thinking. She single-handedly opened up my mind and swept away years of cowwebs that had cluttered up my head."

"Cobwebs," said Lorraine.

"And still she corrects me," said the Russian. "But look at you!" Kropotkin stepped back from the women. Lorraine looked down at herself.

"Lorruska," he said, "you are not dressed for the Russian winter, of which we have an abundance in Moscow...especially at this time of the year. Look at you Lorruska, no boots! And that thin coat."

"I thought it was warm," said Lorraine.

"Pah! It is not designed for a Russian winter. You would soon freeze. Take it off, is time for your Santa Claus's first delivery."

Lorraine removed her wool coat. Kropotkin tossed the garment aside and then produced two gift boxes – one large and the other small.

"Happy Christmas," said Kropotkin smiling broadly, "first you, the cousin."

"You shouldn't be giving us presents," said Lorraine. "You've done enough already paying for Valerie's hospital suite."

Valerie took the smaller of the two packages from Kropotkin. It was wrapped in gold paper with a matching ribbon around it.

"Go ahead," urged Kropotkin.

Valerie undid the paper and opened the box inside.

"Oh, my!" gasped Valerie as she gingerly removed the contents. "This is incredible! A Faberge egg! Do you know what these are worth?"

Kropotkin blushed, and then coughed.

"Not as much as you may think," he said. "It is not an original."

"Of course not," said Lorraine. "Those are practically priceless. But it is exquisite. Those are real jewels. It's too expensive. You shouldn't have, Nikki."

"I hope you enjoy it," said Kropotkin.

Lorraine glanced at him, then at Valerie, then back to Nikki.

"Of course Valerie knew it wasn't an original, didn't you, Valerie?"

Valerie smiled politely. "Oh, of course. I knew it right away. It's still very nice. Thank you."

Kropotkin duplicated her half-hearted smile as she put the egg back in the box. He then regained his enthusiasm as he held the large box while Lorraine opened it.

"A fur coat," said Lorraine.

"Actually, it's mink," said Valerie.

"Siberian sable," corrected Nikki.

"Same thing," muttered Valerie.

Lorraine thanked Nikki again, while Valerie reached out and stroked the coat's sleeve first with, and then against, the grain. Then she blew softly into the nap with the expertise of a furrier.

"Forgive me," said Kropotkin noticing Valerie. "I should have gotten you both coats."

"That's all right," said Valerie. "I don't wear fur. I'm, I'm animal-friendly."

As Lorraine tried to slip on the coat, however, she found her arm blocked where Valerie was still caressing the sleeve.

"Oh, sorry," said Valerie, reluctantly letting go of the fur.

– 55 –
The Last Christmas Tree
You'll Ever Need

An explosion ripped through the snow-covered Idaho forest, echoing off the surrounding hills.

That was a pretty good one, thought Eugenia Bupp, though she wondered if it was too powerful for her intended use. She began to prepare another charge at half the size, her bony fingers struggling in the late afternoon chill.

"Okay," she said to herself, "let's go see what you can do."

As Bupp started crunching through the snow, she came up short when she heard voices.

"It must have been around here," said a man's voice.

Bupp looked up. Coming over the ridge were a man and a woman. They looked to be in their late twenties.

"I hope no one was hurt," said the woman. "Oh, look, over there, there's an old lady."

They scurried to Eugenia Bupp.

"Are you okay," said the man.

"What the hell do you want?" asked Bupp dropping her explosive into the snow behind her.

"We heard the noise," said the man. "Is anyone hurt?"

"What are you doing way out here?" asked Bupp.

"We're picking out our first Christmas tree," said the woman as she smiled and hugged the man. "We've only been married two months."

"What are you doing?" asked the man.

"I'm getting my tree, too, snoopy ass," said Bupp.

"With dynamite?" asked the woman looking at the box of explosives a few feet away.

"That's plastic explosives, dear," corrected the man.

"Where'd you learn about plastic explosives, sonny?"

"In the Army."

"Too bad," said Bupp. They just looked at her. "I mean, too bad you weren't in the Navy, like my late husband. Say, kids, I think there are some nice trees over there, see?"

The couple turned to look at where she pointed. Before they could turn back around, they were both felled by consecutive rounds from Ma Bupp's Beretta.

"Too bad, you didn't stay in the Army, kid," she said returning the weapon to her pocket. "Damn nuisance, dumping bodies. Well, I better get going. No more practice today."

– 56 –
Come Together Over Mink

Russia had its good points and bad points, as far as Valerie Fierro was concerned. It was colder than England, in fact, she thought it was colder than any place she'd ever been before. To compensate for the frigid temperatures, they did have some exquisite furs, or at least the one Kropotkin gave Lorraine was exquisite.

She rubbed her bare thigh against the coat as she writhed atop the bed.

The people seemed cordial enough. On their tour of Moscow earlier in the day they had allowed her and Lorraine to jump to the front of the line at Lenin's Tomb. Of course, she had almost lost her lunch at the sight of the embalmed revolutionary.

Kropotkin was okay, too, she thought. He seemed totally taken with Lorraine, or to be more accurate, taken in by her. Valerie often found it difficult not to laugh in the Russian's face every time he hugged Lorraine. Still, she couldn't fault him for being fooled along with the rest of the world. She could fault him for throwing a boring party, however, which he was doing at that moment downstairs in the Kremlin's presidential residence. Again, like everything else in Russia, the bad seemed to be balanced out by the good.

"Hello, comrade," cooed Valerie pulling the fur coat up around her naked breasts. "Umm, as good as you looked in that uniform, you look twice as…big…out of it."

Andre Tossoff, the Russian Army Captain she had hijacked from the party, stood before her, naked, save for his peaked cap. She liked a man who could wear a hat.

"What's Russian for 'screw my brains out?'" asked Valerie.

"*Izvini?*"

"I forgot, you only know that one English phrase."

Captain Tossoff looked at her sideways and then smiled as if he understood.

"Is hokay with me," he said.

"I bet is hokay with you, big boy," said Valerie flipping the fur off her body to reveal her naked flesh, "isn't it?"

"Is hokay," he agreed, flinging his hat against the wall and pouncing atop Valerie in one athletic bound.

"You Cossacks don't go in for much foreplay, do you?" muttered Valerie, gripping his brushed crew cut as best she could, and holding on with both hands while the Russian heavy artillery went in for a full frontal attack.

"*Vy ochen' krasivy*," growled Captain Tossoff as he nuzzled his face between her breasts and then shook his head.

"I don't know what that means," said Valerie, "but I'm not going out for a translation."

"Is hokay?" he said looking up before making his final approach.

"Da," said Valerie with a wicked smile. "I came halfway around the world to come halfway around the world."

Valerie arched her back and was about to release one of her well-rehearsed moans when a different sound altogether was heard. She froze, as did her lover.

"Wait, shh," whispered Valerie, listening.

There it was again.

Valerie pushed the rigid soldier off her pliant body. Had that been the door to the suite?

"Valerie?" It was Lorraine's voice in the next room.

"Oh, shit, it's him," said Valerie. "I mean, her, oh, never mind you can't understand me anyway. Quick, hide, go hide..."

Valerie's gestures along with his commando training made it possible for Captain Tossoff to leap off the bed and stash himself in the 18th Century armoire in less than five seconds. He was just in time, as was Valerie who managed to cover herself with the fur at the precise moment the door opened.

"Oh, sorry, I didn't realize you were in here," said Lorraine.

"What do you want?" snapped Valerie.

"I came up for my coat," said Lorraine, "besides that, you're on my bed."

"Oh, I, uh...I got confused," she said. Valerie glanced to the far corner of the room and hoped Lorraine wouldn't notice the discarded uniform scattered there. "These Russian rooms all look the same to me."

"Okay..." said Lorraine slowly. She eyed Valerie for a protracted moment. "Well, I'll just get my coat and go." Lorraine reached for the coat.

"No!" said Valerie, clutching the fur to her body. "I mean, why?"

"President Kropotkin is going to show me the view from the balcony. He says it's lovely in the snow at night with all the spotlights on it. Would you like to join us?"

"No!" shrieked Valerie. This cry was not only designed to keep the coat atop her, but also to keep the curious Captain Tossoff from peeking any further out of the wardrobe.

"Don't you want to come?" asked Lorraine.

Valerie bit her lip. "Uh, no, I don't want to, not yet!"

"Sorry," said Lorraine jumping back a half step mentally as well as physically. "I just thought you might want to. Is there something wrong?"

"Damn it, Lorraine! Do I have to be with you every damn minute? Can't I have a little privacy? Do you always have to be around me?"

Lorraine just stared at her. A puzzled look crossed her face. Valerie saw this change in Lorraine's expression and quickly backpedaled from it.

"I mean, that is," said Valerie, "I, uh, I'm not feeling well..."

"Oh...I understand," said Lorraine.

"You, uh, you do?"

"Your little visitor's here."

Valerie's eyes grew large as she glanced towards the wardrobe. She expected to see a naked Russian protruding from it. Another moment's thought made her realize that Lorraine wasn't talking about her little visitor hidden in the armoire. "My little visitor, yes," she agreed, adding a quiver to her voice.

"Cramps?"

"Oh, yes," moaned Valerie.

"Can I get you anything?" asked Lorraine. "I don't know Russian for Midol, but I'm sure they have something."

"No," mewed Valerie. "I'm sorry I took your bed and your coat, but I didn't think you'd mind. It makes me feel warm and ...safe."

Lorraine smiled. "That's okay, stay there." She walked towards the wardrobe. "I'll just get my other coat."

"Wait!" said Valerie. Lorraine stopped; her hand just inches away from the wardrobe handle and the bare soldier behind it. "I mean, wear mine; it's warmer. It's in my closet...in the other room."

Lorraine nodded, as she backed out of the room. "If you need anything," she added just before leaving, "I'll be right downstairs."

Only after Lorraine had retrieved the other coat and the outer door to the suite had shut did Valerie Fierro resume normal breathing. Captain Tossoff, cautiously emerged from the armoire.

"Is hokay?" He whispered.

"No, damn it, she's totally spoiled the mood," said Valerie, punching a pillow. She looked up and stared at the saluting officer for a few seconds. "Hokay," she said waving him on, "let's go, I got it back."

– 57 –
Love Off
a Parapet

Lorraine was standing beside Nikolai Kropotkin as the falling snow enrobed the Kremlin in a pristine blanket of white. The spotlights of the balcony transformed the large flakes into a silent swarm that muffled the sounds of Moscow at night.

"You look lovely tonight, Lorruska," said Kropotkin breaking the silence. "That gown shows off your features very well."

Lorraine looked down at her cleavage, which thanks to a fleshy chest, a roll of duct tape, and Valerie's binding skills, was protruding voluptuously from the top of her full-length beaded gown.

"But where is your sable coat? Did you not like it?"

"Oh, it's beautiful, but I loaned it to Valerie," said Lorraine, wrapping the woolen coat around her shoulders. "She's not feeling very well. It's a shame. She'd love this. She's crazy about the snow."

"And you my dearest Lorruska," he said taking her hand, "for what are you crazy?"

Lorraine took a step backward. "What are you talking about?"

"Confess your passions, my dear," urged Kropotkin moving closer, "and I will confess mine."

Lorraine backed up another step and bumped into the edge of the balcony dislodging some loose bricks. The bricks tumbled over the side and into a snowdrift below.

"Whoa!" shouted Lorraine in surprise as she took a step away from the edge. The Russian president reached out and embraced her.

"Be careful, Lorruska; you could have fallen." Kropotkin held her tightly. "Do not deny it," he encouraged, "Confess your inner desires, Lorruska."

"Have you gone crazy?" said Lorraine. "Did somebody slip you a slice of Wonder Bread when you weren't looking?"

"If I am drunk it is with passion for you."

"You are nuts," said Lorraine, "you've flipped your samovar."

"My samovar could be your samovar! Come, join me in my samovar of love and let us steep the sweet musky tea of heady passion that only a man and woman can steep."

"You've got to be kidding! Where did you dig up that line? You've got to be careful of what you say. You're a respected world leader."

"And I would trade it all; become a lowly peasant...for you, my little Lorruska."

Lorraine managed to wiggle her left arm free, but it only afforded Kropotkin's hand access to her left false breast.

"Oh!" squealed Lorraine. She managed to return her left arm to where it had been. "What are you trying to do?"

"Do not worry, I'm not deflowering, you my sweet little Lorruska."

"Yeah? Well, it's not exactly horticulture either."

"I never called you a whore," he said stepping back.

"Horticulture," said Lorraine sliding back into editorial-mode for a moment, "H-o-r-t-i..." She realized she was giving a spelling lesson to a man trying to rape her, and signaled the end of the class with a scream. Kropotkin muffled her shout with his right hand.

"Do not scream, Lorruska," he said. "I'm not trying to hurt yoooo!"

The last word was given added emphasis as Lorraine bit his pinky. He released Lorraine as he waved his tooth-marked digit in the cold night air. She took a step away from the Russian and leaned over to catch her breath.

"I am not trying to have my way with you," said Kropotkin, "except in the most honorable of ways. I wish for you to become my wife. Please marry me, Lorruska!"

"You've snapped the strings of your balalaika," panted Lorraine. "I couldn't marry you."

"Why not?"

"Well," Lorraine stopped. She couldn't tell him because his Russian parts weren't compatible with her American-made ones. If he knew the truth, he'd go ballistic. Not a good idea with all the missiles he had at his disposal. Of course, she thought, good old Seamus. "I can't marry you," said Lorraine striking the pose of a tragic lover, "I can't marry you, Nikki, because, I'm...I'm already married!"

"No, you're not," said Kropotkin.

She did a double take. "How do you know? I mean, what do you mean?"

"Didn't you read the papers this afternoon?" asked Kropotkin. "No, of course, you didn't, unless you read Russian, which I do not think you do. You are a wronged woman, my dear Mrs. Innis, or shall I say, Miss Ammaccapane. It appears that your husband, Mr. Martin Innis, is in reality, a man of another name...according to the papers, that is."

"Seamus Gynwittie," muttered Lorraine.

"Yes, that is the name they gave. He is already married."

"He told the media that he was already married?" asked Lorraine.

"No, he did not. His first wife, however, did," said the Russian, placing a consoling hand upon Lorraine's shoulder. "The man is a bigamist."

That jerky little potato picker, Lorraine thought. Gynwittie had vowed that he had no family. Apparently, in Seamus' Hibernian logic, estranged first wives didn't count as family.

"I knew something like this would happen," said Lorraine, as she closed her eyes to concentrate.

"Do not worry, my little Lorruska," said Kropotkin as he inched closer. "After all, I long have sensed that this man was not all that important to you."

"What do you mean?" said Lorraine.

"Forgive me," said the Russian, "but how could you love a man who would leave you while you are carrying his child."

"Child?" Lorraine thought back and recalled that the only person aside from Valerie whom she had told about her pregnancy was Kropotkin. "Oh, that," she said with a wave of her hand, "I'm not going to have his baby."

"Much better," he said. "I was going to offer to adopt the infant, but now we can have our own. It will be a little brother or sister for Kateryna. And you will be a new mother to her, will that not be nice?"

"I don't want to be anyone's mother," said Lorraine holding up a gloved hand. "I don't even want to be an aunt to Yuri! I'm not marrying you, or anyone. Let's get that clear. I'm in enough trouble."

"I can help you, my dear one. I have admired you from the first time I saw you. I said nothing then out of respect for your marriage. I had planned to present you with this as a Christmas gift." The Russian drew an envelope out of his breast pocket. "It is the deed to your home in Horse's Neck. I bought it through a former KGB agent who is now working as a Century 21 agent in Manalapan, New Jersey, USA. I was going to give it to you in gratitude for all you have done for me."

"I wouldn't have taken it," she said. "I don't want to live there."

"I can understand that now," said Kropotkin, "given the double-dealing of the man with whom you shared that house."

"That's not it at all."

"But now that there is really no marriage, you can be mine."

"No, I can't, you don't understand. Please," begged Lorraine as she turned away from Kropotkin and again shut her eyes, "I've got to think."

It was obvious to Lorraine that she couldn't marry Nikki. This whole Seamus thing could easily cause everything to unravel before she could finish up the whole Liverot thing. Now she had a whole Kropotkin thing with which to contend. If only they could go back to that October afternoon before the whole Purvis Twankey thing led to all these other things. This, Lorraine thought, is what you get when you try exacting your own revenge. "'Vengeance is mine,' saith the Lord," she recalled Aunt Elinor quoting. If only she'd heeded that simple advice. Or was it justice? Lost in thought, Lorraine didn't notice Kropotkin creeping toward her. She wheeled around just in time to see him lunge for her.

"You are playing hard to get, my little croquette," laughed Kropotkin as he pounced.

"I think you mean 'coquette,'" said Lorraine.

As she corrected him, Lorraine stepped backward, bumping up against the wall opposite where she had dislodged the bricks a few minutes earlier. Reflexively, she thrust out her arms, pushing against him as he sprang towards her. Kropotkin staggered backward towards the damaged part of the balcony. For an agonizing split second Lorraine watched in horror as he flailed his arms, trying to stabilize himself. With his bottom serving as a fulcrum, the attempt was doomed to failure, and a moment later Kropotkin fell backward over the edge of the bulwark with a pitiful yell.

Lorraine stood frozen for a moment as the snow wrapped his cry in an eerie silence. She edged towards the spot from which Kropotkin had plunged. Peering over the side, she saw him buried headfirst in a deep pile of snow. The fact that his legs were furiously wiggling indicated to her that he was relatively unhurt.

"I saved your life by accident, and now I almost killed you by accident," said Lorraine Innis to herself. "I guess this makes us even, Nikki."

Down below, guards scrambled to extricate Kropotkin from the snow bank. Lorraine watched long enough to make sure that he was all right and then went back inside.

– 58 –
Jumping Off the Bubblegum Card

After an unusually harsh winter in Washington, every living thing seemed more alive with the coming of spring. The cherry blossoms, the daffodils, and even the bureaucrats seemed more vibrant than anyone could recall.

It had been a hard winter for Lorraine Innis as well, though there were no hopeful blossoms in her life to mark the beginning of sunnier times. Despite her best efforts to escape her fame, Lorraine's legend continued to grow, as every incident in her life only enhanced her image around the world. And now, finally, Lorraine was traveling to the White House to be honored by President Merton for her service to the nation and the world.

As Valerie drove her new Lexus around the Beltway, Lorraine finally allowed the thoughts that had been racing through her mind to spill out of her mouth.

"Yes," said Lorraine in mid-thought, "I'm definitely getting out."

"What? Here? We're doing over 65."

"No, I mean, I'm going to end it," replied Lorraine.

Valerie almost rear-ended a garbage truck. "End what?"

"My life…as Lorraine Innis."

"That's what I thought you meant. Are you crazy?"

"Not at all," said Lorraine, "after all, I need to tell on myself, before anyone else does. People are counting on me as a role model. I've got to be honest with them. What if I run into another situation like Seamus Gynwittie?"

"Seamus Gynwittie?" said Valerie. "Is that what you're worried about? It comes out that Martin is really some stupid, two-timing Irishman who's already married, and your approval rating went even higher. Are you kidding? Even his real wife felt sorry for you."

"But what if Seamus had admitted that I paid him to pose as Martin?"

"But he didn't," said Valerie. "He kept his mouth shut. You've got to hand it to that Irishman. When you buy him, he stays bought. Besides, who would have believed him anyway? He's a bigamist."

"No he isn't," said Lorraine.

"It was possible. The record shows that Seamus could have married you after he left his wife."

"That's another thing. Where did the record of my marriage to Martin Innis come from? Someone somewhere knows something. What if the person who's created all those phony documents decides to tear the cover off me? No, I need to tell the truth. Don't forget the old adage: honesty is the best policy."

Valerie looked at her sideways. "There's another old saying: don't rock the boat. If they haven't blown the whistle on you yet, they won't. If anyone wanted to cash in on you, they'd have come around already with their hand out. You're just being paranoid. Everyone loves Lorraine. Every time it looks like your popularity has peaked it goes up. Your television appearances get record ratings. Older men and women see you as a daughter; young women as a sister; young men either as a sister or a sweetheart; children as a favorite aunt. The media loves you. The screen rights to your autobiography sold for a record sum. Three Academy Award winners fought to play you."

"Only after I said I wouldn't do it," muttered Lorraine.

"I'm still pissed off at you for turning that down, along with a lot of other good offers. You've thrown away millions!"

"It was just silly to have a university in the Mid-West named after me," said Lorraine. "And that idea of those Japanese businessmen to build a Lorraine-Peaceland theme park outside of Tokyo is ridiculous."

"Nothing's ridiculous if you have the cash," said Valerie."

"Isn't it enough to have the third largest charitable organization in the world? Isn't it enough to generate billions of dollars in the sales of books, toys, and clothing? Women are getting their hair done in copyrighted Lorraine styles that a few weeks earlier would have been simple shags! They're wearing designer clothes that cost three times what their worth..."

"Five times," interjected Valerie.

"Even worse. Five times! Their kids eat Lorraine Innis snacks while watching the animated adventures of Lorraine and her superhero pals. For heaven sake, children think I can fly!"

"You don't fly," said Valerie, "it's a ring you wear that generates a negative gravity..."

"That's what I'm talking about. It's all gotten out of hand."

"Yeah, well, why don't we take a vacation after this is all done?" said Valerie. "I'm always up for a few weeks on some sunny beach.

"Where could I go? I can't even go down to the corner for a paper without getting mobbed by reporters, or tourists, or kids wanting me to autograph their Lorraine bubble-gum cards. How you ever talked me into having my face on a trading card…"

"It brought in over 30 million to the Foundation," said Valerie. "You're helping a lot of people through the charity."

"And I've lost myself in the process," said Lorraine. "I want to get off while there's still a shred of Chesney Potts left. If you recall, I did all this to get the evidence on Peter Liverot. Now, instead of bringing him to justice, I've made him rich beyond his wildest dreams. And I still don't have any evidence on him. Not even Patsy could find any evidence for me. Isn't that what you told me?"

Valerie looked away. "Uh, yeah, that is, she tried, but she told me she didn't find anything. You could have gotten her into a lot of trouble. So, I wouldn't mention that to her again."

"I shouldn't have risked Patsy like that. I'm sorry. So, now, not only don't I have any evidence on Liverot, now I'm partners with him."

"I told you these things take time," said Valerie. "That's another reason why you've got to keep being you."

"So I can make bastards like Liverot wealthy while I lie to decent men like Nikolai Kropotkin?"

"Oh, he's okay," said Valerie, "the neck brace came off weeks ago."

"But the flowers and the gifts keep coming. I can't keep returning them."

"Now you're getting the idea. Keep them! I've said all along that you should."

"But I'd be taking them under false pretenses."

Valerie snorted as she steered up the exit ramp. "You have so much to learn about being a real woman!"

- 59 -
Orthodontist
Heal Thyself

Davis Flemming was reviewing the final preparations for that morning's ceremony when the door of his West Wing office flew open, and a tiny woman stood in the entrance. Flemming jumped to his feet.

"Don't get your balls in a twist, Jockstrap," said the woman. "I guess this ain't the ladies powder room."

"The what?" asked a stunned Flemming.

"The crapper, Nitwit," said woman.

Flemming stared at her. She must have been at least 80, frail and bony, but with the largest bosom he'd ever seen on such a puny woman.

"Who are you? What are you doing here? How'd you get in this area?"

"I'm one of the Cross of what's-her-face people. I walked in through the door down the hall," she said. "I'm the oldest volunteer for whozits. You know the broad with the big nose and nice hooters. I'm not so bad either, eh?" She pointed at her own grotesque figure. "I'm 102, you know, that's my age, not my chest measurement."

Indeed Davis Flemming did know. It was he who had organized the event. Not only to have President Merton present the Medal of Freedom to Lorraine Innis but to invite a large and diverse group of its volunteers. It would be the biggest media circus the White House had ever seen. Every network was airing it live and then replaying it later in prime time specials. Flemming was immensely proud of himself. After months of trying, he had finally been able to spin the Lorraine phenomenon to his advantage. Merton's numbers were up and going higher. Despite being a lame duck, the President would have new clout. Enough clout to handpick his successor, or for Flemming to do it, assuring his secret administration would remain in power for at least another eight years.

"Wait," said Flemming, picking up the phone. "I'll get someone to show you to where you need to be."

"Yeah, do that," barked the woman. "I gotta pee so bad, I can just about taste it. It's floating up on my back teeth." She grinned at Flemming, revealing a hideous, deformed set of teeth. "Like 'em?"

"Charming," muttered Flemming.

"I made 'em myself," said the woman. "I'd make you a set, but it's way too late for that now."

– 60 –
Lorraine Sells Short

"You are the real heroes," Lorraine Innis told the throng of volunteers, curiosity seekers, and media collected at Washington's Inner City Community Center. She had been mobbed upon her arrival ten minutes earlier. Now, as she stood outside the front entrance of the refurbished building, she looked out over the sea of faces giving what she hoped would be one of the last appearances of Lorraine Innis.

"You are heroes, and I now know what it takes to be a true hero," she said. "Many have called me a hero, but I'm not one. At best, I am a celebrity. A celebrity, I've discovered, is a marketable commodity, someone famous or infamous who can be merchandised. I'm embarrassed to say that I've become one of the most merchandised people in history. This is especially troubling because all the books and toys, the lunchboxes and T-shirts are no real indication of my character, be it admirable or villainous. You can't pick up a Lorraine Innis fashion-action figure and determine the moral worth of the person it represents. It can't impart any virtue. It is only an indication of my current popularity and the going price of that fame, which I believe is now set at the suggested retail price of $14.95…$8.98 at most discount toy outlets.

"A true hero is a person worthy of emulation because their actions make this world a better place," continued Lorraine. "We hope that our children grow up to be like these individuals. Not because they accidentally save lives, or give away money, but because they are there every day making the hard, unselfish choices. Heroes are helping children learn to read. They are visiting the abandoned in nursing homes. They are ministering to the sick as hospital volunteers. And they are here in this community center fighting against the triple threats of ignorance, violence, and indifference.

259

"It is my honor to present this check to the Inner City Center, but don't thank me. This is only money that, for some reason, people have sent me to distribute. I suppose they send me the money because they think I'm more qualified than they are to find others who need it. I'm not. In fact, I can honestly say I'm one of the least qualified people to do this. For all those who have so generously sent donations to my foundation, I urge you to cut out the middleman. Look around, find your own local champions, and give them whatever money you would have sent to me. Then after you give your money, get in there and stand in the gap alongside those heroes and heroines, and you'll quickly realize you're a hero as well."

– 61 –
Valerie Sells High and Out

As Lorraine Innis was assailing her own fame and marketability outside the community center, inside Peter Liverot, the mastermind of the selling of Lorraine, was meeting with Valerie Fierro in the office of the center's director. Had he heard his gravy train outside derailing herself, he wouldn't have been so cheery.

"What a day," said Liverot as he peeked through the Venetian blinds at the media event outside. "I gotta hand it to your cousin. That doll sure knows how to work an audience. I dunno what she's dishin' 'em, but they're lapping it up like pit bulls in a butcher shop. And from here, it's on to the White House!"

"I didn't ask you in here, Peter, to discuss pit bulls or butcher shops," began Valerie, "and how dare you call any woman a 'doll!'"

Liverot laughed. "Take it easy. I know you too well to buy that act. Anyway, your cousin's not in the room, so relax. Besides, I didn't mean nothing by it. I'm one of her biggest fans. After this, she's going to accept the Medal of Freedom from the President, and tomorrow we really move into the big leagues. I'm meeting with the Wall Street boys to talk about doing an IPO on your cousin and incorporating her. After that, we'll be in the real dough." Liverot hiked up the right leg of his trousers and sat down on the edge of the desk. "But, like you said, you wanted to talk to me. Have a seat. What's on your mind?"

Liverot gestured for Valerie to sit down in front of him, ostensibly at his feet. She eyed the chair, and then him.

"I can say what I need to say standing up," she replied folding her arms.

Liverot shrugged his shoulders before similarly folding his arms across his chest. He had been expecting a confrontation with Valerie over the Foundation. He doubted she really knew the full story of the entire

Lorraine operation. Instead, he guessed that she was here looking for a bigger cut of the pie.

"So? Say it," said Liverot.

"Lorraine wants out," said Valerie.

Liverot's face fell momentarily before catching himself. She couldn't really want out, could she? More likely it was Valerie's ploy for more money. He decided to play innocent. "She wants out? Out of what?"

"She wants out of the charity business. Out of commercials. Out of books, and licensing, and products with Lorraine Innis on them. She wants out of it all."

"Taking a little break," said Liverot, studying the clear polish on his fingernails. "That's good, a little vacation, a little spring break."

"More like a permanent retirement."

"Really? That's too bad. Not for me, you understand. Oh, I'll miss the pleasure of working with your cousin. It's just that I got an offer that would have been very lucrative...especially for you, Miss Fierro."

"Yeah? How?"

"Well," continued Liverot, "The company that makes the Lorraine cosmetics wants to come out with a little more...sophisticated line of products. You know, something a little sexier, a steamier image for when a woman doesn't want to look like some sort of role model. I told them that's not our Lorraine. I've never met a finer or classier woman than your cousin, but you know, and I know that she's not the type that could be the naughty fantasy of a million men. She couldn't front that kind of product line. You, on the other hand, could do it easily, in a very tasteful way, of course."

"Really," said Valerie.

"Yeah," sighed Liverot, "and of course none of that money would have had to go into any charitable foundation unless you're going to start one of your own. But we'll just forget it, along with the lingerie line.

"Lingerie?"

Gotcha, thought the banker. "Yeah, Lorraine Innis isn't really the kind of woman who the public wants hawking lace teddies. It's not her image. But that's all out now if your cousin's retiring. Face it, I believe you could sell that stuff, but the public won't be interested in Valerie Fierro without Lorraine Innis around. You're just a secondary celebrity, a hanger-on. If Lorraine goes out of the public eye so will you, sorry to say. Of course, if it's money your cousin wants..."

"She doesn't want money," said Valerie. "Lorraine doesn't have a clue when it comes to money. You know she hasn't made a dime off of any of it. Aside from her allowance for a townhouse in Wilmington, she's barely making enough to keep her in mascara. No, *she* doesn't want any more money," repeated Valerie with her hand on her hip.

"I see," said Liverot suppressing a smile. Just as he suspected, Valerie was a free agent. He never knew it to fail. Throw enough money into the middle of any relationship, and sooner or later someone was going to start screaming: "I deserve more!" It reaffirmed his faith in the basic depravity of the human race. "Looking out for number one, eh?"

"*Prima i denti, poi i parenti*," said Valerie with a satisfied smile, "that's what my father always told me."

"Smart man…"

"…And he raised a smart daughter."

"Well, that puts the negotiations on an entirely different footing," said the banker. "You had me worried there for a moment. I'm sure you and I can work out an agreement. We could come up with a little something for your trouble; a small percent right off the top. Free and clear."

"Right," said Valerie, "while you take your 17 percent."

"Yeah, well, I work overtime for that. I got no personal life anymore."

"We won't go there, either," said Valerie. "Look, Peter, there wouldn't be any Lorraine Innis if it weren't for me, and you and your pals would still be doing your laundry on a small scale."

"What?"

"I know what goes on in Gibraltar."

"Oh yes?" said Liverot, perhaps that's why Lorraine wanted to quit. "And your cousin?"

"She only knows what I tell her."

"I see," said Liverot relaxing somewhat. He didn't think Valerie was so foolish as to kill their golden goose.

Valerie sat behind the desk causing Liverot to have to turn to face her. "And I'm the only one who can keep her in line. She'll do anything for me. I get a new deal, or I let Lorraine retire. So, I suppose we can start the negotiations. Eh, Peter?"

"I'm a reasonable man," said Liverot. "Have you ever known me not willing to talk business?"

– 62 –
Two Sides to Every Girl
and One Side of a Bus

An hour later, as a squadron of police restrained the crowds, Valerie Fierro's Lexus inched away from the community center. From the passenger seat, Lorraine Innis waved goodbye to her admirers with a mixture of appreciation and sadness.

"Why is it that whenever I tell them not to idolize me, they do it more?"

"I don't know why you don't just get yourself a limo," complained Valerie as she drove away.

"I thought that's why we bought the Lexus," said Lorraine, "so you could drive me around and write it off as a business expense. Besides, soon you won't have to worry about that, will you? You won't have Lorraine Innis to drive around much longer, will you?"

"Well, yes and no," said Valerie.

"What do you mean? You spoke with Liverot didn't you?"

"Yes."

"And?"

Valerie fell silent.

"Well?" said Lorraine. "Did you tell him I wanted to retire?"

"Yes."

"And?"

"It's not going to be easy," said Valerie.

"Why not? People retire all the time. First I'll retire, and then, after I fade from the public's mind, I'll just disappear. Lorraine Innis will cease to exist, and Chesney can come back to the land of the living. Maybe I'll grow a beard."

"You can't," said Valerie. "Not anymore, remember?."

"Well, I'll wear a false beard. I'll need something to hide my face, at least until people forget about Lorraine."

"Look, it's not as easy as all that," said Valerie taking a right turn. "Liverot said there were long-term contracts and commitments."

"That's too bad, for him," said Lorraine. "Liverot's just lucky that my original plan didn't work out. I've unwittingly made him a lot of money, more than he could have made as a bank president. He's getting off very easily. Besides, he can buy his way out of his contracts with a fraction of the money he's made."

Valerie paused. "Well, what about all the work of the Foundation?"

"What about it? They can still hand out grants from all the funds on hand. That should last them a decade or so. You can still run that. Donations may slack off with Lorraine gone, but that's fine, too. It'll just slowly wind down and disappear…like I plan to do."

Valerie drove in silence for half a minute before speaking. "Right, that's what I told him. One way or another, I told him, my cousin is going to retire."

"What?" Lorraine was surprised. It seemed that Valerie had been arguing why she couldn't stop being Lorraine, now, she was saying the opposite. "You told him that I was definitely getting out of it all?"

Valerie paused again. "Yes, that's what I told him."

"And what did Liverot say?"

"He wasn't too happy, of course, but I told him that it was settled."

Lorraine laughed. "Thank you, thank you. I can finally get off this crazy ride and get back to my life. I've got a speech all written," said Lorraine pulling a worn page from her purse. "I've been waiting for this for months. Now today, at the White House, I can finally read it."

"No," said Valerie, "not today!"

"Why not?"

"It's a lot more complicated than just saying 'thank you,' and 'goodnight.' You've got a lot of legal obligations. If you don't fulfill them, Lorraine would have to stay around a lot longer just to appear in court. Of course, if you just want to disappear and have Lorraine Innis go down as a criminal and a fugitive…"

"No," sighed Lorraine, "that's the last thing I want to have happen to her."

Valerie smiled. "Good, let's just say Lorraine is going part-time for a little while. Don't tell anyone. I'll work out a schedule that will map out how she'll just fade away. Don't worry, I'll make it work."

Lorraine pulled down the sun visor and looked in the mirror on the back of it. She could do it a little longer, she told herself. Couldn't she? Besides, she was already too well identified with Peter Liverot to do him any harm as Lorraine Innis. Perhaps another disguise…

"Okay, I won't make my announcement at the White House," said Lorraine with disappointment in her voice. "I really wanted to get it over with today. But if I have to go on with it all…"

"It hasn't been all bad, though has it?"

Lorraine smiled faintly. "I suppose not. Some of it's been very nice. Especially today, when I really get to meet real people. It's been a good platform. And I suppose it will be interesting to meet the President."

"If I can get us to the White House, that is," said Valerie. "These streets are a real maze. I'd stop and ask directions, but I don't like the looks of this neighborhood."

"Look for a policeman," said Lorraine. "We don't want to be late."

"We're already late," said Valerie. "But they're not going to start without you. Liverot won't let them. He left before us."

"That's true. Mind if I turn on the radio. Maybe they've got some news about the ceremony?" As she fiddled with the dial, instead of a news station, Lorraine discovered a familiar, flat twang:

"What the hell is that?" asked Valerie wrinkling her nose. "Sounds like somebody flushing a basset hound down a toilet."

"It's Purvis!" said Lorraine. "It's his new single."

"Oh, sorry, about that basset hound crack. I should have said it was more like a flatulent cow being run over by a steamroller."

"It's called *There Are Two Sides to Every Girl*. It's ironic, isn't it? It's a remake of an old Jimmy Durante song," said Lorraine.

"Great, now turn that crap off, please," said Valerie before reaching over and shutting off the radio herself. "It's bad enough that he called me the other day without having to hear him on the radio."

"Purvis Twankey called you? What did he want?"

"He called to say he'd figured out a way of telling me what he wanted to say and to watch out for it," said Valerie. "It was pretty sporting of him to warn me, I'll give him that much. Hey, I think I saw the Washington Monument over there, that's near the White House, isn't it?"

As Valerie negotiated a left turn through a congested intersection, Lorraine was confronted with a disturbing sight.

"Oh, good heavens! That bus!"

"I see it, don't worry," said Valerie.

"No, not the bus itself," clarified Lorraine, "the side of it."

Valerie glanced up, then away, and then did a double take. There, plastered along the length of the bus was a fifteen-foot-long advertisement featuring a recumbent Purvis Twankey, stripped to his scrawny waist – though still wearing his cowboy hat. His intent had apparently been to look sexy. Instead, he looked like an appeal for famine relief. In his hands, he was holding a glossy photo of Valerie, which he eyed amorously. Along the bottom of the advertisement were the words: Purvis Twankey's New Hit Album: *To Valerie, Of Who I Dream!*

"To Valerie, Of Who I Dream?" screeched Valerie.

"It really should be 'whom.' Though it's a fairly common grammatical error," said Lorraine. "At least he didn't end the sentence

266

in a preposition. Most people would have said 'To Valerie, Who I Dream Of.'"

"You give him grammar lessons," said Valerie through her clenched jaw, "I'm going to kill him!"

"Watch out, he's coming towards us..." shouted Lorraine.

Indeed the giant emaciated Purvis Twankey was heading straight for Valerie's Lexus as the bus pulled into traffic. Coming in from one of Washington's acute diagonal intersections, Valerie was driving in the bus driver's blind spot. Valerie blasted her horn and slammed on the breaks, throwing the Lexus into a skid. The bus jerked to the side swerving the giant Purvis Twankey directly into the driver's side door with a jarring crash of metal and glass.

"Are you okay?" said Lorraine as both vehicles crunched to a stop.

"I'll kill him," screamed Valerie. "I'll kill that f**king hayseed. That's two times he's hit me!"

"I don't think bus advertising counts," said Lorraine quietly.

"I'll kill him," repeated Valerie raising her left arm then wincing in pain. "Ow! My arm! I'll f**cking murder him!"

- 63 -
Just Like Grandma
Used to Detonate

Two miles away, on the South Lawn of the White House, the visitors were getting restless waiting for the guest of honor to arrive. Inside the Oval Office, President Merton was preparing to go join the festivities when Davis Flemming and an older man in a dark suit entered.

"What is it, Davis," asked the President. "I was just coming out. Is she here yet?"

"No, not yet, Mr. President. Sir, this is Special Agent Rocher of the Secret Service."

"Rocher?" said Merton. "Oh, yes, you were detailed to me during my first election campaign, weren't you?"

"Yes, sir," said Rocher, "the President has a good memory for faces."

"Sir," said Flemming, "Agent Rocher was in charge last October when the attempt was made on President Kropotkin. As such, he also was the first person on the scene to interrogate Lorraine Innis."

"She saved Nikolai, didn't she?" said the President. "Why did we interrogate her?"

"We didn't know she had saved his life at first, Sir," said Rocher.

"Agent Rocher also headed up the investigation on Lorraine and Martin Innis that we had discussed last fall," said Flemming.

"The secret one?" asked Merton looking around as if he were afraid of being overheard.

"Yes, sir."

"Yes, well," said the President, "sorry about wasting your time, Rocher. It would have been a nice if we could have found her husband. Just as well those tourists did, though; after all the man turned out to be a bigamist."

"No, Sir," said Rocher.

"Sure he was," said the President. "It was in all the papers."

"No, Sir, what I mean is that Seamus Gynwittie is not Martin Innis."

"Right, Gynwittie was an alias since he had two wives," said Merton.

"No, Gynwittie is his right name," said Rocher. "Innis was the alias, and he only assumed that four days before the story came to light in the media."

"How do you know?"

"Because there was never a Martin Innis."

"That's preposterous," said the President. "Are you questioning the word of a woman regarding the existence of her own husband, a woman I'm about to award the Medal of Freedom?"

"I don't know, Sir," said Rocher. "I don't know if I'm casting doubt on Mrs. Innis' truthfulness, Sir, because I don't know if there really is a Mrs. Innis."

"Of course there is, she'll be here any minute."

"What I mean, Mr. President, is that there is no record of Lorraine Elizabeth Innis or Lorraine Elizabeth Ammaccapane prior to last October. We don't know who she is, but it's as if she didn't exist before then."

"Well who is she, some space alien dropped down to earth on holiday?" asked the President.

"She could very well be if you believe in that sort of thing," said Rocher. "It would be as plausible as anything else."

"That's ridiculous," said Merton walking back to his desk. "She's one of the most popular women in the world."

"The most popular," muttered Davis Flemming.

"See," said the President. "There are books, websites, television shows... She could be elected president if she wanted the job! A person that public couldn't be non-existent without some reporter finding out. I mean she's got ID, doesn't she? Driver's license, passport, birth certificates, all that stuff."

"Yes, sir," said Rocher. "There is an extensive paper trail that supports all of Mrs. Innis' claims."

"So what are you talking about?" said Merton. "You've seen all these supporting documents, haven't you?"

Rocher looked down at the blue carpet emblazoned with the presidential seal. "Yes, sir, I've seen all the documents because I helped create them."

"Helped create...with who?"

"My operative and I. We created it all based on her own story. Birth records, school transcripts, income tax records, everything."

"What about her house in New Jersey?" asked Davis Flemming.

"It actually belonged to a retired widow who moved to Florida;" explained the agent, "woman by the name of 'Potoski.' We bought the house and backdated the deed a few years to put it in the name of 'Innis.'"

"What about the neighbors?" said Flemming. "Didn't any of them step forward to uncover this fraud?"

"Not one. It's an isolated area, so we didn't have to worry about many neighbors. Those who lived nearby didn't know who lived at 27 Jutland Drive. When they heard it was Mrs. Innis they were delighted to have a celebrity nearby. From that point, psychology took over, sort of like the Indian Rope Trick. You tell people what they'll see, and then it helps them to see it, or think that they do. The neighbors were actually convinced that they had seen Mrs. Innis occasionally...coming to and from work, puttering in the garden..."

"Amazing."

"Actually, we found similar instances wherever we investigated. People were so anxious to say they knew Mrs. Innis 'when,' that they were entirely convinced they actually did know her. They essentially believed what they wanted to."

"If we own the house," said Merton brightening, "then I can give it to Mrs. Innis."

"No, Sir," said Rocher. "Mr. Kropotkin bought it last December."

"Get a good price?" asked the President.

"Actually, no. They found termites in the floor joists."

"Damn Russians! Damn termites!" muttered Quinton Merton.

Agent Rocher then gave a detailed account of the efforts of the Roto-Rooter and himself on behalf of the investigation. By the time he finished, the President was seated behind his desk unconsciously playing with a small rubber squeezy toy.

"So she's a fraud," said the President. "Just when I get to meet her!"

"Not necessarily," said Rocher. "For whatever reason, my operative concluded that everything Mrs. Innis told him she firmly believed to be the truth."

"So she isn't aware that you were creating her past," said Merton.

"No, sir. No one aside from my operative and you two gentlemen, and of course myself, are aware of that fact."

"But why," interrupted Davis Flemming, "why did you go to such lengths to support her story?"

"It wasn't all that difficult," said Rocher. "Realizing her growing influence and potential power we thought she would be more valuable to the government if we knew her secret and no one else did. If Lorraine Innis were exposed, it would be all over in a brief media frenzy. As it is, we have a valuable weapon if we ever need to use her. A sleeper, if you will, since even Mrs. Innis is not aware she's a reserve agent for the United States government. It was actually my partner's idea. He's found her quite impressive, even inspiring, as do I."

"And even she doesn't know her past is phony?" asked the President.

"Not as far as we can determine," said Rocher. "We've had her under fairly close scrutiny, and aside from some uncharacteristic behavior late last October, Mrs. Innis has gone on very rationally and on an even keel."

"What happened late last October?" asked Flemming.

"Her cousin was released from the hospital, immediately following which Lorraine…Mrs. Innis…went into seclusion for several weeks."

"Interesting," said Merton tossing the toy into the wastebasket beside his desk. "And nobody else knows what you've just told us?"

"No, Sir," said Rocher. "Just yourself and Mr. Flemming, and of course my operative."

"Good, forget it," ordered the President.

"Sir?"

"Don't you understand 'forget it?'" snapped Merton. "You guys are trained to take a bullet for your president. I think when he tells you to forget something that's a little more reasonable request. Don't talk about it. Don't tell anybody about it. Don't mumble it in your sleep. Don't remember it. Forget it. Get it?"

"Yes, Sir," said Rocher.

"Thank you, Rocher, good job. You may go," said Quinton Merton.

The President stared out the window as Agent Rocher handed the full report to Davis Flemming and then exited. After a moment's silence, Merton spoke with his back to his deputy.

"I suppose you're wondering why I did that?" he asked his aide.

"You don't think she's an alien, do you, Sir?" said Davis Flemming.

"No, of course not. For one thing, aliens would have gotten the nose right," reasoned the President.

"I meant an alien from another country, but that's highly unlikely," said Flemming thumbing through the report's summary. "That's the first thing they checked."

"Besides," continued the President, "if she were a spy she'd be one for us. I mean she's been all over visiting other world leaders, but this is her first time here. Right?"

"Yes, Mr. President," agreed Flemming.

"So what if she's got a secret past?" said Merton. "We all have something we wouldn't want broadcast, right?" The President looked down. "It's funny, but a few months ago I would have torn the lid off that woman. Now, it's live and let live. Maybe she's had an effect on me, too. Oh, by the way, I haven't seen Dr. Egonski for three weeks now."

"Yes, sir, I know," said Flemming. "Congratulations."

"Thank you," nodded the President. "Yup, if one of our citizens wants to save lives, inspire world peace, and give away millions of bucks, I say good for them. Who cares what shadows are lurking in her cupboards?

"Excuse me, sir," said Flemming pedantically, "but shadows don't lurk, they have no material being."

"Sounds like Mrs. Innis, or Miss Ammaccapane, or whoever she is, is rubbing off on you too, Davis," said Quinton Merton with a smile. "I suppose a little Lorraine is good for us all, eh? Now let's go out and meet this fine lady."

With that, a relaxed Quinton Merton opened the French doors leading into the Rose Garden and held them for his aide. Together, the two men strolled over to the South Lawn and up to the podium where he was informed that the guest of honor was not yet there. Flemming went back inside to check on her estimated time of arrival.

Instead of Lorraine, the President was introduced to Peter Liverot and the handful of volunteers from the Cross of Lorraine who had been selected to appear on the rostrum. As the President moved down the line greeting the guests, Liverot clung to Merton's side carrying on an excited monologue in his ear. Finally, at the end of the line, the President reached a small, old lady.

"Hello, and welcome to the White House," said the President.

"This ain't the house," said the old woman, "it's the backyard."

"Yes," laughed Merton, "I suppose it is."

"Probably standing right over your stinkin' septic tank! That's a great way to entertain your guests. Have 'em stand over the remains of last night's meatloaf after you've run it through your colon!"

"Hey, watch it, lady," warned Liverot. "You're talkin' to the President."

"That's all right," said Merton graciously. "It's good to see our senior citizens so full of life and energetic...Mrs..."

"Bupp," she said, "Eugenia Bupp. Remember the name!"

"It's wonderful to meet you, Mrs. Bupp. You remind me of my own grandmother."

"Really? Did your granny like C-4, too?" asked Eugenia Bupp.

"C-4?" asked the President. "I don't know, what's C-4?"

"This," exclaimed Bupp as she pulled a wire from her blouse, put it between her teeth and chomped down hard.

◆

A second later terror and confusion reigned on the South Lawn of the White House. Eugenia Bupp, having the epicenter of the blast from the plastic explosive known as "C-4" filling her oversized brassiere and set off by the detonator hidden in her homemade dentures, was instantly blown to smithereens. Quinton Merton also had a similarly quick demise and never knew what happened. Peter Liverot, shielded from the direct impact by Quinton Merton's body suffered severe wounds. Others in the immediate vicinity, Secret Service agents and volunteers, also sustained enough severe injuries to fill every emergency room within a five-mile radius.

The Girl in the Diamond Studded Heels

Within days the FBI concluded that the explosion had emanated from the person of one Eugenia Bupp of Coeur d'Alene, Idaho. Though they had screened and searched all the guests arriving that morning, Bupp had gotten past the bomb-sniffing dogs at the gate by applying a trace of ammonia to her wrists and ankles. Though the odor was undetectable to the human nose, it disarmed the canines' sense of smell for a full hour.

– 64 –
Every Confession
But the One I Needed

L orraine and Valerie got the last ambulance in the city dispatched before all emergency vehicles were rerouted to the disaster at the White House. After Valerie was pried out of her Lexus with the Jaws of Life, they were taken to George Washington University Hospital. There as Valerie was x-rayed, the first wave of casualties began to flood in from 1600 Pennsylvania Avenue, along with sketchy news reports of the explosion.

A few minutes later, as Valerie was having her arm set, a doctor approached Lorraine in the hallway.

"Mrs. Innis," said the Doctor, "we have a casualty from the White House who's been asking for you."

Probably one of the volunteers, Lorraine thought. "I'll see them as soon as I'm done here with my cousin," said Lorraine.

"He may not have that much time," said the Doctor. "He's barely hanging on. He says he knows you, personally."

Lorraine followed the doctor down the corridor, past other blast victims, to an examination room. There, lying on a table, his right side mangled and exposed, was Peter Liverot. Lorraine recoiled as she saw her nemesis, the impetus for her disguise, in such a wretched state. As much as she would have wanted to feel some sense of justice, divine or otherwise, Lorraine could feel only pity for Liverot. The banker looked up, noticed Lorraine and smiled weakly. She glanced at the doctor, who nodded that it was okay to get closer, and then approached Liverot's side.

"I'm glad you're here, Mrs. Innis," rasped the banker. "I wouldn't want to see anybody else."

"Mr. Liverot," said Lorraine, fighting back a tear, "don't talk, save your strength."

Liverot feebly rolled his eyes. "I'm done," he said, "but I got to clear the air before I go."

"Do you want me to get you a priest?"

"Nah, I'd much rather have you. I know too many crooked priests. You're different. You're good and honest. You're the best person I know. I've got to get some stuff off my chest before..."

"Are you sure?" said Lorraine. She had been pursuing evidence for Liverot's crimes, now here he was offering her his final confession. Suddenly she would rather not hear it.

"I'm not the guy you think I am," said Liverot.

"Not many of us are," said Lorraine.

"The bank is a front," he continued. "My investors use it to launder money. We'd fund small businesses with loans, then call the loans, get operating control of the businesses and use them to spread out the dough. That was until you came along."

"Me?"

"You were the big one. I set up your charity as the biggest laundry. The biggest we had, the biggest in the world."

Lorraine stared at him. She felt her anger rising anew.

"Funny thing is," continued Liverot, "I didn't need to do it. I mean, after a while we were making more money, legitimate money, from all the stuff I sold with your endorsement. Everybody was so nuts about you. They all love you so much. I guess nice ladies like you will always have the edge over bastards like me. Just be careful, okay?"

Liverot closed his eyes and exhaled. Lorraine watched him for a moment and almost turned away until she realized that she hadn't heard the admission that mattered most of all.

"Is that all?" said Lorraine.

Liverot opened his eyes. A faint look of puzzlement crossed his face.

"Don't you have something else to say?" said Lorraine.

Liverot shook his head feebly.

"What about the murders?"

"Mrs. Innis..." said the doctor.

"If you're going to confess," said Lorraine, "you might as well tell it all...everything."

Liverot labored to sit up, but couldn't even raise his head.

"Mrs. Innis," interrupted the doctor, "really..."

"I wasn't the muscle," said Liverot plaintively.

"Then," said Lorraine, "what about Martina?"

"Who?"

"The girl who worked for you," said Lorraine. "The girl you took to Chicago. The girl who died running away from you."

"Her? She got hit by a bus. She was mailing a postcard to her fat boyfriend."

"That's what you told the police. But she wouldn't have been there if you hadn't wanted her to come along. Martina wasn't supposed to go on that trip, Valerie was."

"So?"

"So you changed the plans. You asked for Martina so you could sleep with her."

A genuine look of surprise crossed his face.

"I didn't change nothing. If I wanted that sort of thing, I wouldn't have asked for a Sunday School teacher like her. My assistant changed the plans."

"Patsy?"

"Al."

Now it was Lorraine's turn to be stunned. "Albrecht Eckner?"

Liverot nodded. "How do you know him? Anyway, what do you…"

Lorraine guessed the banker had started to ask why she was concerned with Martina's death. Before he could finish his sentence, however, Liverot took a sharp intake of breath, followed by a short spasm, and then fell still. Lorraine turned to the doctor who shook his head. Peter Liverot was dead.

Lorraine looked at his mangled form and hung her head. Though he had been there when Martina died, Liverot wasn't responsible for her death. He wasn't even responsible for Martina being there. How could she have gotten it so wrong? It was, Lorraine thought, a bitter irony. For all the crimes Peter Liverot had committed in his life, she had ultimately hounded him to his death for something he hadn't done, perhaps his life's lone act of innocence. And while he wasn't responsible for putting Martina at the place of her accidental death, Lorraine was responsible for Liverot being at the White House that morning. She suddenly thought of Valerie. Even that was ironic. For all the times Lorraine had dreamt of her villain being run over by a bus, it was Valerie who had been hit by one that day. It was wrong. All of it was wrong.

She watched as the doctor pulled the sheet over Liverot's face, and then turned away. Walking into the hall, Lorraine staggered numbly past the attack victims receiving treatment. She didn't quite know where she was going, or even what she would do. She had to think, to reassess everything. Why had Albrecht Eckner wanted Martina to go to Chicago? What about the Cross of Lorraine functioning as the biggest money laundering operation in the world?

And in the light of all that, when, if ever, could she stop being Lorraine Innis?

The End of

The Girl in the Diamond Studded Heels

The Story of Lorraine Innis

will continue in

The Girl in the Aubergine Sandals

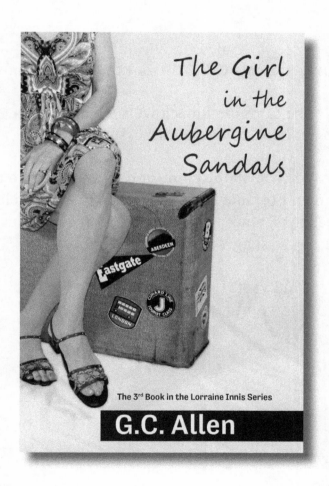

Be a Part of It All!

Daley Into Print LLC
proudly presents G.C. Allen's Lorraine Innis novels.

The Lorraine Innis novels are perfect for
book clubs and discussion groups.

Visit **www.iLorraine.com** for guides on how to throw
your own Lorraine Innis book club meeting including
questions, notes, games, quizzes, and even menu
suggestions from the books!

And visit iLorraine.com's store for fun
Lorraine Innis merchandise.

CPSIA information can be obtained
at www.ICGtesting.com
Printed in the USA
BVHW030723210719
553998BV00002B/268/P